Haymarket

Haymarket

A Novel

MARTIN DUBERMAN

SEVEN STORIES PRESS

New York • London • Toronto • Melbourne

SEVEN STORIES PRESS

140 Watts Street
New York, NY 10013
http://www.sevenstories.com/

IN CANADA

Publishers Group Canada, 250A Carlton Street, Toronto, ON M5A 2L1

IN THE UK

Turnaround Publisher Services Ltd., Unit 3, Olympia Trading Estate,
Coburg Road, Wood Green, London N22 6TZ

IN AUSTRALIA

Palgrave Macmillan, 627 Chapel Street, South Yarra VIC 3141

College professors may order examination copies of
Seven Stories Press titles for a free six-month trial period.
To order, visit www.sevenstories.com/textbook/,
or fax on school letterhead to 212.226.1411.

Book design by India Amos

LIBRARY OF CONGRESS CATALOGING-IN-PUBLICATION DATA

Duberman, Martin B.
Haymarket : a novel / Martin Duberman.—1st ed.
p. cm.
ISBN-13: 978-1-58322-618-6 cl; 978-1-58322-671-1 pbk
ISBN-10: 1-58322-618-4 cl; 1-58322-671-0 pbk
1. Haymarket Square Riot, Chicago, Ill., 1886—Fiction.
2. Parsons, Lucy E. (Lucy Eldine), 1853–1942—Fiction.
3. Parsons, Albert Richard, 1848–1887—Fiction.
4. Trials (Anarchy)—Fiction. 5. Chicago (Ill.)—Fiction.
6. Anarchists—Fiction. 7. Bombings—Fiction. I. Title.
PS3554.U25 H39 2004
813'.54—dc21
2003014163

Printed in Canada

9 8 7 6 5 4 3 2 1

For Sue Grand
with gratitude and affection

Part One

Johnson County, Texas

To watch eighteen-year-old Lucy Eldine Gonzalez cross a room, her step stately and purposeful, her red twill dress rustling dramatically—to see her move was to know at once that she wouldn't take kindly to having her time wasted with quavering inquiries about how long to boil the lye and grease scraps for soap, or whether the missing cowpuncher ought to be searched for in town and given the two dollars more a month he'd demanded, or just let disappear—since he knew as much about cattle as a hog does about a side saddle.

Lucy had to deal with such questions, had to deal with them over and over again, as the woman who ran her uncle's small Buffalo Creek ranch—which was why she insisted the questions be short and kept her answers even shorter. Most of her waking hours were spent feeding the chickens and razorback hogs; pouring candles and knitting socks; making sure the hired hands kept the vegetable rows weeded, the wheat fields tended, the stake-and-rail fence in repair; and overseeing the two Mexican women in the repetitive round of household chores.

But Lucy felt alive not when cleaning out the ash hopper or cooling a prairie chicken in the creek, but when, finally alone in her room at night, she could pore over the *New Orleans Tribune,* read the reports of the latest measures being proposed by the Radical Republicans in Congress to curtail the latest atrocities—a ten-year-old negro boy castrated and cauterized, *made* to live; a white woman rumored to be giving her favors to black men, dragged from her home, hot tar poured into her vagina . . .

Lucy had learned early that most people, including her uncle, worried far more about cattle than negroes—give or take the occasional spurt of outrage over a "stunt" like the Fifteenth Amendment. "Next, they'll want to give the Chinks the right to vote!" one cowpuncher stormed to the others as they sat around waiting for Lucy to put out the evening meal. "It's a damned tyranny, is what! Next, they'll be followin' us into the outhouse!"

"No, next they'll be givin' the vote to women," Lucy said, slamming down a bowl of grits directly in front of the bunk hand. "And a good thing, too. With so many ignorant men votin', we need *some* way to elevate political life."

They stared at her like she'd turned lunatic, then, as if she'd never spoken, turned back to talking among themselves about the familiar staples:

Whether the Texas fever disease would strike the herds again this year.

Whether the Atchison, Topeka, and Santa Fe would build beyond its current terminal, now that the railroad rate wars had eased.

Whether the homemade buggy deserved the jury prize at the state fair, when everyone knew the best wagon known to man was the New Hampshire Concord.

Whether the higher prices they'd been getting by driving the cattle to Abilene instead of Sedalia made up for the longer distance, given the increased risk of stampedes and stealing.

Lucy had nothing to say on such matters. She held herself aloof, moved imperiously from kitchen to table, a silent, smoldering figure. Her uncle often warned her that people thought she was high-falutin'.

"You got the skills to sew yourself a red twill dress," he once said angrily, "but you oughta have the sense *not* to, oughta wear the same flax homespun the other women do."

"And dye it with the same oak bark, I suppose." Lucy made no effort to conceal the contempt in her voice.

"That's right!"

"Oak bark's dull. I like bright colors."

"Well, you might like a husband one day, too, and you ain't gonna find one till you learn to act more everyday-like." Lucy made no answer.

Talk of her "arrogance" wasn't the only disapproving gossip to reach her. She knew that some people thought she was a negro. Her dark skin, broad nose, and curly black hair had long since set people to wondering if Lucy's Mexican uncle wasn't simply her employer, a man who'd hired her as a young girl for her vibrant, lustrous brown beauty—and been helping himself to it ever since. There was even a rumor that Lucy had been born a slave; and another, that she'd married one and then left him.

She refused to respond to the rumors. Once in a great while some particularly obnoxious cowpuncher, the kind that arrived out of nowhere without a pair of spurs or a bedroll to his name and was gone as soon as he had enough drinking money in his pocket, poked his face in hers and sneered something about not taking orders from a "nigger bitch." Then, her temper would burst like a creek flooded by storm, her words splaying him like a Gatling gun: "I don't talk to a man oily as a snake that drags the ground when it walks. Stick this in your ear, mister: You're addressin' a woman of Spanish and Aztec blood. Not an African. My mother was Mexican, my father a civilized Creek. That's all you need to know, or ever will know. Now move! Get!"

If the cowpuncher was belligerent enough to stand his ground, Lucy, composed and haughty, would turn on her heel and stalk off. That might end the confrontation. But not the rumors.

Even Albert Parsons had heard them—heard them long before he let Lucy know it. The two first met when Albert, back in 1869, started traveling to north Texas as a deputy revenue collector for the state, a job few people wanted now that taxes (and tempers) had gone sky-high in response to what the Conservatives were calling the "needless" new Radical expenditures for building roads and setting up a public school system.

When Albert rode into the courtyard of the Gonzalez ranch for the first time that April day two years ago, Lucy had appeared abruptly in front of him, hands on hips, as if daring him to dismount.

"This is the Gonzalez ranch, mister. What's your business here?"

"Excuse me, ma'am, beg pardon for intrudin' on your land . . . My horse Bessie here's got a powerful thirst, and I was hopin' . . ." Albert's words trailed off as Lucy moved into full view, staring up at him. He'd never seen such a woman before—golden brown skin, high cheekbones, a full and sensuous figure, deep, intense black eyes. She moved and spoke with such authority, such concentrated vehemence, that she seemed like some sort—an ancient sort—of queen. *That* was it! Albert thought: She's like a reincarnation of that Egyptian princess—Nefer-somebody—he'd seen a picture of during his school days in Waco.

Seeing Albert looking blank-eyed, as if in a trance, Lucy had trouble fighting back a smile. She knew that look, and what usually followed was some crude attempt to paw her. But she'd seen at a glance that this man had a quiet kind of gentleness about him.

"Well acourse your horse can drink," Lucy said, "if you can manage to get down off the poor beast so I can lead her to the trough."

With a laugh, Albert leapt off and Lucy took Bessie's reins. "You look pretty parched yourself. You head inside there"—she pointed to an archway leading into the long adobe building—"and when I finish with Bessie here I might just find somethin' for you. If you succeed in staying alive that long. You're about the sorriest lookin' cowpuncher I ever seen."

"Ain't no cowpuncher, ma'am, I'm an assessor, a revenue collector."

Lucy's face clouded over, yet the trace of a smile remained. "Are you now? Well then, I guess we'll spare the cheese and currants and give you two soda crackers instead."

She turned away, led Bessie across the courtyard, let her drink her fill, then tethered her to a post. Lucy retraced her steps back to the main house and entered the sprawling but sparsely furnished long room that served as combination parlor, kitchen, and eating area. As she strode into the room, she was already in mid-sentence.

". . . Now just what kind of 'revenue' you fixin' to collect?" Albert jumped up from his chair the moment she entered, but Lucy motioned him impatiently to sit back down again. "Let's hear some figures."

"Well, ma'am, accordin' to my records, Mr. Gonzalez—"

"Señor Gonzalez. I'm his niece, Lucy Gonzalez. And we both expect a proper form of address."

"Yes, ma'am. I do apologize." Flustered, Albert hastily consulted his notes.

"Well, it says here that Señor Gonzalez hasn't paid any kinda tax for two years."

"That's because he don't approve the way the money's bein' spent. 'One year of Radical rule,' he says, 'and there ain't a dime left in the Texas Treasury. They're filchin' hard-earned money from the people and squandering it on schools for niggers and roads to nowhere.'"

"But the State *needs* a school system, ma'am. I'm surprised you feel that way . . ." He saw Lucy flinch.

"I was tellin' you how my uncle feels. That's what matters around here.

Even if I did share his views—and I'm not sayin' I do or don't—why would that surprise you?"

Her twinkling condescension made Albert sputter in embarrassment. "Well, ma'am, can't rightly say why I had that . . . that impression . . ."

"Stop bein' so nervous, boy! Once you learn to speak your mind straight out, people'll respect you more. Anyway, I already know the answer: my brown skin. Which I feel sure you noticed," Lucy added sardonically.

"Yes, ma'am."

"Figured, seeing as how you're not blind. A little glazed, maybe, but your eyes do seem to work okay. Anyway, you guessed right about my views. The negro people may not be my people—I'm Mexican and Creek—but I do believe every child has the right to go to school, and make somethin' of himself, whatever his color. We need for the day to come when dumb white boys like you don't run *everything*." Lucy paused. "Hell, boy, I don't even know your name."

"If you stop callin' me boy, I might jes' tellya."

Lucy laughed out loud. "It's about time you made a protest! Beginnin' to think you hadn't started to shave. How old *are* you?"

"Twenty-one."

"Don't look it. Me, I'm eighteen. And I promise you: *nobody* calls me girl."

"Bet they call you lots of other things. Like beautiful." Albert was shocked at his own boldness.

"If I let 'em," Lucy said impishly. "Now I'll tell you what, as a reward for standin' up for yourself, I'm gonna get you some proper food after all. Maybe even some dried herring, or a piece of cod."

"I'd sure appreciate that. Don't be servin' up no more teasin', though. I can't manage that too well."

"Well too bad, 'cause that's me. Maybe you'll get used to it," Lucy threw back at him as she moved toward the kitchen. Suddenly she stopped and turned around. "Well what *is* your name?"

"Albert Parsons."

Lucy looked thunderstruck. "Albert Par—I don't believe you!"

"Am I famous or somethin'? Maybe for collectin' taxes on time."

"You were proprietor of the *Spectator*. Ain't that right?"

"Didn't know I had a reader this far north."

"You probably had one reader—me. I came across a copy at the general store in Cleborne. They were usin' it to keep the flies off the home-cured meat. I read the first page standin' up. That was it. Read it every week from then on, had to send to Waco for it. 'Albert Parsons.' Now there's somethin' unexpected!"

She paused for a moment. "From now on, you can call me Lucy. As for my brown skin, we may or may not talk more about that some day . . ." She turned into the kitchen and quickly piled some dried fruit, cheese, herring, and lemon crackers on a platter.

"Does that mean I'd be welcome to stop by when I find myself in these parts?"

"That might depend on how much my uncle owes," Lucy said slyly. "He's not likely to offer hospitality to a tax collector."

"Taxes? What taxes?" Albert said with a laugh. He rustled ostentatiously through his papers. "I don't see no Gonzalez on my lists. Either your uncle's all paid up or, as the law do allow, he avoided payin' by workin' on the roads and bridges for a dollar a day. Yup, I guess that must be it."

Lucy returned with the platter of food and put it down in front of Albert. "This ain't cookin' exactly, but it'll hold you till you get to your next place."

He thanked her profusely and began to eat. He'd forgotten how hungry he was.

Lucy was about to join him at the table when one of the Mexican women appeared at the door and called out something in Spanish. Lucy went over to her and the two chatted quietly. Albert knew little Spanish, but he could judge from Lucy's soft tone with the woman that the combativeness she'd leveled at him wasn't the sole way she fronted on the world. Finally, the woman said, "Gracias, señorita," and disappeared.

"A circuit rider's comin' through this afternoon to hold services," Lucy explained. "Amelia wanted permission to leave the fields early."

"A religious service?"

"Methodist. Amelia's Roman Catholic, but there's no church like that 'round these parts. Don't know *what* she gets out of a Methodist service. They hold it in a tiny little place made of logs; was meant to be a schoolroom but the teacher quit after a month. Not even any backs on the benches, so you can't catch up on your sleep. Amelia loves best the outdoor revivals; they get to work themselves into a frenzy under some brush arbor, screamin' like a pack a lunatics."

"Don't sound like you're a believer," Albert said good-humoredly.

"There's lots of things I believe. But none of 'em got to do with angels and a great white father. Are *you* a godly man?" Lucy sounded as if she might just yank the food away if the answer was yes.

"When I was little, my family made me go to church. But that was a *long* time ago!" Albert laughed. He almost mentioned Aunt Ester and how her devout fervor nearly caught him up when he was a boy. But no, he thought, she's not ready for Aunt Ester.

"Glad to hear the superstition didn't catch ya." Lucy sat down beside him at the table and started picking away at some prunes. "The one time I've ever gone to a meetin' was when Dr. Mary J. Walker come through here last year."

"Who's that? Never heard of her."

"Most men haven't. She's a campaigner for women's rights. When Mary J. Walker came to Brenham, a crowd pelted her with eggs at the railway depot. She never did get to give her speech. I had to go to Hillsboro to hear her."

"Sounds to me, Lucy, like maybe you're too quick to think the worst of men."

Lucy looked surprised. She wasn't used to being challenged; it brought a little heat of pleasure to her face. "Well do tell, Mr. Editor."

"Just so you know, I've been a reader of *Woodhull & Claflin's* since it started publishing last year. Do *you* read it?"

"Victoria Woodhull's nuthin' but a high-priced whore," Lucy said loftily, avoiding the question.

"That's what they call every independent woman."

"They wouldn't dare call *me* that."

"Well, not to your face maybe. Besides, you got your facts wrong. It's her sister, Tennessee Claflin, who's mistress to Commodore Vanderbilt. Or at least clysterin' him, as the rumor has it."

"Doin' *what* to him?"

"Clysterin'. Hear tell it's real popular back east, at least in fancy circles. Clysterin's like an enema, but it goes *way* up and massages the prostate, makes the old Commodore feel spry as a youth."

"That's a pretty bold thing for you to be sayin' to me, Albert Parsons. I suppose I should be miffed. Or even kick you out."

"That'd be play-actin', and you know it. I don't think you shock too easy. Fact is, I get the feelin' I could say 'bout anythin' to you."

Lucy tried to conceal a smile. "In time you might be able to," she said. "But you and me, Mr. Parsons, only known each other less than an hour."

"Still, I feel I know you. That don't happen often, but when it does, it happens quick. And please stop callin' me Mr. Parsons."

"Awright, I will. See: I ain't contrary all the time. Now how about some coffee to finish with?"

"Sounds fine."

As Lucy headed back toward the kitchen, Albert called after her: "You still haven't answered my question, you know."

"What question?"

"You read *Woodhull & Claflin's* paper or don't you?"

"No, I don't." Lucy said quietly. "And you know what: I feel shame-faced 'bout it. I *oughta* read their paper. And until I do, I oughta keep my mouth shut about the character of those two ladies."

Having expected a combative response, Albert was surprised at Lucy's capitulation. "Good for you, Lucy Gonzalez!" he said. "Not only a woman of strong opinions, but not afraid to question 'em! Mighty rare." He paused. "You know what?"

"What?" Lucy asked, her voice sounding girlish and happy.

"You and me goin' to get along real fine. As fine as can be. When can I come callin' again?"

"Ain't you the bold one!"

"Well, don't want you to start callin' me *boy* again."

"Bessie do seem a mighty thirsty girl. I'd say you best bring her by often; cain't stand seein' an animal suffer."

"You callin' me an animal?!" Albert said, laughing.

"Can't be that often, though. You're a Waco man, Albert—that's sixty miles from here!"

"Next few months, I'm workin' right in these parts. After that, something'll come up. You leave all that to me, hear? For now, stoppin' by's as easy as slippin' into my saddle."

And stop by he did. Often. He'd complete his revenue circuit in as short a time as possible, trying not to drive Bessie too hard, and when she did tire he'd croon sentimental verses in her ear that made her whinny with pleasure and pick up her gait. But sometimes a full week would pass before he was able to get back to the ranch; the thinly settled north country around Woodson and Elbert made for difficult travel and delays. Hearing a tax collector had arrived, people were far more likely to flee into the fields than to emerge from them to shake his hand. Lucy would grow uneasy with waiting, her ear anxiously tuned for the sound of Bessie's hoofs on the courtyard stones. Sunsets were the worst time; all her life they'd made her melancholy, conjuring up the streaked-red end of things. When Albert was away, she tried to find herself at twilight storing roots in the cellar or checking on the wine corking, chores previously left to others.

Not that she let Albert know the extent of her unease. For the first few months after they met, she remained wary, keeping up her tart, distancing banter, never putting food in front of him that might seem too wifely-complete and setting out the same indifferent wine for him that she served the farmhands. Even when alone with him, she veered the conversation to public questions or to asking him about his family background, while offering only scraps about her own. Albert had little conceit but was as willing as the next man to talk about himself. Eager to please her, he let her set the cues. When Lucy said she wanted to hear all about life in Waco, since she'd never seen the place, Albert cheerfully complied, describing in detail the small, wooden buildings on either side of the town's one commercial street; the steady swirl of dust and horse manure that filled the air; the general emporium that offered denim and calico dry goods and, irregularly, home-cured meats, syrup, butter, cheese, coffee, and, on rare occasions, peppermint sticks for the children; the patent medicine store stocked mostly with quinine and calomel and dispensed in seemingly random amounts by a "druggist" who masqueraded as well as the town's doctor; the many saloons and the lone hotel—a place with more bedbugs than beds, where lodgers were given the choice of doubling up or sleeping in the cowshed.

"You been in Waco all your life?" Lucy asked at one point. "Seems to me I'm hearin' a little Yankee twang when you talk."

"You got a good ear, Lucy. Both my folks came from up north, father from Maine, mother from Jersey. Guess some of it rubbed off."

"Carpetbaggers, eh? Well, there are worse sorts."

Albert didn't know whether she was teasing him or not. "Carpet-baggers?! I'm talkin' 1830! That's when they moved to Alabama, so

Daddy could try his hand at a shoe factory. I was born in Montgomery, lived all my life in the South, most of it right here in Texas. Fought with the Lone Star Grays during the War."

"You—what? A Northern boy and a Southern Confederate! Seems to me you're one or the other."

Albert massaged his arms across his chest, as if shielding himself from an unexpected blast of cold air. "Fact is, Lucy," he said quietly, you can be both. I was, anyway. Thing is, you see, I was only fifteen at the time."

"At the time of *what*?" Lucy could feel her impatience rising.

"When I ran away from brother William's house and become a powder monkey with the Grays."

"Brother who—? How many stories you tellin' me at once? Should I be writin' all this down so I can memorize it later?"

Albert sighed. "Well you asked."

"Didn't ask for the whole family Bible in one readin'!"

"Okay then, it's like this. My folks, you see, both died before I was five. William took me in and raised me. Leastways, gave me a home. But it was Aunt Ester"—whoops, Albert thought, how did that slip out? Too late now—"it was Aunt Ester who actually raised me, taught me my values. I owe that woman everything, everything about m'self that I like anyway. I don't mean William wasn't good to me. He taught me lots of—of practical stuff. Like how to shoot a rifle and ride a horse, how to hunt antelope. Trained me as a printer's devil, too—that was when he was proprietor of the Tyler *Telegraph*."

"Aunt Ester was his wife?"

Albert sat back and sighed. "You sure I haven't told you about Aunt Ester?" Well, he thought, let's just get it over with. "Aunt Ester was . . . was a house servant . . . awright, a slave . . . in my brother's family . . ."

Lucy pushed back her chair and stood up. "Where's this brother of yours now? He still in Tyler?"

"He and his family moved to Galveston. He's a cotton factor now. A big shot. During the War he was a general."

"You sure *he* didn't teach you your 'values'?" Lucy started moving around the room, dousing the candles, picking up loose items from the floor. Albert jumped up.

"My God, Lucy! I was fifteen years old when I joined the Grays! Hot with excitement, that's all, couldn't hardly sit still. Hell, I didn't even know why the War was being fought! Just got caught up in the fever and fireworks!"

"I knew why it was bein' fought." Lucy's voice could have frozen a whole cod for the winter. "The War was fought to keep black people in chains."

"They kept tellin' *me* it was about states' rights. Puzzled me no end. I thought only people had rights, not states. But I didn't trouble m'self much. Before the War I didn't have opinions, I had energy, and needed to do somethin' with it. I grew my ideas later."

"No doubt you'll tell me all about that, too." She snuffed out the last candle. "But not tonight."

And over time he told her about that and more, though never again mentioned the Grays—nor his service in the renowned McInoly Scouts under Major General W. H. Parsons, commander of the Confederate cavalry west of the Mississippi. She wanted especially to hear about the *Spectator*, how in the world he'd ever found the money to start it up and why, in less than a year, he'd closed it down.

"When I got mustered out, I traded a good mule—all I owned in the world—for thirty-five acres of corn standin' ready for harvest. The owner, he was a German man, just wanted to get on that mule and get the hell outta Waco."

"How'd you bring it in?"

"Huh?"

"The harvest. How'd you bring it in? You sure don't look like a farmin' man."

"I hired some black men, freed slaves, who knew the fields like the back of their hands."

"That was nice for you."

This time Albert flared. "Don't know what you're implyin', but I don't like it. Those men were *dyin'* to find work, work where they wouldn't be cheated out of their wages after the job was done. I paid them *on the line*, week after week. The first pay they'd ever had, I'm proud to say."

"All right, then." Lucy laughed. "You got to remember we're jes gettin' acquainted. And I'm a highly suspicious woman."

"I've noticed. About the most suspicious woman I ever met." Some anger still burned in his eyes.

"And with good reason," Lucy said sharply. "But that's a different story. You were tellin' me about that harvest."

Albert decided not to press her further. "We brought it in together, standin' and sweatin' all day in the sun. And you're right—I'm no farmin' man. One harvest was enough to teach me that. But it brought me enough money to start the *Spectator*. Money long gone—or I wouldn't be out here makin' like a tax collector. No one'll hire me as a reporter, or printer . . ."

"Why? You got the skills."

Albert laughed. "Sure do. But I got me a reputation, too. I didn't close down the *Spectator*. People just stopped buyin' it. Called me a low-down scalawag, gone over to 'the enemy.' Seems I printed too many stories about the plight of colored folks. Wrote 'em myself, hell, I did *everything* myself, a one-man operation. It was the story about the eight-year-old black girl they raped to death near Montague—"

Lucy made some strange guttural noise in the back of her throat and got up from her chair so abruptly it nearly toppled over.

"That was the story," Albert continued, his voice an octave lower, "that got me on Cullen Banker's Most Wanted list. He updates it weekly y'know, nails it to the door of the Eagle Saloon in Waco."

Lucy was pacing back and forth.

"You know about Cullen Baker?" Albert asked gently.

"Acourse I know, who don't," Lucy snapped. "The Swamp Fox of the Sulphur, he likes to be called. Kills colored folks for sport. Some whites, too." Suddenly she burst out in a torrent. "It's *worse* than slavery times, that's what it is! *Worse!* And I mean for grown colored women, too . . . don't dare say no . . . White men think it's their right, they don't ask, they choose, like pickin' a cow at auction: 'I'll take this here heifer, brand her, throw her in my wagon . . .' I've heard all the stories I wanna hear, got me stories enuf to back up the bile to my throat! You hearin' me? Don't want no more stories!" She was screaming by then, and Albert rushed over to take her in his arms. The sobbing racked her body, and spittle seeped from the corner of her mouth. Albert had to rock her in his arms for a long time before she was able to dry her tears.

Everybody on the place realized that Albert was seriously courting. And everyone seemed to approve, judging at least from the way the two Mexican women would beam at him the instant he came into sight. Some of the cowpunchers liked to tease him about "bein' so ugly he had to go courtin' in the next county." "Well, fellas," Albert would say genially, "I'm doin' the best I can with what the good Lord gave me."

Only Lucy's uncle was standoffish, barely civil for the first few months. Until the night, that is, when Albert made casual reference to the new tax rolls "due out any day," and tacked on the calculated comment that an upright citizen like Señor Gonzalez, what with being fully paid up and all that, had nothing to feel concerned about. The very next night Gonzalez took Albert aside and, with a patently insincere smile, said he'd been noticing his interest in Lucy and thought they did seem a likely pair. "You're beginnin' to feel like a member of the family." Gonzalez didn't bother to spell out the rest. Tax rolls never came up again and Señor Gonzalez became downright cordial.

At night, Lucy gave Albert two choices: sleep outdoors or in the bunkhouse. He chose the outdoors, knowing that nobody snored like an exhausted cowpuncher. But the time came in late fall when it was too cold for sleeping outside—or for Albert to maintain the pretext that he any longer had enough revenue work to provide a steady wage. He knew he had to find a new job, or at least a new territory, and that meant returning for a time to Waco. To Lucy, he made light of the distance between Waco and the Gonzalez ranch and promised he'd make the trip every two weeks. She believed him, secure in his affections and feeling certain he was an honorable man. Gonzalez told him he'd be welcome to stay over for a few days each visit and could have a small room of his own in the main house.

Both Albert and Gonzalez proved as good as their word, though Albert's probity was put to the harsher test. No stagecoach line ran directly north from Waco—not that Albert would have had the patience to abide the constant breakdowns from rutted roads or flooded riverbanks, or the tedious stops to deliver mail and to change teams. His only option was to ride the sixty miles to the Gonzalez ranch on Bessie. His very first trip coincided with a late, blistering heat wave, and that meant the descent of a horde of black flies not yet killed off by frost and as relentless in their assault as the sweat that poured down Albert's back. In the plains area, the water was so muddy that the locals liked to say they "had to chew it before they could swallow it," and both he and Bessie were parched and suffering until they could find a clear spring. Thereafter, as the weather cooled, the trips became easier, and Albert arrived faithfully at the ranch every two weeks. In between, he found occasional pickup work in one of Waco's friendlier printing shops, giving him just enough money to survive. In early spring he got his job back as a tax collector, and his life with Lucy again took on a smooth daily rhythm.

They ventured beyond the ranch only rarely, usually in response to a neighbor's call for assistance. When a new settler and his wife in nearby Grandview sent out a call for help in raising their house, they knew that every healthy man within a five-mile radius would feel obliged to show up. Lucy and the other women kept the food and drink coming, while Albert joined the men in cutting the felled trees into logs, using pry-poles as levers in rolling the larger pieces onto an ox-cart, and then, at the building site, lifting them into place so they could be notched. Albert had neither the skills nor the acquired stamina of the others, yet insisted on working as long as they did. "Is this what's known as 'fun' around here?" he gasped to Lucy. "It's all we got!" Lucy answered with a laugh. "But cheer up—you're goin' to love the all-night dancin' that follows." A bleary-eyed Albert sank to his knees in mock despair, hands raised to heaven in silent entreaty. "I'm only teasin', silly." Lucy said, kissing the top of his head.

In the tradition of the area, when a family wanted to celebrate some milestone, they'd send out riders to notify the surrounding community that they were throwing a dance. (Once, Lucy told Albert, she'd been at a party where the fiddler had been a negro, a man no one in the area had ever seen before; she'd tried to talk to him between sets, but he quickly moved away.) She and Albert did attend one neighbor's celebration of a daughter's marriage. The fiddler that evening played variations all night long on the same three numbers—the Quadrille, the Virginia Reel, and something called Shooting the Buffalo, which, strangely, proved the most sedate and formal of the three. Albert quickly mastered the dances—Lucy already knew them—and even invented his own special shout when turning his partner during the Reel. Lucy said it sounded somewhere between a hog grunt and a yodel.

Despite the occasional pleasures of the country, Albert no longer felt at home among ranchers and farmers—which he himself thought curious, since he'd lived on the frontier as a boy and had loved the outdoors. He supposed Waco had citified him more than he'd been aware; he'd come to prefer people to unpopulated space, however beautiful, and would rather debate the changing face of Reconstruction than the comparative merits of branding calves at birth versus later. He'd come to think that should he have to leave Waco for good, his preference would be to move to a still larger town, one that might offer the chance to work again as a reporter or typesetter, and to plunge into the daily maelstrom of events.

And might offer, too, the chance to take Lucy with him. He wanted to marry her, to live with her, to set up a place of their own. He'd made that clear many months ago. Initially Señor Gonzalez had been opposed to what he called "too quick a hitchin'" (an opposition, Albert felt sure, based on disgruntlement over losing an efficient housekeeper). But then Gonzalez's fortune took a decided turn for the better: the plague of rust and grasshoppers that had decimated wheat fields across north Texas for five years abruptly ended, with a resulting harvest so bountiful no one could remember its like. An elated, much more prosperous Gonzalez gave his blessing, and promptly hired a third Mexican woman.

But Lucy herself held back, much to Albert's bewilderment, since she'd already told him that she fully reciprocated his feelings. On the evening when he formally asked her to be his wife, her eyes shone with pleasure and she told him in a hushed voice that she'd been certain from the beginning that they were meant to spend their lives together. Albert held her close and kissed her, his heart pounding. But as she clung to him, her face became shadowed in sadness. Lucy knew they could never legally marry, not here in Texas, anyway. Mixed marriage was a crime (though white men forcing themselves on female slaves before the War hadn't been); interracial couples could be imprisoned, deported to Liberia—or burned alive. Lucy had long ago made the decision never to reveal that her ancestry *was,* in truth, part African; she refused to let the world use the information to circumscribe her options or subject her to the scorn and indignities meted out as a matter of course to "inferior people."

Feeling her change in mood, Albert held her at arm's length, the better to gauge it. Lucy did her best to feign a smile, but she'd never been good at concealing emotion. Albert sensed, suddenly and with certainty, that he knew exactly what was bothering her. The time had finally come to talk openly about "the rumors."

He broached the subject farcically, puffing out his chest like a stage buffoon as he announced how lucky Lucy should feel at gaining entrance to a family as accomplished and patriotic as his.

"High-toned folks, no doubt," Lucy sniffed. "Meaning boring and self-satisfied."

"None of them as sprightly as me, that's for sure!"

"Well, my ancestry's just as illustrious as yours," Lucy said tartly—fully realizing what topic they were about to embark on. She gratefully picked up on Albert's farcical tone. "*More* illustrious, come to think of it. Several great civilizations course through my veins. All you got is that thin Yankee stuff."

"What?" Albert mocked. "I'll have you know, young Texas miss, that my great-great-granduncle was the first judge for the Northwest Territory—till he drowned when his canoe capsized. One member of my family lost an arm at Bunker Hill, another a hand at Valley Forge."

"Not too good at holding on to their body parts, are they? Must've been runnin' backwards rather than forward."

"Unlike your Montezuma, they managed to keep their heads at least."

Lucy let out a delighted screech and smacked Albert hard. "Don't you go defaming my people—you hear me, Yankee boy!"

"You dare talk that way to a wild young colt like me?"

"Oh? Ain't noticed no colt 'round here."

Albert grabbed her aggressively around the waist and with a loud puckering sound kissed her on the lips. She stepped away and rolled her tongue around her mouth, as if savoring a candy. "I'd call that a cheerful kiss," she said mischievously. "Fond and friendly. Didn't taste no eager, plucky 'young colt' in it."

"That's 'cause your mouth's set so stern, nuthin' much can get through."

Lucy made a playful swipe at him. "I'm a serious woman," she declared. "Don't want no wild teenager for a husband, so it's a good thing you're a lousy kisser. I'm looking for a man with good cow sense."

"The cow's about the stupidest animal exists."

"But does what it's told. No sass."

"Oh—so you're lookin' for somebody you can boss around. Sorry ma'am, no descendant of Revolutionary War heroes is about to take orders from anyone, not even from an Aztec queen."

"I ain't all Aztec." She gave him a hard stare and decided it was time to get it over with "I love you, Albert," Lucy said solemnly. "Even more, I admire you," she went on, her voice low and resonant. "Your principles, your dangerous work on the *Spectator* on behalf of my—of people who are downtrodden. I want to share that work with you. I want to spend my life with you. I'm a proud woman, Albert. I'm not ashamed of any part of who I am. But you should know that I'm of many parts, not just Spanish and Indian. Do you understand me? To try and marry would mean the other parts might come to light—with hell to pay."

"I understand, I've understood for some time," Albert said, his voice subdued.

"You and I know who I am. We also know that if I want to live with you and stay alive, only you and I must know."

Albert moved to embrace her. "I accept that completely, Lucy, completely." She abruptly pushed him away.

"Better than *I* can, then! I'll do what I have to do, what I been doin', but I curse this land that makes me deny part of myself in order to survive. I *curse* it, you hear?!"

Albert grabbed her and held her close, comforting himself as much as her. "I know, my love," he whispered quietly. She cried bitterly as he stroked her hair. "I know. But we do have each other. That means something, doesn't it?"

Lucy wiped away the tears and disengaged from Albert's arms. "It means everything—especially if they don't murder us." She let out a playful laugh, as Albert marveled to himself at her quicksilver changes in mood. Lucy grabbed his hand and led him toward the house. "Now recite me some verse, my wild colt, like those poems you sing to Bessie. Prove to Lucy that she's in the hands of a safe and singing man."

Part Two

Chicago

1873

"We need to go north," Albert said as soon as the results of the state election became known. "And we need to go soon. With the Redeemers in power, things will go hard with people like us."

"Don't look at me. I'm packed and ready. Been packed ever since we got to Waco."

Albert laughed, then drew Lucy into his arms. "I thought it would be easier than it has been. We can't even touch on the street," he said softly.

"Which, you may remember, is exactly what I predicted. The question is, where will it be any better?" She disentangled from Albert's arms.

"Chicago." He sounded emphatic, like he'd made up his mind long before saying so. "I've been readin' up on it, Lucy. Since the Great Fire two years ago, Chicago's become a boom town. A city. The 'lightning city,' they're callin' it. Within *one day* of the fire, the central post office was delivering mail, even to nonexistent addresses!"

"Well, that sounds pretty stupid. Could'a spent the money findin' people homes."

"And that's not all," Albert continued, ignoring her heckling. "They've made the Chicago River run uphill—and then for an encore, lifted the central business district out of the slime—I mean, literally!"

"What *are* you talkin' about?"

"It was to improve the drinking water!" Albert said exuberantly. "I mean, that's why they rerouted Lake Michigan and reversed the direction of the river. Plus they raised the business district sidewalks several feet to elevate them above the mud and 'road apples,' in local parlance."

Lucy let out a whoop. "Road apples?" City folks sure are delicate! Why not call a turd a turd? Never mind. Sounds to me like lots of headstrong ambition and theatrics. Is Chicago a place where folks can *live*? That's what I want to know. Don't need the heroics."

"There are opportunities from top to bottom."

"It's the bottom I worry about."

"Well, don't. I've been makin' inquiries. Lots of inquiries."

Lucy raised her eyes in surprise. "Thanks for tellin' me!"

He laughed. "Didn't wanna worry your pretty little head more than I had to."

"How about a few particulars, hmm? Like, say, somethin' about jobs and money?"

"Can't get *that* particular. Not yet, but I can tellya this: I've read the Chicago papers, and the dailies are boomin.' They're addin' evening editions to morning ones, some are addin' a woman's page, sports coverage, even serializing novels. What they don't have is near enough skilled hands, especially typesetters. I'll have a job within a week. I'm sure of it."

"No point wastin' my breath, I can see. You're fixin' on us moving there, no matter what I might say."

"That's not true, and you know it."

"All *I* know about Chicago is long, hot summers and dark, cold winters."

"And so many muggers, Mrs. Parsons," he whispered teasingly, "that folks don't dare leave their homes at night—"

"*Mrs.* Parsons? Aren't you the optimistic one!"

Albert's face sagged. "But Lucy, you *promised.* 'Once we're out of the South,' you said—"

"Oh, my silly boy!" She rushed over to comfort him. "Silly, silly boy. *Of course* I still want to marry you. I just don't know that it'll be any easier gettin' a license up north."

"Interracial marriage is legal in Illinois. I know that."

She shrugged. "Well, why should we care anyway . . . We don't need no state to tell us we belong together."

"Now you sound like Victoria Woodhull." He felt exuberant again.

Lucy cupped his face in her hands. "The day we leave for Chicago, Albert, I intend to call myself Mrs. Parsons. Not just to speak the truth of my heart, but to soften our reception. No matter what, people'll despise us for bein' a mixed-breed couple, but bein' told I'm 'Mrs. Parsons' will at least prevent them from despising us for living in sin."

✳

Carrying their overstuffed, shabby valises, Lucy and Albert disembarked from the train at the dilapidated West Side station of the Chicago and Alton Railroad. It had been a grueling ten-day trip from Waco, involving multiple rail changes and maximum discomfort. Yet even as they stepped from the train, Albert—ignoring the peeling paint on the walls and the three-ply carpet of tobacco quids covering the filthy floors—lit up with excitement.

"My God, Lucy, look at all these people!" he shouted above the din. "I never seen so many people in my life in one place!"

"And we don't know a one of 'em. Which I guess is just as well, given how bad they smell." She wrinkled up her nose.

"They're *runnin'*, not walkin'! Where they all rushin' off to?"

"Albert, let's just get *out* of here. My eyes are itchin' so bad, feels like somebody blew pepper in 'em."

Albert's much traveled brother, William, had warned him in advance about the infamous "runners" who infested big-city railroad stations, men eager to steer unsuspecting newcomers to an overpriced hotel or to a "boardinghouse" invariably described as "elegant and inexpensive," but which usually turned out to be a flophouse room with a single cot, locker, and screen. And just as William had predicted, no sooner did Albert lean down to pick up one of their boxes, then he and Lucy were surrounded by half a dozen men, elbowing each other out of the way as they grabbed for the valises and shouted their set hymns of praise about the virtues of this, but not that, place of lodging. Lucy, frightened at the sudden, noisy onslaught, froze, but Albert dealt authoritatively with the situation, shouting that they were already booked into a hotel, while shooing the runners out of their path.

They did in fact have a destination, if not a booking: William, whose factoring business had often taken him to Chicago, had strongly recommended the boardinghouse of a Mrs. Wright, on Harrison Street in the western part of the city. Moving as rapidly as their heavy load would allow, Albert guided Lucy, still a little dazed, out of the station and onto one of the horsecars pulled up in front.

Just getting on board proved a considerable feat. All passengers had to enter through the new, rear-entry "bobtail" cars and then traverse the full length of the horsecar, from back to front, in order to hand the required fare directly to the driver—a difficult navigation, even without boxes, given the overcrowding. Built to carry some twenty riders, the horsecar held three times that number packed together during rush hours. The congestion was only part of the discomfort. The ventilation was poor, and some of the male passengers—especially if it was late in the day and they were headed home from work—would be drunk and think it the height of hilarity to blow cigar smoke in someone's face as he passed by. Inching her way across the filthy straw covering the floor, Lucy was suddenly confronted by a besotted young man, his face and arms streaked with coal dust, who tipped his hat and loudly warned her to "step lively, miss, or the vermin'll be crawlin' up your coochie!" Astonished, Lucy stood stock-still, gaping at him—until the man behind her poked her sharply in the ribs and angrily barked, "Keep moving! Keep moving!"

What with the potholed streets and the frequent stops, it took a full hour for the horsecar to complete the six miles to Mrs. Wright's. Forced to stand the entire trip, eye level with wooden stripping that made it impossible for them to see anything of the city as they passed through it, Albert and Lucy arrived at the boardinghouse utterly exhausted. Fortunately, Mrs. Wright remembered William Parsons well and treated them kindly, immediately ordering hot water for baths and telling the teenaged German boy who did odd jobs at the house to carry their boxes at once to their designated room. It proved pleasantly furnished, airy, and clean, their chief requirements for a planned stay of no more than a month. For three dollars a week, they got a comfortable bed plus breakfast and dinner (hot biscuits, cold meat, and pickles), which they shared with some dozen fellow boarders, mostly overdressed dry-goods clerks, dressmakers with unhealthy complexions, and one mysterious older woman gotten up in flounces and silks, with a fashionably braided chignon and rings on every finger. She held herself apart, never speaking unless the necessity of retrieving some condiment required it.

Thanks to carefully accumulated savings, Lucy and Albert had arrived with $265—the equivalent of half a year's wages for most workers. They had hoped it might prove a large enough nest egg to buy a small house of their own; William had sent them a flyer he'd somehow gotten from the Blue Island Land and Building Company, just south of Chicago, offering lots and houses at 10 percent down. But when they went out to look, on the very next day, they discovered—after trekking a mile on foot beyond the last horsecar stop—lots, not houses, available at 20 percent down.

The whole of the following two weeks was consumed in a discouraging search for housing. They turned quickly away from the rear-lot wooden hovels, without foundations or plumbing, of the Fourteenth Ward; briefly considered a furnished three-story "tenant house," with a family on each floor, in an ethnic Czech neighborhood on the South Side—till they were told that only the cramped, dank basement was available; nearly moved into a neighborhood of unskilled German workers bordering the industrial belt along the polluted north branch of the Chicago River—until Lucy announced that she would have to stop breathing in order to live there. Finally, they decided to stretch their budget and rent a floor in a multifamily "railroad tenement" on the city's central North Side, a district populated mostly by skilled workers and artisans. Three weeks after their arrival in Chicago, they moved into their new home.

During their search for a place to live, Lucy had found herself in a state of astonished indignation the better part of every day. Everything amazed, and much of it repelled, her. The fifteen-year project of raising street levels in the business district was still incomplete in 1873, and the accumulated debris, congestion, and potholes—cavities, really—meant that walking the Chicago streets could be hazardous. The city had given construction firms the right to fence off sidewalks in front of a work site, which meant that piles of stored equipment and materials cluttered or wholly blocked some downtown streets. Contractors were required to build temporary wooden crossing bridges around their work areas, but these were often insubstantial, narrow, cheaply constructed passages that packed pedestrians together and forced them to inch their way forward.

And this was during the *day*. When they first arrived in Chicago, Mrs. Wright had given them a stern lecture against ever going out at night. "The downtown streets," she warned, "are infested with con men, brazen whores, drunks, and 'footpads.'"

"Footpads?" Lucy had asked.

"Muggers so stealthy they move without a sound, silently grabbing you from behind." Albert and Lucy felt sure that Mrs. Wright, who seemed to have a decided theatrical bent, was exaggerating the city's nighttime perils. But it hardly mattered; after trudging around the city all day, they were exhausted by evening and intent on retiring early.

One day, as Lucy and Albert were turning the corner at Haddock Place, they saw looming just ahead of them an entire four-story building being carted off on a jack down the street, with dozens of shouting workers tightening pulleys, adjusting cranes, and barking orders to the gathered crowd to clear the way.

Lucy let out a gasp and clutched at Albert's arm. "It's going to topple over!" she yelled, tugging him toward a nearby alleyway. "We've got to get out of here!"

Albert managed to reassure her that moving buildings, however unknown in Waco, had long since become commonplace in Chicago, with only an occasional mishap. "Try to think of it as an army of ants on the march, resettling their colony," he said genially, wondering where this newly authoritative voice had come from.

"This city's crazy! Everything's unfinished, never will be finished," Lucy said, trying to regain her composure. "You got me to move here by ravin' away like some dry-goods salesman about 'Chicago's triumphant rebirth,' or some such twaddle."

"Well it *is* a rebirth, Lucy. Now be fair. The whole world's agog at what Chicago's managed to do in so short a time."

"Right! Collect more filth, create more noise in less space than ever known to man. Not to mention producing a most remarkable stench!"

"Rumor is," Albert said, trying to tease her into a better mood, "that the city fathers are plannin' to attach 'odor-cutters' to the tugboat prows."

"Ha ha," Lucy said glumly.

"Plus the papers say that the surface grime on the river is so solid that builders are cuttin' it into foundation blocks, preferring it to concrete."

Lucy tried to conceal a smile. "But it don't do a thing to get rid of the nausea in my stomach or stop the burnin' in my eyes."

"Oh, c'mon, sweetheart," Albert said, putting his arm around her. "Everything you say about Chicago is true, absolutely true. It's a foul place, no doubt about it. But here's what I think: in no time at all, we're gonna get so used to it, we won't hardly notice any more—and then we'll start seein' some of the good things about the place."

Maybe, Lucy thought to herself. But not now, that was for certain, and not for a long time to come, she suspected. But she held her peace and allowed herself to be comforted.

It mystified her how Albert remained unruffled, how little he seemed affected by the assault of smells, filth, and noise. How could he take it all in stride, Lucy wondered, while she, who thought—no, knew—herself a strong person, felt actually ill much of the time? Between the stench from the river, the foul smells from the smokehouses, the faulty gas lamps, and the thick bituminous coal pouring from thousands of chimneys and darkening the sky at noon, she felt in constant danger of retching.

She longed for the pure Texas air. And the uncluttered stretch of horizon. There'd been hubbub aplenty on her uncle's busy ranch, but it had felt connected to purposeful activity, to tasks that could be completed, and it existed in counterpoint to the dense, faraway stillness of the unlimited land. In Chicago, the noise came at her from all directions, unidentifiable in origin, never giving way to a quiet interlude. The downtown area produced a ceaseless, capricious din, emanations of the perilous disorder everywhere in sight—the unruly, shouting crush of workmen; the aggressive army of food vendors hawking oysters, baked pears, or spiced gingerbread; the icemen hauling hundred-pound blocks between the jaws of their tongs; the scissor grinders ringing handbells; the scurrying hollers of competing hordes of ragpickers. Should two horsecarts collide, a carriage overturn, or a runaway team of horses break loose—everyday occurrences—traffic would abruptly deadlock, and stay deadlocked until limbs could be untangled, tempers cooled, and the calliope whistle announced the deafening arrival of a patrol wagon, officers hanging off its sides, determined to arrest *someone*.

The filth of the streets was as overwhelming to Lucy as the noise. Debris and garbage were piled everywhere, and in the more poorly paved areas, where the inefficient sewerage system failed to drain properly, store owners had to pay "crossing sweepers" just to clear a path through the muck in front of their establishments.

"What's wrong with these people?" Lucy irritably demanded of Albert one afternoon, as she stooped down for the fourth time that day to wipe slime off her shoes. "The city's worse'n a pigsty! Why do they put up with it?"

"I guess they don't much care," Albert replied blandly, irritating Lucy further. "Too busy racin' around makin' money to bother with a little dirt."

"Only the big shots are makin' money, and they don't see the dirt, sittin' in their parlors on Prairie Avenue, cooled by the lov-e-ly breezes from Lake Michigan—or in summer, sittin' in the same kinda parlor somewhere in Europe. I'm talkin' about everyday folks, people that got to slog to work everyday. Why do *they* put up with it?"

"I guess they don't have much choice. Or maybe they expect to live on Prairie Avenue themselves one day."

"I think they're too damned tired from workin' fourteen-hour days to care about anything, including themselves—" Lucy suddenly interrupted herself. Her face reddening, she pointed across the street. "Now just look at *that*, willya?"

A janitor from an office building across the way was blithely dumping five-gallon containers of ashes from the building's furnaces directly into the street. As the flaky gray specks started to settle on her hair and clothing—her one good dress—Lucy became so angry that Albert had to restrain her from crossing the street and directly confronting the man. He held her tightly as she and the janitor got into a shouting match across the street, ending with the janitor calling her "a no-good nigger bitch" and spitting in her direction before disappearing into the building's tunnel.

If Lucy felt assailed by Chicago's chaos, Albert, from the beginning, seemed enlivened by it. "This city's out-of-control," he said to Lucy cheerfully one day, looking up at a new eight-story office building—the city's largest to date—with life-size griffins plastered in terra-cotta around its circumference. "These people don't know when to stop," he chuckled. "The papers say a ten-story building, the Montauk, is already on the drawing boards. I hope they skip the griffins this time."

"What is a griffin?" Lucy asked anxiously.

"It's a mythical creature."

Lucy frowned. "Then griffins is just right for this place. The whole city's unreal. A river with no fish and birds walkin' on top of it!"

"I sorta like the excess," Albert said, sounding a little guilty. Yes, he thought to himself, that's it; the place does the bustin' out for me; the one thing it isn't is neutral! "Yeah, even that new hotel we walked through yesterday."

Lucy shuddered. "That Palmer House? Ugliest thing I ever saw. All those plaster statues up the entryway, then you get inside and it's just one big hall crammed with people talkin' money and spittin' on each other's shoes."

"Well, I liked those fancy electric annunciators they got for room service. Now that *is* special."

"They probably don't work, or won't work for long. I'll bet they never even finish the place. Or if they do, it'll burn down again. These people *like* bein' unfinished. Helps keep 'em frantic."

"Now you're bein' silly," Albert said, taking her hand.

Lucy pulled away. "And how come nobody talks about the lives lost, people crippled and homeless, thanks to all this tearin' down and buildin' up. Chicago don't want a past *or* a present—just some future that never arrives. It's like bein' in the middle of a hog auction that goes on forever."

"Oh, soon you'll be runnin' for Mayor." Albert put the back of his hand gently across her cheek. "You don't fool me, miss."

That made Lucy smile. She hated the way she'd been feeling since they arrived—uneasy and insecure, more deeply afraid than she could account for. She'd fought against fear all her life; she'd insisted on acting in charge even while knowing that her actual circumstances made a mockery of her commanding ways.

"That's a sweet thing to say," she said, kissing Albert on the cheek. "I wish I could figure out why I'm so on edge and you're so damned calm. It's not like you been livin' in New York all your life, or even Galveston."

"It's temperament," Albert shrugged. "You're quick to the boil, I'm low-keyed." He laughed. "The strong, silent type—like the heroes of yore." Lucy tried to give him a good-natured kick, but he skirted nimbly out of the way.

On one matter, though, Albert had been quick to flare up from the first day they set foot in Chicago: the city's barbarous treatment of its horses. Eighteen seventy-two, the year before they arrived, had seen the calamitous "Horse Epizootic"—an undiagnosed illness that had killed more than a thousand horses in a six-week period and had continued to rage on for months; oxen had to be brought in as a partial replacement for horse-drawn commercial wagons, but for a time traffic had been brought to a near halt.

Albert felt sure he knew the cause of the horses' "undiagnosed" illness. It was plain and simple mistreatment. Back in Texas, there'd certainly been times when he'd seen an animal ill used, but he'd felt able to personally intervene or remonstrate. In Chicago, the scale and frequency of the abuse made him feel helpless. He couldn't be stopping the dozens of horsecart drivers he saw every single day ferociously lashing their animals or pushing them beyond their strength. Besides, here—unlike in Johnson County—he wasn't sure who was in charge, who was responsible. Was an individual driver to blame or was it a horse-car company? Even if the driver was self-employed, perhaps his frantic brutality came from necessity, from himself being under the lash to make enough deliveries to keep food on his table . . .

All Albert knew for certain was that he couldn't bear to see the trusted companions of his childhood treated so badly. When he saw a horse being harshly beaten on the street or forced to pull heavy weights that brought the animal to its knees, the image of his beloved Bessie would come to mind and bring tears to his eyes. Few of Chicago's horses had any meat on their bones; fed a starvation diet in hard times, in sickness or old age they were simply turned loose and abandoned.

Albert wasn't the only one concerned: a group of citizens, just a few years back, had formed the Illinois Society for the Prevention of Cruelty to Animals. Maybe if enough people protested conditions, Albert thought, the city fathers would pass a law ensuring better treatment for the animals. Maybe. Brought up to rely above all on himself, Albert knew he wasn't the likeliest candidate for banding together with anybody to do anything. It didn't come naturally to him. Still, he signed up for membership in the ISPCA. It was the first organization he'd ever joined.

The second was Typographical Union Number 16. Just as he'd predicted earlier to Lucy, Albert found work almost immediately, as a substitute typesetter on the *Inter-Ocean* newspaper. Always a quick study, within six months he'd mastered enough of the new steel-engraving techniques to find full-time employment as a typesetter on the *Chicago Times*. His eventual goal was to become a reporter again, but he knew that would take time. Meanwhile, he kept his membership in the typographical union a secret: the *Times* was notoriously anti-union, and besides, he himself remained ambivalent about the utility, perhaps even the morality, of collective organizing.

Lucy insisted on working, too. Albert's sixty-dollar-a-month salary was considerably above the working-class average but not enough to allow them to have children, which they both wanted, without risking poverty. Besides, Lucy had never had any intention of spending her life at home—"I've spent too much of it there already, too much time preparing lye, shifting ashes, and emptying chamber pots."

Albert encouraged her to find work, but there were few options for women, other than becoming a live-in domestic or a prostitute. He teased her about the opulent attractions that awaited in the higher-class brothels, the elegant parlors, the cultured pianist, the French cuisine and the (post-coital) games of blind man's buff. "To hear the lads at the paper tell it . . . Why, at Carrie Watson's House they provide the girls with free liquor and morphine—enough to bring home a little extra at night for your old man."

"And *I* hear," Lucy shot back, "that she charges her girls a dollar a towel. No, I'd do better sitting in an open window on Clark Street and leaving my blouse off. Exotic Aztec Queen. I'd be rich in no time. Marry myself a ty-*coon*!"

"Perfect!" Albert laughed. "Wealth would make you eligible to become a Nervous Woman with sick headaches, palpitations, and morbid chills. Then you could get yourself shipped off to the mountains with the other fancy ladies for a rest cure."

"Where I would lie abed"—Lucy thrust back a nonexistent bustle on her dress and piled her hair onto the top of her head in some vague approximation of a chignon— "and regularly dose myself with laudanum and Bakers Stomach Bitters, with perhaps a bit of cocaine hydrochloride on the side—quality-controlled, of course." She collapsed in a burst of laughter.

"Just one minute, young woman!" Albert said, thrusting a hand through the breast of his jacket in imitation of a pompous physician. "You do realize, I trust, that your sexual organs are at the root of all your troubles. Medical Science has proven that sexual desire in a female is a form of derangement, a danger not only to herself but to any man with whom she might come in contact." Lucy silently insinuated her hands into Albert's pants' pockets, stroking his thighs through the wool.

"You must learn to restrain and retrain your body, curtailing abnormal sexual desire, making the will of the male your own." He pulled her hands out of his pockets, then gently put his own around her waist. Lucy pretended to swoon, going limp in his arms.

"Yes, m'lord," she said faintly. "Do as you like with me. I'm yours to command. But may I first ask one small question?"

"Well, be quick about it," he whispered in her ear as he began gently nibbling on the lobe.

"It's just this, sire: how do you know when a woman is exhibiting 'abnormal' sexual desire?"

Albert stifled a laugh. "A simple test, madam. I take my finger—like this—and mechanically stimulate the breast and clitoris." He moved his hand slowly down her body.

"That does not feel mechanical, m'lord."

"Aha!" Albert cried in mock horror. "You're responding to my touch! A clear sign of degeneracy! You must be sent at once for gynecological surgery. Only a clitoridectomy can cure so hysterical a condition!" He kissed her passionately on the lips, as their bodies slid slowly to the floor.

✳

With Albert away at the *Times* all day, Lucy began to make a few friends among the neighbors in their tenement, and particularly with a woman named Lizzie Swank who lived alone in a one-room flat on the floor above them. Like Albert, Lizzie came from a family whose members had fought in the Revolution and then moved west, in her case to Iowa. Her whole family, including her mother, was actively engaged with public issues, and Lizzie herself sometimes wrote for the libertarian press. Far better read than Lucy and Albert—Lizzie had a high school education—she started to loan them books, including a dictionary, which they avidly consumed.

Lizzie had moved to Chicago only a few years before them and supported herself by working at home as a dressmaker. "You don't have a lot of choice," she told Lucy, when they discussed job possibilities. "Some saloons have begun to hire female servers, but the wages are low and the jobs are, how shall I put it, of 'questionable character.'"

"Meaning what?" Lucy asked, her eyes mischievously alight. "That I have to get the customers drunk?"

"Exactly. Though the standard description is 'Encourage the male patrons to imbibe, using all female wiles necessary.'"

"If that's the case, I might at well sit in a fancy brothel and make some real money."

"Of course, you could always try factory work." Lizzie's frown made her opinion of that option clear enough. "The women put in a minimum of ten, a maximum of fourteen, hours a day."

"Those are farmhand hours," Lucy said indignantly.

"But *without* room and board. One of my friends makes lace collars for twenty-two cents a dozen; a twelve-hour workday brings her in sixty-six cents. She has a complexion like chalk from malnourishment."

"But that's slavery!" Lucy stormed. "I thought they'd freed the slaves."

Lizzie gave her a quizzical look, not knowing whether Lucy's remark was offhanded or meant to inaugurate an intimate conversation.

"Some stories are far worse, believe me. Another girl I know is a carpet-sewer. Her hands are blistered and raw but she has to keep going to support her invalid husband, disabled on a construction site. The boss makes her sew the carpet borders for free—they're 'chucked in,' part of the job, he told her. They're always 'chucking' things in," Lizzie added with a sigh. "My friend Mary Perkins makes coats for a living and has to dampen them in starch water and iron them without any extra pay. She works half the night, near every night, just to keep food on the table. Count yourself lucky, Lucy, that you've got a man who brings in money. There are lots of women living alone in this city who are starving to death."

"I'm determined to work," Lucy said dejectedly. "I must."

"Then you'd best be thinking about being a domestic. Like it or not, that's about all that's open to you."

"Is there any such thing as a part-time domestic? Then I wouldn't have to live in and could come home to Albert."

"I've heard of such jobs once in a while. But too many Irish girls are in need of a bed and willing to settle for room, board, and some second-hand clothes. Why should the fine ladies hire someone who won't be there to light the fires in the morning and turn off the gas lamps at night? Ah, Lucy, you'd never last anyway! You don't have the gift for kow-towing, I can tell."

"I don't have many gifts," Lucy said quietly. "Never was given a real education, just taught my numbers and how to write a more or less complete sentence. But I got plenty of grit and energy," she added, her spirits rising with her words. "Maybe I could become a burglar or a mugger."

"That's a man's field," Lizzie said with a laugh. "And there's a long waiting list."

"Well then, I got no choice. I'll just have to find out if any such thing as part-time domestic work exists."

"Give it a try, why not! But stay away from the employment agencies. They're mostly fly-by-night. They take your 'application fee' and then disappear. I'll get the name of a respectable intelligence office for you, a place that specializes in matching up servant girls and employers."

Lizzie was as good as her word, and one afternoon Lucy took herself to Mrs. Burke's Intelligence. In one room sat three or four elegant, impatient ladies bedecked in velvet dresses and overskirts of lace. One wore a white llama jacket, usually reserved for evening, her face painted with a compound of bismuth and arsenic that gave her skin a fashionable deathlike pallor. In an adjoining room, which had no chairs, a horde of unhealthy-looking young girls, most of them newly arrived immigrants, crowded together hoping to be picked, on any terms, for one of the few jobs available.

The woman in the llama jacket strode into the room where the girls waited, looked them over with the barest glance, and announced in full voice, "This is disgusting! There isn't a single one in the whole lot fit to enter a decent house." With that, she swept up her skirts and turned to leave. "And how would *you* know what a decent house is," Lucy yelled after her, "all gotten up like a whore!" Within seconds, a burly man appeared from nowhere, grabbed Lucy hard by the arm and pushed her out the front door.

That decided her. She'd stay at home and take in piecework; better lower wages than the daily humiliation of having to cater to the whims of idle women—or the predations of their sons and husbands. Lucy had learned sewing as a child and become skilled with the needle, able to make braid rosettes, velvet or ribbon trimmings, tarlatan interlinings—even Medici collars. She was confident she could succeed as a dressmaker, especially since Lizzie could promise a network of fellow seamstresses for contacts, advice, and customers. The downside of working at home was finding herself forced, against all inclination, to attend to a string of household chores that an outside job would have obviated.

During their first year in Chicago, Lucy and Albert were able to afford only a few pieces of furniture for their flat. A large metal bed with a roll-up mattress took up most of the smaller room; a washstand with bowl and pitcher for daily ablutions (with a strip of oilcloth underneath to catch any spillover), one straightback chair, and a footlocker for storing clothes consumed the rest of the space. The second room, the "living" area, had two kerosene lamps; two squat, undersized armchairs (bought thirdhand from a German peddler); and on the wall, one of the popular "chromos" of the day—a color lithograph that reproduced an oil painting of the western plains. Most of the remaining space was soon given over to Lucy's dressmaking. Albert folded a board over the washtub and pinned oilcloth around it to create a worktable for her. Lucy crocheted a bureau scarf to cover the table when not in use and, as an added nicety, sewed curtains for the window to conceal the garbage-strewn back alley it faced out on.

The kitchen alcove, dominated by a small ice chest and a large coal stove, made up the rest of the flat—and generated most of the repetitive chores that Lucy so deeply resented. Once a day, she had to lug fresh water into the house and more than once had to carry out cooking slops, dirty dishwater, and lamp soot, as well as collect human waste from the outdoor privy in a small shack behind the tenement. She also had to make frequent trips to the local lumberyard to buy kerosene for the lamps; filling and wiping them, plus trimming and replacing the wicks, were daily, sometimes twice-daily, necessities. The coal stove required even more attention—laying and tending fires, sifting and emptying ashes, scraping and blackening the stove's surface to prevent rust.

To escape spending what remained of her day in shopping for food and preparing it, Lucy avoided the markets and relied instead on the numerous street peddlers who conveniently passed near her door. It wasn't just a matter of conserving time: Lucy had heard the growing rumors—soon proven true—that the leading grocery stores were artificially dyeing decayed fruits and vegetables, then wrapping them in colorful gauze; and that meat was being adulterated with everything from ground entrails to wood chips. Food from the vending carts was usually fresher and less contaminated. From the peddlers, often Italian immigrants, Lucy could buy dairy goods, a variety of produce and meats, ice and coal; and from the Alsatian Jewish peddlers, the occasional personal item or inexpensive piece of clothing—a decorative hair comb, woolen stockings for winter.

Within a few months Albert and Lucy had become more or less acclimated to the city, Albert more, Lucy less. The basic routines of newspaper life had long been familiar to Albert and although the *Chicago Times* operated on a far larger scale than anything he'd previously known, he found the expansive new challenges exhilarating. The *Times* offices were located in the Haymarket area of Randolph Street, near the heart of the frenzied downtown commercial district. Yet Albert managed to maintain his own calm rhythm.

After the first few weeks, Lucy rarely went downtown. When she did, on some special errand to find corset stays or the like, the deep canyons and the smoke-darkened sky invariably brought back feelings of uneasiness. She couldn't understand why, and that annoyed her. On the ranch, she'd always been intrepid, even nervy, as quick to chastise faintheartedness during a flash flood as she was fearless in facing down a drunken cowhand.

This anxious new sense of unease was so unfamiliar that Lucy decided it couldn't possibly be a true part of her. She sternly admonished herself to stop being foolish and weak and decided that she would act like the Lucy of old—the Lucy of Johnson County—and thereby hasten her return. She was determined to stay away as much as possible from the strangely intimidating menace of the central city.

Both she and Albert were coming to terms with Chicago, in their own distinctive ways.

*

One morning in late September, as Albert was at his typesetting station laboring to master the "shooting stick"—a tool for unlocking pages of type from the metal frame that held them together—an employee from another department burst into the room shouting the news that "the financial house of Jay Cooke and Company in Philadelphia has suspended operations!" Everyone realized at once that the economic disaster long feared had come to pass. All work in the typesetting room stopped as the men huddled together, speculating in hushed tones about the likely firings soon to follow, how extensive they would be, and who would be left standing when the smoke cleared.

Within a few weeks, it became apparent that the devastation would be widespread. The collapse of Cooke and Company precipitated a stock market panic that radiated out into a rash of brokerage, insurance, and bank failures. A full-scale crash was at hand. Seemingly overnight, an army of the unemployed, many evicted for nonpayment of rent, was wandering the streets of Chicago, and every other major metropolis, in search of work, food, and shelter.

Albert and Lucy considered themselves fortunate in comparison with their neighbors. Within a few weeks of the economic collapse, all the families in their tenement were to varying degrees in straitened circumstances. Lucy managed to hold on to some of the piecework she'd been doing for a nearby textile mill, though at reduced rates. And Albert, too, was able to continue working. The *Times* did fire a fifth of its employees, but Albert, known for his speed and dexterity in composition, was among those kept on, though with a cut in pay from sixty to forty-two dollars a month.

Of all the families, the worst off were Joe and Margaret Hennessey, devout Catholics with five children, who lived in the cramped basement quarters. Joe was a stonecutter, Margaret a pieceworker. Both lost their jobs within a week of each other. Having no savings, having barely managed the rent each month, the Hennesseys were terrified of actual starvation. They immediately pawned their only two items of value: Joe's silver belt buckle, bought with money he'd earned as a young man working in the Butte, Montana, mines; and Margaret's cherished enamel brooch, her mother's parting gift when, at age fifteen, she had emigrated from Ireland.

The Hennesseys' three eldest children contributed a modicum of money from part-time work. Their nine-year-old peddled wooden matchboxes on the street and their eleven-year-old worked as a newsboy. Sheila, fourteen, belonged to a posse of teenagers who picked rags after school, collecting bits of cloth from factory discards and reselling them for conversion into paper or for use as upholstery stuffing. The three children's combined pennies and nickels were enough to put eggs, thin slices of cheap meat, crackers, and black coffee on the table in the morning.

Providing food for the rest of the day was problematic. Margaret sought help from the Chicago Relief Society, but it initially turned her away; on the basis of its "scientific" formula for determining who was or was not worthy of aid, the society adjudged the Hennesseys capable of being self-supporting—if the family mended its "irregular habits and spendthrift ways" (specifically cited were Joe's use of tobacco and Margaret's having once taken the children, at two cents a head, to view the mound of melted metal from the Great Fire on display at the Relic House).

"You mean to say," Lucy sardonically asked Margaret after she'd recounted what had happened, "they didn't reprimand you for having breakfast *every* morning?" She encouraged her to make a second appeal and—perhaps because an unusually harsh winter had set in, with people found every night frozen to death on the streets—the society did, when Margaret reappeared, partially relent: it agreed to provide the Hennesseys with a food basket and some firewood every other day. But Margaret couldn't abide the lectures on abstinence and hard work that accompanied the hand-outs and after a month refused further help from the Society.

Lucy and Albert insisted on giving the Hennesseys a "loan" of two dollars a week, all they could spare, and every other week Lizzie Swank chipped in half a dollar from her own meager income. But bad luck continued to dog the family at every turn. They had long been relying on credit not only for grocery purchases, but for almost every item in their barren flat—including the dishes, the pots and pans, the stove, and above all, the precious Singer sewing machine. Unable any longer to meet payments, they watched helplessly as their household items were repossessed one by one. The sewing machine was the last to go, and Lucy held a tearful Margaret tightly in her arms when the collectors arrived to take it away.

Still worse was to come. One afternoon, as Lucy was absorbed in stitching a waistband, a tearful Margaret rushed in, barely able to blurt out the news that her eleven-year-old, Tom, had been arrested for trying to pawn stolen goods. In the investigation that followed, Tom was linked to a gang of street children—several such gangs had sprung up in the city—who'd been employing an arsenal of inventive survival tricks. One of them had mastered the epileptic fit, convincingly collapsing in convulsion in the middle of a crowded street; horrified passersby would drop a few coins into the boy's outstretched palm before fleeing the scene. Another, a girl of twelve, had become a pathetic "cripple," hobbling down the street on broken-down crutches, her hand held out for alms; sometimes, bored with her own performance, she'd substitute a fake prosthesis or swath herself in filthy bandages. In the same high spirits, the gang would leave their own brand of calling cards at the mansions along Prairie Avenue: they rang the doorbells and unhinged the gate at the Marshall Field residence; and on the lawn of the Pullman mansion, they planted a large "Tripe and Pigs' Feet" sign.

The police treated the children as dangerous criminals. Tom, without a trial, was sent at once to Dunning, the notorious three-story brick building situated nine miles outside the city that simultaneously served as jail, madhouse, and shelter for the indigent poor. A sobbing Margaret told Lucy, who'd never heard of Dunning, that it was Chicago's most dreaded institution. "I used to threaten my Tom with the place when he misbehaved."

Lizzie, outside Margaret's hearing, told Lucy some additional horror stories about the place. "A girlfriend of mine," Lizzie said, "had a nervous collapse from too much work and not enough food, and they sent her to Dunning. The staff members—not a respectable soul among them—stole every single personal item she had, down to her ripped stockings. The only two 'doctors' in the place were inexperienced students who prescribed the same medications for all ailments. And the meals, every meal, consisted of watered-down soup, moldy bread, and some sort of 'meat' concoction so tough it got nicknamed 'B.A.'—'blacksmith's apron.'"

"I wouldn't have stood for it!" Lucy said indignantly.

"Ah, Lucy, you still have a lot to learn about Chicago! Who would you have reported it to? The warden of Dunning?"

"Yes, to those in charge."

Lizzie shook her head with amusement. "You weren't here a few years back when the Dunning scandal broke."

"What scandal?"

"Promise you won't start cursing and yelling, but it was discovered that the warden had appointed his seventeen-year-old daughter as head of housekeeping, and that the chief physician, under cover of night, had for years been digging up the corpses of newly deceased inmates and selling them, at twenty dollars each, to medical colleges. It was apparently a lucrative trade."

"What did he do with the empty coffins," Lucy said evenly. "Use them to start the Great Fire? You see, I don't *have* to curse and yell."

The very day Tom was sent away, a tight-lipped Margaret told Lucy that "my Tommy will not be long at Dunning. That much I swear."

"But how will you get the court to release him?" Lucy asked, misjudging Margaret's intentions. "That costs money. Lots more money than any of us have."

Three days later, when Lucy went to knock on the Hennesseys' door, she found it wide open, the apartment stripped of its few remaining items, and the Hennesseys gone. At first she thought the landlord had turned them out, but he proved as mystified as everyone else at their disappearance.

It was only months later that they learned from an unemployed neighborhood youth named Kruger, who'd "gone tramping" but had returned briefly to Chicago to visit his parents, that he'd spotted the entire hollow-cheeked Hennessey clan, including young Tom—somehow spirited out of Dunning—on a boxcar freight traveling west from Des Moines. They were part of the growing army of vagabonds, homeless and jobless, wandering the nation. "I seen folks," Kruger said, "sleeping under bridges, in hayricks, barns, and hen roosts. In Iowa, heard about one family of five—went to sleep in an old lime kiln and was crushed to death that night by a cave-in."

"How do people get food, what do they live on?" Lizzie asked, sounding dazed.

"An occasional dole from town officials, a few days' work as farm laborers or street sweepers or coal carriers," Kruger said. Then he smiled slyly. "And stealin'."

He told the Hennesseys' Chicago friends that in fact he'd been able to speak with the family for only a minute or two. He'd caught up with them during a brief train stop when they were frantically trying to wash up in a nearby canal. When he greeted Margaret, she looked at him blankly, then turned away. Joe Hennessey would say no more than that they were heading west, where he hoped to work once more in the mines.

Lucy never saw the Hennesseys again. Nor heard a word about their fate.

"That Mr. Gianni was on the street today," Lucy told Lizzie. For companionship, the two women had taken to doing piecework together in the Parsons's apartment.

"Gianni?"

"You know—the produce man who comes around sometimes with his horsecart. His stuff's not the freshest, but he looks so worn down I try to buy a few tomatoes at least. I asked him how his daughter was, and he almost burst into tears. 'My Sophia,' he said—he doesn't know much English—'has much too hard in factory . . . material bad . . . break needle . . . must pay.' I couldn't catch his meaning at first, but he rubbed the heavy material of his overalls between his fingers and somehow got me to understand that that was the kind of rough material his daughter sews. It often breaks the machine's needle and sometimes even the throat plate."

Lizzie shook her head knowingly.

"The foreman fines Gianni's daughter and the others girls five cents per needle, fifty cents per plate. Sometimes they bring home no money at all at the end of a week's work."

"And the breakage isn't even their fault," Lizzie said.

"What *is* their fault?" Lucy scoffed, "that they were born poor? The girls aren't even allowed to talk to each other to help pass the time! It's even worse with Gianni's son. The boy's only eight and has to work ten-hour days filling sausages and cleaning casings—all the while breathing in disgusting air and standing on a stockyard floor flooded with water. The child came by on the cart one Sunday a few weeks back. He looks like a little old man. Oh, Lizzie!" Lucy wailed. "We've got to do something! If only I could think what . . ."

Albert took off his coat and dropped wearily into an armchair. "It's awful out there," he groaned. "The suffering's worse'n anything you can imagine."

Lucy stiffened a bit at the implication she hadn't had enough misery in her own life to understand. But she'd rarely seen Albert so upset and decided to go easy. "I can imagine," she said, keeping her voice neutral. "Lizzie and I were talking about it most of the day."

Albert got up from his chair and started to pace the room. "The *Times* won't print but a small part of what's going on. I complained to one of the reporters today, tried to tell him about a scene I'd witnessed during lunch break. He just shrugged and looked past me. 'The proprietors don't want to alarm the public,' he said, 'with too many unpleasant stories.' Hell, don't they think the public's alarmed already, what with families sleepin' in horse stalls and going to jail for stealin' a little food?" With a groan, Albert slumped back into the armchair. "It's an outrage, that's what . . ."

"Which is just what Lizzie and me were sayin' . . . the big shots don't seem to care and the rest of us don't know what to do . . . What happened at lunchtime?"

"Oh God," Albert said, "it'll just make you more miserable . . . never mind . . ."

"Tell me, Albert. I want to hear."

Albert paused a moment. "It was this young girl . . ." he began, and then stopped.

"*Tell* me, Albert."

"There was a crowd gathered around the back of a parked grocery wagon . . . I thought maybe they were sellin' fresh produce, so I edged towards the front, thinkin' I'd surprise you with a few pieces of fruit . . . and then I saw her . . ." Albert's chest started to heave. "Just a little slip of a thing . . . no more'n thirteen or fourteen . . . she . . . she was . . . frozen to death! The only lodging that poor child could afford was the back of an empty wagon—"

Albert started to sob, his body shaking. Lucy rushed over and took him in her arms, cradling him and rocking him back and forth until he slowly began to breathe more easily. He took a handkerchief from his pocket and dried his eyes. "I'll get you some tea," Lucy said softly and went to the kitchen. When she came back, they sat side-by-side holding hands and talking quietly.

"Lizzie says they've started to let some homeless sleep in police stations at night. That means a few less deaths . . ."

"For *one* night," Albert said. "Ten to a cell so small two of 'em have to stand up. At the stroke of six, the police throw 'em back out on the street—no breakfast, no chance to wash or even relieve themselves. The papers are full of praise for Superintendent Washburne's 'humanity.'"

"Where do they go?" Lucy asked, her expression stony.

"Where does who go?"

"After they're thrown out of the police station."

"Oh. Well the desperate ones go to the Tramps' Lumber Yard, where they can—

"The tramps' *what*?"

"Haven't you seen all the signs posted up on buildings?"

"If I had, would I be askin'?"

"Now don't get testy," Albert said. "I'm in no mood."

"Was I?" Lucy seemed genuinely surprised. "Sometimes I don't think I hear the sound of my own voice."

"Often, my pet."

"Well, why don't you hold me more to account, then?"

Albert smiled. "The problem is, I like your ardent ways. You want people to have better lives. And you want it right now." He let out a chuckle. "Still, it's true, you can sound like an awful harpy sometimes."

"Oh Albert, that's terrible! No, no, stop laughin'. This isn't funny. I don't like it at all— you have to help. Help me be better."

"Awright—I will! It's a promise."

He gave her a loud, wet kiss on the cheek.

"I hold you to it. Now, what is the Tramps' Lumber Yard?"

"The propertied class is gettin' alarmed at the number of jobless men roaming the city. So the Relief Society's opened this yard, where any man who saws and splits a cord of wood will get three meals and a night's lodging, worth in total, about fifty cents. It's work that ordinarily pays two dollars and seventy-five cents."

"How generous."

"Even less than you know. It takes an experienced lumberjack ten hours to split a cord of wood. Most of the jobless have never done that sorta work. Besides, they're weak from lack of food and sleep. So all they can usually manage is to cut enough wood for a single meal."

"And it's probably pigs' feet."

"The Relief Society has declared itself enormously pleased with the lumber yard experiment. They're callin' it a touchstone, an infallible way of finding out whether the masses of men 'loitering about' really want to work or not."

"And those who refuse this grand opportunity?"

"If a man won't work in the Lumber Yard, he's officially branded a professional beggar—and turned over to the police."

"Albert, this is monstrous! Something must be done!"

"Yes, *something*. But what, what?!"

"Horror stories from Lizzie! Horror stories from you! And here we sit, soaking 'em up with our tea as if we were at a Prairie Avenue social . . ."

"Some protests are being organized . . ."

"Oh? Why haven't you told me? Why haven't I heard anything about them?"

"I'm just beginning to hear things myself. I should be learning more very soon," Albert said enigmatically.

"Hearing what? Tell me, tell me!"

"Well, I've been exchanging greetings—just a nod of the head or a few words—for some time now with a young carpenter working in the *Times* building. Then just this week, he asked if I'd care to share lunch with him at one of those nickel-and-dime counters downtown for workingmen. So I did. By the way, they *chain* the utensils to the counter."

"Nothing surprises me any more." Lucy said matter-of-factly. "So who is this carpenter? What did he tell you?"

"His name's George. Won't give me his last name. He recruits for the Knights of Labor, but he's also, secretly, an organizer for the First Inter-national. He's very intense, very—"

"What's the First International?"

"It's a Marxist group."

"Followers of Karl Marx?" Lucy asked. "But isn't he very—"

"Yes *very*—radical, that is. George says Chicago's had a section of the International for a decade, mostly made up of German workers. But now, since the crash, the membership's jumped upwards."

"To how many?"

"George says about four hundred."

Lucy laughed. "The *Times* probably employs more people than that"

"It's a large enough number to scare the hell outta the rich. The papers are writin' up the International as if it's the Paris Commune all over again. Here, look at this."

Albert tossed a copy of the *Chicago Tribune* on the table.

Lucy picked it up and read aloud: "Men claim they can find no work, yet somehow they have money enough to get drunk and threaten every description of trouble. They are a thriftless and improvident lot."

"Well," said Lucy, putting the paper down, "too bad the *Tribune*'s edi-tor never met the Hennesseys. What a bunch of drunken rotters they were, eh?"

"My own dear employer, the *Times*," Albert said, "is demanding that a National Guard garrison be set up to put down what it calls the imminent revolution. My carpenter friend George agrees. He's sure the Revolution will come any day now. To tell you the truth, Lucy, he scares me a little.

I feel more and more in sympathy with the Knights of Labor, they're right that a fair day's work ought to bring a fair day's pay. And they're embracing all workers, skilled and unskilled . . . But the International—leastwise as George describes it—wants to get rid of capitalism altogether. He thinks any man who's ever made a large amount of money is, by definition, a scoundrel."

"No, only the white ones." Lucy tossed in.

Albert shook his head. "That goes too far for me . . . But I am feeling more and more sympathy for the Knights."

Lucy eyed him suspiciously. "You said that already. Somethin's goin' on here."

"Well," Albert said sheepishly, "truth is, I've been going to their meetings downtown, during lunch break—"

"You've been going to meetings? When did you intend to tell me—after the revolution?"

"I needed to feel sure about what I was doin' before I involved you. You can understand that."

"I could if we had a bad marriage. Anyway, you won't involve me. From what I hear about the Knights, they're just a bunch of silly men who like dressin' up in strange outfits."

"Well, then, you haven't heard nearly enough," Albert replied. "And, by the way, that's a good example of the harpy tone you wanted me to point out."

"What?" Lucy was instantly indignant. "All I said was that the Knights seem more interested in costumes than politics."

"That isn't what you said, though it's just as bad. Besides, it's your tone I'm reacting to."

"Oh, I see. Women shouldn't have opinions on public questions, let alone express them with passion."

"Lucy! You're the one who asked me to point out when you're bein' a bit more tart than necessary."

"That doesn't mean you'll be right every time."

"No, it doesn't. But I am right this time."

"Maybe yes, maybe no," she grumbled, beginning to back down. "How long've you been goin' to those meetings?"

"Coupla weeks. I've never kept any other secret from you in all the time we been together." Albert said fervently. "To tell you the truth, I can't really say why I kept it from you. Maybe I thought you'd talk me out of it. Anyway, I promise you that from now on, I'll—"

"Oh, don't make so much of it, for heaven's sake. *I'm* not!" She loved leaving Albert with his jaw hanging open. "If we told each other every single thing we did or thought," she breezed nonchalantly on, "we'd bore each other to death in a week. And don't think for a minute that by bein' so sincere and repentant, you're gonna get me to change my mind about the Knights!"

"Lucy, you are a maddening creature."

Chicago

1875–1876

The man didn't offer his name. He instructed Albert to wait in the ante-room—the Outer Veil, he called it—that adjoined the meeting hall. The small space was bare except for a line of chairs along one wall and, near the closed set of doors that led into the hall, a triangular altar on which sat a globe, a closed copy of Scripture and a red basket filled with blank cards. The man removed two of the cards, handed one to Albert, and told him to write his name on it. Then he himself wrote something on the second card.

"When you hear a rap on the door," the man said solemnly, "you will rise and follow me into the inner Sanctuary." He then sat on a chair distant from Albert's and the two waited in silence. Albert felt uncharacteristically jumpy, alert to every sound.

Within minutes the rap came, and the door leading to the meeting hall swung open from the inside. Without a word, Albert's companion moved toward it, beckoning him to follow. Standing there awaiting them was an impressive figure of a man, his face—except for the corners of a large, drooping moustache—concealed behind a mask and slouch hat, his body draped in a black cloak. He was known, so Albert later learned, as the Unknown Knight (his informer adding good-humoredly, "I never met a member who knew what all these rituals and symbols are supposed to mean—some say one thing, some another").

The shrouded figure wore a large triangular gold medal on his cape. Despite the dim light, Albert could make out a pyramid at the center of the medal, with the letters *S, O, M,* and *A* etched on its sides and base, standing for Secrecy, Obedience, and Mutual Assistance—the Knights of Labor's official tenets. The man in the black cape took Albert's right hand in his own and pressed his thumb hard against Albert's fingers; as previously instructed, Albert returned the pressure and then received two quick, light taps on the hand.

The Grip having been successfully exchanged, the man then placed his closed hand under his own chin. Again as preinstructed, Albert announced, "I am a stranger." To which the man responded, "A stranger should be assisted," and swept his cape aside to make way for Albert to enter the hall.

Albert peered expectantly into a gaslit chamber only slightly larger than the waiting room. He could make out some dozen men standing in a semicircle, several of them wearing robes of different colors with elaborate ribbons, tassels, and medallions attached to them. No man was dressed like any other. Though Albert was too nervous to cast more than a hasty glance at the exotic outfits, his eyes did fix briefly on one brilliantly fashioned badge—a large coral column with an open hand fashioned out of ivory on it, plus carvings of leaves, fruit, and the words "Hear Both Sides, Then Judge."

After Albert had entered the inner room, a lance was placed on the door and it was pulled closed behind him, thus announcing that the meeting was in progress. Two men, one on either side of Albert, took hold of him firmly under his arms and moved him to the center of the room. The others closed in around him, forming an unbroken circle. In quick succession, they exchanged a series of complicated hand grips, signals, raps, and passwords.

The series completed, the man in the black cape spoke a few hushed and, to Albert, murky words. He could barely catch their drift, though he did distinctly hear the first sentence, "Open and public associations having failed, after a struggle of centuries to protect or advance the interests of labor, we have lawfully constituted this assembly."

Beyond that, Albert was able to pick up only an occasional fragment: ". . . Opulent monopolists are a power greater than the State . . . sapping foundations of democracy . . . moral worth not wealth is the true standard of greatness . . . ," and the concluding sentence, spoken fervently by the entire group, "An injury to one is the concern of all." The ceremonies ended with everyone joining hands and singing the Knights of Labor anthem, its sturdy chorus reverberating four times over:

Storm the fort, ye Knights of Labor,
Battle for your cause;
Equal rights for every neighbor,
Down with tyrant laws!

At the close of the song, the gas lamps were turned up. Albert was greeted with smiles and bear hugs and given a copy of the booklet *Adelphon Kryptos* (Secret Brotherhood), which somewhat better explained the principals and rituals he had fleetingly glimpsed and only partly understood.

*

"Secret handshakes, fancy robes—oh, Albert!" Lucy laughed derisively. "It sounds like the Klan—or a bunch of not so bright schoolboys tryin' to scare the neighbors."

"You're not payin' attention to the principles." The degree of Albert's frustration was always best gauged not by the rising volume of his voice, but by the way its characteristic mellowness bleached into a colorless monotone. "'An Injury to One Is the Concern of All.' *That*, he said evenly, "is the essence of the Knights' philosophy. There's no other platform that can bring together working people who don't like each other's manners and ways."

Lucy remained unconvinced. "Then stress the principle, instead of burying it beneath all those ridiculous trappings! 'The Outer Veil,' The *Adelphon Kryptos*—ugh! It sounds like one more superstitious religion to me. And a particularly dumb one at that."

"Forget the mumbo jumbo," Albert said; he did want to persuade her. "It's no different from the Masons—or the Roman Catholics, for that matter. The men need it. It gives them some sense of specialness, importance. Exactly what they don't feel in their lives. Don't be so hard on the poor fellows. Let them feel a little exalted for once."

That softened Lucy, but she didn't want to show it just yet. "'Injury to one, the concern of all,' eh? Just who does 'all' include? Any women at the meetin'? Did you see a black face?"

"The only people excluded from membership are bankers, lawyers, gamblers, speculators—and liquor tradesmen."

"Liquor tradesmen?" Lucy fairly shrieked with glee. "That mean the German beer halls are off limits? Now *that's* an effective tactic for unity!"

"You're not listenin'. The ban is against those who monopolize the *sale* of liquor. No one intends to ban *liquor*! Now stop bein' foolish."

"I surely will—just as soon as you answer the question about women and negroes."

"I saw none of either group at this particular meeting." Albert looked uncomfortable. "But it was a small meeting, and I've been reliably told—"

"Told by who?" Lucy interrupted, feeling confident he'd have no answer.

"The chief man." (Albert couldn't get himself to volunteer his actual title, the Master Workman, knowing it would set Lucy guffawing till morning). "After the meeting, I put the question to him directly."

"And his answer?" Lucy knew Albert wouldn't lie to her.

"They are welcome, they truly are," Albert said fervently. "Women and negroes. You must believe me about this. Though it's true that Uriah Stephens, the—"

"Who?"

"Uriah Stephens, the founder of the Knights. He—"

"What a name! Sounds like a pinched bookkeeper."

"Stephens did want to exclude women. He thought they were incapable of keeping secrets." Albert smiled sheepishly, expecting Lucy's wrath.

But she simply laughed. "Oh my, yes! We're also incapable of reading serious books without overtaxing our weak brains and having breakdowns. You men have got it all figured out."

"That's not fair, Lucy, not in regard to the Knights, anyway." He suddenly reached for the *Adelphon Kryptos* lying on top of the table and opened it to a page he'd earlier marked. "Listen to this, now just listen for once: 'I can see ahead of me an organization that will include men and women of every craft, creed and color.' Do you know who said that, do you know whose words those are?"

"God's."

"Uriah Stephens! You see—the man's capable of changing his mind. His views aren't set in stone. He's struggling. And even if he personally ends up on the wrong side of things, it won't matter. In the seven years since the KOL was founded, more and more local chapters are actively recruiting women and negroes as members. The call is for "universal brotherhood." And it's not just words. I tellya, within a few years there'll be tens of thousands of female and colored members."

"Well," Lucy said derisively, "ain't nobody else recruitin' nigras—'ceptin' as peons."

"I give up."

"Oh, don't get all edgy. I do want to hear more about this universal brotherhood stuff . . . Truth is, I read some of those Knights pamphlets you leave around—taxin' though it's been for my feeble brain. Noticed some pretty nasty stuff in 'em about the Chinese. Coolies, the pamphlets call them. 'Vice-ridden, human locusts, pagans'—that's how one writer describes 'em. Says they work so hard for so little money that they're takin' the bread outta the mouths of real Americans. Now is this what you Knights mean by universal brotherhood?"

Albert sighed. "It's not what *I* mean. And you know it. But okay, you're right. Most Knights do despise the Chinese, just like the rest of the country." He fell silent for a moment, tongue-tied with discomfort. Lucy said nothing, wanting him to stew a little longer.

Albert finally blurted out, "What else is there, Lucy? No labor organization—no elected official, for that matter—is sayin' anything different about the Chinese. The white man is what matters. You taught me that."

"Gotta be pale white—no Jews or Italians, thank you."

"At least the Knights are *aimin'* at something better, even if they haven't fully taken hold of their own principles. Yes, they got a long way to go. The question is, Do we try to help 'em get there, or do we turn up our superior noses—and give up?"

Lucy broke into a warm smile, and her voice was emphatic. "We try to help 'em get there, of course." She hugged Albert. "I like to make you sweat. But I'm with you, sweet boy."

✳

"Eight hundred marchers and twenty-nine floats—just imagine, folks!" the speaker thundered from the platform. "Two years ago a beer garden—a small beer garden—would've been enough to hold our numbers!

Today we've filled the lawn of the Colehour picnic grounds to capacity! We finally got us a Fourth of July picnic that does represent the spirit of independence!"

The crowd roared in delight. Albert and Lucy were standing near the front, his arm around her waist; he squeezed her so hard with excitement that she let out a little squeal, then playfully smacked him on the arm.

"The Knights," the speaker went on, "cannot be stopped—not by the government, not by the police, not by the monopolists—until we reach our goal of a decent life for everyone!"

Albert leaned down and whispered in Lucy's ear. "*Everyone*. Hear that?" Lucy swatted him again.

A tidal wave of enthusiasm swept through the crowd, the earsplitting roar of approval rolling on and on. Dozens of banners and placards—"THE LAND FOR THE PEOPLE; UNITED WE STAND"—waved through the air like low-flying flocks of birds. Fathers swung their children into the air. A drum corps beat out roll after roll. One of the two bands started playing "Hold the Fort, Ye Knights of Labor," inspiring a top-of-the-lungs sing-along. The speaker kept raising his arms in a futile plea for quiet, but soon gave up. Cupping his hands over his mouth, he good-naturedly yelled out to the crowd, "On to the picnic, folks! Time to enjoy! . . . footraces! . . . crafts! . . . barbecue! . . . don't forget dancing at the lake pavilion! . . . and the greased pigs! . . . beer enough to float Mayor Colvin out to sea! . . ." The notables descended from the platform.

Albert and Lucy had come to Colehour with Lizzie Swank, and as the crowd began to disperse in search of various amusements, the three of them started across the lawn.

"It's too hot for dancing," Lizzie said. "It's bound to be the polka, and then more polka."

"I say it's time for beer and pretzels," Albert offered.

Lucy agreed. "A glass of beer would save my life."

As the three of them turned in the direction of the beer garden, Lizzie bumped into a man passing close to her on the left. "I'm so sorry," she said, stepping back. Then her face lit up with pleasure—"Why for heaven's sake—it's Mr. Spies!"

"My dear Miss Swank, what an unexpected surprise!" The man's English was impeccable, though unmistakably flecked with a German accent. In his early twenties and strikingly poised and handsome, he had an athletic build and a face so classically sculpted that it might easily have appeared inert—were it not for a luxurious, thick moustache and deep-set azure eyes that sparkled with ironic humor. He was in the company of another man.

"This is August Spies," Lizzie said, introducing him to Albert and Lucy. "He has a small upholstery store near the dress shop where I once worked. We used to stop now and then to chat." They exchanged greetings, and Albert congratulated Spies on being self-employed.

"Only recently," Spies said. "My mother and sisters have come over from Landeck and I must try to make more money to support them."

"Aha!" Lucy said, smiling, "You're a budding capitalist!"

"Alas," Spies replied, "I earned more when working in someone else's furniture store. But perhaps sales will pick up soon."

Spies turned and introduced his companion, a large, brawny man, somewhat older than he, with thick eyebrows and a full black beard. "This is my friend Samuel Fielden, who works in the stoneyards."

"There isn't a street in Chicago," the smiling Fielden said tipping his hat, "on which I haven't dropped my sweat." His powerful voice and physicality might have been intimidating were it not for his modest manner, the warmth in his eyes, and the neutralizing trace of an English accent.

"I should warn you," Fielden said with a twinkle. "I'm saving my pennies to buy a team, to become a hauler of stone rather than a lifter. I suppose that makes me a potential capitalist, too."

"Nonsense," said Lucy. "That simply makes you a hard-working man—which *dis*qualifies you from membership in the capitalist class."

They laughed together with an easy sympathy that led Albert—who felt himself immediately and powerfully drawn to Spies—to impulsively suggest that the two men join them for beer and some food, and they readily accepted his invitation.

Lizzie wondered whether she shouldn't stop off on the way to have a look at the pagoda housing handicrafts and needlework. That prompted Fielden to say that he, too, was tempted to join up with them later, since he wanted to have a go at the fifty-yard fat men's race.

"You're not fat, Mr. Fielden, you're strong," Lucy said in that definitive way of hers. "Why, it wouldn't be fair to the other contestants." Both Fielden and Lizzie were easily persuaded, given the heat, to relax first and take in the fairgrounds later.

The beer garden was set in a cool, shady grove of trees with a big banner stretched across its entryway: "UNION THROUGHOUT: UNION CIGARS, UNION HELP, UNION MUSIC, UNION BEER."

"I know what union music is—loud and brassy," Lucy joked as they seated themselves at one of the few vacant tables, "but what is union *beer?*"

"It's beer," Spies said solemnly, "brewed during a workday not longer than eight hours."

"Which means beer that don't exist," Albert replied. "No one I know works an eight-hour day—except a lucky few in the craft unions." He was surprised at his own earnestness and wondered if it was appropriate to sharing a light-hearted drink with brand-new acquaintances. But the newcomers picked right up on it.

"No employer has to make concessions now, not even to the craft unions," Fielden boomed out. "There's an army of unemployed men more than glad to work twelve-hour days for half the regular wage."

"Wages fall, but prices don't," Lucy chimed in.

"Least of all the price of food," Lizzie added. "Over half my wages go for food these days. Add in the rent, and I don't have enough left over for a bolt of calico."

"Not to mention the cost of a draught of beer," Lucy said, lightening up the conversation. "That means one of you fine gentlemen will have to treat this poor"—she gestured toward Lizzie—"working girl."

Spies and Fielden vied to outdo each other for the privilege, their voices overlapping with Lizzie's indignant protest, "For heaven's sake, Lucy, I've got my own nickel to spend."

Lucy held up her hand for quiet. "Thank you, thank you," she nodded to Spies and Fielden. "Lizzie *and* I accept your kind offer—Albert can pay for his own. And the second draught is on us!"

"Meanin' on me," Albert said, laughing.

"No such thing." Lucy replied in a flash. "I make my own wages, I'll thank you to remember, and am just as independent as you."

"Oh my dear," Albert said with a huge, concluding smile, "you're far more so."

Beer was at once ordered for all but Spies, who said he preferred Rhine wine. Fascinated by Spies's educated tastes and speech, Albert was keen to know more about his background and started plying him with questions.

It turned out that Spies had emigrated from Germany just five years earlier, at age seventeen. "I had a happy childhood," he said. "I played and studied. In my country children must go to school for eight years and during that time cannot, by law, be utilized by parents or employers for profit."

"Whereas here I'd wager," Albert said, "poor children attend school for two, three years—which is why I sometimes still feel like a country bumpkin. Like now." He grinned ingratiatingly at Spies, who smiled back sympathetically but said nothing.

Lucy filled the silence. "Some children," she said, "get no schooling. They're slaves from birth, even now that slavery's ended." She was aware that Fielden was suddenly staring at her intently, and felt sure she knew why: he was wondering if this was a subject he could broach. Fielden hesitated a moment, then turned instead to Spies, who had started to describe his father's work as administrator of a forest district, a career for which he, too, as a youngster, had been preparing.

"I even had private tutors now and then, and for a time studied at the Polytechnicum in Kassel."

"You sound like a rich boy," Lizzie said innocently.

"I certainly never saw the kind of poverty and suffering that I've seen since coming to this country," Spies replied.

"Why didn't you become an administrator?" Albert asked.

"Father died suddenly when I was seventeen and as the eldest of six, I didn't feel justified in continuing my studies. And so I immigrated to the States, first to New York and then, the following year, here to Chicago. From forestry to furniture—that about sums up my journey thus far," he said with a sardonic laugh.

"May I put a direct question to you?" Albert asked, a bit belatedly.

"Yes, of course. I'm all for bluntness." There was a detectable edge to Spies's voice. "But I think I've guessed your question and the answer is, No, I'm not married."

Lucy let out a delighted hoot and said something about "being able to fix that soon enough."

Albert looked a little offended. "That was not at all my question," he said.

"Everybody asks the handsome Mr. Spies that," Fielden affectionately explained. "Nobody ever asks *me*. But in case you had, I'd have told you

I have a wife and three children. And love 'em dearly."

Lizzie gave Fielden's arm an approving squeeze.

"I'm so sorry," Spies said to Albert. "Do ask me what you wanted to."

"I wanted to know your philosophy. Your politics. You needn't answer, of course."

"Oh do attempt some answer, Mr. Spies, or how will we ever get to know you?" Lizzie said, her eyes weighty with sincerity.

"I ask as a novice," Albert added, "as someone just beginnin' to feel his way politically."

"But that's how I feel." Spies laughed.

"I think you're being modest," Lucy said. "You're a learned man; anyone can see that."

"Well, I've read many books; that's true," Spies replied, his tone dejected. "But they've filled my head with many more questions than answers. If I have a basic philosophy, I suppose it's simply this: the object of life is to enjoy it. And to make sure that other people can as well."

"But what about your politics?" Albert asked, his disappointment transparent. "You and Fielden seem to care about the plight of the poor, but—"

"—we *are* the poor," Fielden interrupted, with an amused grin.

"Well then," Albert went on, "what political means do you favor for improving your lot? There are so many competing organizations and ideologies."

"Yes, and each wants single-minded allegiance," Spies said. "But why give it? Why commit exclusively to the Knights of Labor, say, or the International, or the Lehr-und-Wehr Verein, or any of a dozen others, when all are doing valuable work? I simply don't understand the need to—"

"—excuse me for interrupting," Lizzie said, "but what's that last group? I've never heard of it. What did you call it?"

"The Lehr-und-Wehr Verein?"

"Yes, that's the one. What does it stand for, what does it do?"

"There's no reason you should know it. My apologies. The first Verein is only now getting organized." Spies went on to explain that the German words roughly translated into "education and defense society."

"They're modeled," he said, "on the Turnverein, a gymnastic association popular in Germany."

"What's the 'defense' part all about?" Albert asked.

"The members drill," Spies said matter-of-factly, "to provide guards for meetings and parades. And to prepare for self-defense."

"Against what?" Lucy asked, full of interest.

"Against any threat to the safety of working people." Spies's unambiguous reply took them by surprise, contrasting as it did with the elusive sophistication of his earlier conversation.

"But as I was saying before," Spies continued, immediately softening the impact of his words, "I find no real need to choose among the various organizations. All have valid messages, however partial; all have valid contributions to make."

"Then why not join them all?" Lucy asked in a vexed tone, nettled at what she took to be the condescending way Spies kept shifting his position, as if he didn't consider them enlightened enough to be trusted with consistently straightforward talk. The sensuous way he kept stroking his moustache added to her suspicion.

"Because there aren't enough hours in the day," Lizzie explained, puzzled at Lucy's vexation. "Why, just deciding to come here today means I'll have to put in overtime all next week to meet my rent."

Spies had caught the hostility in Lucy's voice, and to placate her—though he wasn't sure why he felt the need—he said he did constantly push himself to become more politically engaged. "But I have to add, in all honesty," he continued, "that I'm not convinced humanity yet knows what is best for it. It isn't humanity's fault, of course. Most workers have been turned into automatons, incapable of understanding what their own best interest is."

Lucy's distrust went up another notch. He *is* arrogant, she thought to herself, likes to play the visionary, the man above the fray.

"You do sound like a rich boy," she said.

"I'm as confused as the next man. Which is what I was trying to say before you pushed me into this pompous recitation about What I Believe. All I know for the moment is that I can clarify my thoughts better through study rather than through organizational affiliation."

"Rubbish, I say." Lucy was delighted to see Spies flinch. "In my opinion, you learn more by joining with others in struggle than by sitting alone under the gas lamp."

Albert had remained silent during the exchange, his hands thoughtfully cupped under his chin. He now turned to Spies. "I agree," he said, carefully measuring his words, "that it's difficult to know which struggle to join. The movement for an eight-hour day? For trade unions? For government ownership of—"

"All right, Albert!" Lucy cut in. "You're reciting the platform of every group that ever existed."

Albert laughed. "I guess I *could* go on all night! Everybody has a theory, it seems . . . "

"Besides," Lucy abruptly declared, "the Knights already have the answer."

Albert nearly jumped in disbelief. "Lucy, you're teasing again!"

"I most certainly am not," she replied.

"Not long ago you were denouncing the Knights."

"Well, I've changed my mind. Been readin' their stuff and goin' to their meetings. And what I've learned is that they're the only organization open to all workers. And that's the only approach that can save us. I got no trouble at all pledging allegiance to that," she said, staring boldly at Spies.

Albert was dumbfounded, but pleased. "Well, my dear," he said with some amusement, "I suppose you might have first told me all this in private, but I can understand why the announcement of your major conversions requires a larger audience than your dull old husband."

Lucy ignored his affectionate gibe. "And the Knights are trying to live up to their principles. A woman's just been elected to a leadership position in a Philadelphia local, and an assembly of negro coal miners is forming out in Iowa. I'm even beginnin' to see more colored folks at meetings right here in Chicago."

Fielden looked up with sharp interest at Lucy's mention of negroes. He decided he *would* attempt a private word with her at some later time.

"No other group," Lucy went on, "is even trying to overcome the old prejudices."

"No other group wants to," Albert said.

"I believe you could end up playing a leadership role yourself, Lucy," Spies said. "You've got the fire for it."

"Yes, I think that might be right. Couldn't do worse than you menfolk, that's for sure! And Albert's going to make a fine mother—he's the kindest person I know."

They all laughed, Spies a little skittishly, not sure if he actually approved of Lucy or was simply trying to appease her. Albert gave Spies a reassuring smile, as if to confirm that it was perfectly safe to play with the tiger cub.

"Well, in my opinion," Fielden declared, "the Knights aren't radical enough. They don't want to destroy the monopolies, they want the government to regulate them in the name of fair competition—whatever that is. If the Knights have their way, all that will happen is that private property will be safeguarded. I want it abolished."

Fielden stopped as abruptly as he'd started, and a respectful silence followed.

"Eloquently put, Mr. Fielden," Lucy finally said. "You speak with great force."

"Thank you, ma'am." Fielden blushed deeply, a shy youngster peeking out from his powerful frame.

Another lull followed.

"Well," Albert finally said, "I hope we can keep talking like this. It . . . it . . . well, for me, it's been—just grand." He felt utterly foolish, like a Texas clodhopper. No one else seemed to notice, which surprised him.

"Let's not keep talking *tonight*," Lizzie said, laughing. "I've got to be up at five." She moved her chair back from the table and started to rise. The others followed suit, though Spies seemed reluctant to leave. As the group headed out of the garden, he took Parsons aside and the two strolled together toward the park gate. Spies was quick to reopen the question of the Verein.

"Am I correct that you don't speak German?" he asked.

"That's right, I don't. But I'd better start learning, given how active the German community has become."

"'You understood, I hope," Spies said, lowering his voice, "that the Lehr-und-Wehr Verein I spoke of back there is still a small organization, founded only a year ago."

"Are you a member?" Parsons asked.

"I attend meetings and I'm attracted by what I see and hear," Spies answered. "The emphasis is on education—the Social Question—though the Verein is also a militia."

"Do you drill with actual weapons?"

"Yes, when we can afford them. We're trying to raise money to buy more, and uniforms as well. Some of the socialist clubs have made donations."

"Frankly, I think any use of violence will backfire." Albert was feeling confident again, no longer the stammering yokel talking to his intellectual superior. "I've read enough to agree with the author who called violence 'a form of revolutionary romanticism.' A destructive form. And as for socialism . . . well, I believe in less government, not more."

"The Verein doesn't sanction violence, either!" Spies said vehemently. "Our weapons are for self-defense *only*." He took firm hold of Parsons's elbow. "Surely you've seen the willingness of the Chicago police to use force in breaking up protest meetings that were entirely peaceful."

"I have, yes. Several times."

"Besides," Spies continued, "the Constitution itself sanctions the militia system, the right of the people to bear arms."

"But Spies," Albert said solemnly, "if the Verein grows in strength, you must realize that the authorities won't stand idly by."

"A strong-armed militia patrolling workers' meetings, leading their protests and parades, will give the police pause. Our goal is to prevent violence by demonstrating that we have the strength to resist it."

"It's more likely, I think, that armed workers will frighten the moneyed class so much that the government will intervene. You'll bring about a violent confrontation, not prevent one."

"Possibly. But tell me, Parsons," Spies sounded cooler, more aloof, "Do you have another suggestion for stopping the police from interfering with our right to assemble and to speak our minds?"

"Well," Parsons offered hesitantly, "maybe electing our own people, so they can pass laws to end such abuses?"

"Ah, my friend! Where are the numbers for winning elections?" The hint of condescension was unmistakable. "The workers in this country are divided and disinterested. Besides, even if we could gather the needed votes for success at the ballot-box, the authorities would find a way to disallow the results—a benign way, hopefully, through some legal technicality. But I wouldn't *count* on it being benign."

"I think you're too cynical," Parsons said quietly. Spies jerked his head with impatience, but kept silent.

Albert decided to be bold. "I must say, Spies, you seem much more deeply engaged in questions of the day than one would have guessed from your conversation back in the beer garden. There, you sounded like a somewhat skittish bookworm—and managed to get my wife rather upset at you in the process."

"Lucy's quite remarkable," Spies chuckled. "She has a keen scent, picks up on the most delicate clues—especially the unintended ones. I don't believe she took to me at all. Thinks I'm snotty and highfalutin'. I give that impression sometimes, which is regrettable. People think me arrogant. But I'm not. As you'll come to see when you get to know me better."

"Which I look forward to."

"I have the strong sense that we're going to end up great friends. And allies."

"I feel it, too," Albert said.

The two men embraced, then walked silently side by side for a few moments.

"I do try my best, in public, to be prudent," Spies suddenly remarked. "And that isn't entirely a pose. I feel I have much to learn before solidifying my commitments. After all," he said, smiling enigmatically, "unlike you, I haven't even joined the Knights of Labor."

"Even? To me, it's the most advanced group around."

"Well as to that, time will tell, eh?" He looked as if he was tempted to say more.

They had reached the gate, and looking back saw Lucy, Lizzie, and Fielden approaching.

"Let's talk more about all this," Parsons said.

"Yes, we must," Spies said earnestly. "And soon, I hope."

The conversation between Lucy, Lizzie and Fielden had been no less intense. It began with Lizzie asking about his early life in Lancashire.

"We were a family of hand-loom weavers," he said. "I went to work in a cotton mill at age eight. It was a place of torture. Ten hours a day stripping full spools from the spinning jennies and then replacing them with empty spools. I tell you, exhausted children is a pitiful sight. I often had tears streaming down my cheeks, hands bruised and skinned from the revolving spools, rushing from machine to machine to meet our allotted quotas and avoid beatings."

"How awful," Lizzie said.

"I was one of the lucky ones. At ten, I was already a strong lad, so I got shifted from the spinning machines to carrying the heavy spools from the carding room to the jennies. Eight years ago, at twenty-two, I finally quit the mill and came to America."

He went on to tell them how important it had been to his education to hear "several colored lecturers" speak, on different occasions, about slavery in the United States. "One of those gentlemen was named Henry Box Brown. Do you know of him, Lucy—er, Mrs. Parsons?"

"You've been calling me Lucy all evening, Mr. Fielden. Why stop now?"

Taken aback, Fielden began to stutter an apology. But Lucy cut him short.

"I'm not one for formalities," she said, sounding decidedly formal. "Isn't that right, Lizzie?"

"Sounds right to me," Lizzie responded, puzzled at the undercurrent of anger.

"Yes, I've heard of Henry Box Brown," Lucy said. "Who hasn't?"

"I haven't," Lizzie said innocently.

"He had himself shipped to freedom," Fielden explained, then paused, uncertain whether to leave the topic entirely.

Lucy continued the story herself. "Henry Brown was a slave in Virginia, Lizzie. He had himself boxed into a container with holes bored in the top for air, and with provisions of food and water. He was shipped via Adams Express to abolitionist headquarters in Philadelphia, where he arrived safely twenty-six hours later."

"Goodness!" Lizzie said. "What a brave man."

"His lectures had a great effect on my mind," Fielden said. "They awoke me to the horrors of slavery. I read a great deal about it . . . Harriet Martineau . . . Fanny Kemble . . . *Uncle Tom's Cabin.* During the American Civil War, you know, the people of Lancashire suffered grievously for lack of cotton, but we remained staunch supporters of the North."

"As indeed you should have," Lucy said, her voice only a shade warmer.

"When I came to this country in '68," Fielden continued, "I had to work for a time in the South, and I discovered that in many instances the so-called freedman was as much a bond slave as ever. Sambo had confidently looked forward to the government giving him forty acres and a mule, but instead—"

"Sambo?" Lucy bristled. "*Sambo* is a Southern term, a mocking term, Mr. Fielden—or should I say Sam, now that we're all on such familiar terms. Sambo. Sam. How curiously close the two names are."

Fielden felt as if he'd been knocked to the ground. "I . . . I had no idea that . . . that your people took offense at the term . . . at the word . . . Sambo," he offered haltingly.

"My people? Oh, I see . . . yes, now I see!"

So did Lizzie, who let out a small groan.

Fielden, however, remained mystified. Where he had meant to express sympathy, he had somehow managed to give offense.

"This isn't a subject I discuss, Sam. Ever. But since it seems possible we might be working together in some fashion politically, I'll make an exception. This once. After I've finished, I don't intend to return to this topic again." Lucy was breathing fire. Lizzie took hold of her friend's hand in an effort to calm her, but Lucy sharply withdrew it.

"Yes, of course, Lucy . . . whatever you say. I'm so very sorry . . . I had only meant to express my deep concern for the plight of—"

Lucy interrupted him. "I recognize your concern. It does you honor. It's a concern I share. The negro's plight in this country is a tragic one, and we must all work to alleviate it. But though it will apparently come as a great surprise to you, Sam, I am not myself a negro. My looks do allow for that mistaken impression—I mean my dark complexion, the broad base of my nostrils, and so forth. But my ancestry is Spanish and Aztec. Not African. I'm a great admirer of the negro race. In my judgment negroes are a superior people, decent and kind, far superior to whites in ordinary relations. But I don't happen to be one of them."

Fielden looked utterly stricken. Lucy's heart went out to him, despite herself, and as if to say as much, she let her arms, which had been tightly folded across her chest, drop to her sides.

"Doubtless my dark skin," she said, her tone decidedly more conciliatory, "misled you. It does many people."

"Oh yes, many people, Sam, I can assure you of that!" Lizzie was quite overwrought.

Lucy raised her eyebrows in surprise. She stared hard at Lizzie. "Many people?"

Having said more than she'd intended, Lizzie now busily backtracked. "Oh just neighbors, you know . . . a few of the neighbors."

Lucy took in a deep breath. "I don't want to know their names," she said regally.

"There's bound to be talk, you know that," Lizzie said, intending comfort but falling far off the mark. "You and Albert have different skin color . . . it sets people to wondering, that's all . . ."

"Yes, that is all. I suggest we consider this subject closed. Permanently closed. Why don't we return to some lighter matter—like dynamiting police headquarters, say."

Lucy's humor was so unexpected that Lizzie burst out laughing. Fielden managed a weak, tentative smile. Within a minute or two he regained enough composure to beg Lucy's forgiveness for his "stupidity," and to express the hope that they might yet become good friends. Lucy said she was sure of it.

They had now reached the gate.

Part Three

The Diary of
Albert R. Parsons

I have this day, May 3, 1877, decided to keep a daily journal, or as nearly so as I can manage. With my increased involvement in the new Workingman's Party, Lucy says I have a responsibility to record what I see and hear. The lives of working people like us don't often get written down; our stories and struggles don't get passed on to the next generation, or into the textbooks. The monopolists control history to the same extent they do the economy. Since I aim to keep this record as honest as I can, I need to confess at the start that I also have my vanity; this diary will help to preserve my name for posterity. No man wants to leave without a trace.

I'm aware that the passion I've begun to feel about what's going on in this city and country might color the truth of what I set down. Yet I believe my concern allows me to see a side to events that the disinterested might miss. Anyway, I vow to do my best to create an accurate chronicle of events. Alas, I'm not a writer. I don't have the imagination for it. The best writers can invent whole stories. Perhaps it's just as well I can't.

Of late, I've become in demand as a speaker. People want to hear what the Workingmen's Party stands for and are kind enough to say I have an oratorical gift, that I'm able to explain complicated issues in a way they understand. I suspect the prime reason I'm beginning to be pushed front and center is because there are so few American-born speakers in the Chicago section of the WP, other than John McAuliffe, Philip Van Patten, and myself. The concern is that the party will be stigmatized as "foreign-run" and that native-born workers will shun it on that account.

I've already been as far east as Philadelphia and have seen a lot. Enough to know that Spies is right: many of our fellow wage-earners are ignorant of their own best interests and blind to the value of organizing. Their employers encourage this by misrepresenting the WP's purposes. The capitalist press is starting to label me a "labor agitator." So be it—though I wouldn't like to lose my job at the paper.

May 4

I should set down some facts about the Workingmen's Party. There are about 2,500 members in Illinois alone. Our basic aim is to appeal to all workers, no matter their national or religious backgrounds. In this, we're like the Knights, but we're more politically minded. Most of the WP's fifteen Chicago sections are German speaking, plus three Bohemian, two Polish, and one Scandinavian. We had an Irish club, too, but that disbanded. The Irish decided that the WP is godless. They prefer the Knights, with its mystical rituals and the secrecy that reduces the risk of getting fired. The Knights, unlike the WP, is almost wholly dominated by Irish-, British-, and American-born workers.

I suppose the Irish are right—most of us in the Workingmen's Party are godless. I like the way Spies summarized our attitude the other day. "The church," he said, "serves the oppressor. It keeps the masses in line with talk of a Natural Order and with the promise of a better life in the hereafter." Sam Fielden confessed that as a young man in England he had been a Methodist preacher and prominent at revival meetings—"caught in the snares of superstition" is how he put it.

But I'm losing track of my point. Maybe that's what diary-keeping is, letting oneself wander from thought to thought. It makes me uneasy, though, as if I'm not fulfilling my purpose.

To continue, the WP's leading paper is *Der Vorbote*. It does a fine job of gathering news about labor activities around the country and has a circulation of some 3,300. That's pretty good considering that trade union membership—which just five years ago was at three hundred thousand—is now down to about fifty thousand. How can an unemployed man pay dues to help a union bargain for jobs that don't exist?

Der Vorbote's office is a small second-story space on the west side of Market Street. It's become a gathering place for many of us "labor agitators." The mainstream press loves to portray it as a den of thieves and revolutionaries. I'm not exaggerating. The *Times* described it the other day as "a dingy little den, a narrow, dirty stairway leading to the hive, a constant stream of idle drones buzzing and snarling in their various languages. Not one of them bore the marks of a decent workingman. Sallow Bohemians and Poles, dirty and ragged renegade Frenchmen, stupefied by idleness, and Germans, outcasts from the society of their own nation, mingled in a filthy, snarling crowd." That is what they think of us, and what they want the world to think of us.

Der Vorbote's editor somehow heard that I'd worked as a reporter in Texas and asked me to write for them. Oh, how I'd love to! But right now I don't have a moment to spare. On top of everything else, the *Times* is making its typesetters put in extra hours (at no extra pay) to learn the new point system of printing. Now that the Marder-Luse foundry has adopted it and patented the first type cast, it's generally assumed that within a few years the point system will become universal. Well, at least the typesetting industry is undergoing a revolution even if society isn't! Anyway, I need to master the new system, and quickly, to hold on to my job—already threatened by my politics.

May 5

I'm going to run for public office! I'm as surprised as anyone. It happened last night. I went to the WP meeting at Odd Fellows Hall to discuss the upcoming local election, and the idea somehow took hold that despite the lateness of the hour, we ought to test the political waters by running a few candidates of our own. I was one of three chosen to run for alderman. I'll stand from the Fifteenth Ward, where Lucy and I live. I didn't feel I could say no to the fellows, so great was their ardor. But the decision was made in such a rush of enthusiasm, we never did talk through all the implications. I did say flat out that, in my view, running for office might not be the best way to use our limited resources.

Our friends are much divided on the issue. Those who follow Ferdinand Lassalle (at Lizzie's urging, I've started to read him—it's arduous) insist that success at the ballot-box is all-important. But others are just as adamant that politics is a waste of time. Everybody argues about it. At a recent Knights meeting—I still go as often as my schedule allows—I heard one speaker eloquently insist that middle-class Americans will side with us once they learn the truth about working conditions, and that together we will become the political majority.

Among our closest friends, Spies is the most skeptical. He's not against taking part in politics, but thinks it's useful solely as a means for propaganda, a way to educate the public about the harshness of working conditions. The electoral process by itself, Spies insists, will never bring about fundamental change. That, he says, can only come through economic struggle, with the general strike our best weapon and the Paris Commune our best model. The more I come to know Spies, the more outspoken and radical he seems. I guess his "study" phase is over. I'm not far behind him, but am moving at a slower (southern?) pace.

June 14

So much for my good intentions about keeping a daily record. More than a month has gone by since I last wrote. The election used up every minute. Canvassers came to help from all over the city; the *Tribune* called them "carpetbaggers" and "imported foreigners." Lucy did the work of a dozen, knocking on doors, passing out leaflets. She's got twice my energy, and I have plenty. During the campaign we mostly stressed local issues, like the need to have open bidding on city projects, and shorter work hours. It was an exhilarating few weeks, to tell the truth. So much fervor. Also, I learned a lot about our ward, and met many new people.

Oh, I forgot the results! I didn't win. But then nobody thought I would, not even Lucy. I did get some four hundred votes, about 15 percent of the total, which everyone says is amazingly fine for a new party and a last-minute campaign. Spies, in his ironical way, said, "And don't ever expect a better showing." Sometimes I think he's too cynical. Maybe with more time for organizing and education, we could actually win enough political offices to make a real difference.

June 15

While the election was consuming all my time, the larger world refused to stand still. A railroad crisis is brewing. Railroad stocks started to sink a few months ago. The owners tried to recoup their losses on the backs of their employees. The Boston & Maine cut wages 10 percent—then turned around and paid its usual 6 percent dividend *and* raised the salaries of its president and superintendent. That woke up even the stodgy Brotherhood of Locomotive Engineers, which has been spending more of its treasury on the temperance cause than on helping the unemployed. The Brotherhood went out on strike and asked for a raise of ten cents a day for the engineers. The B&M only has sixty-seven engineers, so the total cost per day to the owners would have been $6.70. Yet they rejected the increase. So the Brotherhood stopped the trains. But management was too smart for them. Within hours the B&M had replaced the engineers with nonunion standbys, and now, just four months later, the trains are running on schedule. The Brotherhood, meantime, is still out on strike, but its treasury is running low. Some of the railroad bigwigs have decided that now is the time to break the union altogether. Charles Francis Adams II—yes, of "the" Adams family—claims that the Brotherhood "has become a mere common nuisance . . . a standing public menace," and must be destroyed. A *menace*—because they asked for *ten cents* more pay per day.

Meanwhile here in Chicago, hotel owner John B. Drake is staging his annual Game Dinner. At staggering cost, he imports, slaughters, and serves up hundreds of wild animals from around the world. The Dinner is always oversubscribed. Today's *Tribune* hails the upcoming event as "a high point in the social calendar of the city's polite classes and a mark of Chicago's growing sophistication as a metropolis." If we become any more sophisticated we'll be killing and serving up each other.

June 16

Reports are coming in from the eastern states about "wealthy gentlemen" forming vigilance committees, hiring mounted police, and, in Pennsylvania, issuing every "respectable" resident a horn and a watchman's rattle and a club to promote a "war on the tramps." An easier way to get rid of tramps would be to find work for them.

June 17

Some of the railroads are hiring private detectives to "protect property." Meaning, Lucy says, "to protect any working person from ever owning any." The Allan Pinkerton Agency, having exposed what it claims is "a secret band of labor terrorists"—the so-called Molly Maguires—is now so well known that all private detectives are being called Pinkertons. Nobody I know ever heard of a group called the Molly Maguires, though ten of their number—coal miners who protested working conditions in the Pennsylvania pits—are now awaiting the gallows.

June 20

Lucy got Spies to agree with her—he's trying hard to earn her good opinion—that I've been working too hard of late and needed to take all day Saturday off. She cajoled me so prettily that I said yes. Her first choice was for us to try out the new "roller-skating" craze. Spies went along with that, but asked that later on he be allowed to take us to a Turnverein; he thinks we need to take better care of our health through regular exercise. My suggestion, since the day was beastly hot, was that we go for a swim in the lake off Gutchow's beach at the foot of Erie Street. Lucy said we'd get arrested, since Gutchow's is a private beach. Spies agreed. He said we'd be getting arrested soon enough and should save it for something important. I let them have their way, but a swim would have surely been nice. I remember back in '73, the year we arrived here, the health department asked the Lincoln Park commissioners to create a public beach for the poor; the park board insisted that the health department pay for it—and that was the last we heard of the beach.

We didn't last long with the roller-skating. It's an amusement for the rich. We had to pay twenty-five cents each just to gain admission to the rink, and then another twenty-five cents to rent wooden-wheeled skates. And to do what? To go dumbly around and around in a circle on a hard maple floor that, when you land on it, hurts like the dickens. I fell twice, much to Lucy's merriment. "Got to trot before you can canter!" she yelled as I lay flat on my back.

Then we had to go to Spies's Turnverein. The one he attends is among the few that admit women. *Turnverein* sounds fancy, but it was just a big exercise room. There were odd items all over the place, and Spies insisted on demonstrating most of them—hoops, rings, rowing devices, pulley weights, and something called the Indian club, which looks like a bowling pin (Lucy thought it was great fun to swing it around her head). Spies says many physical fitness devotees also have strict notions about diet—no alcohol or tobacco, regular mineral water purges—all to avoid the dangers of something called "autointoxication." "What a word!" Lucy said, "sounds like someone pouring liquor down their throat!" Spies told us he sticks to the exercises and forgets about the diet part. "Glad to hear it," I told him, "I wouldn't want a friend *that* well-disciplined." Spies does have a fine physique, but if it takes this much pushing and sweating to get one, I'll keep to waxing my moustache.

June 21

Sam Fielden's just returned from Pittsburgh with news of a newly formed
Trainmen's Union. Its ranks are open to all who work the railroads—engineers,
conductors, firemen, brakemen, switchmen. Members pledge that during a
strike no worker will agree to fill in for another. And when men are working
on a line that isn't on strike, they will refuse to handle struck equipment. This
is great news! The railroad owners have combined to defeat worker demands;
now the trainmen have shown that two can play that game.

Fielden also reports that Robert Ammon, a brakeman, has been elected
the TU's "grand organizer" and will be traveling the country to propa-
gate the faith and sign up new union members. He's got the gift of gab,
Fielden says, and trainmen are already rushing to join up. Fielden warns
me that Ammon has a mixed reputation. He fought in the cavalry against
the Blackfeet, has a strong taste for bonded rye, is rumored to have taken
part in a swindle involving a diamond mine in Arizona. Stubborn, sure of
himself, and doesn't take kindly to contradiction. Sounds like everybody
I ever knew in Texas, I said. I expect we'll get along just fine.

June 22

The ten Molly Maguires were hanged in Pottsville, Pennsylvania yesterday
morning. The state militia patrolled the streets with loaded guns the whole
night because of rumors that there'd be an attempt to rescue the men
by force. Nothing came of it, and just as well—we don't need any more
dead workers. Thousands of miners and their families gathered quietly in
the rain as the traps were sprung. Spies angrily pointed out the contrast
between the State's unhesitating use of violence and the way it screams
bloody murder if workingmen so much as puncture the ground with
unloaded weapons.

June 24

We can forget about the farmers and the Granger movement as potential
allies. The prospects all across the country are for bumper crops. There's
talk of wheat and corn yields going higher than any in history, and the
Grangers have rapidly traded in political rallies for pie socials and oyster
suppers. It puzzles me how the smell of money can turn men away from
a just cause. Once their own agony's passed, fellow feeling seems to
pass with it. Lucy says that's what fellow feeling is: commiserating with

someone who shares your plight. I don't accept that, and Lucy herself is a good example of why. Now that word of her dressmaking skills has spread and her earnings are up to nearly five dollars a week, she's busy giving most of it away to families in greater need than us. If she hears of a family that can't put food on the table or whose child is sick, she's the first to help—and does it anonymously, slipping cash in an envelope under a door. She likes to play the cynic, but like most cynics, her sarcasm is protective covering for a tender heart.

Lucy recently got her first commission from a private client. And a wealthy one, which is why she almost refused it. It all came about through Lizzie. A distant relation of hers is a woman of some means, and she periodically asks Lizzie to duplicate a dress she's seen in a shop or in *Godey's*. This time around, Lizzie was overburdened with piecework and enlisted Lucy's help in constructing the bustle. The woman was amazed at how skillfully Lucy interwove two fabrics, silk and organdy, and two shades of magenta as well. She declared Lucy a "seamstress of genius."

The relative recommended Lucy to a Mrs. L. B. Risberg, wife of a prominent Astor Street physician. Mrs. Risberg promptly sent her carriage, and Lucy reluctantly agreed to go. She wanted to satisfy her curiosity, she said, about what the inside of a Prairie Street mansion looked like, but swore she'd never lend her skills to making the upper class look attractive.

We'd all seen pictures of the Risberg mansion in the newspapers during the various stages of construction, but Lucy, after she got back from the place, said the pictures don't begin to do it justice. She was a mess of conflicted feelings. "No one can gainsay the beauty of the house," she said, her eyes a warring mix of admiration and anger. "And I have to give Mrs. Risberg her due—though aloof and formal, she was polite enough to show me around most of the main floor. And Lord, what a sight it was! The mahogany entrance hall alone nearly took my breath away. You've never seen such fine woodwork, floor to ceiling. Missing, of course, was a plaque with the names of the Czech and German artisans who worked their fingers to the bone creating it. The Risbergs probably paid them five dollars a week and made them eat their lunch in the stables."

"If they got a lunch break," I said.

"Oh—and the front parlor!" Lucy exclaimed. "You wouldn't believe it! Tapestries, a red-and-gold ceiling, flowered carpets, and, above the fireplace, a stained-glass overmantel depicting the five Muses in various poses—like bathing beauties!"

To compensate for her guilty excitement, Lucy ended with a proper dose of indignation: "They live like European barons!" she bellowed. "While all over Chicago children are going to bed hungry, clutching some pathetic rag doll for comfort! And I'm supposed to make glamorous clothes for such creatures? I'll never do it! Never!"

"Don't be so high and mighty!" I said. "Making money through honest labor is no crime."

Lucy gave me a withering look. "Of course you feel that way with the *Chicago Times* paying your salary."

I swallowed hard, and couldn't think of a thing to say.

"Short of forming a printers' collective," Lizzie chimed in, "which would fail of course, thanks to the huge type foundries, exactly where *can* one find untainted, 'honorable' work? I'd love to know so I can put in an application myself."

"Spies has found it," Lucy said quietly. "He's self-employed. And Fielden is trying to buy his own team of horses."

"But they still have to rely on *customers*," Lizzie mildly pointed out, not sure whether she was trying to convince me or Lucy. "And they can't afford to pick and choose among them on the basis of their political opinions. I tell you, in this society, there's no such thing as an honorable living. To survive, we all have to participate in the corruption."

Eventually, after several more go-rounds about the "morality" of the thing, Lucy finally decided to accept Mrs. Risberg's commission. Since then, the Risberg carriage has been arriving regularly to carry her off for fittings. Lucy's guiltily proud of her black silk dress. Even in its unfinished state, Mrs. Risberg has pronounced it a "triumph," commending Lucy for incorporating whalebone to bind the waist (the latest word in fashion, I gather) and a bustle of iron that requires a cushion of fifteen yards of cloth. Lucy triumphantly insists that the dress is in fact a "monstrosity," constricting breathing and movement. "It's better suited to a medieval soldier than a modern woman," she huffed one day to Lizzie, who shrugged. "The more misery it causes her the better," Lizzie said. "Only well-to-do women can afford to torture their bodies in this way." Their giggling reached me in the kitchen.

June 25

Ammon is in Chicago. We met at Fielden's place. A fourth man was there, invited by Fielden. Name of George Engel. He's older than the rest of us—at least forty, I would say. German born. He's had a hard life. Lost both his parents when just a boy, and was hungry all the time. Says nobody ever cared about him. Finally got himself apprenticed to a house painter, and that's how he survived. He immigrated to America at a time when there wasn't any work in Germany and he'd "given up all hope." He's married with two children, and until last year worked in a wagon factory. Now he and his wife run a small toy store. Says it's a poor living, but it gives him more time for reading. I've written this much about Engel, because I find him compelling, in a fierce, direct sort of way. He's not an easy man to warm up to, though. Serious and silent.

But easier to like than Ammon, a blustering type. Talks so much you can't tell what he's feeling. What a contrast to Fielden, who's undisguised in all his dealings. The more I see of him, the more I admire him. He's a truly frank and pure fellow; a deep goodness radiates from him. Lucy told me she got angry at Fielden back when we all first met because of a remark he made about "Sambo," but she's come to feel that he said it in innocence and cares deeply about the plight of negroes.

Ammon told us that Tom Scott and the other railroad magnates have refused to even meet with a committee to hear worker grievances. He believes there will be a general strike sooner or later, probably sooner. Many of the brakemen are refusing to go out on "double-headers," a term I didn't know. It means having to handle twice as many cars as is usual. As it is, he says, brakemen have the most dangerous job. Not that anybody has it easy. The firemen shovel coal for hours on end into furnaces "hot enough to melt glass," as Ammon puts it. And even the engineers, who have it the best, face plenty of drudgery and danger. They have to stay alert for every blind curve and grade crossing during shifts that last twelve hours—and are paid three dollars and twenty-five cents. That's "down to hard pan," to use Ammon's railroad lingo.

But the brakemen, he says, risk actual loss of life or limb. Most companies refuse to spend money on safer equipment like the new air brake or automatic coupler. A brakeman has to climb up the side of a car using handholds that are never inspected and sometimes break off; and as he moves between cars, he runs the constant risk of catching his foot in a switch frog and often can't free himself before the rolling wheels have sliced off a leg. As he races along the top of a car to spin the brake wheels or guide a coupling link into place, he can get his head chopped off by a low bridge. "There aren't many brakemen," Ammon said angrily—holding up his own right hand, which showed a stub where the index finger should have been—"who have both hands or all their fingers. If they do, they're new on the job." In Massachusetts alone, some fifty railroad men die every year from one kind of accident or another. The widows get nothing. And if you're maimed, not killed? Their regular pay must cover all liability, with no added compensation for injury. "We're scum to them," Ammon told me. "And now they want us to go out on double-headers. Now they've found a quicker way to murder us."

July 7

There's been a strange lull these past two weeks, and I figured there was no point filling up these pages with idle talk. Maybe it's the heat. Its been blazing, day after day. Some of the old brick sewers are backed up and the stench in the streets has got everybody worried about another outbreak of typhus or cholera. In Baltimore 150 children died of typhus just last week. The rich, of course, are off to the cool breezes of White Sulphur Springs or the Adirondacks. For a change of pace, they're hunting bears instead of workers.

To protect against disease, Lizzie and Spies both urge us to purge once a week, but I can't stand prunes and bran, and as for Spies's recommendation of sauerkraut, I'd rather have a torpid liver than an upset stomach. The peddlers are selling so many different kinds of syrups, elixirs, and tonics, and making equal claims for all of them, my guess is they're equally worthless. But to humor Lizzie, I let her pour Fletcher's Castoria down my throat—once!

July 11

The lull has ended. President Garrett of the Baltimore & Ohio has announced yet another reduction in wages for employees, this time a full 10 percent. What does he expect the men to live on—old shoe leather? A storm is brewing.

July 17

The storm has broken. And where? In Martinsburg, West Virginia! Who would have dreamed it? Ammon organized a small TU lodge there last month, but told me it was probably for naught, that the men were too passive ever to engage in a walk-out. And now they've done it! Lightning does strike in unexpected places.

The news we have is sketchy. Apparently some firemen began deserting freight trains, word of their action quickly spread, and a crowd gathered to urge the men on. They uncoupled train engines, ran them into the roundhouse, and told the local B&O officials that not another train would leave Martinsburg until the pay cut was rescinded. President Garrett demanded that Governor Henry Mathews provide military protection, and he's dutifully dispatched the Berkeley Light Guards.

July 18

The strike is spreading over other divisions of the B&O. Conductors, brakemen and engineers are joining the firemen. Seventy engines and six hundred freight cars are now jammed into the Martinsburg yards, though the strikers are letting passenger and mail cars go through. They're behaving in an orderly, restrained way, refraining from threats of violence. Yet the *New York Times* has come out with an editorial condemning the strike as "a rash and spiteful demonstration of resentment by men too ignorant or too reckless to understand their own interests."

July 19

Governor Mathews telegraphed President Hayes requesting troops "to suppress this insurrection" and "protect the law-abiding citizens of the State" from the "unlawful combinations and domestic violence" of the strikers. All of which stands reality on its head. Federal troops will create violence not currently in evidence.

July 20

Hayes has sent the Second United States Artillery to Martinsburg—more than three hundred troops. Today freight trains are moving freely out of the yards, staffed by strikebreakers brought in from Baltimore. Governor Mathews announced, "The insurrection may be regarded as suppressed."

Sam Fielden came by with some sad tidings. His middle child, Ephraim, has succumbed to dysentery after an illness so brief no one realized the child was in serious danger. Fielden couldn't hold back the tears. His wife, of course, is utterly bereft. She's taken to consulting a medium. Spiritualism has grown exceedingly popular but thus far our rational-minded crowd has been immune to it. At first Fielden tried to dissuade his wife from such "nonsense" but soon realized that any comfort would be a blessing. She's become convinced that their son will "pass back over" and "materialize" if she follows the medium's strict instructions. These include burning locks of hair, carrying the child's portrait over her heart day and night, and paying for "treatments" that utilize the "positive magnetic energy" of the right hand. Poor soul.

July 21

Though all remains quiet in Martinsburg, new protests are breaking out elsewhere. It's as if a dying ember leapt into a nearby thicket of parched woodlands. The boatmen of the Chesapeake and Ohio Canal have docked their vessels and shut down all canal traffic. Thousands of coal miners have gone out and railroad workers in various locales have been boarding and detaining trains, taking off the crews and pulling out coupling pins. Only one of the sixteen freights sent west from Martinsburg has gotten through; the rest were stopped at Cumberland, Maryland, where the rolling mill is idle, many unemployed, and some starving. The crowd there displayed a real fury. Shots were fired and a trainman hit.

In Baltimore, a mob formed in front of the regimental armory, hurling rocks at the doors, shattering nearly every pane of glass, and panicking the 180 soldiers inside. When three companies tried to get out and were met with brickbats, the soldiers leveled their breechloaders and began firing directly into the crowd, which fell back and scattered. Before the shooting was over, ten men and boys had died—none of them strikers. The enraged crowd, now grown to fifteen thousand, turned its fury on the B&O depot, setting passenger cars afire and exchanging pistol shots with the police.

And in Pittsburgh, the state militia has committed outright slaughter, firing into a crowd of people gathered in the Twenty-eighth Street area, killing a dozen and seriously wounding more than fifty, several of them small children. The city's gone mad with grief and anger. Scores of loaded oil and coal cars have been torched, creating an immense inferno. Violence doesn't shock the American people—not after the everyday carnage of the Civil War.

The mainstream press uniformly condemns the strikers and exonerates the soldiers. Hardly a surprise, since most of the papers are owned outright by the monopolists—Jay Gould controls the *New York Tribune*, Tom Scott, head of the Penn Central, dictates policy to the *New York World* . . . The railroads, the editorialists proclaim, are essential to the nation's economic health—though the health of those who work on them goes unmentioned—and a general stoppage, therefore, cannot be tolerated. For those among the "unpropertied rabble" who dare to trespass on railroad property, the proper response, according to the *New York Tribune*, is the Gatling gun. When asked about hungry strikers, Tom Scott is quoted as saying, "Give them a rifle diet for a few days and see how they like that kind of bread." He said it shamelessly, as if talking about killing off diseased livestock. The *Chicago Tribune* has managed to top him, calling for the use of hand grenades against the "mob."

The strike is rapidly spreading westward, and with mounting bitterness and determination. Capital and labor have collided with greater speed and force than any of us thought possible. We can thank the monopolists for speeding up the process, for insisting—for the first time in the nation's history—that federal troops be called out in peacetime, and to attack its own citizens. Spies says it is sheer folly on their part, that they've succeeded where we have failed in mobilizing the working class against them. We're all holding our breath for what might follow.

July 22

The escalation continues. Our private lives hardly seem to exist, or matter, any more. Franklin Gowen's arrogant boast that his Philadelphia & Reading would never be touched by the Great Strike (as people are calling it), has been made a laughing-stock now that the city of Reading is in an uproar. Some fifty men in work clothes, faces blackened with coal dust, have torn up the tracks, jammed switches and, joined by a larger crowd, burnt down the Lebanon Valley Bridge, choking the Schuylkill and Union Canals. The country is being shaken to its roots. And with no end in sight.

July 23

The Workingmen's Party has assumed the lead. I'm just back from seeing Philip Van Patten, the wp's national secretary, to plan a mass meeting in Market Square. We drafted a flyer. Like me, Van Patten's in his late twenties and one of the few prominent party leaders of "old native stock." (I put that in quotes because when Lucy heard me use it last week, she rightly derided me. "Well bless my stars! Here I've been living with you going on six years and I never knew you were an American Indian. Who would have guessed it, what with that pale face of yours!").

Van Patten is certainly prepossessing, with deep-set eyes, long black hair, stand-up collar, and flowing necktie. He carries himself with the air of a poet but is as practical and straightforward as a horse trader. We got right down to it. He says a violent eruption in Chicago is imminent, since this is the railroad capital of the country and some thirty thousand unemployed men are walking the streets in search of work and food. The railroad owners know the city is a tinderbox, despite their nonchalant statements to the press.

July 24

How can I begin to re-create the feverish excitement of last night?! A huge crowd—some estimates go as high as thirty thousand—gathered at the intersection of Market and Madison in response to our call. Torchlit processions marched in from every section of the city. A thrilling sight. Lucy held my hand so tightly I thought I'd be crippled.

During the speeches, I had to leave her and mount the platform, but she was in good hands, surrounded by Lizzie, Spies, and Fielden. John McAuliffe spoke first. He was going at it with a white-hot fury, announcing that this strike was "labor's Fort Sumter" and vowing to raise his "voice, thought, and arm for bloody, remorseless war!" That sort of talk, in my view, is foolishly inflammatory. I caught the disapproval in Van Patten's eyes, and he moved quickly to take McAuliffe's place at the podium and lower the crowd's temperature.

Then it was my turn. It made my knees shake to hear Van Patten announce me as "the main speaker of the evening"—that's a first! But fortunately my mouth opened before my brain had a chance to shut down. Mostly I argued against the use of violence, championed an eight-hour day, and emphasized the importance of using the ballot-box to gain our rights.

McAuliffe looked disgusted, and spat out a glob that damned near landed on my shoe. But the crowd seemed with me, yelling out their approval over and over. Van Patten later congratulated me for "setting the right tone" but then added, his eyes darkening, "I must tell you in all honesty, however, that at several points in your speech you sounded more like McAuliffe than I should have liked."

My guess is that he disliked my saying—it was my most heated moment, but I don't regret it—"If the proprietor has a right to fix the wages and say what labor is worth, then we are slaves, bound hand and foot, and we should be perfectly content with a bowl of rice and a rat a week apiece." I have the words exact because Lucy, standing in the crowd, immediately grabbed a pen from Fielden and scribbled them down—says she's going to sew them as a sampler and hang it in the living room.

For once, she said, I sounded fiery enough to suit her, didn't lurch back and forth in my usual "fair-minded" fashion.

Her sarcasm annoyed me. Some people, I thought to myself, would praise me for remaining open-minded. I do share some of McAuliffe's views, but that doesn't mean I have to swallow all of them whole. I told Lucy that she's too quick to make up her mind and then to hold her ground no matter how much circumstances change.

"It *is* bloody war!" she responded. "McAuliffe's got it right!"

"Is that so?" I said, feeling my anger rise. "Maybe you wouldn't think 'bloody war' is so desirable when you get your first look at a teenage boy with his face blown away, as I did many a time, during the War."

"Hey, mister, you ain't the only one's seen atrocities," she fired back. "I've seen plenty of blood spilt, most of it spurtin' out of negro bodies."

I had no recourse to that, other than to feel ashamed . . .

July 26

A whole day has gone by, one of the most momentous of my life. I'm exhausted and ill, but before getting some sleep—it's 2:00 A.M.—I have to try and get down at least an outline of what's happened.

Early yesterday morning I met with Van Patten to work on our "Manifesto to the Workingmen of Chicago." We're aiming to strike a balance between caution and determination, urging the avoidance of rash action during the current crisis while also urging a nationwide general strike for the eight-hour day and a 20 percent increase in wages.

I managed to arrive on time again at the *Times*, knowing I'd be allowed no leeway. It turned out not to matter. I found that my name had been stricken from the roll of employees. I'm not only discharged, but blacklisted—apparently for the crime of speaking at the rally. In today's editorial, the *Times* makes its position clear: it refers to the Michigan Central switchmen out on strike as "an uncombed, unwashed mob of guttersnipes and loafers."

The wonder, I suppose, is that the *Times* kept me on as long as it did. I ascribe it to my job performance. I read every issue of the *Paper and Printing Trades Journal* and stayed abreast of all the new graphic innovations. Trying to make myself indispensable, I even mastered the Nonpareil six-point type! Yet in the end, they've turned me out anyway; better to do without a skilled worker than to have an "agitator" on the premises. I gathered my few things quickly, got some hearty pats on the back from the fellows, and there I suddenly was—standing in a daze in front of the *Times* building. Feeling numb, I started to walk home, heavy with the thought of having to tell Lucy the news. With two-thirds of our income gone, and me blacklisted from finding work on another paper, I don't know how we'll pay the rent, let alone afford to have the children we're so eager for. Lucy's dressmaking business continues to pick up, but it's not at the point where we can look to it as our main source of income.

July 27

When I pushed open the door to *Der Vorbote*, I found a beehive of activity. The room was crammed with strikers, many of them asking how they could sign up for the Workingmen's Party. I took off my coat straightaway and started taking down names and addresses.

I soon learned that the strike had spread throughout the city. The *Tribune*'s headline this morning says it all: IT IS HERE. Freight stoppage is general. The crews of several lake vessels have struck for a dollar fifty a day, forcing the North Chicago rolling mill to shut down for lack of coke. Crowds are moving about the city closing down the rail yards, shutting factories, even succeeding in calling out workers from several packing houses. Business is at a standstill. Gun stores are reporting brisk sales and Mayor Heath has—wisely, I think—closed the saloons. He—unwisely—called on all "upright" citizens to organize patrols and has authorized issuing the new Remington breechloaders to volunteers, most of whom are Civil War veterans. And he's accepted the offer of an anonymous "private citizen" to pay for extra policemen; as a result several hundred "specials," with even less training than the regulars, have been sworn in.

At noon, I was still enrolling WP members when suddenly two threatening-looking men yanked me up from the desk. They'd been sent, they brusquely informed me, to take me to Mayor Heath's office: "He wants to speak to you." Startled, I decided not to resist, thinking that just possibly the Mayor was genuinely interested in working with us to prevent violence (even if his messengers seemed to personify it).

I accompanied them to the street, where they set a brisk pace, one on either side of me. The wind was strong and their flapping coat-tails flying revealed that both were armed. This flustered me, and I was relieved when we arrived at City Hall; until, that is, they took me not to the Mayor but to Chief of Police Hickey. His office was filled with prominent citizens, several of whom I recognized, plus a large number of unfamiliar police officials. Hickey I knew.

Everyone in Chicago knows Hickey, given the number of times he's been brought up on charges for everything from running bail-bonding rackets to protecting Mike McDonald's deluxe gambling emporium, The Store, to personally stealing the collection of diamonds owned by Lizzie Moore, proprietor of a leading bagnio. Just last year the City Council launched an investigation of him that turned up evidence of shady real estate deals and bribe-taking from a slew of fences and thieves, and from the penny-ante faro games that operate out of second-floor storerooms along the wharf. Mayor Heath "studied" the evidence, pronounced it flimsy, and retained Hickey in office.

No, I didn't like for one moment finding myself in that man's office, surrounded by scowling faces. Hickey is capable of anything. I held fast to the sides of the chair they'd deposited me in, and tried to prepare myself to stand tall against the bullies. Hickey started right in on me. His bulky body looming over me, he accused me of bringing "great trouble" to Chicago, of having "come up here from Texas to incite the working people to insurrection," of the Workingmen's Party having been responsible for starting the strike—and so on. My voice still hoarse from speaking outdoors two nights ago, I croaked out the facts as best I could. The strike, I told him, had erupted from the same conditions that produced the Workingmen's Party—from exploitation and poverty.

I could hear some loud muttering from others in the room. "What're we waiting for?" one man yelled, "Let's lock him up and get it over with." Another actually shouted, "Let's lynch the bastard!" Fortunately, a third man replied that any harm done to me would incite the "revolutionaries" to further violence. That calmed things down, and Hickey went back to grilling me. Where was I born, where were my folks from, did I have a wife, children? I'm sure he had all that information already. I did my best to stay calm, but felt several times that I might pass out.

Hickey finally left my chair and went to consult with several of the notables in the room. Eventually, he strode back, pulled me up, and snarled in my face, "We've decided to let you go—this time." He grabbed me hard by the arm and moved me toward the door. "Let this be a warning, Parsons," he said, his voice thick with rage. "From this moment on, consider your life in danger. If you had a drop of sense, you'd leave Chicago on the next train. Don't fool yourself: our men will be at your back from this hour on, trailing your every movement. Everything you do, every word you say, will be made immediately known to me."

With that, Hickey turned the spring latch, shoved me through the door into the hallway, and yelled after me, "You've been warned!" The door slammed in my face.

I felt suddenly dizzy and wobbled like a drunk down the vast corridor, trying to find a way out of the building.

This terrible day was not yet over.

Once downtown, I passed a news hawker and my eye caught the huge headline in the afternoon *Times*: "PARSONS, LEADER OF STRIKE, ARRESTED!" I felt paralyzed, unable to put one foot in front of the other. Was I on the street or in a jail cell? Am I a Famous Revolutionary or an unemployed typesetter? I finally tottered onward, feeling I might collapse at any moment. I must have been walking in that aimless fashion for more than an hour when I looked up and saw that I was in front of the *Tribune* building.

I abruptly snapped out of my trance, rescued by a concrete thought: perhaps I could get a night's work in the composing room. I went up to the fifth floor and was warmly greeted by the men, who had seen the headlines and were amazed to find me in their midst. By now it was nearing eight o'clock. Suddenly, as I was talking to Mr. Manion, chairman of our typesetters union, three men grabbed me from behind, spun me around, and asked if I was Parsons. When I said I was, two of the men took hold of my arms, the third held on to the back of my shirt, and they shoved me toward the door. This time I felt angry, not befogged, and I loudly protested that I had come in the door as a gentleman and refused to be dragged out like a dog. They responded with curses, pushed me through the door, and started to lead me down the interior staircase. One of them suddenly put a pistol to my head and said, "I have a mind to blow your brains out right here and now—if I thought you had any." As we passed a window on one of the landings, the second man threatened to throw me out of it to the pavement below. When we reached the bottom of the five flights, the men loomed threateningly over me for a minute or two, then kicked me into the gutter. Expecting a bullet in my back, I ran down the street, but this time rage, not fear, propelled me, rage at the easy violence these people commit against us even as they denounce us for violence we haven't committed.

Safely out of their view, I slowed my pace and turned down Dearborn Street, which looked deserted. I sat down on the curb for a few moments to collect my wits, but quickly got up when I saw pockets of men, muskets in hand, leaning against some of the nearby buildings. Then I realized that these were Illinois National Guard troops. A terrible chill ran through me. Today I was threatened with violence; tomorrow, I fear, many will directly experience it. I instantly left the area and hurried home to Lucy. Lizzie, it turned out, had shown her the headlines and she'd been frantic. She'd insisted on going down to the Cook County jail and Lizzie, unable to dissuade her, had gone along too. At the jail they were told that no prisoner named Parsons was there, and baffled, they'd reluctantly returned home.

I wasn't back more than an hour and already dead asleep—collapsed really—in Lucy's arms when a knock on the door roused us. It was Abel Hinson, one of the *Tribune* printers. He'd come by to tell me that after I'd been dragged from the building, the men in the composing room had threatened to go out on strike then and there. The proprietor himself, Joseph Medill, had had to appear before the men and calm them down. He swore that he'd known nothing of my mistreatment and had not sanctioned it. But as Hinson said, "The men aren't the dumb animals Medill thinks they are. They know he's lying to them and they're biding their time."

I fear a bloody dawn awaits us.

Utterly exhausted . . .

August 1

It has turned out worse, far worse, than could have been imagined. At this point, an uneasy calm has settled over the country. But what a nightmarish few days it's been. I myself witnessed enough brutality to last a lifetime. I don't put entire blame on the soldiers and police for the hundreds of deaths and injuries; in some places they were strongly provoked by teen-age gangs pelting and taunting them. Still, they were too quick to pull their triggers, far too quick. Why do so few of them seem able to understand that they're firing on *fellow workers*? More than half the police force of Chicago is made up of men of Irish and German descent. Many have shared the hard immigrant life, worked under a factory taskmaster, lived in the tenements, and even now earn a miserable fifty or sixty dollars a month. Yet they dutifully follow orders from the corrupt ward bosses—the "Bathhouse" Coughlins and Mike McDonalds, the "gray wolves," as we call them, who in turn take orders from the propertied classes. That's where responsibility for the mayhem finally rests. For a decade, the magnates have haughtily ignored the workers' peaceable pleas for improved conditions, treating them as mere pests, a passing plague of locusts. When, desperate to be heard, the workers grew more clamorous and the owners could no longer stop up their ears, they turned to their politician cronies and hired thugs to shoot men down with as much pause as you'd give to sweeping away poisoned rats.

My hands tremble as I think back on incidents I myself witnessed. It is too much for me to set down all the details here. Still, the purpose of starting this diary was to create a record of events, so I must steel myself.

The night following my run-in with police chief Hickey and the thugs at the *Tribune*, I attended another outdoor meeting called by the Working-men's Party. Throughout the day, there'd been innumerable skirmishes. Roving groups of angry workers closed up factories, stoneworks, and tanneries, and stopped the Burlington Railroad from delivering any grain to the elevators (but not before a fusillade of police bullets had killed three and wounded nine). At the Michigan Central yards, the police charged directly into the crowd, clubs flailing, sparing no one. Even the *Times* reported that the sound of clubs falling on skulls was "sickening; a rioter dropped at every whack, it seemed, for the ground was covered with them." If the bloodshed sickened the *Times*, one can imagine the extent of the onslaught.

Still, the three thousand workingmen who turned out for the WP rally that night were entirely peaceful in demeanor. Van Patten had taken the precaution of going to police headquarters that morning to assure them that the rally would be calm and orderly—for which pains he was given what they called the "Parsons treatment," including a threat to hang him from a lamppost. At Lucy's insistence, I stayed *off* the platform and we mingled in the crowd, greeted over and over with delighted shouts and slaps on the back.

Then, as soon as Van Patten opened up the proceedings and began his speech, a squad of police cavalry charged the assembled crowd from behind. In their rush to flee, people crashed into the flimsy platform, reducing it to splinters, scattering the torches, and injuring Van Patten. At that very moment a procession of one thousand workingmen, arriving late, entered the meeting grounds with a blaring fife-and-drum corps at their head. The police "mistook" them for an army, fired a warning volley, and then collided with the crowd in a series of skirmishes. Miraculously, only a few were killed.

The next day, Mayor Heath called for federal assistance and President Hayes authorized the use of the Illinois National Guard. Their ranks were swelled from elsewhere. Some business leaders and railroad heads organized armed companies from the lists of their employees. They served, I like to think, against their will, but I've learned not to trust too much in the "logic" of worker solidarity.

Hundreds of Civil War veterans eagerly lined up for blocks to get deputized as "special" police officers. That, I confess, did confound me. Having experienced the miserable carnage of war, why were they so eager to reenlist in it? Did they blot out memories of suffering in order to taste again the intensity of feeling and purpose now absent from their lives? I suppose when you've marched with Grant from Donelson to Vicksburg, being a clerk or a bricklayer twelve hours a day is like trading in cognac for tea.

The climax came at the Halsted Street viaduct, where an angry mob of some five thousand clashed in open combat with the police. I was in a different part of the city during the melee, but Spies found himself trapped in the middle of it. He reported seeing man after man fall in his tracks with a bullet in the head or chest, or mercilessly clubbed into unconsciousness. One striker, blood and brains oozing out of the back of his neck, was so caught in the frenzy of the moment, according to Spies, that he staggered forward for several blocks before falling over dead. He also saw a teenage boy standing upright and immovable, blazing away at the police with a pistol in each hand—until he suddenly crumbled to the pavement, shot through the head. When Frank Norbock, a leader in the Bohemian section of the Workingmen's Party, was likewise felled with a bullet in the neck (or as the *Times* described it the next day, "with a bullet through the base of his uncultivated brain"), the crowd started to scatter. And no wonder, with eighteen dead and thirty-two wounded—not counting those dragged anonymously away by friends.

Still the police weren't satisfied. They headed straight for Turner Hall on Twelfth Street where some 250 members of the cabinetmakers' society, the Harmonia Association of Joiners, were engaged in an orderly discussion of how to achieve an eight-hour working day. Without warning, the police roared into the meeting, guns drawn, and brutally brought down their clubs on any head within striking distance. It was all over in a matter of minutes: one cabinetmaker shot dead, a score of others seriously injured. A few tried to escape by jumping out of the third-story windows. The press today praises the police for their "quick action." The *Tribune* urges that every boiler be equipped with a hose attachment that could be used to direct a stream of scalding water at the "Communistic rabble."

Despite the bloodthirsty press, the sheer horror of the Turner Hall incident produced a shift in public mood. As if the breath had been knocked out of them, people took a gasping step backward. In the three days since, there's been a rapid de-escalation on all sides. Scattered incidents are still being reported, but terror has loosened its grip on the city.

Indeed, on the country. St. Louis remained at fever pitch a few days longer than most places. The Workingmen's Party there is one thousand members strong. I felt proud to read that when a negro man took to the platform at one of the St. Louis rallies, saying he wished to speak for all his people who worked on the levees and steamboats, the crowd listened attentively. According to the *Vorbote*—no other paper even mentioned the event—the colored man told the rally, "We work in the summer for twenty dollars a month and in the winter can't find the men we worked for." Then he asked the crowd, "Will you stand with us regardless of color?" It roared back, "We will!"

Those are thrilling words, but I don't need Lucy to tell me that what's said in the passion of the moment is soonest forgotten. Still, I'm hopeful ("You always are!" my dear wife says). In late July, negro longshoremen in Galveston struck for—and won—equal pay with white workers on the docks. And just two days ago, in that same city, it was the negro tracklayers who persuaded their white counterparts to demand a raise in pay to two dollars a day. And they got it!

On the other hand, in San Francisco white workers are demanding that all Chinamen be discharged from the railroads and are randomly attacking Chinese people on the street, setting fire to their washhouses and ransacking their homes for valuables. Even the Knights of Labor call the Chinese "vice-ridden racial inferiors"—even "human vermin." It's disgusting to me, but these attitudes are so widespread that if I were to await a *pro*-Chinese platform, I'd have no labor organization to affiliate with. Only the most radical groups, the Marxists or anarchists, show a broader tolerance. But they're too ideological for my taste. The Marxists especially seem too sure about what the past means and what the future requires. To me, so much seems unknowable, and unpredictable. Perhaps the fault is mine. I started late on my education, certainly as compared with Spies. These days I read widely but it's mostly hit-and-miss. Lucy insists I'm better off for it.

But I'm wandering far from my topic.

The rest is quickly summarized. We must face facts: the Great Strike has collapsed. Among those who scrambled to join the Trainmen's Union, it turns out, were a number of private detectives and informers; management soon had its hands on our membership lists. Now many workers are worse off than before. That is surely true of me. I have no job and no prospects of one in a city where I'm denounced as a "leader of the mob." The railroads have fired and blacklisted anyone who played a prominent role in the strike. The Trainmen's Union has collapsed, and Ammon has started getting chummy with a few railroad officials—I never did trust the man, even while admiring his courage. The Workingmen's Party, its membership dwindling and under threat of repression, is lying low.

On the positive side, the propertied classes have been severely shaken even while their hatred of the "lower orders" seems undimmed. Just last week, the Reverend Henry Ward Beecher told his New York congregation that the strikers represented a "tyrannical opposition to all law and order." Can you believe it?!—the *workers* are now the tyrants! Beecher went on to say that "it is true that a dollar a day is not enough to support a man and five children, if the man insists on smoking and drinking beer. Is not a dollar a day enough to buy bread? Water costs nothing. Man cannot live by bread alone, it is true; but the man who cannot live on bread and water is not fit to live." This from a seducer of women, a sybarite living in the lap of luxury.

At least labor has seen what can be accomplished when its numbers and organizations are strong. And resentment among the workers is more fierce than before, though for the moment forced underground. It will soon enough find new expression. Of that, I am certain.

Part Four

Chicago

"It's such a risk. And I'd rather not be taking it," Lucy said, her voice piqued and strained. "But how else are we supposed to survive?"

She and Lizzie were standing in the vacant ground-floor space of their tenement building. The room was a bleak, empty rectangle, seven by eight feet, the flooring rough-hewn boards, the space devoid of all ornamentation and amenities—no molding on the walls, no basin for washing, no ice chest for food or stove for heat. Which was precisely why it had stood unrented all these years, though priced at only four dollars a month.

The room's one attraction was a large window that faced onto the street. It was the window that had first given Lucy the idea. Passersby would be able to see directly inside, and could be drawn in, hopefully, by the merchandise on display.

"Lucy, you'll freeze in the winter, and during the summer, with the sun beating down on that window, this place will be an inferno."

"I'm not going to live here, I'm going to work here. I'll keep the door open for ventilation."

"You'll be living here more than half of every day," Lizzie said fretfully.

"Do you think I like the idea? Give me an alternative, just one, anything. With Albert blacklisted and bringing in no money except the occasional pittance for an article in the *Vorbote*, how do you expect us to live?"

"It's just . . . just that a dress shop in this neighborhood is such an unlikely—"

"—after all, Albert can't develop new skills overnight, much as he might like to become a cooper or a blacksmith!"

Lizzie simply threw up her hands rather than attempt a reply.

"No," Lucy went on, "Albert is a writer and a speaker, and that's how he should spend his time, not as a day laborer or a barker for some dime museum."

"I completely agree," Lizzie said, as if humoring a five-year-old. "Albert's doing important work that only Albert can do."

"You agree? Then why are we arguing?"

"I wasn't. I was only trying to raise a few practical considerations. Almost every woman in this neighborhood knows how to sew, and makes her own family's clothes. Who will your customers be? How many women can find the extra pennies to buy a skirt, let alone pay you to lay in pleats or fix a hem? Or are you expecting commissions from Mrs. Risberg's crowd for tennis outfits and riding habits?" Lizzie mordantly added.

Lucy snorted. "I've yet to get a referral from her. There must be a new 'Creole genius' in town. And don't think that I couldn't make tennis and riding outfits! I could copy them straight out of *Arthur's Magazine*. In case you've forgotten, I happen to be a very fine seamstress."

"I have no doubt on that score. It's customers I worry about."

"I'm going to charge very little. I can make a basic housedress for two dollars, and using decent material too—sateen at twenty cents a yard. I could remodel an older garment for even less. Working cheap, I'll get some customers from the neighborhood. Then, if I get lucky, word'll spread about 'the wonderful seamstress who works for practically nothing.'"

"Oh Lucy, you are something!" Lizzie said, appreciatively. "Nothing can keep you down."

"Nothing yet." Lucy suddenly recalled the dread she felt during their first few years in Chicago whenever she had to go downtown. "Oh, and I forgot!" she said, brightly. "Albert says if I make up a flyer, he'll distribute it at political and trade union meetings. The men greatly admire him. They know we're in trouble. They'll come forward."

"I want to help, too," Lizzie said evenly.

"You?" Lucy was taken by surprise, and touched. "But how can you help, dear Lizzie?"

"I'm *almost* as fine a seamstress as the world-famous Lucy Parsons." Lizzie said with a grin.

Lucy smiled, some of the strain draining from her face. "You're better than I am with buttonholes. And I might even give you the nod with linings. But, Lizzie dear, where could you possibly find the time?"

"I have my Sundays, and an hour or two in the evenings."

"You don't have a moment for yourself as it is. You need to go to more picnics and socials. You'll never find a husband helping me stitch borders."

"That will come when it will. I'm in no hurry," Lizzie said firmly. "What matters now is making some contribution."

"Do you want children some day?" Lucy abruptly asked.

"Why do you bring that up?"

"I very much want children," Lucy said gently. "So does Albert. But we have to make sure we have enough food for two before we can add a third." Her voice sunk to a confidential whisper. "That's another reason for the shop . . ."

"Well then!" Lizzie said, her eyes widening with excitement. "You and I had better get down to work. I've already thought about approaching the widow Arnstein who lives over on Kinzie Street. With age, her eyes have gone bad and her husband left her comfortably off."

"We'll give an honest price for honest labor. We'll never overcharge." Lucy said, as if addressing a crowd.

Her solemnity somehow made Lizzie merry. "Speak for yourself," she said. "I intend to charge you considerably more than the going rate for piecework. After all, I'm a white woman working for a *negress*. It's unheard of!"

Momentarily stunned, Lucy burst out laughing.

Chicago

"I want to offer a toast," Albert said, lifting his draft beer, his face beaming. "Or, rather—if time and our bankrolls permit—a whole series of toasts."

He was seated with Spies and Fielden at Mackin's, the popular North Side saloon that drew a varied ethnic crowd. Not wanting their talk interrupted by the piano-playing at the back, the three men had taken a table close to the swinging doors at the entrance, near the front window, which was so clotted with advertising posters that the potted ferns, desperate for light, leaned perversely *into* the room. Directly opposite their table, Mackin's famous mahogany bar stretched the full length of the room, with a brass footrail at the bottom.

"Yes," Spies said, "there's much to celebrate, at least for the moment."

"Now Spies—no German pessimism tonight!" Albert noisily clinked his glass against Spies', as if to insist that festivity would reign.

Fielden's kindly eyes twinkled with pleasure. "I insist on my prerogatives," he said, leaning into Parsons. "As the eldest person at this gathering, I claim the right of proposing the first toast. You must cede the honor."

"But my glass is in mid-air!" Parsons said, instantly raising it into that position.

"Then hold it there," Fielden said, quickly raising his own. Spies followed suit.

"Let us drink to the most momentous of all the momentous events of late," Fielden toasted, "To the birth of Albert Richard Parsons! Let the world take note, a new generation of Parsons means a new generation of agitators!"

With a loud "Albert Jr.," the three men drank. Then Spies, his tone characteristically wry, asked if Albert Jr. was enrolled yet in the recently formed Socialistic Labor Party. "Or are you and Lucy sticking with the Anglo-Saxon Knights?"

"Albert Jr.'s going to have a difficult time getting signed up for *any* group," Parsons said, with a seriousness that surprised the others.

Fielden, puzzled at Albert's shift of tone, tried to restore the comic mood. "Do you mean the lad's turned his back?" he asked with feigned horror. "Imagine—two weeks old and already crossed over to the capitalists."

"Very sensible of him," Spies chimed in. "The child wants to eat regularly."

"Truth to tell, my friends," Parsons said, "Albert Jr. won't have many options, as child or adult."

"You're talking in riddles, Albert," Spies said.

"All right, then. To the point. At the Lying-in Hospital, Albert Jr. was officially registered as 'a negro baby.' As you may imagine, that'll make it difficult to enroll him in a decent school, even."

There was a stunned silence. Parsons felt it was up to him to ease the tension. "I'm exaggerating, of course. Not *every* door will be closed. Why, in these enlightened days he might even aspire to become a waiter. I hear the august Palmer House is now employing a few negro servers—what difference if they have to enter the hotel through a separate alleyway?"

"Was this Lucy's doing?" Fielden asked hesitantly, unsure, after his earlier brush with her on the subject, whether to risk going near it again.

"You mean in creating a negro baby, or in registering it as such?" Albert said with a strained chuckle. "Lucy doesn't register *herself* as 'negro.' You can be sure she wouldn't put that label on her son. His complexion's much like hers, tawny, bronze. But—" Albert stopped in mid-sentence; his mind had caught up with his tongue.

"That's enough about Albert Jr.," he said with finality. "He's a fine, healthy baby and Lucy and I are thrilled to have him." To forestall further discussion, he quickly raised his glass. "I have a toast of my own to propose: To Sam Fielden's new team of horses—a self-employed stonemason at last!"

"And a leader of the teamsters' union!" Spies added, raising his own glass.

From there the toasting proceeded to memorialize every imaginable instance of recent good fortune: a toast to Lucy's double success in turning a modest profit on the dress shop even while helping to found the Working Women's Union; a toast to the steady growth of the Knights and to the many semiskilled railroad workers who'd been signing up in the wake of the Great Strike; a toast to the appearance of several new labor newspapers, with a special toast to the *Socialist* and to Albert's being named its assistant editor; and finally a series—a stupefying series—of toasts to the new Socialistic Labor Party for filling the shoes of the defunct Workingmen's Party, to its willingness to accept negro members, to its active campaign to enroll women, and (eyes now blurry) to its promising foray into electoral politics with the recent election of Frank Stauber to the City Council.

Spies proposed the final toast, rising to his feet and speaking with solemn, if slurred, grandiloquence, of Albert's own near-election, in his recent second run for office, to the Council from the Fifteenth Ward. "The whole city knows that the corrupt ward bosses had to stuff the ballot-boxes to count our comrade out, to cheat him from a victory he'd clearly won."

Uncomfortable with the flush of pride he felt, Albert shifted the talk to the upcoming spring election. He spoke about it so coherently that Fielden accused him of having poured half the toasts down his shirt front instead of into his mouth. "Shucks, partner, we ain't had more'n a couple pints," Parsons replied, affecting his boyhood accent, "'T'ain't nuthin', m'boy—not if you've had a proper Texas upbringing!" Mounting a figurative platform, he then announced, this time in textbook English, that "the coming election will prove once and for all that trade unionism and political action go together"—here he hiccuped loudly—"and pursued together will bring our people to power and put a, put a . . ." Albert suddenly went blank.

"Put a stop," Fielden prompted.

"Yessir, yessir, that's it! . . . Put a *halt*!"—his deliberate substitution made all three of them howl—"put a halt to turning this country into a land of paupers, tramps, and menials."

Fielden and Spies loudly applauded, startling the tables around them. All three were now well on their way to being drunk, since they'd shifted, after the first few rounds, from nickel beer to the rare extravagance of ten-cent whiskey. And they'd drunk it down straight, followed by a chaser of water—except for Spies, whose delicate stomach dictated a buttermilk substitute.

And it was Spies's stomach, as the evening careened to a close, that displaced politics as the consuming topic of discussion. "You care too much—that's the cause of nervous indigestion, m'lad," Fielden said affectionately. "It overexcites the nerves."

"No, no, no!" Albert laughingly insisted. "It's because you live with your mother and sisters. Just how old are you, Spies?"

"I'm twenty-four."

"Good lord, Spies, you're practically middle-aged—you must marry at once, before your loins give out! The trouble is, you're too dashedly handsome. With so many to pick from, you can't pick at all."

They went on teasing Spies as if he wasn't there, while he basked in the warmth of having doting older brothers. "You're wrong, Parsons!" Fielden roared happily. "Spies's nature is *much* too delicate to bear up under the strains of marriage. Why, look at me," he said, pounding his chest and breaking into a broad grin, "an ox of a man, yet old before my time thanks to the loving ministrations of the wife and kiddies. Take it from me, lad," he said to Spies, trying to look glum, "stay single, that's the ticket. You're an intellectual, you need your time to yourself for reading and such matters."

"'Delicate' is he? Now that's a joke!" Albert laughed. "This man is vicious, he, he's joined the wicked Lehr-und-Wehr Verein, believes in armed revolt! I read all about it in the *Chicago Tribune*."

"When you've sobered up," Spies said, trying, with marginal success, to sound pulled together, "I'll explain—yet again, since you native Americans are so *thick*—that the Verein views armed struggle as a disservice to the workers'—cause—yes, rejects all talk of class war—"

"Yet drills with fancy Remington and Springfield rifles," Albert threw in. "And those cost a pretty penny. Bet the money's comin' straight from Karl Marx and his gang in Germany."

"Karl Marx lives in London," Spies said, grinning broadly.

"Same thing," Parsons said with another loud hiccup, which they all found hilarious. "It's foreigners what's ruining this country," Albert yelled, briefly silencing the tables nearby. "All these filthy anarchists piling up on our shores!"

"And what about those uniforms?" Fielden demanded, spittle trickling down his shirt front. Not even the ladies of Prairie Avenue spend as much on finery as the Verein does!"

"Just so you know," Spies said, "our money comes from fund-raising balls, picnics and voluntary contributions."

"My God, he's still talking in full sentences," Albert said loudly to Fielden. "Uncanny. It must be that buttermilk."

Spies laughed. "Tonight is obviously not the night for any——" He pushed his chair back and started to rise.

"Where do you think you're going?" Fielden bellowed. "I haven't even toasted the queen——to say nothing of Uriah Stephens!"

"Both of them will forgive you," Spies said. Going around to the other side of the table, he helped Albert and Fielden stand up, then managed to propel all three of them out the door.

Chicago

"As we agreed, I'll give you thirty minutes of my time," Parsons said, sitting down opposite Richard Andrews in his office at the *Chicago Tribune*.

"That should prove more than enough, Mr. Parsons. And let me thank you for coming." Andrews's meticulous courtesy was undermined by the sing-song insincerity of tone. When he'd initially asked for the interview, Albert had dismissed the idea. But Spies had convinced him that the risk should be run: "If only a few half-truths make it into print," he said, "that would be an advance. Besides, you yourself worked for the villainous *Times*. Perhaps Andrews, too, will turn out to be a secret sympathizer."

Andrews turned out to be primarily interested in the upcoming Socialistic Labor Party rally at the huge Exposition Building to celebrate the eighth anniversary of the Paris Commune, a rally that had already prompted alarmed editorials demanding that the National Guard be called out. Andrews approached the subject circuitously, however, complimenting Albert on his growing prominence in, as he put it, "the struggle against capitalism."

Ignoring the remark, Albert chose a generalized reply. "I believe in the importance of unifying the working class through both economic and political means. Organizing trade unions and voting to elect SLP candidates are two means to the same end."

"Then I take it you disagree with Paul Grottkau, at least as he's expressed his views in *Der Vorbote*." Confident that the depth of his information would take Albert by surprise, a smug blush suffused Andrew's face.

"I see," Parsons said evenly, "that you follow our internal debates and publications with some care."

"Yes, yes, we must keep abreast of the competition," Andrews said with a chuckle.

Annoyed at Andrews's condescension, Albert felt determined to stay focused on the issues.

"Paul Grottkau is a most learned man," he said. "I hold him in the highest regard. We agree on much, especially on the importance of strengthening the trade unions."

Andrews, like a man who's been sitting poised with a fly swatter above his head waiting for the annoying little buzzer to land exactly within range, came down hard. "Yet Grottkau has insisted that economic action should always take precedence over political action. How do you reconcile that view with the amount of energy you've spent running for a City Council seat?"

"With no more difficulty," Albert replied, striving to maintain his equanimity, "than you might have in reconciling *Tribune* editorials that refer to Chicago's unemployed workers as 'prowling wantons' with your own *obvious* sympathy for men desperate to feed their families."

Seeing Andrews redden, Albert spoke rapidly to maintain his advantage. "People who band together in common cause don't share all views in common. Besides, you seem not to have grasped the full subtlety of Grottkau's position. He doesn't oppose political action per se, but only the notion that it can, by itself, free the working class from economic servitude. He advocates political action when anchored to a solid trade union base. So you see, Grottkau and I are not so far apart. And who knows? The future may bring us still closer together—especially if the ruling class continues to use fraud and intimidation to block our law-abiding efforts to produce change through the ballot-box."

Albert had spoken at such a clip that Andrews felt like the victim of one of those high-wheeler maniacs currently threatening the pedestrian population with their new fifty-four-inch bicycles. He retreated to a simple question: "Does that mean you will or will not be running again for municipal office?"

"Having been counted out by fraud last year, I'll be devoting my time to the candidacy of others, mostly through my editorial writing in the *Socialist*."

"Ah yes, I've heard you've been named the assistant editor. I haven't yet seen the little journal in question. Isn't it one of those ethnic publications?"

Albert met him toe to toe. "The *Socialist* is the English-language organ of the SLP. Since English *is* an ethnicity, I suppose we could fairly be called an ethnic publication. Our focus, however, is on organizing all workers into one political party."

"I suppose you have a very large subscription," Andrews said, knowing full well that all the labor papers struggled along with minimal support.

"We're growing all the time." Albert spoke so emphatically that he sounded threatening.

Not that Andrews was fazed. "And is there any one candidacy this year that interests you more than the others?"

"The main race is, of course, for Mayor."

Andrews seemed genuinely surprised. "Does the SLP intend to contest that office? You've never run a candidate for any municipal post higher than alderman."

"We feel ready to move up in the world." Albert's smile was tight and pointed.

"And who might we expect the SLP candidate to be? Yourself, perhaps?"

"As I said, my contribution this time around will be through my writing. There was a move to nominate me for the Presidency, but—"

"—the Presidency of the SLP? But isn't Phillip Van Patten still the—"

"The Presidency of the United States."

Andrews literally gasped. His reaction was so flagrantly comic that Albert had trouble suppressing a laugh. "Why do you find that prospect so astonishing?" he asked in pretended innocence.

"Well, my dear sir, I mean surely it . . . it makes no sense for . . ." Andrews was sputtering—and furious at losing control of the reins.

"I refused, of course," Albert said quietly, trying not to look like a Cheshire cat.

"Well, of course. I should think so." Andrews nodded vigorous assent, as if a sense of propriety had been restored.

"I'm too young."

"I beg pardon?" Andrews again looked dumbfounded.

"The Constitution, you know. One must be thirty-five years of age to run for the presidency. Four years to go, alas. But I'll be of age in time for the '84 canvas."

Andrews rose to his feet with such a rush of anger that he nearly knocked over his chair. "I believe, sir, that our allotted thirty minutes has passed."

"Right you are," Albert said cheerfully, rising to his feet. "Nothing like small talk, very small talk, to make time fly, eh? Are you sure you have all you need?"

"More than enough," Andrews replied stiffly. If a powdered wig had somehow been at hand, he would doubtless have jammed it on his head in a desperate gesture to restore the proper distinctions of rank.

"Some day," Albert said, "a person from the working class *will* head this government. That is, if the working class doesn't lose all faith in it before then."

With that, he turned and left.

Two days later, Andrews's article appeared in the *Tribune*. The headline read, "ANARCHIST PARSONS PLANS UPCOMING SLP RALLY TO LAUNCH 1884 CANDIDACY FOR PRESIDENCY OF THE UNITED STATES."

Chicago

Spies stepped purposefully to the front of the group of fifty or so men, a signal for them to fall in and close ranks. They were one of several units of the Lehr-und-Wehr Verein designated to serve as marshals for the march to Exposition Hall. They'd gathered here at the Ogden Grove picnic grounds to run their drills while there was still some daylight and to review their plans for keeping order along the march route. Spies moved easily among the men, chatting in German with this one, in English with another, coaxing them into formation, his eyes shining with excitement. Though he looked (and sometimes acted) the aristocrat, Spies, like Parsons, was comfortable before any kind of audience and with people of varied backgrounds.

Next month would mark Spies's twenty-fifth birthday, yet he had the commanding presence of someone much older and people seemed quick to defer to him. Some of his natural authority emanated from his physicality. Even as a young boy in Landeck, a mountainous region of Germany dominated by the ruins of medieval castles, he'd spent much of his time out of doors, often accompanying his father, a forester, on his rounds, but almost as often scampering off alone on forbidden explorations. He would joyfully clamor over the rocky terrain of his favorite ruin, Castle Wildeck, unafraid of the omnipresent bats and adders, bursting with happiness when he reached its highest point and could stare down into the fertile valleys and cozy villages below. Only once did he feel afraid—when he stumbled on the remains of an old torture rack, its corroded spikes encrusted (so he imagined) with human blood. As an adult, he converted the fear into philosophy, drawing confident parallels between the barbarism of the medieval knight and the agony inflicted by the policeman's brutal club.

Today at Ogden Grove, the splendor of Spies's outfit amplified his natural charisma. He wore the full, striking LWV uniform: a tufted cotton jacket and heavy dark pants for protection against the winter wind (in summer the pants were white), a blue linen blouse, a light-colored sailcloth sash across the chest, and a black Sheridan hat. Few LWV members could afford the outfit, and it had taken many a fund-raising petition and much scrimping for most of the men even to approximate the official garb. A good number of them wore frayed undershirts rather than blouses and carried old muzzleloaders rather than breechloading Springfields or Remingtons. Still, the LWV was known as the smartest-looking and best equipped of the various workers' militias—though the gray dress uniforms of the Bohemian Sharpshooters had their decided fans.

Spies and his men were proud of the responsibility they'd been given. The long-awaited Exposition Hall rally, designed to demonstrate the potential power of an aroused working class, had galvanized the poorer districts of the city and scared silly the wealthier ones. The *Tribune* had spoken for the propertied elements in characterizing the prospective participants as "the dregs of the slums, the choicest thieves and the worst specimens of female depravity."

On an ordinary Saturday, the Ogden Grove picnic grounds would be packed with thousands of working-class people thronging to the various stands, booths and tents for food, dancing, and carousels. Today, it was nearly empty. Most of the regular patrons had gone to one of the numerous other assembly points that the SLP had assigned to each of the different trade unions and organizations that made up the constituent sections of the march.

For weeks, details regarding the march and the Exposition Hall proceedings had been thrashed out at popular working-class gathering places in Chicago's North Side, at Thalia Hall, Zepf's Saloon, Greif's, Neff's, and a dozen other smaller places, like the Labor Hall at West Twelfth Street—and on plenty of street corners and vacant lots, too. Night after night, exultant discussion had rung out over details small and large: the wording (and stitching) of a banner, approval (or denunciation) of a chosen speaker or political plank, skirmishes over an organization's place in the line of march, the number of torches needed, whether or not to carry arms, and so on.

One of the few booths open that day at Ogden Grove was the wine bar, famed for 1873 Riesling from the royal caves in Stuttgart; and several of the LWV men on arriving at the grounds headed directly for it. But Spies put an immediate stop to that. "Liquor consumption of any kind is forbidden," he reminded the men, his voice gentle but firm. "We've been given a mission of supreme importance and must remain true to it. Our senses must be clear and our minds alert." A few good-natured curses were thrown Spies's way, but the men dutifully headed off to a second tent, this one serving coffee, buttered almond cake, and the sweet yeast bread Topfkuchen.

The LWV and all the other worker militias would be marching with the chambers of their rifles empty. The Citizens Association, an organization of the city's leading businessmen, had seen to that. Alarmed at the militancy shown during the Great Strike, and convinced that the Exposition Hall rally marked "the possibility of a dangerous Communistic outbreak in Chicago," the association had successfully pressured the state legislature into passing a bill that made armed workers groups illegal.

The leadership of the Socialistic Labor Party was itself divided on the wisdom of militaristic display. Van Patten carried the day with the argument that the appearance of armed groups of workers would, whatever their actual intention, primarily serve to frighten the general public, confirming the long-standing propaganda that the SLP was intent on outright revolution and distracting attention from its just grievances. But when Van Patten banned even the carrying of empty weapons, the party's militant Chicago section rejected his order and a fissure was opened in the SLP that would continue to widen.

At the exact stroke of 5:00 P.M., Spies's LWV unit marched smartly out of Ogden's Grove to link up with the other militias—the Bohemian Sharpshooters, the Irish Labor Guards, the Jaegerverein, and a variety of LWV groups. Together they formed ten units, totaling more than five hundred men. Trade union flags waved in the brisk breeze alongside red flags and the Stars and Stripes. Whole families accompanied their marching kin and, galvanized by the Jaegerverein's two brass bands, cheered them on vociferously from the sidelines. Together the militias represented a diverse mix of ethnic and trade groups—from laborers and factory hands to boxmakers, bakers, machinists, and teamsters.

Following the militias in the parade line were the tableaux vivants— floats, most of them bathed in red calcium lights, depicting heroic episodes from the final days of the Paris Commune uprising. The most ambitious one, mounted through the combined efforts of the Furniture Workers' and Iron Moulders' Unions, depicted government lackeys shooting General Jeroslas Dombrowsky and his falling back into the arms of wounded freedom fighters.

Fielden was marching with the teamsters' brigade, and when he and Spies spotted each other along the route, they broke ranks for a warm embrace. Fielden had only a few seconds to introduce Spies to the man marching next to him. His name was George Engel—the same impressive man Fielden had introduced Albert to a year or so back. Engel's stolid intensity caught Spies's attention. But there was no chance to talk; the line of march began to move forward again, and the men rejoined their respective units.

As the procession swelled in numbers and headed toward the lakefront, the sky darkened and the human serpent grew bright with an endless string of bobbing torches that stretched out for miles along the shore. So huge was the turnout that the approach to Exhibition Hall soon became blocked with an undulating sea of humanity. Albert, as a featured speaker, as well as Lizzie and Lucy (who was holding Albert Jr. wrapped in blankets in her arms), were already inside the hall. They stood looking out at the massive crowd from the second-story stairway of the gigantic building.

"It's beyond anything I dreamed possible!" Lucy gasped.

"Truly amazing," Albert said in a near whisper, his eyes ablaze with excitement. "Humanity awake."

Lizzie worried that the crush of bodies might lead to injuries, that someone would get trampled underfoot.

"No, no," Lucy reassured her. "Just look!" She pointed out the window. "It's entirely orderly. No one's pushing or shoving. They're patiently waiting for admittance."

"But how will they all fit in?" Lizzie asked anxiously.

"They won't," Albert said. "There could well be forty thousand people, or more, out there. Not even this barn can hold that many. But no one will leave and no one will get hurt. Somehow I know that. People simply want to tell their grandchildren that they were part of this glorious occasion, the day when working people realized their numbers and power. Getting inside to hear the speeches is the least of it. Which reminds me—I should get to the platform and see if we're running anywhere near schedule. Don't forget: there are places reserved for the two of you in the first few rows."

Albert embraced the women, kissed his infant son, and hurried off.

Spies's Verein unit was near the front of the line of march, directly behind the brass bands now playing the "Marseillaise," as the crowd sang lustily along, to accompany the marchers as they passed into the building's vast expanse. The interior of Exhibition Hall was draped wall to wall with flags and banners, the largest of which read "THE GRAND ANNIVERSARY OF THE DAWN OF LIBERTY: PARIS, 1871." Within an hour, every inch of available space, including the platform, was crammed to overflowing with exuberant humanity—with twice as many people stirring on the grounds outside.

The militia groups had been scheduled to perform a drilling exhibition, but given the press of the crowd, the men simply stacked their guns into pyramids and took up police duty to ensure order. Acrobatic and dance performances had also been planned as entr'actes to the speechmaking, but the lack of space meant that most of the elaborate opening program had to be abandoned. No one was even sure whether, given the dense crowd, the speeches would carry beyond the main floor.

By now it was nearly half past eight, a half hour after the official program had been scheduled to start. The organizers huddled on stage and made a quick decision to send out the tried-and-true crowd pleasers W. B. Creech and John McAuliffe. Creech, the "untamed troubadour," often provided an opening song or poem for large labor gatherings and on this night he declaimed his latest composition in a strong, clear voice that carried straight up to the galleries:

> So come, my friends, and join us,
> And you'll never rue the day,
> For we'll change this present system
> To the Socialist way.

Creech sang on for a dozen stanzas, got a rousing cheer at the end, and returned the compliment with several grandiloquent bows. Before he'd even returned to his seat, John McAuliffe bounded across the stage. He was running for Congress on the SLP ticket and his vibrant tenor voice rang through the crowd: "Let us yank, and thunder, and roar, and storm, and charge, at the ballot-box, and having thus peaceably, yet boldly, won the victory, we will enjoy it, *or know the reason why*! Fellow workers, be true to yourselves, desert the enemy, and the morn following election, Labor's sun will rise radiant with glory!"

Lucy and Lizzie were seated so close to the stage that McAuliffe's voice reverberated through them as though in an echo chamber. When he shouted "radiant with glory!" Lucy—handing off Albert Jr. to Lizzie so quickly that she nearly dropped him—leapt to her feet as if struck by lightning. Throwing her arms over her head, swaying from side to side, she shouted "Hurrah!" after "Hurrah!" up into McAuliffe's face. Her voice was so powerful that he actually heard it above the din and turning in her direction, threw her a kiss.

"Next year!" Lucy yelled exuberantly at Lizzie, who was trying to comfort a bawling Albert Jr., "next year there'll be a woman up there on the stand and"—her eyes blazed with anger and bravado—"that woman might just be me!"

The assembly meeting carried over into the next day, a Sunday. Many families camped out on the grounds for the night, and a constant stream of men went back and forth into the city to get food, blankets, and other provisions. The police, armed with formal complaints from the Board of Trade and the Stock Exchange, tried to remove people from inside the building, but most refused to budge. They caught a few hours' rest on the hardwood floors or sat up all night in excited talk.

When it finally came time for Albert to speak, the crowd had thinned—Lizzie and Lucy had themselves been forced to leave in the early morning hours, after Albert Jr. developed diarrhea—and the thousands who still remained had by then heard the impassioned drone of so many speeches that the repetitive words barely penetrated. Fatigue and anticlimax were rapidly becoming the order of the day.

Albert began by saying that what the Chicago working-class wanted in 1879 was the same as what the German workers had wanted in 1848 and the French in 1871—"to establish a self-governing republic, wherein the masses could partake of the civilization which their industry and skill had created." That produced a wave of applause and spurred Albert on to an energetic argument in favor of electoral politics. But the shift from talk of pistols and bayonets to the vote didn't suit the audience's bleary, raw-edged mood. It wanted a few bold shots, however figurative, across the bow. The crowd's restlessness dampened Albert's spirit, made him feel muddled and heavy. "The ballot-box must remain our first remedy," he said, his muted tone managing to make the tactic sound as tired as his voice. Light applause gave way to scattered booing when he went on to say, "In our current situation, with the power of the army at the beck and call of the propertied classes, strikes ultimately cannot be won, cannot bring lasting change."

The booing thoroughly unnerved him. He'd never before experienced anything like it. A popular orator, a tried-and-true audience pleaser, he'd grown used to warm approval. Shaken, feeling a sudden evacuation of energy, he brought his speech to a swift close. "Independent political action is, I repeat, the answer. We must elect our own representatives to implement our social program through legislation. And that program, I want to emphasize in closing, is *not*—as our enemies claim—a communistic call to abolish or equalize property ownership. Rather, it is a socialistic call for government ownership of public utilities and an end to the wealth of the country being drained off into the pockets of the few while the masses go hungry."

To a limp smattering of applause, Albert moved shakily off the podium, almost losing his balance and tripping as he disappeared into the sea of people.

✳

By the time he arrived back home, not having slept for two nights and having eaten little, he still felt bewildered and sorely in need of comfort and rest. But Lucy was in too belligerent a mood to provide much of either.

"Well what did you expect? You misgauged their mood, and they let you know it. All week long I tried to warn you! But as usual, you refused to listen."

"What are you saying, for heaven's sake? I value your opinion above all others, and have nearly always heeded it. Why are you being so unfair?" he said, his frustration and exhaustion bringing him near tears.

"Electoral politics! The ballot-box!" Lucy, hands on hips, started to move agitatedly back and forth across their narrow living room. "Why can't you understand that those with power never yield it up peacefully. They'll stuff your ballot-boxes. They'll discard your votes. You and Spies prattle on like old women about 'peaceful change' through the ballot. At least Spies has bought a rifle . . ."

"Oh, is that what you think I should do?" Albert asked, flaring. "Go out there and kill a few people?"

"Maybe," Lucy said quietly.

"Oh fine . . . just lovely . . . like the wonderful results violence gave us during the Great Strike . . . ending with the men stripped down to the status of slaves."

"There are slaves and there are slaves," Lucy said. "Fifty years ago, one of them was named Nat Turner."

"I know as much about Nat Turner as you do!" Albert shouted. "And I know what happened to him, too. He ended up on the gallows, his rebellion a failure."

Lucy turned on him in a fury. "As *you* measure failure, maybe. But in the hearts of his own people, Nat Turner is a living source of inspiration."

She turned away. "I must tend to the baby." And with that, she swept off into the other room.

Chicago

Lucy agitatedly paced the floor in front of Albert. "I want to write. And so does Lizzie."

She was making a declaration, not opening a discussion. "And I intend to start immediately. Between the dress shop and taking care of Albert Jr., I'm home all day anyway."

"But how will you find the time?" Albert was startled at Lucy's sharpness, but tried to hold to a neutral tone.

"The same way you and Spies and Grottkau and Van Patten—and all the other men—find the time. By not getting enough sleep. By taking your meals standing up. By rushing through the day. By seeing your spouse only when your heads hit the pillow at night. Why do you even ask? Do you think I'm less resourceful or energetic than you?"

Albert got up from his chair and went over to embrace her. "Sweetheart, you have more zest than the rest of us put together. And I want you to do this. You have strong opinions and they need to be heard."

"So does Lizzie."

"Lizzie doesn't speak out as forcefully as you, so her commitment isn't as apparent."

"It's apparent to me. We talk all the time. And not about fabrics and stitching."

Albert laughed. "And I thought a sewing circle was the apex of both your ambitions," he teased.

She wasn't amused. "I want you to get Frank Hirth to publish our articles in *The Socialist*. And I want him to pay us for them."

That took Albert aback. "Lucy, I'm only his assistant! He's the editor, he makes the final decisions."

The telltale flush that preceded a major outburst starting to ascend from Lucy's neck, and seeing it, Albert shifted his tone. "Of course Frank does consult with me. But all I can promise is to put the idea in front of him."

"Tomorrow."

"Tomorrow—what?"

"Speak to Hirth tomorrow."

"I will if I can get his attention long enough."

"Oh Albert!" Lucy wailed with frustration.

"I will, I will. You have my word. I *want* you to write for the press. Yes, and to speak out at public forums too. Surely you know I don't doubt your right, or your ability." He was sounding frustrated himself, which softened Lucy.

"I do know," she said quietly. "And I also know how lucky I am to have you for a husband—even if you were pigheaded about your Exposition Hall speech." Albert decided not to reply.

"Most men," Lucy went on, "would suspect their wives of neurasthenia if they showed any interest in public questions. I'm very lucky to have you." She stroked his cheek and put her arm around his waist.

"Well, I'm glad to hear that," he said, still holding himself at some distance. "Lately you seem angry with me most of the time."

"I've been angry with myself—and take it out on you," Lucy said simply. "I feel I have so much to contribute, but no way to do it."

"We'll find a way, I promise." He was touched by Lucy's admission. "If it doesn't work out with Hirst, we can take your articles to the new *Arbeiter-Zeitung*. Did I tell you the paper might use some of the five thousand dollars it raised at Exhibition Hall to hire Spies? As its business manager."

"Lucky man! I'm sure he'd love to stop stuffing chairs for a living."

"Don't tell him you've heard the rumor. He hasn't a firm offer yet. I'll start by approaching Hirst."

"Tomorrow."

"Tomorrow." They smiled happily at each other.

"Now tell me," Albert said, "and I'm asking this as a serious question. What are some of the things you want to write about? Some of the topics."

"My first subject," Lucy said, "will be the egotism of reformers. Too many of our male friends, it seems to me, care more about their own glory than the cause."

"We're probably all driven by a little personal ambition."

"I didn't mean *you*, for heaven's sakes. You're the most modest man I know! But there's a big difference between you and Mr. Philip Van Patten."

"Oh? I thought you liked him."

"I do. But what the man wants above all is to remain the president of the SLP. To that end, he'll compromise his principles."

"I think you're being too hard on him. Van Patten's human, that's all. We all like to see our name in the newspaper."

Lucy visibly stiffened. "*I* don't. I couldn't care less if Lucy Parsons, the individual, is ever mentioned. In fact, I have no intention in my articles of ever talking about myself. I refuse to."

"My, my," Albert said, trying to sound impish, "I didn't realize I was living with a saint."

"Don't make fun of me."

"Very well. Then I'll tell you what I really think. I think you have a great deal of ambition." He surprised himself with his own directness. "And what's more, there's nothing dishonorable about it. I take ambition as a given. What matters is how you use it—in what cause, for what end."

"I never said I wasn't ambitious." Lucy felt she'd trumped him. "All I said was that I'd do nothing to push myself forward, nothing for personal notoriety. Self-importance is the first, nearest, hardest, most contemptible of our enemies."

There was a momentary silence. Faced with Lucy's righteous, almost ceremonial declaration, Albert decided against discretion. "You know what I think, my dear Lucy?"

"I'm eager to hear."

"I think you have the makings of a first-class revolutionary fanatic."

He'd hoped to sound a waggish note, but Lucy's response had no playfulness in it: "I dearly hope you're right. I've gotten a late start."

"What will happen, I wonder, if I fail to keep up with you?"

"I'll chuck you out, straightaway, that's what!" Lucy's smile signaled her agreement to end the exchange with humor. "Anyway," she added, "that's the first thing I would write about."

"Chucking me out?"

"Egotism—you goose." With mock exasperation, she swatted him on the arm.

"And your second topic?" Albert asked. "Something tells me you have several dozen already laid out."

"My second article will be about the semislavery of female servants. About the elegant Prairie Avenue ladies who work their maids sixteen hours a day and then dare to keep strict records of their weekly tea and sugar allotments. I want more women to know about the Working Women's Union, to know they have a place to go with their complaints. The article would summarize what I said at the WWU public meeting in the spring."

"Remember how surprised we were at John McAuliffe's response?"

"He was right to castigate the SLP for having only five women members in Chicago."

"Well, at least the party has endorsed women's suffrage."

"But done nothing to implement it. If the SLP doesn't include a suffrage plank in its next platform, women should refuse all aid to the party."

"The silly part, I thought, was when McAuliffe urged women to refuse even to *dance* with an SLP man. What next? Refusing to cohabit?"

Lucy's eyes narrowed. "Don't start me up again. We were beginning to have a civil conversation."

"The first move you make to quit my bed and—"

"Yes, *and?*"

"And, I immediately resign from the SLP."

"That's my dear husband!" Lucy threw her arms around him, then quickly disengaged. "And my third article will be aimed directly at you."

"Now what have I done?"

"You won't admit that you're wrong about electoral politics. Didn't the recent results teach you anything?"

"The SLP got twelve thousand votes for Mayor—20 percent of the total, nearly half Carter Harrison's winning tally!"

"And if you'd won? Your assignment would be to license wharves and farmers' markets!"

Albert had had enough arguing for one day, but his glum expression all but handed Lucy the unspoken victory. "As you well know," he said, "most of my spare time these days is going to the eight-hour movement.

I'm rethinking a lot of things."

"Well, I've already rethought them. The essential struggle's economic, not political."

"Thank you, Karl Marx."

"You're indeed welcome. My advice is yours for the asking. It might speed up that 'rethinking' process," she said with a taunting smile. "What helped me was a phrase from Mirabeau that Lizzie—your quiet, 'unforceful' Lizzie—showed me: 'You cannot reform the world by the sprinkling of rose oil.'"

The Diary of
Albert R. Parsons

January 17, 1880

I'm more dispirited these days than in a long time. Even as the SLP loses strength, it's breaking into antagonistic factions. An implacable stubbornness is in the air. I don't feel comfortable with the brass-bound inflexibility emerging on all sides. I ascribe it mostly to disillusion; wretchedly disappointed in our hopes, we take out our frustration on the nearest targets. I'm sure the much-touted "return of prosperity" has also played a role. The newspapers exaggerate the recent improvement in conditions, but times are better. Farmers are reaping good harvests again, railroad construction has greatly expanded, some factories have reopened, the demand for labor has grown, and in some places wages have risen.

But for most of us the purported prosperity has been pretty thin gruel and will turn to water soon enough, as the next cycle of market manipulation begins. The upswing this year has mostly profited people like Jay Gould and his circle of high-flying financiers; they're having a grand old time, with the balance of trade turned favorable, with Congress nullifying the income tax and restoring the gold standard, and with interest rates down and stocks up. For those of us who toil for a living and have no assets, "prosperity" has been marked at best by a two-dollar-a-week raise—with no guarantees about next week's paycheck.

I keep trying to explain this to people when I go out to give a lecture or talk at a trade union meeting. But my audiences have dwindled by half, and that half is less than fiery in its response. A lot of workers seem to feel that "the system" has proven itself sound after all. It's as if their memory of the horrors of the past decade has been wiped clean. Maybe this is the way people—black slaves or factory slaves—manage to survive:

they blot out their suffering or tell themselves that it's their own fault or that nothing can be done about it (and that, besides, the joys of heaven await and will ultimately compensate). Certainly the pulpit and press cooperate with the plutocrats in pressing home the biblical message that "the poor always ye shall have with you." It's God's will. How convenient. Only in times of desperation, it seems, does the wool drop from people's eyes, and the woodenness from their limbs.

The widespread decline of interest in politics and trade unionism makes me despair. The comparative few who had joined the SLP now seem bent on deserting it. Given the party's recent high hopes, the leadership is understandably sick with disappointment. It's further fed by the deaf ear we get from the powers that be. Last week, for example, the Chicago Eight-Hour League sent me to Washington, DC, as a delegate to a conference of labor reformers. I presented a resolution calling on the government to explain why the federal eight-hour law passed back in 1868 has gone unenforced at a time when Washington is vigorously pressing legislation of all kinds favorable to the demands of the railroad barons. The conference adopted my resolution and I stayed on in Washington for a full week trying to lobby the issue in the Congress. I mustered no sympathy at all, let alone action. Probably this should cure me of any hope that politics will solve our problems. Yet that hope stubbornly stays with me. For how much longer?

January 18

Spies called an emergency meeting of our friends to discuss growing factionalism within the SLP; as its ranks decline, the rancor rises. Grottkau insists that building a strong trade union movement must precede political action. Spies insists that workers' militias are an absolute necessity to protect against police brutality. Van Patten denounced them both for taking the SLP off course; he continues to insist that the party focus solely on political action. Spies later told me that Van Patten has actually threatened to expel him and others if they persist in their views. How utterly misguided! He's jeopardizing long-standing ties forged against great odds.

January 19

At the meeting yesterday, a yeast salesman named Oscar Neebe, who helped establish the *Arbeiter-Zeitung*, was particularly outspoken against any accommodation with Van Patten. I hadn't met Neebe before and was impressed with his strong commitment to trade unionism. But he, and some others at the meeting, too, seem to regard me with suspicion because I refuse to take a tooth-and-nail attitude toward Van Patten. I can't for the life of me understand why people who share the same social goals can't disagree without personally vilifying each other.

February 5

I'm proud as punch of Lucy. She—and Lizzie, too—have pushed their way forward in the male world of politics, making their voices heard more and more. And their writings in various labor publications have been drawing admiring comments. I've always known how smart she and Lizzie are, but I wasn't prepared—I admit it—for their articles to be so vigorously written and argued. I was more worried about Lucy, in truth, since Lizzie has had a good education, and has also had the advantage of being brought up in a family of free-thinkers. Yet Lucy has set the pace. She pulls no punches about the plight of her sisters. "It's a fact," she wrote the other day, "that women are paid less, driven a little harder, have less chance to cry out, are actually slaves of slaves."

February 15

Lucy's written a powerful piece excoriating the emerging Greenback Party for assuming that a "natural harmony" exists between capital and labor. As she put it, "That's the same as saying there's a natural harmony 'twixt robber and robbed." Most American workers have been taught to believe that what's good for the rich is good for the country as a whole. But the propertied class cares only for its own interest and defines "harmony" as the worker meekly accepting whatever terms are dictated to him. And what terms they are! You can't pick up a labor newspaper these days without reading some heartbreaking account of mothers dying of tuberculosis and their children of malnutrition because they couldn't afford to pay for medical care, or of penniless Civil War veterans being denied charity.

February 18

Lucy confided to me that Lizzie has been courting. And who should her swain turn out to be but William T. Holmes, a man I'd recently met at an SLP meeting and had immediately liked. He's English-born, like Fielden, but migrated here with his parents when five years old. Scholarly by nature, he had to drop out of school after his father became an invalid. He worked for a time as a sawyer in box factories and now, having taught himself shorthand, makes his living as a stenographer. His story is like so many others in our ranks: gifted people meant for a life of study and contemplation, but unable to follow their natural bent.

At thirty, Holmes is a year younger than Lizzie and three years younger than me. He's a calm, modest man, with a temperament much like Lizzie's own: both are peaceful, generous souls, born mediators. They're a wonderful match, even though I've never been one to assume that similar temperaments guarantee a happy union (not that anything does). Look at Lucy and me—a hot-headed, cool-tempered mismatch if ever there was one, judged superficially. Yet my (comparative!) placidity helps cushion her hurtling energy, and her passion helps ruffle my calm.

Lucy has sworn me to secrecy about Lizzie and Holmes. They have no immediate plans for marriage and want to maintain their privacy. I'm delighted for Lizzie. She's such a good soul, and so deserves this happiness.

May 1

More than a two-month break in my journal keeping. Lucy and I have had to move. We were not, like so many unfortunates, forced out of our flat. Rather, we decided to see if we could find a place with a bit more room. Albert Jr. has taken his first steps—and in our cramped space he's banging himself into a mass of bruises. Besides, Lucy, much to our delight, is with child again, and we'd like to be settled in our new flat before she comes to term this winter. With a little more money coming in these days, thanks to my increased editorial work and to Lucy's dress shop, we decided this was the right time to try and find a bigger place.

At first we thought of buying one of those six-hundred-dollar four-room cottages being built just south of Chicago. I guess we still have some nostalgia from our Texas days for wide-open spaces and greenery. But we realized that the urban din is part of our own rhythm now, for better or worse, and that to move outside the city would remove us from our friends and political work. "With only seventy-five dollars to our name," Lucy said one day with a laugh, "no building and loan society is about to lend the notorious fanatics Lucy and Albert Parsons one penny. Besides, something tells me that those cottage communities of white homeowners aren't likely to take kindly to a woman of, ahem, tawny hue. Especially a woman who thinks nobody should own a home until everybody can."

Nonetheless, thanks to Sam Fielden, we got lucky soon enough. He told us about friends of his who were high-tailing it out to California to make their fortune, leaving a three-room apartment on Grand Street with a rent just a few dollars more a month than we've been paying. Best of all, it's just two blocks away, so Lucy would still be near her shop.

All we had to do to secure the place was to make a little "offering" to the landlord. We bought him and his wife an expensive (ten-dollar) colored lithograph—a chromo. Fielden warned us that they had "refined"—that is, petit bourgeois—tastes, and recommended we buy Robert L. Newman's mawkish *Blue-Fringed Gentians*. For a moment in the chromo store Lucy got a wild gleam in her eye and said we should really get them Currier and Ives's *Darktown*, with its depiction of negroes as feckless imbeciles. "That ought to confuse the hell out of them," she said gleefully. "*Is Mrs. Parsons making fun of us or of herself?* That might at least close their traps—in front of us, anyway, which is all I ask—on the whole subject of race." In the end we played it safe (for once) and bought the Newman—which Lucy promptly retitled *Violets in the Shape of Female Genitals.*

Moving day was a nightmare. It seemed as if all of Chicago had chosen the tenth of April to exchange apartments. It took us the better part of a day to travel two blocks, locate missing articles dropped on the way (some never found, others broken beyond repair), and complete the unloading and carrying of our possessions up three flights. Never mind—we're beginning to settle in and feel very content with the grand amount of space. To celebrate, we've bought two second-hand armchairs for the living room, a draped center table, and a pine bookcase.

Until now, we had books piled in every corner, many of them gifts from Spies. At our urging, he took our education, or I should say, our lack of it, in hand, and we've been gratefully—and to tell the truth, often with great difficulty—reading our way through various European social thinkers. Glad as I've been for the increase in knowledge, I've felt some sadness about it, too, as if I've been moved still further away from my roots. I never did sound like a true Texas lad, but thanks to High European culture I no longer sound like one at all. I comfort myself with thinking how pleased Aunt Ester would be. She used to shake her finger at me and scowl away: "You best be attendin' those schoolbooks, boy, or for sure you'll end up powerful ignorant."

It's been the anarchist writers—about whom we'd never even heard—who have most appealed to us, especially Proudhon and Prince Kropotkin. They've opened up new horizons, even a new view of human nature. It suits those with money and power to justify their ruthless ways by arguing that selfishness and aggression are part of the law of life, which they define as a race in which the ablest (which happens to be them) win the prizes. Kropotkin argues that evolution has relied more on cooperation among people than on vicious competition between them. He insists that we are social creatures; we crave harmony and connection with each other. The State and other forms of imposed authority, like the Church, interfere with our natural bent toward mutual aid. Voluntary association will be the basis of the free society of the future. It's a noble dream—Good Lord, I was in the middle of writing about moving day and here I am getting carried deep in the meshes of philosophy!

Where was I? Oh yes, the new items we've purchased. I think the bookcase completes the list. We firmly ignored the landlord's sniffy "suggestions" that we cover the mantels with lace paper, put doilies on the backs of chairs "to protect your fabrics from greasy pomades," and fill a dozen vases with bouquets of homemade paper flowers. He was annoyed at our failure to heed what he called his "discerning eye for fashion," but we were hardly going to spend our hard-earned money on such silly stuff. Our flat remains sparsely furnished, but it's been filling up enough for Fielden to comment that "the landlord's petit bourgeois ways seem to be climbing up the stairs." I doubt that Lucy and I are in serious danger of contamination. Neither of us cares much about possessions, maybe because we never had many. But we're not puritans about it, either. I believe it feeds the soul to have a few beautiful objects around—would that we could afford a few—but it destroys the soul to fill one's space with fashionable clutter.

The single drawback we've discovered to the new flat is that the police department has installed an alarm box right in front of our tenement. It's one of the multiplying pine boxes, about seven feet high by three feet in diameter, being installed all around the city as part of a police "call system."

Inside each box is a telephone and an alarm dial with a pointer that can be moved to one of eleven choices—such as "riot," "thievery," "murder," etc. The boxes are fastened to telegraph poles with a direct line to the police station; when the alarm sounds, a wagon and two policemen are rushed to the site. And guess who gets to have a key to the alarm box? "Citizens of good standing." As defined by the police, that is. Which means that ward bosses and their flunkeys are far more likely to get keys than ordinary citizens. No one's offered Lucy and me one, nor anybody we know in the neighborhood. Lucy says the police might as well have put the box in our living room.

I confess that I thought the telephone would be one of those wonders of the world, like the velocipede bicycle, that fades away overnight. But the gadget seems to be spreading like wildfire. I read in the paper yesterday that in just two years the city of New Haven has already gotten enough subscribers to install a switchboard (though the article said that the young men employed as operators are so rude and rambunctious to callers that "hello girls" are going to replace them). In Chicago the telephone is still a plaything of the rich; there aren't more than a thousand of them—telephones, I mean.

June 1

The new apartment finally feels like home. Since we're still in the same neighborhood, it wasn't that much of an adjustment—except for getting used to the damned alarm box going off in our ears day and night. We've now turned our full attention to the pending Greenback convention, just a few weeks off. Those of us who will be representing the SLP are determined to pass a platform with real socialist teeth in it; otherwise, we won't consider any kind of merger. But what we're hearing from various quarters is that the only labor planks the Greenbackers are likely to support are watered-down, vague calls for "better working conditions." Spies says they're basically "heartland patriots," who don't want to acknowledge how much is wrong with our economic system and so have put their faith in an unsound cheap money scheme that won't do a thing to help the poor. What it would do is produce inflation, and the country's farmers are eager to see a rise in food prices. But how would inflation benefit the city worker, who has trouble affording a decent diet as it is? We'll see what the convention brings . . .

June 10

Great news!—Spies has been elected superintendent of the *Arbeiter-Zeitung*, with the likelihood that he'll soon be asked to become its editor as well! The paper's been on the verge of bankruptcy due to mismanagement. Saving it, and I'm certain Spies will, means saving an important voice for the movement. We have too few labor papers, and even fewer with staying power. *The Socialist*, in which we had such high hopes and which was hospitable to women writers like Lucy and Lizzie, has given up the ghost—and we are now without a single paper for English-speaking socialists.

June 20

We've had a terrifying two days, which fortunately have ended happily. On Friday, Albert Jr. suddenly started to run a high fever. Lucy immediately gave him our tried-and-true home remedy, a compound of willow and meadowsweet, which produced some improvement. But it proved temporary; within a few hours, the fever had returned full force, he had difficulty swallowing, and the glands in his neck appeared swollen. The sounds from his tiny throat were awful to hear, a deep, gurgling noise. Lucy and I became frantic. We felt there was no alternative but to seek medical help at the hospital dispensary, though like all people without money we've long known that staying at home usually provides better odds for survival.

We rushed him to the Central Free Dispensary, and were fortunate enough to land in the hands of a Dr. John Zeigler. He immediately diagnosed Albert Jr. as having diphtheria and told us that it was essential to dissolve the "pseudo-membrane" that had formed in his throat. He warned us that should his efforts fail, he'd have to intervene surgically and insert a small tube into Albert Jr.'s throat—at which point Lucy burst into tears, as I nearly did myself.

The next twenty-four hours were a grim vigil. Zeigler first tried a spray of limewater and pepsin, but it had no effect. Nor did chloride of iron. Lucy became terrified, inconsolable; her lamentations filled the corridor, rending my heart. Then, just as we were about to give up hope, Zeigler decided to give the baby a dose of calomel and bichloride of mercury, and within minutes, miraculously, the hideous sounds issuing from his throat eased. Within a few hours, he was breathing far more easily, though he continued for some time to regurgitate a vile-smelling viscous substance.

With Albert Jr. out of danger, Dr. Zeigler kindly sat with us a little while to explain what had happened. He ended up telling us far more, in our exhaustion, than we wanted to hear. The good doctor, it became clear, is exceedingly proud of his up-to-the-minute medical knowledge and was determined to display it at length. We felt so much gratitude towards him for saving our boy that we felt obliged to sit still for what turned into a considerable lecture. At least I did; Lucy was still so distraught that after a few minutes she excused herself, saying she felt faint and needed to find a place where she could lie down.

Dr. Zeigler, it seems, has recently studied in Germany and is a convert to the new "germ theory," derived from the work of a Frenchman named Louis Pasteur. Zeigler predicts that "germ theory" will soon produce a revolution in how we explain and treat disease. Unfortunately, he says, it's being met with strong resistance within the medical profession, with many doctors holding firmly to earlier ideas, like glandular theory or spontaneous generation. As for diphtheria itself, they continue to ascribe it to "miasma"—to the odors of putrefaction that are the bane of Chicago and other large cities. But miasma, Zeigler explained, his eyes alight with excitement, isn't the root cause of diphtheria, or of most other diseases, either—"though it's certainly true," he said, "that the lack of pure water and air, as well as decent sanitary disposal, do create ideal breeding grounds for germs." Although I admired the doctor's passion, I was still too consumed by the ordeal we'd passed through to feel much of anything at the moment, other than apprehension and relief.

But the next day, with our boy safely home, I did think back on what Zeigler had said, and especially about how little the city does to correct the conditions that carry off so many young lives. Yes, health inspectors dutifully make the rounds and dutifully issue detailed reports on the "horrendous" conditions in poor areas of the city—the widespread use of oil lamps because the city hasn't provided the needed connections for gas lighting, the polluted backyard wells, the use of unlicensed plumbers who "upgrade" antiquated wooden pipes, the toilet facilities that consist of little more than a pit in the basement floor: the "sewer" in the Nineteenth Ward literally pours into a hole in the ground. I could go on.

Yet nothing is done. About the foul air, either. For years citizens' groups have been lobbying for the passage of an ordinance that would force factories to install high-heat furnaces or add smoke-consuming devices to inefficient boilers (since they refuse to shift from bituminous coal to the less polluting—and more expensive—anthracite). The response of the city and the press, unbelievably, is to place primary blame on the poor themselves, accusing them of "vicious, slovenly habits" and a "peasant" mentality that indifferently cohabits with filth. And in the meantime, the city continues to herd people like cattle into packed tenements (in truth, we never confined cattle that closely in Texas) where disease rages, and children die. On a day like today, the air full of choking smoke, the streets full of shoving, unconcerned people, I can still get to feeling a little homesick for the open spaces of Waco. I've become a city boy for certain, but now and then the pure breezes of the Brazos will sweep across my mind's eye, carrying me back to another time, a freer time . . .

The city's health problems never seem to affect the rich or inhibit their pleasures. The papers have proudly announced that the "sporting crowd" may now savor live lobster at the Boston Oyster House or dine on the wonders of Viennese cooking at Henrici's. And our grand hotels are outdoing each other in pampering their wealthy guests. Potter Palmer has inaugurated a private coach line to greet arrivals at the railway station and deliver them safely to his hotel's splendid entryway—thereby avoiding unnecessary contact with the hoi polloi.

Our precious baby, at least, has been saved. He's now entirely free of fever and has quickly rebounded. Would that all the afflicted were as fortunate. I was afraid the ordeal might endanger Lucy's pregnancy, but fortunately she seems unaffected.

June 28

The new mayor, Carter Harrison, has unexpectedly chosen William McGarigle to head the police department, a man with some reputation as a reformer. After the City Council finally voted Hickey out of office two years ago—running a bail-bonding racket out of the Armory Station proved too much of a scandal for even the Council to swallow—we had a series of temporary incompetents (meaning minor rather than major thieves). McGarigle has ten years' police experience and a college education. I still have this habit of thinking that an education guarantees a certain level of wisdom, or at least rectitude. "No," says Lucy, "a college education provides a larger vocabulary with which to justify one's crimes."

July 3

A few of us met in our flat last night. Spies, Fielden, Lucy, Lizzie, and that toy store owner George Engel, who both Spies and I met through Fielden. In his quiet way, Engel is a fierce fellow. He insists that the notion of a "free ballot-box," which he once believed in, is a dupe and a delusion. He looked straight at me when he said this, as if I was the Leading Dupe.

At the end of the evening Lizzie surprised us with a big birthday cake to celebrate Lucy's birthday—and Lucy announced to all gathered that she is again with child. She told everyone that she's hoping for a girl and has already picked out a name: Lula Eda (*very* Southern). We fussed and hollered over her, and she sat there looking like the shyest little twelve-year-old, so happy she might burst into tears. Then adult Lucy reemerged and mockingly accused us of making her far older than she was. "So how old are you?" the literal-minded Engel asked. Lucy flushed and said, "That's none of your business, sir." Of course she hasn't but the vaguest notion herself . . .

July 12

The Greenback convention is over. Our group was put politely but firmly on the sidelines—and with Van Patten's help. Now that the SLP's in decline, he's apparently decided to save himself by jumping on the Greenback bandwagon. Lucy and I were on the platform committee, and it refused even to consider our resolution in support of women's suffrage. When Lucy tried to gain the floor to argue for the measure, the "points of order" and "questions of privilege" were thicker than whortleberries in fly time, and she never even got recognized.

When the forty-four SLP delegates caucused to discuss the final plat-form, Lucy and I both raised hell about the absence of any socialistic planks, other than a few absurdly vague phrases like "the divine right of every laborer to the results of his toil." I offered a formal resolution that the SLP withdraw from the convention and field an independent ticket in the coming election. The caucus sided with Van Patten.

What now? Do we resign from the SLP? And if so, to go where? Spies counsels patience a while longer. He doesn't feel that the argument within the SLP is concluded.

August 1

In the midst of all this turmoil, parties rising and falling, old friends denouncing each other, confusion on all sides, the Knights of Labor—with its call for "one big union"—has emerged from its recent dormancy. For years, it's been chugging along, a secret little band of true believers, with grand rhetoric and next to no influence, constantly skirting extinction. But now people are beginning to say, "Hey, maybe the answer's been under our noses all the while," maybe it's time to chuck all our fine-spun ideological differences, which have given us more parties than members, and gather under a banner that emphasizes the one basic truth: that we're all working folks, skilled and unskilled, and must unite to fight a common oppressor.

A slew of small splinter groups have already begun to fold themselves into the Knights. And its membership is slowly changing, too. Most Knights used to be native-born, skilled city workers. Now some mine laborers are signing up, particularly in the coal fields of central Pennsylvania, and even a few agricultural workers are joining. Women, too, are being cordially welcomed; Frances Willard, Susan B. Anthony and Elizabeth Cady Stanton have all been Knighted, and the first all-female chapter is getting under way among Philadelphia shoe operatives. Lucy disapproves of separate locals for women, and I agree with her. We've heard rumors of a few all-negro locals as well, especially in the coal pits around Ottumwa, Iowa. The KOL has long proclaimed a belief in racial solidarity as a prime aspect of Universal Brotherhood, but rhetoric and practice haven't much coincided.

Though I can't remember the last time I actually went to one of their meetings, I've never lost my emotional attachment to the Knights' founding principle: An injury to one is an injury to all. That still seems to me what the labor movement is all about, or should be. Unfortunately, though, the Knights have elected Terence Powderly as their new Grand Master Workman. He's a mere reformer, preferring arbitration to strikes, eager to downplay class antagonism rather than organize around it.

September 5

I walked in on Lucy and Lizzie having the most amazing discussion. There they were, cutting out and basting the body of a dress—and casually chatting away about the comparative merits of spermicidal douches versus pessaries (which I'd never heard of), and of sheaths made from animal intestines versus rubber condoms! I tried to beat a hasty retreat as soon as I got a whiff of the conversation, but Lucy practically ordered me to sit down. "Why you old prude," she said, laughing out loud. "You're like all the others—quick enough to do it, but not at all quick to talk about it! You're as bad as Anthony Comstock!"

"What's *it*?" I asked, bidding for a little time to regain my composure.

"Sex, of course. I thought that much was obvious! Lizzie needs some advice, and though I'm far better equipped than you to provide it, you might have something worthwhile to contribute." Lucy was enjoying herself hugely, and I was beginning to have a pretty good time myself. No Texas farm boy is really shy about sex; he learns to play coy in the city.

Still, when they told me the actual news, I was flabbergasted: Lizzie is pregnant. By William Holmes, of course. It seems they've been amorous since first committing themselves to each other, but neither is eager to get married. Lizzie has been married before—another piece of surprising news—to a Mr. Swank (I had thought that was her family name). He died of tuberculosis after they'd had only a few years together, so her associations with marriage are morbid. For his part, Holmes feels a strong responsibility to his invalid father; the whole family migrated here from England twenty-five years ago and remains close-knit. Marriage not being an option, not for now, anyway, Lizzie and William have decided on abortion. Lucy urges her forward: "There'll be time for babies later on," she told Lizzie.

Turning to me, Lucy said, "These days you can't even find out how or where to get the procedure done. It's become a scary business since Comstock persuaded Congress to mandate a twenty-year sentence for the death of an aborted fetus."

"Comstock drove that New York abortionist to suicide two years ago," Lizzie reminded me. "Since then skilled practitioners are so fly-by-night you can't find out who's a quack and who isn't." She sounded frightened.

"Meantime, our upright medical community," Lucy heatedly added, "has no hesitation performing clitoridectomies on women who have what they call 'over-excited' sensual appetites—meaning, God help us, that they enjoy sex! The whole subject makes me crazy! They've gotten women to believe that sexual passion's a sign of disease, so the poor souls end up willingly offering their bodies for mutilation. Well, the doctors might persuade middle- and upper-class women, but us poor women know better. We've got few enough pleasures—they ain't takin' sex away from us, too! Being poor is in their minds already a hopeless disease."

Lizzie herself sounded more resigned, maybe because she's from a middle-class family, to say nothing of being from pioneer stock. One of the most endearing things I ever heard Lizzie say was, "I'm as American as a person can be who's not a full-blooded, copper-colored Indian." I got the feeling she's letting Lucy lead her in all this; she fidgeted with her hair the whole time we talked, and didn't say much herself.

"Comstock won't stop us, try as he might," Lucy said. "The papers are full of advertisements for 'infallible French female pills' and the like, and I been asking around among our women friends. Several told me that the most reliable is a quinine extract called calisaya, and that it could be purchased commercially, no questions asked."

"Lucy bought a supply this morning," Lizzie said timidly, "and I took the first pill just before you came in the room."

"Do you feel okay?" I asked her. She looked pale and guilty.

"I suppose so," she answered, getting up from her chair and collecting her sewing materials. "But my Puritan forebears are kicking away in there," she said, patting her stomach, "letting me know they don't approve." It was a brave little joke, and Lucy and I tried to laugh, though it came out sounding hollow. Lizzie looked more unwell with every passing minute, and said she thought she'd better go home. Lucy insisted on accompanying her.

"Poor Lizzie," she said after she'd returned, her eyes filling up. "She loves children as much as we do, and badly wants some of her own."

"It will happen," I said, trying to comfort her. "She and William have many years together."

"Isn't it strange that she and I got pregnant at nearly the same time? It makes me feel a little eerie, like I'm carrying both our babies."

September 12

Lizzie's had a most difficult time. We don't know whether it was the calisaya that caused the bleeding, or some deformity in the fetus itself. But two days after starting on the pills, she soaked through the mattress and, in great pain, discharged a small mass from her uterus that we presumed was the aborted fetus. But the pain didn't abate, and she started to run a high fever. Holmes—at Lizzie's bedside every second—insisted at that point that we take her to the hospital. None of us wanted to risk the Central Free Dispensary, but we didn't know if we could collect enough money for one of the small private facilities operated by doctors or religious groups that give far superior care. In fact we raised the money quickly and with no trouble; every friend we asked immediately gave us all they had. Sam Fielden even took out a lien on his team of oxen.

Lizzie refused to go to any hospital run by the religious, and our first choice among the physician-run hospitals, Garfield Park, refused to admit her. The desk nurse claimed they didn't handle cases relating to "female trouble," but the sneering way she looked us up and down made it clear that what they didn't handle was poor people.

We had better luck at Woman's Hospital, and a good choice it turned out to be. Oh, a few of the nurses there turned up their noses, too. One of them picked up Lizzie's garments as if she was handling hot coals; maybe she thinks pregnancy—or poverty—is catching. But an agreeable (at least initially) young doctor named Michael Fenton took charge of Lizzie's case and quickly managed to control her bleeding. Within a few hours, her fever subsided.

Once Lizzie was out of danger, Dr. Fenton sat down by her bedside and politely asked permission to discuss "with you and your husband a number of delicate matters." Lizzie and William gave their consent, without pausing to correct Fenton's assumption about their marital status. But Lizzie did say that she'd like her two closest friends—us—to remain in the room during the consultation: "We have no secrets from them," Lizzie said sweetly, "and their reactions to your advice will greatly assist our future determinations." Fenton looked disapproving but reluctantly agreed, on condition that Lucy and I refrain from speaking until after he'd gone. I saw Lucy raise her eyebrows, but she held her peace—even after Fenton informed us, with considerable pride, that he'd taken his medical training in Paris, completing it "just before the barbaric Communards nearly destroyed that beautiful city." Lizzie thanked her stars at that moment (she later told us) that she hadn't offered our last names; the good doctor, on hearing the name Parsons, might well have called for our eviction.

Dr. Fenton's ensuing lecture was such a patronizing mixture of high-flown theory and practical absurdity that we had difficulty holding our tongues, but mostly succeeded. He began with a general statement—apparently the latest word in Paris—that "marital intimacy should occur only when the two parties are in a calmly rational state of mind. The blood must be unheated, and the stomach empty." ("He wasn't describing sex," Lucy said later that evening when we were alone, "he was describing a discussion of the family budget.")

Fenton then offered a truly odd prescription for producing "strong and beautiful children when you feel the time has come to raise a family." The prescription consists of the wife eating large portions of red meat while preparing for conception and the husband lying in hot baths while drinking orangeade. If Fenton hadn't already saved Lizzie's life, we would have whisked her out of there on the spot. Lizzie dryly responded, "Red meat's a bit expensive for us, but as we prosper in life we'll hold your excellent advice in mind." By this point Lucy was so tickled that I was afraid she might laugh out loud. Having the same thought herself, she moved to the far corner of the room, out of Fenton's immediate view.

He next warned Lizzie to steer clear in the future of all abortive preparations currently advertised in chemists' shops or by traveling salesmen, and to focus on "preventative" methods. The need to turn to dangerous abortion nostrums, he said, could be avoided simply by avoiding pregnancy in the first place. He pronounced "extra-vaginal ejaculation" as "far and away" the preferred method of contraception. "If your husband," he said, looking sternly at Holmes, "refuses that practice, then I would urge you to employ the barrier method. The condom, you know, now costs but a few pennies, and is most effective."

"And as for you, sir"—here he turned directly to William—"let me offer some blunt advice." (Before he even heard it, William flushed crimson; unlike the three of us, he's apparently never discussed such intimate matters openly). "I presume," Fenton went on, "that you're familiar with established scientific facts about the perils of self-emasculation." William quickly nodded his head in the affirmative, but the truth was that none of us had ever heard the term before. Sensing our confusion, Fenton elaborated: "A man's semen, which is purified concentrate of blood, is of precious and limited supply. Excessive emissions through masturbation will unbalance your spermal economy, destroy your life force. May I ask you, sir, if you have noticed bloodshot eyes, fetid breath, or any rise in pitch in your voice?"

"No, sir," William replied, blushing so deeply that I thought he might burst a vessel.

"I'm glad to hear it," Fenton replied. "Those would be the first symptoms of excess. You might want to hold them in mind. Well then," the good doctor said, rising from his chair, "I've laid out all the essentials, I believe. I now leave it to your own good judgment, reinforced"—here he nodded toward Lucy and me, a slight sneer at the corner of his mouth—"by the wise counsel of your dear friends, to avoid a second unhappy episode such as this." Dr. Fenton bowed slightly and left the room.

Lucy immediately went over to Lizzie's bed and embraced her. "I'm surprised he didn't tell you to wash out your privates with lye," she said. It wasn't an especially humorous remark, but we all started to laugh—with relief, really, that Lizzie had passed safely through her terrible ordeal. She was back home the next day. Now she's on her feet but still feeling melancholy over the loss of the child. She says the experience has deeply shaken her—and "put an end to my modesty." To which Lucy, trying to coax a laugh out of her, added, "but not, I hope, to your sex life."

I thought Holmes handled himself impressively throughout. He never left Lizzie's bedside. He's a quiet man, as unpretentious as Lizzie herself, yet deeply attentive and affectionate. A fine mate for her. I'm glad to have gotten to know him better, however awful the circumstances.

September 20

We decided to give ourselves a full day's outing in celebration of Lizzie's recovery. Lizzie's sister, who returns back east today, offered to take care of Albert Jr., so we jumped on the chance to have ourselves some fun.

The four of us spent last night planning the day—and it took all evening! Lucy refused absolutely to go to any of the dime museums. She said the exhibits were all shams, and what's more, she couldn't stand the idea of fat people and other unfortunates, like "Krao, the Monkey Girl," being displayed as "freaks."

We all agreed with that, but then Lizzie started to giggle and confessed that when she was a girl, before the Great Fire of '71, her aunt had once taken her to Colonel Wood's famous Chicago Museum (which burnt to a cinder in the fire). Some of it, Lizzie declared, was actually educational, especially the cases of birds, reptiles, and insects from around the world. At that, Lizzie stopped, looking vaguely ashamed, but we egged her on and insisted on hearing about the *non*educational stuff.

"Well, there was a reconstruction of the Parthenon," she said hesitantly, "lots of ship models and, in a display case of its own, Daniel Boone's rifle."

"Wonderful, wonderful," Lucy said. "Now let's hear about the *really* silly stuff."

And for the next half hour Lizzie regaled us with descriptions of the mummified Egyptian princess who rescued Moses from the bulrushes—"but changed her mind and tossed him back again," Lucy added with a chuckle—and the Great Zeuglodon, a ninety-six-foot-long skeleton of a "prehistoric whale."

"When its authenticity was challenged in the press," Lizzie said, "Colonel Wood organized a group of 'scientists' to present erudite testimony on its behalf. But then, alas for Colonel Wood, a ten-year-old boy who'd briefly escaped his mother's surveillance, dug his knife into one of the Great Zeuglodon's ribs and gleefully exposed the pine wood underneath the coat of paint."

We had a great laugh over that and William, opening another pint of beer, offered a toast to the "Great Wooden Zeuglodon." "And," Lucy interrupted, "to the disobedient ten-year-old who brought him down!"

William, it turns out, is something of a horse-racing fan, which surprised me in so gentle a man, and he suggested we spend part of the day at Garfield Track, where we could have lunch at the café while watching the sport.

"It isn't a sport," I said, my voice a bit sterner than I'd intended. "It's a form of cruelty to animals. Their trainers beat them, their stalls are foul, and their food is the worst kind of slop. These are noble beasts, and they're being treated worse at Garfield Track than any place I've ever seen. Do you know who Garfield's chief owner is?"

William, taken aback at my vehemence and looking chagrined, meekly shook his head no.

"Mike McDonald." I paused to let the shock sink in. "Yes, King McDonald."

Everyone in Chicago, of course, knows who Mike McDonald is, though that didn't stop me from rubbing in the facts a little. "Thanks to his alliance with the police, he now controls all forms of gambling in this city—horses, dice, cards—he's packed the County Board with his supporters, controls every type of bail bond and, come election time, pays wagonloads of repeaters to drive precinct to precinct voting for his dear friends."

"You sound pretty self-righteous," Lucy said, out of nowhere. "Who doesn't know that Chicago politics are corrupt? And since when are games of chance really one of life's major sins?"

"When helpless animals are involved," I replied. "Speaking of self-righteous, who was just denouncing innocuous little dime museums as if they were Satan's own creation?"

"Mike McDonald has done what all American—sorry, white American—boys are told to do: make money any way they can," Lucy responded blithely. "He started out as a boy selling candy and magazines at the railroad station, and now he's got a lovely brownstone and holds court with cigars and brandy at The Store. It's a classic American success story." Lucy spoke with airy mockery, the tone, as she well knows, that most provokes me.

"The store?" William asked weakly. He looked downright ashen, having never seen Lucy and me go at each other before, and having been brought up to believe that social decorum between husbands and wives was the clearest sign, if not the only guarantee, of a good relationship. He'd never met a woman like Lucy, for whom passionate engagement was the lifeblood of a happy home.

Lizzie, on the other hand, was long familiar with our ways. She knew that although I was far more even-tempered than Lucy, I could be just as tenacious in an argument. I flared less, but probably yielded less. With Lucy, Lizzie understood, the point was never to calm her down, but to move her along, to sidetrack her into a new topic.

Turning to William, Lizzie explained, "The Store is McDonald's deluxe gambling establishment downtown. It's a large townhouse with everything you can think of inside—an elegant dining room, a cigar store, a saloon, expensive antique oak furniture, and gambling tables offering every form of cards and dice known to man."

"*That's* where we should go tomorrow!" Lucy shouted triumphantly.

"They don't allow women on the premises," I said, laughing. Lucy frowned, but with the hint of a friendly twinkle that signaled the end of contention.

Lizzie immediately sensed the shift. "I think it's time I took charge," she said with benign firmness. "After all, I'm the one whose recovery we're celebrating."

"That seems fair to me," Lucy said, suddenly the picture of docility. William let out an audible sigh of relief.

"Here's what I suggest." Lizzie plunged ahead, knowing that Lucy was unlikely to remain compliant for long. "I suggest we buy tickets to the new panorama on Michigan Avenue, and after that we get some beer and toast *everyone's* continued good health."

And that's precisely what we did. And with great pleasure all around. Lucy and I had never managed to see a panorama when they were at the height of fashion a decade ago, and now that they're becoming popular again, it was a chance—for a steep fifty-cent price of admission—to find out what the hullabaloo is all about. I must say, we were more impressed than we expected. The panorama was a gigantic painting of the beauties of California, accompanied by verbal descriptions, and it was unrolled in long strips from giant upright scrolls placed in front of the audience. The effect was quite startling, like actually having the visual experience of seeing California from, say, the seat of a moving train.

Afterward, Lucy had the sudden inspiration that we should have a drink of "soda water," the newest sensation, at one of the fountain parlors that have sprung up. They use some sort of artificial carbonation, sodium bicarbonate or baking soda, and combine it with various syrups and extracts. We chose sarsaparilla. None of us was much taken with it. It tickled my nose and made me burp, and surely the miraculous medicinal powers ascribed to it are poppycock. The breweries needn't worry about competition.

Lizzie then decided that we should buy tickets on the fancy Citizens' Omnibus Line, which has been running for five years and owns some twenty-five hand-carved buses and two hundred head of healthy horses. They make the trip around the lakefront in thirty minutes! When we passed Haymarket Square, all of us were amazed at the bustle of activity since we'd last been there. Filled with stalls set up by hundreds of wagon drivers from outlying truck farms, Haymarket seems to have suddenly become as large as the markets on West Randolph and South Water Streets.

Toward evening, Lizzie announced that she'd been celebrated enough and now wanted to celebrate *us* for having taken such good care of her. She especially wanted to do something nice, she said, for her "dear William." She came up with the notion—pretty far-fetched, I thought, but held my peace—that, in honor of William's Yorkshire background, we go for our final drink of the evening to one of those concert saloons the English favor.

"I left Yorkshire when I was five years old!" William protested, "and besides, those saloons, which aren't confined to Englishmen, are mostly dens of iniquity." Even as he protested, William blushed with such obvious pleasure that we concluded at once to go. On impulse, Lucy stopped a police officer on the street and—he didn't even blink—boldly asked him to recommend a more or less safe English or Irish concert saloon. The stern-faced officer, nattily dressed in his blue uniform coat, politely suggested we try Sullivan's, located just to the south of the downtown area.

"But that's where the Patch is," Lucy said indignantly. "It's the center of the prostitution trade!"

"The Patch, madam, is located to the south*west*." The officer seemed deeply offended at the implication that he'd given unreliable advice. "Suit yourselves," he said, and strode off.

So on to Sullivan's we went, and the officer proved entirely dependable. The place serves up (along with a wonderful malt beer) a less than bawdy Punch and Judy show, a few naughty song-and-dance routines, and a couple of wiggling "legmania" dancers—one kicked so high, she exposed her drawers, which made Lucy hoot out loud. But it was all sham vice, about as daring and dangerous as learning to dance the Minnehaha.

We didn't get home until nearly midnight, good spirits and morals intact. But we found Lizzie's sister, not used to big-city ways, in a state of real concern over our safety—the only genuine fright anyone had had all evening.

October 5

Well, Van Patten's gone and done it. He's expelled ten members of the SLP, including Spies, Paul Grottkau, and Oscar Neebe, because of their opposition to the Greenback alliance. How sad that it's come to this. Especially since Van Patten misrepresents our views. Yes, we've become more and more disenchanted with the ballot, but we've never condemned politics as "mere parliamentary chatter," as the New York SLP branch has. They've announced that from now on they intend to focus on union organizing, strikes, boycotts, general work stoppage and, should those efforts meet with outright repression, preparations for self-defense. But here in Chicago we've continued to maintain that native-born workers regard voting as the touchstone of democracy and that to scorn it out-of-hand would risk our being viewed as un-American.

Van Patten may not realize it, but by expelling those who resist an expedient alliance with Greenbackism, he's effectively killed the SLP. Our faction will survive. We retain the leading journal, the *Arbeiter-Zeitung*, and the bulk of the radical readership. But the dream of a broad-based, unified party is gone.

Who can predict what's on the horizon? The plutocrats seem to dictate the agenda, while the workers go for each other's throats.

✳

February 15, 1881

I pick up the diary again to record wonderful news: we are the proud parents of a healthy six-pound girl, Lulu Eda! Lucy came to term earlier than expected. She was brought to bed on February 2, attended by a number of neighborhood women, with Lizzie orchestrating the group. For precaution's sake, we had a midwife in attendance, too. But at one point, when Lucy's pain became intense and Lizzie asked the midwife to administer chloroform, the wretched woman refused and even dared to quote the Bible at us—"In pain thou shalt bear children." Our polite Lizzie became furious and practically shoved the midwife out the door. Happily, Lucy's pain soon subsided and her labor lasted but four hours. She's made a rapid recovery and now seems entirely herself. We smile all day long over our little girl.

Part Five

Pittsburgh
October 18, 1883

My Dear Wife,

It's been a glorious Congress, Lucy—historic in its importance, I'm certain. It's also been, for Spies and me, a considerable nightmare. We've been locked away day after day with none other than Johann Most himself, battling over the final draft of the Manifesto. If this pen could sputter and gasp you'd have some sense of my state of mind. The man's impossible. Until I get home, I can give you only a bare outline of what I mean.

Do you remember when you and I briefly met Most last August? How we'd both found him strangely reserved and fastidious? Well, that Most was downright charming compared to the verbally ferocious, posturing, bullying Most that Spies and I have had to contend with here. When it comes to polemics, he seems more feral than human—a lion's roar comes out of that sparrow's beak. At one point he gleefully referred to dynamite as "the good stuff," and gloated that "we must bring war to the throne, war to the altar, war to the money bags—to the whole reptile brood" (his pet phrase for the bourgeoisie).

Spies reprimanded him for "irresponsible hyperbole," then added, "As telling as your attack on the cruelties of capitalism is, I can't accept your advice to become just as cruel."

"Alas," Most sneered, "the propertied classes don't share your scruples about the use of force and murder. As for myself," he went on, "I'm proud to say that when Czar Alexander was assassinated two years ago, I publicly praised the act—and paid for it with sixteen months at hard labor."

"No one questions your courage," I said.

"Tell me if you can," Spies asked Most, "precisely what the Czar's assassination accomplished."

"If you do not know," he haughtily replied, "then you're not fit to call yourself a revolutionary."

Spies actually laughed. He's Most's equal in learning and eloquence and isn't at all intimidated by him, which I can't say about myself. "The czar's assassination," Spies said, "failed to make Russia one whit less brutal than when he was alive."

Most threw up his hands in mock resignation: "There's no point engaging men like yourselves in general philosophical debate; you've been too corrupted by bourgeois values. I remain in this room for one purpose only: to complete work on the Manifesto."

Do you get the picture? Is it any wonder my hair's gone gray at such a pace that I've had to apply the black dye you gave me (again, please don't tell even Lizzie) twice this week—and even so, look as if I've aged ten years?

But of course, despite Most's vow, we were soon back to arguing general principles. I insisted that the Pittsburgh Manifesto has to reflect the view of most American workers that our main goal is to build a strong trade union movement and to achieve an eight-hour day.

"The eight-hour day," Most shouted, "is a mere sop! The workers' lot might become an iota better, but at the cost of encouraging them to believe that their masters do care, thus diluting the ardor needed for revolutionary struggle."

"It's unwise and immoral," Spies replied, "to ignore the workers' current misery. The Manifesto has to give priority to winning better working conditions now. They're desperately needed. What you don't seem to understand is that by championing trade union demands, we'll attract recruits for the long-range struggle to revamp the social order."

When it became clear that Most wasn't going to budge an inch, Spies and I took our case directly to the convention floor, with mixed results. The delegates did pass a resolution declaring trade unions "the advance guard of the coming revolution," but only slightly modified Most's declaration that "the first principle of this Congress must plainly and simply be the destruction of existing class rule by any and all means." On one matter, we did get an outright victory. Over Most's strenuous objection, the delegates approved a pledge to work for "equal rights for all without distinction to sex or race."

"In my experience," Most later told us, his voice dripping with disdain, "women show up at revolutionary meetings primarily to search for eligible husbands, and once found, both disappear." I offered you and me as an example of a couple who have helped each other evolve toward a better understanding of social questions. To which Most replied, "Can she cook?" (I can hear your bloodcurdling yell all the way from Chicago.)

Regrettably, some needlessly inflammatory language does remain in the final document. The worst is a clause stating: "It is self-evident that the struggle of the proletariat with the bourgeoisie must have a violent revolutionary character." This can, and I hope will, be read as relevant only if the moneyed classes remain deaf to our pleas for amelioration. Still, I fear the language could alienate many more workers than it attracts.

The best thing to come out of Pittsburgh is a new organization, the International Working People's Association, and, finally, a stated vision very close to our own hearts. "The ultimate goal of our struggle," the Manifesto reads, "is the creation of a society based on the cooperative organization of production, the exchange of products without profit-mongery, the regulation of all public affairs by free contracts between autonomous groups linked in a federal system, and a secular system of education based on the principle of the equality of the sexes." (Most announced that "the unsuitability of women for higher education will become so quickly apparent that I need not waste energy opposing it.")

Whether the IWPA can successfully unify the many bitterly divided factions, socialist and anarchist (and everything in between) remains, of course, to be seen. But at least it marks a fresh start, a new hope, and both were desperately needed. For the moment, at least, everyone seems buoyant.

As for Johann Most, I doubt that I'll ever resolve my deep ambivalence about the man. As infuriating as his performance here has been, we need to remember that it was his brilliant articles in *Die Freiheit* that helped us to understand for the first time that the anarchists, and not Marx, are right about the State—that it's inevitably an instrument of oppression, no matter who controls it, that power itself, the habit of ruling others, deeply corrupts. The anarchist dream of a decentralized society based on voluntary association *is* the best dream.

You and our babies have been constantly in my thoughts throughout these tumultuous days. It's hard to believe that dear Lulu is nearly two and a half. How it saddens me to be away from home so much, how I miss its joys and comfort. And now I am off yet again; as I telegraphed you, dearest, I go straight from here, along with Spies and several other comrades, to meet with Terence Powderly in New York City. The meeting, as you know, comes at his suggestion. We're all eager to find a way to forestall another bout of factionalism down the road.

When next I write, it will be from amidst the fleshpots of Gotham. I toyed with the idea of simply boarding at one of the brothels—I'll be pressed for time, after all—but finally decided that settling down among a mere twenty or so women would foolishly limit my options. We anarchists, after all, must give full and free expression to human possibilities. I only hope that my strength is equal to the task!

Oh, I almost forgot a juicy tidbit that I know you will savor. Van Patten has disappeared, leaving behind a suicide note declaring his despair at the disintegration of the SLP. We were distraught at the news. That is, until word arrived two days later that he had been spotted in Washington. He's taken a job as a minor federal functionary. Since you always distrusted the man, our hats are off to your intuition.

You can write to me c/o Powderly at the Knights of Labor office, 119 Grove Street, New York City.

Believe me, ever your devoted husband,
Albert

*

Chicago
October 21, 1883

Dear Husband,

I rejoiced to get your letter, though not at some of its news, and gave your babies big, big kisses from you. Albert Jr. does miss his papa mightily. Lulu and I are indifferent. (Are you silly enough to believe that?)

Some of your news I'd heard just yesterday from Michael Schwab, who got the full text of the Manifesto off the telegraph. You've never met Schwab, have you? He moved to Chicago only two years ago. I met him through Lizzie. You will like him. He's gentle and mild-mannered, though a little dry and scholarly. Spies can tell you more about him; he's just hired Schwab as a reporter for the *Arbeiter-Zeitung*. Schwab does agree with Most that the ruling class will never abandon its privileges peacefully. I do, too. I think you're doing what you always do—torturing yourself with scruples about the possible necessity of force—which I can assure you, my dear, no capitalist has ever felt when murdering us. Lizzie agrees. That ought to impress you. You've always viewed John Brown's insurrection as an act of heroism. Why can't you apply his logic about the lords of the lash to the lords of the loom? Well, we've been over this ground many times. You sometimes think me hard, I know. And I sometimes think you faint-hearted. We must be patient with each other. Together we will find the right path.

Lizzie and I have both been working hard to organize Chicago's sewing girls. Lizzie's gone into the commercial sewing shops and found conditions there even worse than the ones we were familiar with. The women sit at long tables in filthy fire traps. In shops where steam provides the power, the sewing machines are bolted to the table. Bits of fabric, along with grease and dust, fill every cranny. Signs are posted on the walls: "No Talking or Laughing Permitted," "Injured Goods Will be Charged to Employees," "Extra Trimmings Must be Paid For," and so forth. And for twelve to sixteen hours a day of such humiliation and drudgery, what wages do these poor souls take home? The range is a dollar fifty to ten dollars a week. How lucky for me that my dark skin made it impossible to get a commercial sewing job and forced me to work at home, where I don't have to ask permission to go to the toilet or stop for a cup of tea.

High-minded ladies of charity visit the shops to lecture these wretched women about "improving their housekeeping habits and paying more attention to their children's upbringing." How dare they, these fancy, idle women, who in their own homes have domestics performing every one of life's chores for them! It makes my blood boil. It makes me willing to do *anything*—yes—to end this barbaric system. Lizzie and I feel we will soon be able to claim success in organizing the very first strike of Chicago's sewing girls.

I've also reached a decision this week to refuse to sew for any of the wealthy clients that have occasionally come my way. Though we need the money, I can no longer bear to be in their overstuffed homes and listen to the chatter of their empty minds. I do make one exception, and one only—the Van Zandts, mother and daughter. For them, I'll willingly continue to make clothes. I've told you about them before, their intelligence and kindness, their genuine interest in hearing about conditions among the poor. (It's amazing to me how little information finds its way into the cocoons of the rich.)

The daughter, Nina—yes, she insists I call her Nina, can you believe it?—has a kind of innate egalitarianism—can you imagine, a wealthy young debutante schooled at Miss Grant's and recently graduated from Vassar! If only we could figure out why some few traitors (well, potential traitors) to their class do emerge, we might be able to produce more of them. Anyway, when I was fitting Nina yesterday, she actually wept when I told her about the conditions Lizzie had found in the commercial sewing shops. Whether her empathy will ever take any political form remains to be seen. You can be sure I'll do my best to bring tears to her eyes whenever possible.

I cannot warn you too strongly, dear husband, to be on your guard against Powderly, especially since I'm told he has a great deal of personal magnetism. By now you may well have had your meeting with him. But if not, let me remind you that the man is on record urging workers to shun strikes whenever possible in favor of "negotiated settlements" with their employers. Oh yes, I know, he acknowledges that strikes are a legitimate weapon of last resort and can be an effective organizing tool, but his emphasis is on caution and conciliation. What he fails to tell us is how we are to "negotiate" when we have no power, or how to "conciliate" someone who has his boot on your throat. Powderly's counsel of patience feeds the workers' already profound sense of fatalism. Taught to believe from early youth that whatever happens to them is either ordained by heaven or the result of their own character defects, they discount their ability to influence their own fate.

And something extraordinary—Lizzie is giving piano lessons! She used to be a music teacher and never told us! She says she'd put that part of her life behind her and has returned to it only because, with economic conditions worsening again, she's forced to piece out her income. She's a marvel, our Lizzie. I heard her lecture the other night on "The History and Philosophy of Music" and it was as if I was in the presence of a learned professor.

You will much oblige your loving wife if you avoid patronizing Gotham's prostitutes. I care not a fig for your virtue, but rather for my health! On the other hand, I insist that you see as much of the rest of the city as possible, and describe it to us in detail when next you write. Do not waste your entire visit on the likes of Terence Powderly—you can be bored to death right here in Chicago. I want to hear all about the latest fashions, the Coney Island Loop-the-Loop, the grand new Opera House, and the electric arc illumination on the city streets. And before blowing up J. P. Morgan's Madison Avenue mansion, be sure to take copious notes on its incandescent lighting!

      Ever your devoted wife,

      Lucy

*

New York City
October 25, 1883

Dearest Assassin,

Have you and Lizzie yet picked a candidate whose murder will "awaken the people to their liberation" (as your new mentor, Johann Most, might put it)? Shall it be another President? The current incumbent, the honorable Chester Alan Arthur, seems rather too rotund to be successfully pierced with any ordinary weapon; perhaps a forced diet of baking soda and saltpeter would do the trick.

Or do you have your heart set on the arch worker-traitor himself, Mr. Terence V. Powderly? You sound ferocious enough about him to have settled on death by cannibalism. That might also satisfy your penchant for melodrama. You will admit, my dear, that you have a tendency to see people in theatrical terms.

Yes, I intend to lecture you a bit. I hope you'll sit still for it. It's important not to caricature Powderly. I've now spent two lengthy evenings with the man and I admit that on sight he looks like a timid tee-totaler, with his Prince Albert frock coat, starched standup collar and tie. But his views are more complex—even his attitude towards strikes—than we've been led to believe. The labor movement can't continue to demonize people with whom we disagree on particular points. We've seen far too much of that. It does the work of the enemy for them.

I want to remind you that Powderly has been outspoken against all discrimination based on sex or color. Just last month, as you know, one of the Knights' key demands in the telegraphers strike against Western Union was equal pay for the female operators who make up a quarter of the workers. True, Powderly, unlike us, believes that labor and capital can ultimately be harmonized. But he's no Pollyanna. The man may be slow to go to war, but he's not afraid to fight, and his ultimate goal is the same as ours: a cooperative society. Contrast Powderly's views with those of the craft unions, especially the up-and-coming Cigarmakers International under Gompers and Strasser. They mock our determination to overthrow capitalism as utopian fantasy. Powderly told Spies and me that he thinks the craft unions and the Knights are on a collision course—both growing rapidly in numbers, but committed to very different social visions for the future.

Given his temperamental dislike for extremism of any kind, Powderly may one day end up denouncing us, or we him. But let's not declare him an enemy in advance of a rupture that may never prove necessary.

There, I'm done lecturing you. Have you already torn my letter to shreds and gone raging off to Lizzie? I know your stubbornness prevents you from taking kindly to criticism, but we must be able to say everything to each other. You are my closest friend. If I've been too harsh, you'll let me know. Of that I can be sure!

Another important matter: I hereby report that your beloved husband has *not* returned to the scenes of his "wild youth." Being thirty-five does, alas, take a fearsome toll on energy. And I knew I had to conserve it—not for anything as trivial as politics (or our pending reunion) but, as you so firmly instructed, to view and report on the wonders and horrors of the great metropolis.

The truth is, I got to see precious little of those wonders, for reasons of time and finances. Everything costs so much! Most of what I viewed was from the outside, in the free air, avoiding entrance fees and the like. New York is a maelstrom of commercial construction, yet a great deal of the building going on is speculative; the tenants may never materialize. Signs of a renewed economic recession are already apparent here. Rumors of a general collapse are spreading, the unemployment rate already way up. Meanwhile, prices are rising, thanks to John D.

Rockefeller joining forces with his rivals to create the virtual monopoly of the Standard Oil Trust.

But I've slipped back to politics, I see, and I was supposed to be taking you on a sightseeing tour. Well, my love, in all essential ways New York City strikes me as very similar to Chicago, especially the sense of frenzied growth and the focus on material accumulation and display. The new buildings here, like ours, grow ever taller—the Produce Exchange, at ten stories, is as high as our Montauk Building. They're commonly called "temples of labor"—not *to* labor, mind you!

Fashionable New Yorkers would sniffily deny the suggestion that their city has anything in common with Chicago. They consider us a barbarian outpost, without a proper (which is to say, opulent and outsized) concert hall, symphony orchestra, art museum, or opera house. Why, we do not even have, according to the *New York Times*, a proper elite. That is, an upper class capable of erecting Renaissance chateaux staffed with a small army of menials, and cognizant of the importance of retaining footmen in livery, exchanging engraved calling cards, taking afternoon brougham rides in Central Park, and taking sides in the world-shaking struggle for social primacy between Caroline Astor and Alva Vanderbilt. The Metropolitan Museum of Art is open one day a week—Sunday, when most workers are too exhausted to do more than attend church, have a pint, and fall into bed.

As for the rapid advance in electrification that seems to fascinate you— could it be connected, my dear, to your own highly charged self? The cable car has quickly become as omnipresent in New York as in Chicago. I still prefer the horsecar. At rush hour yesterday, I was nearly knocked to my feet by the horde of riders. They put such a weight on the steel pulleys that the cable of one car snapped and another got so tangled that the driver lost control and, abruptly grabbing the switch, threw the passengers to the floor. Besides, just like back home, the moving cable makes such a racket that one can hardly talk above it. And the mounting demand for electricity and telephones has meant an astounding proliferation of utility poles, with a thick network of power lines strung on top that actually darken the sky. This is known as Progress: electricity turns night into day and the network of overhead wiring turns day into night!

But I have to admit, the electrification of the streets is a stunning thing to behold. They're a good deal ahead of Chicago in this regard. It's been nearly three years since New York began experimenting with arc lights.

Mounted on ornamental cast-iron posts twenty feet high, they already stretch all along Fifth Avenue and across Fourteenth and Thirty-fourth Streets, and are rapidly multiplying. Where people were once fearful of leaving their homes at night, they now gather on the streets to gawk at the illuminated hotels and shops. The famous entertainment emporium, Niblo's Garden—Spies and I couldn't afford the entrance fee—apparently boasts chorus girls who wave electric wands as they dance, and there's an illuminated model of the Brooklyn Bridge on display, designed by the Edison Electric Light Company.

The outdoor arc lights are far too bright for domestic use, but Edison's incandescent lamp for the home has proven practical. Your great personal friend J. P. Morgan installed a generator in his garden some three years ago, thus becoming the first (as he wishes to be in everything) to convert a private dwelling entirely to electricity. Fashionable New York has speedily followed his lead. Nearly a thousand wealthy homes are now electrified, and several thousand commercial establishments. The city stock exchange has installed three "electroliers" of lamps above the trading floor, and the new Mills Building has its own electric generating plant. The papers have reported the claim of one architect that the use of electricity in residences is leading to an outbreak of freckles.

Onward to Coney Island. At your behest, I've made the obligatory journey to see the Loop-the-Loop. Spies, gracious gentleman that he is, offered to accompany me on our one afternoon free of meetings, though we agreed that we would have preferred to catch up on our sleep. But off we trudged on the Culver Line to catch a steamer for West Brighton. Once there, the astonishing variety of sights and sounds soon woke us up. The two-thousand-foot Iron Piers are an amazing engineering feat. But then there's the Elephant Hotel! It's more like a free-standing sculpture of the animal, a gigantic creation built of wood and covered in tin that dominates the skyline. It has thirty-four rooms scattered in its various body parts, a cigar store in one front leg and a diorama in the other, a dairy stand in its trunk, and spiral staircases in its hind legs that lead up to an observatory in the head. What next? A clothing store in the shape of a frock coat?

As for your adored Loop-the-Loop, it may satisfy the age's fascination with speed and motion, but to Spies and me the ride's rickety twists and turns seemed like an invitation to suicide; we declined the experiment, though you, doubtless, would have climbed instantly aboard. As I always tell you, women are braver than men.

We expected the Coney Island beach itself would be deserted this late in the season, but thanks to unusually warm weather, it was packed with people, the women covered head to foot in interchangeable flannel suits, the men sporting straw boaters, and the children busy burying each other in the sand or disappearing into the crowd—inciting their frantic parents to race up and down the beach in search of them. At the height of the season, we're told, the general chaos is far greater. During summer, there are hundreds of food vendors, saloons, sideshows, crayon portraitists, and fortune tellers whose tents and pavilions (many of them shuttered today) line the beachfront, plus the assorted con men, thugs, and prostitutes who prowl the side streets just beyond. Even today, late in October, there was the din of barkers shouting out the wonders of their wares, daring us to test our skill at catchpenny games, horseshoes, shooting clay ducks or—a horrifying sight that I hesitate even to tell you about—hitting a negro on the nose (the poor man's head is stuck through a hole in a cloth and he must continuously bob and duck to avoid the rubber balls eagerly pitched at his face). Coney Island is widely hailed as a "working-class pleasure ground." I pray that in a less barbaric future, we may come to hold a different definition of pleasure.

We set out for home day after tomorrow. I am eager to hold you in my arms and to embrace my beloved children.

Till then, my dearest,
Albert

Chicago

"I can't get a close measure, Nina, unless you stand perfectly still. The garment *must* be snug under the arms, and you keep shifting your weight. I have to get the tape line exactly right."

"Oh, Lucy, this is all so tiresome!" Nina said, her voluptuous, almost plump face creased in a frown. "A tea gown! Why in heaven's name do I need a tea gown. I'll wear it once, if at all."

"You need it because your mother says you need it. Now please try to stand still."

"My mother also thought I needed to go to the Vanderbilts' fancy dress ball in New York. On *that* I put my foot down."

"Oh? I should have loved to have been there, seen that Hobby-Horse Quadrille described in the newspapers." Lucy said. "I couldn't figure it out—elaborately gowned guests seated on top of life-size wooden horses covered with genuine hides—how could they even move, let alone perform a quadrille?"

Nina started to giggle. "I think the horses were on wheels and the servants pushed them around."

"So it was the servants who had to learn the quadrille?"

"Just the footwork, I suppose. I heard that for months before the ball, groups of little ninnies all over New York City were practicing the quadrille arm movements—oh, I don't know, it makes no sense at all, does it? The entire ball, in my opinion, was a silly calamity."

"My dear Nina, you're beginning to sound like a socialist. And you're waving your arms around like one, too. Please! How am I to measure?" Lucy put Nina's arms quietly at her side.

"Well, I'm not a socialist. But Mother agrees with me that Mrs. Vanderbilt's 'event of the century' is the best argument she's ever heard for revolution. Can you imagine?—dozens of servants lining the walls in maroon livery, enough palm fronds and bougainvillea to beautify all of Fifth Avenue, and the guests—good gracious, the guests! There were so many gorgeously gowned Marie Antoinettes and Mary Stuarts that if I had decided to attend, I would have been tempted to appear in the costume of a guillotine! Do you think you could sew *that*?" Nina laughed so merrily that the braided chignon coiled at the back of her head threatened to come loose.

"My dear young lady," Lucy said with mock solemnity, "you've lost all sense of propriety. How I pity your poor parents."

"Well, don't. They feel the same way I do. Well, almost the same way. Papa and Mama may be 'socially acceptable,' as the old biddies say, but they have some decidedly advanced views on social questions. Can't you tell just by looking at this house?"

"What do you mean?"

"The way they built it."

Lucy shook her head uncomprehendingly—managing to drop several pins onto the carpet. Exasperated, she got down on her hands and knees to retrieve them. "You can relax for a minute," she told Nina.

"Are we nearly finished? I can't bear standing still for very long."

"See—you *are* a socialist," Lucy said laughing. "Ah! Here they are," she said, holding up the two pins triumphantly. Old sharp eyes. Come, miss, your reprieve is over."

Nina sighed.

"I'm almost done. All I need to do now is mark the bodice. What were you saying about this house?"

"The open veranda all across the front. There isn't another like it in the entire neighborhood."

"So having a porch means that you have advanced political views? I don't understand. Albert and I don't have a porch."

"You're making fun of me," Nina said, with a touch of petulance.

"What? Believe me, dear Miss Van Zandt," Lucy said, sounding more arch still, "I know the difference in our stations and I would never presume to—"

"Now stop it, Lucy!" Nina actually stomped her foot in frustration. "I insist on being taken seriously. By you and by everyone else."

"And quite right, too. I apologize if I offended you."

"Now if you'll open your mind and concentrate," Nina said, "I'm sure you'll be able to understand what I mean." Lucy silently filed away Nina's patronizing overtone. Condescension, she told herself, was second nature for rich young debutantes. This one, at least, had a supple mind and some humane sympathies.

"I'm listening carefully," Lucy said evenly.

"It's perfectly simple. Every other house on the street is a stone fortress, sealed off from the world. Our house is the opposite, open and welcoming. People walking down the street can see us sitting on the porch, going about our lives. Just like ordinary people."

If they're allowed on the street, Lucy thought to herself. Still, she wanted to acknowledge Nina's generous-minded innocence.

"I see your point. Yes, definitely. But isn't your family afraid?"

"Of what?"

"I don't know. Of intruders, of people being able to see into your home . . ."

"We don't even have a vestibule to keep out salesmen!" Nina said with a self-congratulatory laugh.

"Maybe your level of trust is too high."

"Who should we be afraid of? Are you and your socialist friends planning an attack?" Nina was highly amused at her own remark.

"No," Lucy said solemnly, "but your neighbors might be. That is, once they get wind of your advanced views."

"Oh, they know all about us. The downstairs maid next door told me her employers—they're a branch of the Cyrus McCormick family—were talking about us over dinner just the other night, discussing my parents' trip to Detroit to see that five hour play, *Monopoly*. We can't imagine how they found out."

"Why didn't they see the play in Chicago?"

"Oh, it'll never be performed here, Lucy. It's all about a strike for an eight-hour day. At one point in the play a superintendent tries to bomb a factory so he can put the blame on a radical labor agitator." Nina paused for a second, trying to accurately recall the plot her mother had described.

"And?" Lucy asked impatiently; she was finding it hard to believe that such a play existed, let alone that it had been performed.

"And . . . I think I have this right . . . all's well in the end because the industrialist becomes an enlightened convert to the workers' cause after he discovers that the labor agitator is his own long-lost son, kidnapped at birth."

"I should have known," Lucy snorted, "A soppy melodrama . . . in real life there aren't any enlightened industrialists."

"Well, I can't disagree with you there. At least *we* don't know any, my own dear papa excepted of course. . . But there will be. I'm sure of it . . ."

"Yes, I know," Lucy said sardonically, "'every day in every way we get better and better.' Progress is inevitable. Which means we don't have to lift a finger to work for it. Ha! If anything gets better it'll be the result of more and more agitation."

In a sudden wave of revulsion, Lucy decided to end the conversation then and there. She liked Nina, admired the spunky way she could take issue with her own class values. But her pie-in-the-sky optimism sometimes irritated Lucy beyond bearing.

She stood back and looked at the tea gown. "Yes," she said, "it's perfect. We're finished. You're free to go."

Chicago

MAY—JUNE 1884

"Didn't you think it strange that Adolph Fischer showed up?" Albert asked, after the small gathering of the American Group at Greif's Hall had adjourned and he and Lucy were back home in their flat. "The others I expected— Neebe, Fielden, and of course Lizzie and Spies. But Fischer—?"

"It surprised me, too," Lucy said, as she brought over some biscuits and toys for the children. "After all, he and Engel dominate the North-West Side Group, a much bigger pond. The American Group's probably the smallest section in the IWPA."

"Small, but needed. It's important to have at least one English-speaking club in this city."

"Why?"

"Oh, Lucy. You know perfectly well why. English-speaking workers feel confused and out-of-place when they go to an IWPA meeting and it's all in German and they can't follow what's going on."

"I suppose so," Lucy said vaguely. "I like Fischer. He's an affable man."

"He and Engel don't fully approve of us," Albert said, his face creased with annoyance at Lucy's sometimes baffling contentiousness. "They mock the notion that trade unions can help create a cooperative society."

"Well, Fischer probably just wanted to see what we were up to. He won't come back."

Albert decided to let it go at that. He reached into his pocket and took out a clipping. "Have you seen today's *Tribune*? It has the report of the Citizens Association."

"Why would I waste time on anything those jackass businessmen have to say? Besides, there's an account in the *Arbeiter*."

Albert unfolded the clipping. "They start by explaining that rumors of widespread suffering among the poor have led them to undertake an investigation."

"Undoubtedly expecting the rumors would prove false."

"Perhaps. But give them some credit. They did decide to investigate."

Lucy, determined on indifference, sat down in the armchair and began stitching some white lace edging she was making for Lulu's party dress.

"And what's more, they concluded that conditions in the tenements are wretched. These are prominent citizens who could exert a powerful influence on Mayor Harrison."

"Yes, but in what direction? Will they tell Carter Harrison that we must promptly abandon capitalism? Not likely. They'll recommend more health inspectors and will piously exhort the poor to mend their slovenly ways." Lucy shook her head. "I can't believe you're still looking for help from people with a prime stake in maintaining this wretched system. Haven't we learned anything in ten years?"

Albert mumbled something about being "willing to accept help from anyone to relieve the current suffering."

Deciding to be merciful, Lucy made no answer. After a moment or two, she went and got the *Arbeiter* from the table. "This has a different version of the Citizens Association's little tour. It's by Michael Schwab. He accompanied the conscientious citizens day after day. Care to hear a bit of it?" Albert nodded a distracted yes.

Lucy began reading. "'There are hovels where two, three, and four families live in one room, where the only light comes in through rents of wall, where human beings sleep on rotten straw or rags, where broken chairs and tables are luxuries, where no fire is in the stove although it is bitter cold and three or four members of the family are sick. And how do these people live? From the ash barrels they gather half-rotten vegetables; in the butcher shops they beg for offal and make sausages out of that. Diseases of all kinds kill them wholesale, especially the children.'"

Lucy looked up from the paper. "A little more pointed than the Association's report, eh? Here's how Schwab concludes: 'This is a *murderous* system—yet it dares to lecture workers against the immorality of violence!'" She slapped the paper back down on the table. "Now there's a voice I can respect!"

"I admire Schwab, too. What I don't admire is your holier-than-thou tone."

Startled at Albert's bluntness, Lucy was momentarily silent. Finally, Albert said quietly, "Why are we taking out our anger on each other?"

"I don't know," Lucy said simply. "We have nobody else to yell at."

Albert went over and embraced her. "My only point, dear, hardly an inspiring one, is that the Citizens Association is in a position to do something. At least a few members of the elite have declared themselves appalled."

"But they don't represent their class—any more than Nina Van Zandt and her parents do." Lucy's temper was heating up again.

"I didn't say they did."

"And it's absurd to think the Citizens Association will argue for *real* changes in a system that keeps them on top of the heap."

"But they could demand that conditions be improved."

"Oh, Albert! The Association wants everyone to believe that the current misery is due solely to a 'transient' depression, and not to capitalism itself. But the lives of working people were wretched long before."

"You make it sound as if I disagree with you." Albert said, trying to avoid another escalation. "I am *not* Jay Gould."

"You're right. He's handsomer."

"Oh, I see!" Albert caught her around the waist. "Now I know why you're so angry: Jay Gould has refused you a private tour of his grand new yacht."

Lucy freed herself from Albert's grip and did a coquettish turn around the room, her skirt billowing out. "It just so happens I disembarked from the *Atalanta* after a single day. Jay was so angry. But I found the decor in such bad taste that I simply couldn't abide it any longer. Imagine! Strawberry curtains on the portholes and wood paneling in the dining saloon featuring carved groupings of—fruit!" Lucy danced giddily around the room. "My sensibilities were horribly offended by such nouveau trash."

She collapsed on the floor in a heap of laughter, and Albert was instantly down by her side, caressing her, kissing her face and neck. They'd never lost their passion for each other, not even after the arrival of the children, commonly viewed as the time when women were freed to pursue their real interest, domesticity, and men were freed to search for real sex outside the home. Lucy liked to joke about her being *unnatural*, since she liked sex and no "normal" woman was supposed to. "I guess it's because of my African blood—you know, we're all sex-crazed animals. Perhaps when we get rich you can send me to the mountains for a rest cure. But of course when I'm rich, my passion will shift to jewels and gowns."

✳

As economic depression and social unrest deepened in the early months of 1884, the American Group's regular Wednesday night meetings at Greif Hall became so crowded that it was decided to add Sunday afternoon gatherings at the grassy lakefront area. Before long, thousands were flocking to the open-air meetings to hear Parsons, Spies, Fielden, Neebe, and others address the great questions of the day: What accounts for the poverty of the masses? What is the origin and purpose of government? Is socialism or anarchism the best remedy for alleviating the sufferings of the poor? At some of the meetings, a woman presided—and often it was Lucy or Lizzie.

Having heard all the American Group orators many times over, Lucy announced one evening to Albert that he was the best of the lot.

Charmed at the serious way she pronounced her verdict, as if having deliberated on the matter for some time, Albert asked if a prize accompanied the designation—"a gold cup, perhaps, or maybe a chain link to adorn my vest."

"Selfless revolutionaries don't get prizes, or covet them."

"See—I'm a fake. Unworthy of your praise," Albert said, his eyes twinkling.

"You don't fool me. You want me to defend my compliment, and itemize your particular virtues as a speaker, one by one."

"Oh, *do*!" Albert said, exuberantly.

"Well, they're very specific. You have—how shall I put it?—a certain boyish charm, an unflagging geniality."

"You forgot my much-commented-on lyrical, lilting voice, especially when reciting poetry."

"If only I *could* forget. If I have to listen to one more of your renditions of McIntosh's 'The Tramp'—that wretched bit of sentimental claptrap—or your beloved 'Annie Laurie,' I might be seriously tempted to leave the movement."

"I'll never give up my 'Annie,'" Albert laughed. "That's my favorite poem in all the world."

"And thanks to you, all the world has now heard it."

"I'm sticking with 'Annie,' like it or not. After all, I've only got a few arrows in my quiver. I can't lay claim to anything like Fielden's bellowing power, or to Spies's learning."

"To say nothing of Spies's ardent blue eyes and gymnast's body, both of which the ladies discuss with some frequency."

"Really? How shocking! They can't be proper ladies at all."

"Oh, they're much too refined to understand the real source of Spies's appeal."

"His intellect?"

"His controlled sarcasm—an infallible indicator of a darker, more sexual energy." Lucy looked utterly delighted with her own boldness.

"Am I supposed to fall over in a faint?" Albert said blithely. "Remember, I live with a sarcastic person."

"Count your blessings."

"Oh, I do, my dear, I do." They smiled giddily at each other.

"Now, Lucy," Albert said, after a pause, "If you hadn't started all this banter the moment I arrived home, we'd already be celebrating my big news."

"You sound serious."

"I am."

"Well what is it, for heaven's sake? Tell me."

"The IWPA has decided to start a new paper. The *Alarm*. And you are looking into the face of its new editor."

"Oh, Albert—no!" Lucy squealed with delight. She threw her arms around his neck and covered his face with kisses.

"Stop!" Albert said, holding her out at arm's length. "That's only part of my news."

"I don't think I can bear any more," Lucy said, sitting down to catch her breath. "Your first full-time newspaper job since the *Times* blacklisted you. And the coincidence of it! Spies just appointed editor of the *Arbeiter-Zeitung*, and now you. It's too good to be true!"

"Now, now, let's keep things in proportion. The *Alarm*'s never going to achieve the numbers or influence of the *Arbeiter*. Their circulation is twenty thousand. We'll be lucky if we can come out once a week rather than fortnightly. We're the only radical English-language paper in the city, but how many English-speaking radicals are there?"

"You can play it down if you want, but I say your appointment is a miracle."

"There's yet another miracle," Albert said mischievously. "The IWPA has also named two assistant editors. Can you guess who?"

"Do I know them?"

Albert burst out laughing. "I'd say you know them rather well. The new editors are Lizzie Swank and—Lucy Parsons."

Lucy let out such a shriek that little Lulu, who all this time had been playing quietly with her brother in the corner of the room, burst into terrified tears. Lucy rushed over to comfort her, but was so excited she tripped on the scatter rug and very nearly fell on top of the frightened child. That set Lulu to more screaming, but eventually, with much patting and hugging, she quieted down and everyone caught their breath.

"Oh, Albert," Lucy said, sitting down beside him and taking his hand. "I'm so happy. It's a dream come true for me: I will have some influence on the world in my own right, not just through my husband."

"You deserve it; you've earned it." He kissed her sweetly on the forehead and put his arms around her. "There *was* some opposition to your appointment. I'd rather be the one to tell you, since you're bound to hear about it eventually."

Lucy didn't seem the least bit surprised, or deflated. She knew she wasn't, unlike Albert, everyone's cup of tea. "*Some* opposition to me?"

"Only a few people on the board objected. It was more an objection to us. You know, 'As husband and wife, they of course hold the same views, and as a result the *Alarm* will fail to represent the wide range of opinion that actually characterizes the IWPA membership.'"

Lucy laughed. "They can't know us very well. Anyone who's spent two hours in our company would have heard one of us shouting disagreement at the other."

"*You* shout. *I* reason." Lucy swatted him gently on the top of his head. "Besides, we do agree on a lot, if not everything. We do need to make sure that the *Alarm* prints the whole spectrum of views within the International. Yes, even views as extreme as yours."

She gave him another swat, and this time a big kiss as well. "I can't wait to begin."

"Could we have dinner first?"

"I suppose I can hold off for an hour. But let's eat quickly . . ."

✳

Two days later, Lucy burst in on Albert as he was cleaning out a nook in the small *Alarm* office. She was brandishing a newspaper over her head with one hand and holding on to Lulu with the other.

"I can't believe it!" she shouted, "It's an invitation to murder!"

"What is?" Albert asked, as he took Lulu in his arms.

"The *Chicago Times*. About the most villainous thing I've ever read!"

"Try and be calm, dear." He motioned her to a chair. "Sit and read it to me." Albert sat down opposite her and put Lulu on his lap.

"You've never heard anything like this: 'The best meal that can be given a ragged tramp is a leaden one. When a tramp asks you for bread, put strychnine or arsenic on it and he will not trouble you any more, and others will keep out of the neighborhood.'" She looked up in triumphant fury.

"Good lord!" Albert said, "that's monstrous. And they accuse *us* of fomenting violence."

"And for once," Lucy said, removing a piece of paper from her pocket with a flourish, "they're going to be right."

"What does that mean?"

"I've written a response. I don't expect you to publish it in the *Alarm*, but I'll see if the *Labor Standard* will take it. Steel yourself," she said, picking up the page. "Throughout the bitter winter of 1884, you, the homeless and unemployed, have had to keep bonfires lit all night long to avoid freezing to death. Many of you have died of exposure anyway. Others have drowned themselves in Lake Michigan. I beg of you: Stay your hand! If you decide to kill yourself, take with you a few of the rich. It's their heartlessness that's made you so desperate. Every hungry tramp who reads these lines should avail himself of those little methods of warfare which Science has placed in the hands of the poor . . . *You must learn the use of explosives!*"

Lucy put down the page and glared defiantly at Albert.

"Lucy," he said, "I beg you to reconsider. This will confirm every stereotype our enemies have of us."

"Predictable."

"This isn't you speaking," Albert said, raising his voice. "It's Johann Most. A part of you has always been secretly drawn to his views. I've long known that. But you must get it under control. Self-defense is one thing, individual terror, precipitating violence, is another. It's wrong, Lucy, it's plain and simply wrong!"

"Yes sir, Mr. White Man," Lucy spat out. "Next time they lynch a nigger I'll climb up the tree as the noose tightens, and whisper in his ear, 'Congratulations, my man, for never having *precipitated* violence. It's a bit late now for self-defense, but at least you go to heaven with clean hands!'" She hovered above Albert for a second, then like a tornado abruptly veering off, grabbed Lulu and swept from the room.

Lucy's Manifesto ended up a month later on the front page of the *Alarm*, When Albert called in his two assistant editors to tell them his decision to feature it, his tone was matter-of-fact and the words he chose clearly designed to forestall discussion. He simply said, "The reigning policy of the *Alarm* must be to print the full range of views held within the International, thereby allowing readers to make their own informed judgments."

Lucy bit her lip and said nothing. Lizzie, smiling broadly and deliberately interjecting a non sequitur, said she'd been meaning to ask Albert for some time now what their salaries were going to be.

"The International has fixed my salary at eight dollars a week and both of yours at four dollars. Is that acceptable? Frankly, it doesn't seem fair to me, since you'll probably put in as many hours as I will."

"It's acceptable to me," Lizzie said. Seeing that Lucy was still speechless at hearing that Albert would print her piece, Lizzie added with a grin, "It's acceptable to Lucy, too." That made them all laugh, and there was a round of hugs and tears.

South Bend, Indiana
October 12, 1884

My Dear Wife,

This is such a short trip that I had no intention of writing, but I'm so shaken up at what's happened here that I wanted to put words to paper while the experience was fresh.

Little did I know that the local chapter of the Knights here is underground. And with good reason. Any person daring to join a labor organization, or suspected of being connected with one, is instantly discharged. This town is the property of the Studebakers, Ollivers, and Singers. Those who still have jobs are working for eighty cents a day, and hundreds are walking the streets without employment of any kind.

Despite the reigning terror, more than *one thousand* men and women gathered to hear me speak. An astonishing show of courage—and desperation. Mr. Frank Avery, who lives outside the jurisdiction of the Studebakers, introduced me. He told the crowd that he was sure they'd heard terrible things about Anarchists, Communists, and Socialists. "Well," he said, "tonight you can see and hear a man who is all three and judge for yourselves."

Picking up on his theme, I began by saying that no single label could adequately represent the whirlpool of ideas swirling through our movement. Some in our ranks, I said, believe that the "purification" of our republican institutions is all that's needed to set the country to rights. Others emphasize the need for government ownership of the railroads. Still others put their faith in a general strike. And so forth—you know the lengthy litany. What we all share in common, I told the crowd, is the belief that the average person deserves a better life, that the paradise of the rich is made out of the hells of the poor. We believe too, I said, that if the current desperation continues, the working class will be driven, against its will, to outright revolt.

Then I turned to conditions right here in South Bend. "I've been told," I said, "that just two months ago armed men with whips and lashes drove seventeen so-called tramps out of town." ("It's true! It's true!" various voices called out.) "And I know it as a fact," I went on, "that at the Olliver Plow Works steel filings and sand dust can destroy a man's lungs within a year." That wasn't exactly news to them, either. "Olliver consumption," they called out. "It's killed hundreds."

At this point I called up one Valentine Ruter, who'd volunteered himself to me earlier, and who now jumped up on the platform and stood next to me. "Look at this man," I said. "Along with his four able-bodied brothers, he worked in the Olliver grinding mill for three years. During that time all four of his brothers died of consumption. When Valentine's health also broke down this year, Olliver put him on the streets. Awaiting death, he's fed his wife and three children on the *one dollar and fifty cents per week* given him, as a charity case, by the town trustee."

"Nor do these horrors happen only at Olliver," I said. At which point I called up another volunteer, Martin Pauliski, who replaced Ruter at my side. "This man," I said, "worked for the Studebakers' wagon and carriage factory for eight years. When exposure and overwork brought on rheumatism and he was unable to stand for more than short periods, the company discharged him. Last winter, his family nearly froze to death, and his wife, in desperation, went directly to the Studebakers. They gave her a cord of wood. Soon after, Pauliski was told that he could come back to work. Though in considerable pain, he did so—only to be again discharged as soon as his labor had paid for the wood. Both Olliver and Studebaker gave large sums last year for the erection of a new church in town. The gospel they preach to you there is that you must be content with the station in life to which it has pleased God to call you. Is that what God wants for his children—mutilation and early death?"

My words, and the terrible visages of the two broken men, produced a sensation. The crowd pressed in close, and on the outskirts a cry went up that I was a lying atheist and should be made to answer for it. Somebody yelled out, "Lynch him!" A workman jumped to my side and shouted at the crowd, "If you try to harm this man, then you, not him, will dangle from a tree limb." Shouts and applause went up from the crowd.

When order was more or less restored and I was able to continue, I assured them I was speaking the truth, that they all knew the examples of Ruter and Pauliski could be multiplied many times over. What they might not know, I went on, is that the Grand Army of the Republic is at this very moment also being employed in Wyoming Territory, in East Saginaw, and in Cleveland to break skulls and bust strikes—that the power of the State was being employed wherever and whenever the capitalists called for it. "The result," I said, "is that workers are being robbed of any peaceful way to present their grievances."

By now, the crowd was pretty fired up, and so was I. "The people," I told them, "are being *driven* to violence as their sole recourse. A storm is brewing, a storm that will break forth before long and destroy forever the right of a few men to exploit and enslave the majority of their fellows. Agitate!" I shouted. "Agitate! Organize! Revolt!"

Suddenly a man in police uniform stepped up behind me, laid his hand on my shoulder and said, "Sir, if you continue to incite the people, I will arrest you." I asked the officer what his name was, and he answered, "It is none of your business, sir." At this point pandemonium ensued, the crowd erupting in a kind of frenzy. Before I knew what was happening, a phalanx of wagon and plow workers had formed a protective wedge around me and had swiftly removed me from the officer's grasp. On the sidewalk, a group of armed men—no one recognized them—attempted to assault me, but my stalwart bodyguards saw me safely to the hotel. Three of these noble men insisted on sleeping on the floor of my room throughout the night.

I'm exhausted and exhilarated. The workers do understand what must be done.

Soon after you get this, I'll be home and holding you in my arms.
Your loving Albert

Part Six

Chicago

In a police department notorious throughout the country for its free use of the club, Captain John Bonfield, commander of the Des Plaines Street Station, had become the first among equals. He proudly declared that he'd rather slug a few bystanders than run the risk of a striker getting away unbloodied. When asked, as rarely happened, to justify his innumerable raids on IWPA and union meetings, Bonfield laughingly cited the "absence of a visible American flag" or the "flaunting of a red one."

He'd recently led fifty policemen in breaking down the door and storming Greif's Hall in order to terrorize a gathering of the members of a socialist publishing society. The police smashed cabinets, ripped the society's silk flag to shreds, and, with clubs flailing, seriously injured half a dozen men. The publishing society brought suit. The presiding judge decreed that "the police had acted without prejudice, in the staunch belief that these people belonged to the dangerous group known as anarchists."

A few months prior to the Greif Hall incident, Bonfield broke up a strike of streetcar conductors by ordering his men to charge the crowd gathered at the corner of Madison and Western and to club everyone in sight, whether strikers, onlookers, store owners, or passersby. The police assaulted the crowd with zeal, and Bonfield personally beat two men, neither of them strikers, into unconsciousness. The assault directly defied Mayor Harrison's standing order to avoid unnecessary confrontations with the citizenry, and he promptly called Bonfield into his office for an explanation. During the interview, Bonfield refused a proffered chair and throughout stood threateningly erect over the seated Mayor. Before being asked a question, Bonfield delivered an answer: "I did it," he said, "in mercy of the people. A club today to make them scatter may save use of the pistol tomorrow." Harrison angrily terminated the interview and decided on the spot not to yield to the intense pressure building among the group of police officers loyal to Bonfield to appoint him to the vacant Superintendent's job. He would offer it instead to Frederick Ebersold.

But Bonfield was a hero to the cabal of police officers he led. Like him, they were entirely out of sympathy with working-class grievances—though themselves of working-class background—and were deeply beholden to certain allies in the business community for a generous array of gifts and a host of opportunities for graft to augment their meager salaries. Ebersold knew all this, knew of the cabal, the bribes, the graft, and the endemic brutality when he accepted the position of Superintendent, and he decided to do as little as possible to antagonize Bonfield and his supporters.

Ebersold was no coward. He'd fought with Sherman at the battle of Shiloh, and before that had been a decorated soldier in his native Bavaria. And he had no doubt, when he got the nod from Mayor Harrison, that he was more deserving than Bonfield. After all, he told himself, Bonfield was a man who'd failed twice over in business, at running a grocery store and a small fertilizing company, and had become a policeman by default at age forty-one. Ebersold had a report on his desk that, if he decided to use it, would have a devastating impact on Bonfield's reputation. It contained eye-witness affidavits and detailed complaints itemizing Bonfield's excesses, as well as a petition—a copy of which the signatories had sent directly to Harrison—from a thousand citizens demanding that Bonfield be dismissed from the force. The most startling of the letters came from Captain Michael J. Schaack, a member of Bonfield's own inner circle, directly accusing his fellow officer of "needless brutality."

It was Schaack's letter that convinced Ebersold to request an appointment with Harrison "to discuss the citizens' petition." When the two men met, the mayor told Ebersold that he agreed with the petition and believed that Bonfield had engaged, "with some frequency," in abominable behavior. "He should be disciplined," Harrison announced, "perhaps removed." A pleased Ebersold started to commend the mayor for his bold leadership in the matter, when, with the raising of a hand, Harrison cut him short. "Unfortunately," he said, his voice sounding strained, "a number of influential persons have intervened on Bonfield's behalf, emphasizing above all his superb work in keeping the city from falling into the hands of terrorists and foreigners. After weighing the conflicting testimony carefully," the mayor said, "I've found myself coming down on their side of the argument."

Stunned, Ebersold could barely stammer out, "Do you mean, Your Honor, that John Bonfield is not—not to be—disciplined?"

"Not for now at least. What the future might bring I can't predict. For now Captain Bonfield will be allowed to retain his command. However, I will expect you to keep a much closer eye on him."

＊

"Frankly, I find him a puzzle, unfathomable really," Spies said. Michael Schwab, who worked with Spies at the *Arbeiter*, nodded in agreement. "But he's a most intriguing puzzle, as impressive a young man as I've ever met." The two had come from the *Arbeiter* office after putting the paper to bed and were drinking beer with Lucy and Lizzie in the Parsons's flat.

"There's something of the monomaniac about him," the gentle Schwab added. "He's deeply silent, deeply compelling."

"Maybe Lingg is silent because he doesn't understand English," Lucy suggested, looking up from the white cambric skirt she was sewing for Nina Van Zandt. "He's only been here a few weeks."

"No, not having the language is the least of it," Schwab said. "The man lives inside himself."

"He's hiding from the ladies, Spies added with a twinkle. "Lingg is remarkably handsome. A man of natural poise and physical assurance."

"And does that make you uneasy, my dear Spies?" Lizzie asked teasingly, "August Spies finally has competition, and from a younger man, no less, for female attention."

Spies laughed. "Lingg wins hands down, I promise you. He has the most extraordinary eyes you've ever seen—steel gray, penetrating, somehow all at once ice cold and burning with intensity. He's the sort of man who assigns no value to his attractiveness, and thus enhances it. "

"He sounds quite terrifying, if a boy of twenty-one can be terrifying," Lucy said.

"You're the one person, Lucy, he probably wouldn't intimidate. He's a fierce champion, incidentally, of women's rights. Insists that in a true civilization the female sex would be absolutely independent of the bearded half of humanity—and that only then would we see pure and free love."

"Which probably means," Lucy said, "that he has a girlfriend who dutifully darns his socks and gratefully kisses his toes."

"And he's to the *left* of Engel and Fischer," Spies added. "He thinks they spend too much time talking about bombs and not enough time building them. Rumor has it that Louis Lingg's created a veritable arsenal in his room."

"Which isn't, I trust, too close to here," Lizzie chimed in.

"He boards on the North Side with a man named William Seliger and his wife," Schwab said. "Both men belong to the Carpenters' and Joiners' Union."

Five-year-old Albert Jr. suddenly burst into the room, bawling from a scary dream during his nap. Lucy jumped up to comfort him. Without breaking stride in the conversation, she put him on her lap and rocked him back and forth. "What do we know of Lingg's background?" she asked. "Has it entered your heads that he might be an agent provocateur?" Albert Jr.'s whimpering began to subside.

"No, no, nothing like that," Spies assured her. "We're in touch with people who knew the whole Lingg family in Baden. He's been a furious little rebel ever since his father, who worked in a lumber yard for years, had a disabling and ultimately fatal accident and the company denied his mother aid of any kind. She had to raise her two young children in extreme poverty, and the boy nursed a bitter hatred of existing society. Which has only grown with time."

"I want my papa," Albert Jr. suddenly sobbed. "I want my papa!"

"I know you do, sweetheart," Lucy said, wrapping her arms around the boy and continuing to rock him gently in her lap. "Papa will be home very soon, I promise you. What is today, eh?"

"I don't knooow," the boy howled.

"Yes, you do. Today is Tuesday. Then comes Wednesday, then Thursday, then Friday. And before the sun sets on Friday, Papa will be back home with you."

"I want Papa."

"Of course you do, sweetheart. This has been a long, long trip. We all miss Papa. But think of it!—just three more days, my brave boy, and he will be home."

That seemed to comfort Albert Jr. He stopped sobbing and began to doze in his mother's arms.

"Have you been hearing regularly from Albert?" Spies asked.

"Yes," Lucy said. "He knows how concerned we are for his safety and writes nearly every day. Though how he finds the time, I can't imagine, since he goes from one meeting to the next. He must stay up half the night."

"Did he go beyond Lemont?" Schwab asked in his reticent way.

"Albert goes where he's called." Lucy laughed. "On this trip alone, he's been in Ohio, Missouri and Kansas. I can't even remember all the towns. And somehow he manages to write me fifteen page letters." Lucy reached above Albert Jr.'s head, momentarily jostling him awake, to retrieve a thick packet from the nearby table. "Here's the most recent one."

"May we hear some of it?" Spies asked.

"We're going to publish it in full in the *Alarm* next week—all but the billing and cooing parts, of course. But I can read you a portion. I warn you," she added, "most of it is pretty grim stuff."

She unfolded the letter and read, "The Lemont stone quarry owners quickly broke the strike. It was swift and brutal. The militia opened fire directly on the assembled townspeople. They killed two men on the spot. Andrew Stulata, a popular young man in the village, was standing with both hands stretched out trying to hold a group of twenty-five or thirty children back from the street. A shot from the troops blew off the top of his head and his blood and brains scattered all over the little ones. A man named Jan—"

Lizzie abruptly rose from her chair. "Enough, Lucy, enough. I can't hear any more," her voice quavered.

Lucy quietly put the letter down.

"It's pitiful," Schwab said.

"The workers are too afraid to organize," Lucy said. "There isn't even a chapter of the Knights anywhere in the region."

"They're absolute pawns in the hands of the quarry owners," Spies added.

"That's not what Albert thinks," Lucy responded stiffly. Albert Jr., now the quietest person in the room, slid out of his mother's arms and wandered back to bed.

"What would you have these poor men do?" Spies asked in surprise. "The quarries are the only source of work in the area."

Lucy started to pick up the letter from her lap, but Lizzie grabbed it out of her hand.

"I told you—I can't hear any more."

"Here's a new Lizzie," Lucy said stonily. "I've never known you to deny reality." She folded her hands in front of her.

Lizzie blanched at the rebuke. "I'm sorry if . . . if I've disappointed you . . ." She was near tears again.

"The part I was about to read you," Lucy said, "has nothing to do with horror. It shows Albert at his finest." She sat erect and unmoving.

For a moment no one spoke. Then Lizzie stepped forward and put the letter back in Lucy's lap. "I'd like to hear it," she said softly.

After a moment's hesitation, Lucy picked up the letter. "Very well . . . Albert is writing about a meeting called the day after the killings."

"'I spoke briefly at their meeting,'" Lucy read, "'mostly about the need to organize. But several of the men angrily rebutted me, said that if they tried to organize, the bosses would starve them out. "Then you are slaves," I said quietly. The men hung their heads. Several had tears in their eyes. Finally one of them said, "Alas, sir, it is too true." But when a vote was finally taken, the men, to my surprise, did decide to strike. It was short-lived, just as my antagonists had predicted. The men had no power to back up their demands, and had to return to work on the quarry owners' terms.'"

"So things are just as before in Lemont, or worse," Lizzie said with a sigh.

"Not at all," Lucy answered sharply. "The quarry workers now understand that next time they'll need a stronger organization and a willingness to engage in the very lawless acts that the Knights and Terence V. Powderly caution them to avoid."

Lucy snorted derisively. "Powderly's goal is what he likes to call 'class reconciliation.' As if any such thing were possible."

Schwab, usually somewhat timid, felt he had to defend Powderly. "I think he's concerned that the imbalance of power between owners and workers is so great that few strikes can hope to succeed. It's a point not easily refuted."

"Nonsense!" Lucy cried out. "Assess the workers ten cents a week, build a strike fund so the men can afford to stay out, proclaim a general strike."

"We have to remember," Lizzie said, inadvertently throwing more coals on the fire, "that the average worker prefers caution to apocalyptic hellfire."

"Most workers," Spies added, "aren't even willing to join unions, let alone be assessed. And what happens when an undernourished strike fund runs out? Or if nobody responds to the call for a general strike?" Spies knew the questions had no answers, but he was annoyed at what he considered Lucy's glib militancy.

"Given the workers' fear and reluctance," Schwab said mournfully, "the odds in places like Lemont are too heavily stacked against us."

"Nat Turner faced greater odds," Lucy snapped. "That didn't stop him."

"But would you say, then, that Nat Turner succeeded?" Spies asked Lucy, with careful provocation.

"Black folks are free, aren't they?" Lucy barked.

"I'm surprised you think so," Spies replied.

"They're not in slavery." Lucy emphasized each word. "And they'll achieve greater freedom still, once more of them recognize that their essential struggle revolves around class, not race. The outrages still leveled at the negro will cease on the day capitalism is defeated."

Spies tried to modulate his incredulity. "Surely you, Lucy, of all people, know that racism has a history and a life of its own."

"Me of all people? What can that possibly mean?"

Realizing he'd invaded a sanctum Lucy kept sealed, Spies glided off the point. "I mean, having grown up in Texas, having personally seen the depth of racial hatred. That heritage, I fear, will be with us even after class divisions no longer exist. Those of us in the American Group are among the few socialists or anarchists who seem to care about the negro's plight."

"You're quite wrong," Lucy snapped. "The Knights are making far greater strides in welcoming negroes into their ranks."

"I'd say making some strides," Schwab threw in. "Negroes are invited to form separate, not integrated, assemblies." Schwab hoped to dampen down the undercurrent of hostility between Spies and Lucy. He had a strong need to believe that a commitment to socialism automatically created serene bonds of comradeship, and any evidence to the contrary made him deeply uncomfortable.

Lucy continued as if she hadn't heard him. "And on this matter—and only this—I give Terence Powderly considerable credit."

"Powderly has also said," Spies emphasized "that he doesn't expect black people to be received into the homes of whites."

"But he himself socializes freely with negroes," Lucy shot back.

Annoyed that Lucy refused to yield an inch, Spies reminded her that T. Thomas Fortune, editor of the New York *Age* and the most prominent negro in the country, had himself lambasted the racism he found endemic in the Knights. "Not that I think," Spies went on, "that the IWPA is doing much better. Just two weeks ago, a comrade much respected for his learning confided to me that lynching may be the only way to keep what he called the 'nigger brutes' in line in the South!"

"I don't wish to talk any further about the subject of race," Lucy announced. "The comrades are not where they should be on the issue. Nor are negroes where they should be in regard to the class struggle." Her voice was frigid. "You're entitled to your opinions. Let us leave it at that." Soon after, Spies and Schwab took their leave, but Lizzie lingered behind. Lucy busied herself with clearing off the table, not having entirely forgiven what she felt had been Lizzie's earlier sentimentality.

"Albert's energy is a wondrous thing," Lizzie said.

"Yes, it is," Lucy curtly replied.

"Lucy, there's . . . there's something I need to say," Lizzie hesitantly offered.

"You have nothing to apologize for," Lucy said, continuing to wipe down the table. "You should always speak your mind with me. I know you as a thoroughly truthful woman and that is what you were tonight."

"It isn't about tonight," Lizzie said. "I regret hurting you . . . if in fact I did. But I agree it would have been wrong for me to disguise my honest reaction to Albert's letter."

Lucy stopped doing chores and sat down in one of the armchairs. "But then what is it, my dear?" The aloofness in her voice had evaporated, replaced by puzzled concern.

"It's about William and me," Lizzie said softly, sitting down in the other chair.

"Have you set a date?" Lucy asked, suddenly full of interest.

"As a matter of fact, yes." Lizzie said, looking strangely unhappy.

"What wonderful news!" Lucy said, grabbing her friend's hand. "But my dear, why in heaven's name do you look so . . . gloomy?"

"Because we'll be moving out of the city," Lizzie blurted out, and the tears gushed from her eyes.

Lucy reacted as if physically struck. "Moving? Moving where, for heaven's sake? Your place is here, here in Chicago, in the movement, here with us! You're my dearest, dearest friend!"

"We're not going far," Lizzie said, dabbing at her eyes with a handkerchief. "And we'll still be active in the struggle; William feels as strongly about that as I do. But . . . it's not like being around the corner from you . . ." She started to sob, and Lucy put her arms around her.

"Where are you moving to—Alaska?!"

"Geneva . . . It's only some forty miles away. And now there's daily commuter service on the Illinois Central."

"But why, why Geneva of all places?"

Trying to get hold of herself, Lizzie disengaged from Lucy's arms. "William's inherited a small house there. He hopes to open a school for shorthand and elocution. I could give music lessons." She hesitated for a moment. "The doctors have told him that the country air will do wonders for his health."

"I didn't know William was ill. My word, tonight's been one surprise after another!"

"Digestive problems. The doctors haven't been able to come up with a clear diagnosis and none of their potions have helped."

"Oh, Lizzie, how I'll miss you!" With a sudden wail, Lucy buried her head in Lizzie's lap. Lizzie had never seen her friend cry before and the shock of it was profound.

"Oh, my love, my love . . . it'll all come right . . . I'm sure it will . . . nothing can keep me away from you . . . you'll see . . . And I'll be at every meeting, every one!"

Gradually stifling her tears, Lucy sat back up. "You are very dear to me . . . do you know that? Do you realize how important you are to me, Lizzie, how much I love you?"

"I do. Truly I do. As important as you are to me."

"Because if you didn't know, I would have only myself to blame. I can be so rude and angry."

"That's because your soul is so large, dearest. It registers all the world's hurt. And in your own life you've had to experience more wrongs than most of us. Your anger's been earned."

She hugged Lucy fiercely, then eased away. "And you needn't worry about the dress shop, either. If it continues to grow, I could do some piecework in Geneva. It would be a nice relief from all those talentless piano students."

Tears started pouring down Lizzie's cheeks. The two women again embraced, holding each other in silence for a long, long time.

✳

Lizzie and William Holmes's departure from Chicago in November 1885 coincided with the height of the economic depression—and the rapid spread of worker resistance. Strikes, speeches, rallies, organizations, publications, and parades multiplied. Hundreds of thousands of workers, many unskilled or semi-skilled, flocked to join the Knights of Labor. Others, more militant, joined the International and founded a host of new IWPA chapters, while still others, with the privileges of a professional craft to protect, lined up behind Samuel Gompers in focusing on the rights of skilled workers. Parsons, declaring himself a "revolutionary socialist" as well as an advocate of trade unionism, stressed in his speeches the importance of organizing, whether the channel be the unions, the Knights, or the International.

The movement for an eight-hour day, long dormant, also sprang back to exuberant life in the winter of 1886. "Eight hours for work, eight hours for sleep, eight hours for what we will!" became the dominant rallying cry of an aroused working class, the central metaphor for achieving a better life. Albert was among the first in the IWPA to awaken to its appeal, and he soon brought Spies—who initially feared siphoning off political energy into so "limited" a demand—with him.

"After all," Albert argued, "we don't want to be seen as stubborn utopians who refuse to lend our weight to a movement that promises immediate relief from daily suffering."

"I suppose we can view the eight-hour movement as historically inevitable," Spies said, finding for himself a palatable argument, "a necessary stage in the evolution of worker consciousness."

Parsons didn't believe in "inevitabilities," but did want Spies on his side. "Think of it this way," he said, "the drive for an eight-hour day could well create the class unity that up to now has eluded us."

*

Inspector John Bonfield was feeling enormously pleased with himself. He'd hatched yet another scheme for securing future income. With a contribution of five hundred dollars from each of the officers in his cabal, he'd bribe the state legislature to pass a lucrative pension bill that would guarantee policemen with twenty years of service a retirement sum equal to half their salaries. True, five hundred dollars was an enormous amount of money for an officer to raise whose yearly salary was only slightly more than double that, but Bonfield had a canny solution for that little dilemma, too. For those interested in joining up, he would make loans available at minimal interest; the money would come from the police department's substantial slush fund, built up from the sale of unclaimed property, saloon licenses, and fines collected for assorted violations of the law. Bonfield felt confident that with hearty support from his fellow officers, the legislature would pass the pension bill at its upcoming session.

Several other enterprises currently commanded his attention. All emanated from his close connection to Mike McDonald, the city's gambling czar, a man with fingers in so many pies that doing any bit of illicit baking in Chicago without his first lighting the stove was very nearly impossible. McDonald controlled dozens of wholesale liquor distributorships, owned an off-track betting emporium, was deeply invested in various bail-bonding rackets, and was the sole owner of a high-stakes gambling establishment that catered to the more affluent of the city's sporting men, offering them dice, cards, brandy, cigars, and gourmet food. McDonald employed dozens of "bunko men"—hustlers—to hang out at railroad stations and hotel lobbies to entice prosperous-looking out-of-towners to an evening of chance. Chicago's lesser gaming establishments were allowed to remain in business on the stipulation that they pay McDonald a monthly percentage. In 1885, he bought a splendid mansion on Ashland Avenue, one of the city's most fashionable areas.

Bonfield was one of the key officials McDonald relied on for protection from police interference, for ensuring suspended sentences for any of his bunko men who might end up in a police court, and for securing friendly and influential witnesses on the rare occasions when McDonald himself might be brought into court for a legal infraction. In return, McDonald saw to it that Bonfield and other cooperative officials were handsomely compensated, sometimes through direct payments, sometimes through shares in one of his enterprises, whether it be counterfeiting, loan sharking, fencing, or the routine shakedown of street peddlers and prostitutes.

*

Bonfield disliked visiting the Harrison Street lockup. He didn't approve of police stations being used as places of shelter for the city's homeless. Many were recent immigrants, meaning, to Bonfield, troublemakers and radical scum, too lazy to stick to a job or too high-and-mighty to do manual labor. Still, once a month, in his role as inspector, he was required to visit the Harrison facilities.

As he walked down the row of cells, his questions to the guards were, as usual, perfunctory.

"You're not allowing any of the homeless to spend more than a single night, are you?"

"No, sir. We tell 'em that when they arrive asking for shelter: 'Just one night, after that it's the workhouse.'"

"How many to a cell?"

"Most times, ten. It's all we can squeeze in, the space being five by seven."

"Vermin under control?"

"Usual number of rats and mice."

"I meant the vagrants," Bonfield said laconically.

The turnkey dutifully laughed, not having heard the joke for a full month. "Yes sir, we lock 'em in all night."

"Each cell has a bucket for bodily functions?"

"Yes, sir."

"The air smells foul. Probably coming off the vagrants, not the buckets."

"I expect so, sir."

"What time are they chased out?"

"Six A.M., sir. After breakfast."

"You give them breakfast?" Bonfield looked outraged. "Who authorized that? Breakfast's not required by law."

The turnkey smiled slyly. "It's only for them we rouse early to polish our boots."

From the cell behind Bonfield, a voice suddenly pierced the gloom. "I spit it in your face."

Bonfield whirled around. Peering into the dark cell, he yelled, "Who said that?"

When no one answered, he turned to the guard. "Did you recognize the voice? It had a thick German accent."

"Yes, sir," the guard answered wearily. "He's been giving us trouble most of the night. Wanted water, things like that."

"Bring him out here at once!" Bonfield ordered, fingering his club.

The turnkey opened the lock, but before he could enter the cell, a young man stepped forward voluntarily. He was an imposing figure, despite the dirt on his clothes from having lain all night on the floor. Strongly built, with a handsome head, his eyes were at once hooded and intense.

"Yes?" he said staring directly at Bonfield, as he stepped from the cell.

"What's your name?"

"Louis Lingg."

"Where are you from?"

"Ich komme gericht von—"

Bonfield swung his club hard against Lingg's shoulder, causing him momentarily to lose balance. "Speak English, you god-damn Kraut! This is the United States of America!"

Lingg's facial muscles twitched with anger. Bonfield circled around him, slapping the club against his palm as he alternately cursed Lingg and plied him with questions. Lingg stood silently erect, glaring straight ahead. He refused to say another word, even when Bonfield pushed the club painfully into his ribs.

"Don't you know who I am, you stupid bastard? Bonfield's the name. Ever hear it? All your anarchist friends have." There was something in the obdurate way Lingg faced him down, silently, that convinced Bonfield on the spot that he was dealing with one of those terrorist swine. "'Black Jack' Bonfield, in honor of my fondness for smashing your kind in the head. Black Jack Bonfield. Don't forget it!"

With that, Bonfield turned and marched back up the line of cells. As he reached the door, Lingg's voice sounded loudly at his back: "I will remember."

Bonfield whirled around, tempted for a moment to march back down and give Lingg a thorough beating. "Not worth my time," he told himself, and without another word he turned and left the cellblock. He would remember, too.

Lingg had landed at the Harrison Street lockup through a series of unpredictable circumstances. That morning, at the barrel factory where he worked, he'd refused to take over the job of a striking worker and had been discharged on the spot, his paycheck for the week withheld. Unable to pay the rent to his landlord, William Selinger—a fellow carpenter who'd once befriended Lingg but had now turned ugly—he found himself on the street. The bitterly cold weather had forced Lingg to seek shelter for the night at the police station.

He cursed himself afterward for not having known better, since his girlfriend, Ida Miller, had warned him never to accept "public charity." When a newcomer to Chicago, Ida had worked for a tailor on the North Side sewing buttonholes at two cents a piece. But when the slack season came, she'd been laid off and was unable to come up with her three-dollar weekly rent. The landlady had thrown her out.

Penniless, Ida had gone to the Atheneum, a refuge for homeless women, but after one night was denied lodging because when she washed up, they told her, she "made the towels too wet." She then tried the Home for the Friendless but was told it only took in children and old people. For the following ten days, she slept on a bench in Lincoln Park. Then she found work at three dollars a week as a clerk in a fancy-goods shop, which allowed her to secure a room at the Working Woman's Industrial Home on Fulton Street. Since room and board was $2.50 a week, she agreed, as a way of getting a reduced rent, to sleep on a mattress in the corridor and to get up at 5:00 A.M. to help prepare breakfast. "So much for refuge," she later told Lingg bitterly. "If I'd known what I do now, I would have worked the streets as a prostitute instead."

Chicago's august West Side Philosophical Society, aware of the agitation throughout the land, decided that the time had come to schedule an open debate at Princeton Hall on "Socialism." Albert Parsons was invited to present the case.

"That's like the Pope opening the Vatican to the Pharisees," Lizzie said when she heard the news.

"Don't go," Lucy said, "You'll be Exhibit A at the freak show."

"I have to go," Albert said, "it's a unique opportunity to speak my mind to people who are convinced I don't have one. Don't worry: I have no illusions that anything I could say will find favor, or even comprehension, among the stuffed shirts."

"Good," Lucy said, "because you won't change a single person's mind."

On the night of the debate, a sizeable contingent of IWPA comrades, including Lucy, Lizzie and William, Spies, Fielden, and Neebe, grouped tautly together at the front of the imposing and packed auditorium. The seats immediately surrounding them remained unfilled; though it was a standing-room only crowd, none of the fashionable attendees would dream of sitting in proximity to such notorious rabble-rousers.

Reacting to a tap on her shoulder, Lucy turned around to find herself staring into the smiling face of Nina Van Zandt.

"I just wanted to say a quick hello," Nina offered. "I'm so looking forward to hearing your husband speak. So is my mother." Nina pointed to a woman seated in the middle of the audience, dressed in a full-length gown with shirr pleats across her right shoulder and velvet trimming on her left—the latest word in Continental elegance. Mrs. Van Zandt waved cordially—she and Lucy had briefly met during Nina's fittings—and Lucy, still open-mouthed at Nina's audacity in publicly acknowledging her, waved back.

"Thank you for . . . for coming," Lucy managed to stammer.

"I'll see you very soon," Nina said over her shoulder as she went to rejoin her mother.

At just that moment, Albert mounted the podium. He paused for a moment to survey the sea of satins and shawls, felt top hats and Prince Albert long coats, the members of the audience spread out before his eyes like a sea of long-necked albatrosses.

"Ladies and gentlemen," he began, his voice benign and melodious, "it very seldom happens that I have a chance to speak before a meeting composed of so many gentlemen with nice white shirts and ladies wearing elegant and costly toilets. I am the notorious Parsons, the fellow with the long horns, as you know him from the daily press. Well, I am from Texas, where longhorns—cattle, that is—are indeed common, so perhaps the image is not entirely inappropriate."

That produced a few titters, and some unease. The ladies tended to think Parsons's smile uncommonly sweet; the men found his emphasis on longhorns vaguely threatening, somehow conjuring up the image of heads on pikes.

"I'm in the habit," Albert continued, "of speaking before meetings composed of people who by their labor supply you with all these nice things you wear while they themselves are forced to dress in coarse and common garments; of such people who build your fine palaces, with all those comfortable fixtures, while they themselves dwell in hovels or on the street. Are not these charitable people—these *sans culottes*—very generous to you?"

The only response was some low hissing. The ladies made a quick reevaluation: the sweet smile belonged to a villain—just as they'd been warned.

"We've often heard," Albert said, "that in this country fifty-five million people live in ease and plenty. Yet in its last issue, *Bradstreet's* states that two million heads of families are in enforced idleness and without any means of support—and *Bradstreet's* is certainly not a lying communistic sheet." There was a renewed, louder wave of hissing.

Motioning for quiet, his voice less mellow, Albert moved directly—he knew this audience wouldn't listen for long—to his charge: "Here in this city of Chicago alone, there are thirty-five thousand men, women, and children living in a condition of starvation, driven to—"

He was again interrupted, this time by loud booing from several different sections of the audience. Albert's voice rose insistently above the din: "You may choose to deny that so many in your midst are starving to death, but that will not make the fact less true."

"Give us proof!" a man shouted from the back rows. "Prove that what you say is fact!"

"Proof? Do you lack eyes and ears, sir? Or do you employ them only when guaranteed sylvan sights and sounds? Proof, my dear sir, is easily come by. Take yourself to a police station on a bitter winter night and you will see what passes for charity in Chicago—cold, bare flagstones for sleep, a 5:00 A.M. slice of bread for breakfast, or none at all. Or if you fear visiting a police station lest you be detained for *real* crimes, have a look in the city's damp tunnels at night, where you'll see men—yes, and many women, too, and they are not prostitutes, as you may prefer to believe—trotting up and down all night to keep from freezing to death. If none of that persuades you as proof, then you might try—"

Dozens of men in the audience were now on their feet, stamping and shouting insults at the platform. The chairman of the event hastened to the podium, banged the gavel, and called for order. As the frenzy began slowly to subside, the chairman gestured frantically toward the wings, and two frightened young ladies, with their musical accompanist, timidly appeared on the stage. But before they could begin to sing, Albert, taking advantage of the lull, managed to yell out a few final words:

"You are driving the people to revolution. I do not advocate force, I merely predict it. Violence will come not because we want it, but because you make it inevitable!"

As the auditorium broke into an uproar, Lucy, Spies, and the other comrades rushed Albert through the back exit behind the stage. Once on the street, they quickly dispersed—but not before Lucy caught a glimpse of Nina and her mother standing silently on the sidewalk, alone.

*

In late March 1886, Mayor Carter Harrison announced that as of May 1, all city employees would work no more than eight hours a day. "May first" instantly became a national rallying cry, and labor organizations across the ideological spectrum united in endorsing a general strike on that date to pressure for an extended compliance with the eight-hour day.

When the long-awaited day arrived, it dawned cloudless and cool. Across the country, some three hundred thousand people left their jobs and answered the call to march. In Chicago, eighty thousand gathered and exuberantly wound their way through the city's downtown area. Armed police, Pinkertons, and militiamen lined the rooftops, and rumor had it that 1,350 National Guardsmen had been put on alert in the city's armories. The Parsons family—Albert Jr., now six, and Lulu Eda, four—marched at the head of the line. The children soon became tired, but Lucy and Albert took turns carrying them, and periodic purchases of ice cream and soda water from street-side vendors stifled their yawns and refueled their energy.

The Citizens Association, which Albert had once hoped might prove a progressive force, became convinced that the march marked the onset of revolution and that Chicago might "fall to communism." Accordingly, leading Association members placed themselves at strategic points along the line of march where, at the first sign of trouble, they could instantly alert the police. But the members found startlingly little to report. All was brass bands and exultant singing, high spirits and smiling faces, the happy crowd dispersing at Ogden's Grove to enjoy a round of picnics, sporting events, and inspirational speeches.

Spies and Parsons gave the keynote addresses. Intoxicated at the size and liveliness of the crowd, Albert rose to passionate heights: "After evolving for 109 years under the Republic, the people are about to throw off their economic bondage!" The crowd roared its approval and a group of men, to deafening cheers, hoisted Albert on their shoulders and carried him from the platform through the crowd.

That same evening, he left Chicago for Cincinnati, insistent, though exhausted, on fulfilling his pledge to speak at the eight-hour rally there the following day. That duty performed, Albert then headed straight back to Chicago, arriving home in the early morning hours. He fell into a deep sleep on the couch, only to be shaken awake by Lucy at noon. She and Lizzie, who'd come down from Geneva to stay with them for the duration of the May demonstrations, were "worried, very worried," she told a groggy Albert. He propped himself up on one elbow, hoping to get the blood circulating in his befogged brain.

Lucy agitatedly paced back and forth. "The momentum's fading. I can feel it," she said. "People are signing up for the trade unions or the Knights, not the International. That means it's all going to end with our rulers tossing us a few token reforms."

Lucy now had Albert's full attention. She'd touched a raw spot he rarely allowed himself to acknowledge. He'd long feared—and once in a great while had publicly said—that a major barrier to progress lay in the passivity and conservatism of the American working-class itself.

"I know what you mean," he said grimly. "In Cincinnati, one worker denounced me, and all revolutionary socialists—as *enemies* of the working class! 'I want nothing to do with communists and anarchists!' the man shouted. I have no idea how he was defining either," Albert wearily added, "since *we* can't! He got some applause, too."

"It makes me crazy," Lucy said. "Here, for the first time, we have the opportunity for real insurgency, a time that may never come again, and it's slipping away. If the sewing girls are any gauge, it may already have passed. They're frightened and wavering, terrified of losing their livelihood. We must convene a meeting of the American Group for tonight, before another day is lost, to try and figure out some way to bolster the girls' fighting spirit. Please, Albert, we must!"

Though bone-weary and desperate for sleep, Albert agreed. He threw some cold water on his face, downed a quick breakfast, and headed out to place an announcement in the afternoon editions calling for a 7:00 P.M. meeting at 107 Fifth Avenue, home of both the *Alarm* and the *Arbeiter-Zeitung*.

Instead of then going home to rest, Albert decided to stop off at the *Alarm* and catch up on recent events. He ended up spending the entire day. Spies came by to welcome him back and sat for several hours filling him in on developments.

"A lot has happened," Spies said, "almost all of it bad. And the worst of it at the McCormick plant."

"Again?"

"Much worse than the skirmishes of the past few months. If only Cyrus McCormick Sr. was still alive. Things were better back then."

"That's because he was born poor. And smart enough to walk the plant floor and talk to his workers."

"Unlike his benighted son," Spies added. "They don't come more arrogant and misguided than Cyrus Jr. Bringing in those non-union scabs and hiring three hundred armed Pinkertons to guard them—idiotic provocation. No wonder the men now call the place Fort McCormick. And the machinations of Bonfield aren't helping."

"Is he up to some new tricks?"

"Well, you know how much Bonfield wants Ebersold's job and has been trying to discredit him as pro-union."

"That much I know, yes."

"Ebersold has caught wind of it and to burnish his image as the Protector of Property has stationed three hundred and fifty Chicago policemen, nearly a third of the force, at the McCormick works."

"When I left for Cincinnati," Albert said, "there were only a few hundred scabs still on the job, despite police protection."

"True, but yesterday," Spies said, "was the worst confrontation yet at the plant. I was out that way and saw some of it myself. I went to give an open-air talk to a large group of workers gathered at Black Road, a few blocks from the McCormick works. I was speaking to them from the top of a boxcar, and wasn't having much success. I was dead tired—I've been giving two or three speeches a day for weeks, plus the newspaper."

"What?" Albert asked good-humoredly, "August Spies's famously fiery oratory failed for once?"

"I was more like a burnt-out cinder," Spies laughed. "As soon as the three o'clock whistle blew at the McCormick plant, my audience had an excuse for leaving, and hundreds rushed off to heckle the scabs between shifts. I tried to get them to hear me out, but the crowd continued to dwindle. Then, suddenly, a number of patrol wagons raced by us, heading toward the plant, and before long we heard distinct sounds of a struggle. At that point, the remnant of my audience took off for McCormick's."

"Did you say anything to incite them?" Albert asked, knowing that Spies could get carried away.

"Albert, I was so down-in-the-mouth, I couldn't have incited Louis Lingg! I simply urged them to stick together and not retreat in the face of McCormick's threats. You're as bad as the reporter from the *Chicago Herald.*"

"What's that mean?" Albert asked.

Spies handed Albert the morning edition of the *Herald.* "He quotes me as telling the crowd to 'strike while the iron is hot—arm yourselves and forcibly drive the scabs out of the McCormick yards!'"

Parsons broke into a smile. "Maybe he was exhausted too, got you confused with Lingg, or Engels or Fischer?"

"None of whom were there."

"Just listen to this." Spies picked up the *Herald.* "'By the time the McCormick bell tolled at three o'clock, the fiery Spies had worked the crowd up to such a pitch that they filled the air with bloodcurdling cries of "Kill the scabs!" and in a fever of excitement rushed towards the plant, sweeping across the vacant lots in disciplined phalanxes.'"

Parsons burst out laughing. "That would mark the first time in history that a frenzied mob managed to maintain a disciplined phalanx. What *did* happen?"

"What—you don't believe our free, democratic press? For shame! Well, it's simple: deserted by my audience, I decided to follow and see for myself what was going on at the plant." Spies turned somber. "It was a sight, I can tell you. A horrible sight. Something I'll never forget."

"The strikers didn't attack the scabs, did they?" Albert sounded seriously worried.

"They did bombard them with stones when the shift let out, driving them back into the factory. Nobody was hurt."

"Well, that's a relief."

"But the stoning gave the police an excuse to call for reinforcements. The new detail arrived within minutes and some of the strikers surrounded the patrol wagon. The captain got out and started lashing at them with a whip. Then he—"

"A *whip*?" Parsons almost gagged on the word. "Where in God's name does he think he is, in the Deep South?"

"It gets worse. He ordered his men to wield their clubs freely and to fire their revolvers directly into the crowd. And fire they did, round after round, even though the crowd rushed to disperse. No one has reliable casualty figures. Some reports have six workers dead, with others close to death."

Spies gestured contemptuously toward the copy of the *Herald* lying on the table. "The press, of course, insists that the police gave warning—'Disperse or we'll fire.' The *Herald* even dares to claim that initially the police shot above the strikers' heads and resorted to direct fire only after the strikers attacked them. The reporter doesn't bother to explain why no police officer was wounded, let alone killed."

Parsons was on his feet, agitatedly pacing the room. "Then what happened, what happened? This is an unspeakable outrage!"

"I must've been in a state of shock. I raced back to the *Arbeiter* office and drafted a circular, both in English and German."

"Do you have a copy?"

"Right here." Spies pulled the folded circular from his pocket. "*This* can justifiably be called fiery."

Parsons took it from his hand and quickly scanned it. "No, no, it's just right," he said, having read it at a glance. "It's grand." He patted Spies on the back. "The language is strong, but necessary."

"And that last line?" Spies asked apprehensively.

Albert hesitated a beat. "It can be misread—'To arms we call you, to arms!'—but then, our masters deliberately misread everything we say or write anyway."

"You do have some doubts about the line, don't you? I can tell from your tone."

"I know how you meant it—as a summons to preparedness. Our enemies, of course, will insist that it's an overt call to violence."

"The German version," Spies said sheepishly, "is stronger still. I don't think you'll approve. But then, I'm not sure I approve, now that my rage has subsided. Especially one part." He paused, doubtful whether to continue.

Parsons pressed him. "What part? Did you invoke Johann Most and advocate dynamite?" he asked kiddingly. Albert didn't dream that the answer might be yes.

Spies looked away in embarrassment. "I didn't specify the means. But I did advocate 'annihilating'—alas, I'm now quoting verbatim—'the beasts in human form who call themselves rulers!' What can I say? I was nearly out of my mind with anguish. To make matters worse, one of our compositors, a friend of Fischer's, took it upon himself to insert the word *revenge* in bold letters at the top of the circular."

Parsons sucked in his breath with apprehension, then tried to cover over his unease. He knew that Spies, for all his occasional pridefulness, was as tender-hearted a man as ever lived; he knew, too, that even the tenderest, pushed too far, can become maddened. "Well, wait'll Lucy reads your words. She'll knight you on the spot!"

The attempt at humor failed.

"You're disappointed in me, I know." Spies said quietly. "I've let you down. I've let a lot of people down."

"None of us was there," Parsons said firmly. "None of us saw young men with their faces blown off for daring to go on strike for a few cents more a week. I wouldn't think of judging you. And anyone who does, refuses to see that violence of language is not violence of deed." He put his arms around Spies and hugged him tightly.

"Thank you for that, dear friend. I'll not forget your kindness."

"I'm being truthful, not kind," Albert said.

"Saying that is part of your kindness." For a moment there was an awkward pause, then Spies said, "I can at least say in my own defense that I didn't go as far as the North-West Side Group."

Albert froze, deeply alarmed.

"A small group of Most's followers, plus some members of the armed auxiliaries, met last night at Greif's Hall to figure out how to respond to future police attacks. Both Engel and Fischer were there. From what I've heard, Engel presented some sort of general contingency plan—the accounts I've had vary—for a coordinated reaction to police aggression. They left the specifics for some future meeting. What dominated the discussion, I'm told, was the outrage at McCormick's. In the upshot, it was decided to call a mass protest gathering for this evening in Haymarket Square. Fischer was chosen to oversee the printing of a handbill announcing the meeting and . . ." Spies paused ominously. ". . . and . . . and Fischer—unauthorized, mind you—inserted into the flyer, in bold print, "WORKINGMEN ARM YOURSELVES AND APPEAR IN FULL FORCE!"

"Fischer's a compositor at the *Arbeiter*, isn't he?"

"That's right."

"So didn't he have to show you the flyer before printing it?"

"He came to me this morning and asked if I'd let the handbill run in today's edition. When I saw it, I flared up and denounced it as ridiculous." Spies caught Albert's puzzled expression.

"Yes, I know, I'd expressed very nearly the same sentiments in my own circular of the day before. But overnight, I'd come to my senses. Which may be why I got so angry at Fischer—why hadn't *he* come to his senses? Plus, I was furious at my own earlier stupidity. I told Fischer that unless he removed the offending line, I'd neither run the handbill in the *Arbeiter* nor speak at the Haymarket meeting, as he'd asked. He agreed, but I sensed his resistance. Then I learned, to my horror, that some copies—with the offending line included—had already been printed. I immediately ordered them destroyed, only to discover a few hours ago that several bundles of the original handbills, probably a few hundred in all, had been distributed in various working-class bars."

Spies was so upset his eyes misted over. "Let's hope they fell into the hands of our more peaceful-minded brethren."

Parsons tried to quell his own alarm, in the name of comforting his friend. "You're needlessly worried, Spies, I'm sure of it. Try to remember, after all, that most workers abhor the idea of violent protest and have vigorously rejected the views of Most and his kind. The meeting at Haymarket tonight will, I feel sure, be entirely peaceable."

"I'm counting on you to be there," Spies said, his voice still heavy with apprehension. "We're expecting upwards of twenty thousand people, and tensions have been running high in the city all day. People are saying that the class war is finally at hand."

"A one-sided class war has been going on for some time," Albert added dryly.

"And no one longs to precipitate it more than Black Jack Bonfield," Spies said, "as sadistic a brute as ever lived. With the defenders of law and order themselves lusting for violence, the workers become mere cats'-paws. Though some are ready enough to scratch back. And I count myself among them."

"You've always advocated self-defense. Is that what you mean?"

"I mean"—Spies's voice unexpectedly went up a notch—"that despite all the remorse I've just been claiming, I found myself not two hours ago writing an editorial for the *Arbeiter* that was as inflammatory as my circular of yesterday. I'm veering back and forth like a drunken sailor."

"Let me see it," Parsons said with trepidation.

"I know it by heart: 'There must never again be a slaughter of workers like the one that took place at the McCormick plant.' Next time, 'we must fight back with *weapons*, not stones!'"

"That's strong language," Albert said quietly, "but the sentiment's not new."

"What worries me is that the language is *so* strong, it can be construed as the same as, or uncomfortably close to, a call for violence."

"Words are not acts. Yelling at a man is not the same as shooting him."

"How much more *can* we take?" Spies unexpectedly burst out, possibly in relief at Parsons's consoling attitude. "Should we simply lie down and be slaughtered?"

"You've been through too much these past few days." Parsons had never seen his friend this mercurial and decided to tread lightly.

"I don't recognize myself," Spies said, as if he'd read Albert's mind. "I've never felt so erratic, unstable really. I think my nerves must be shattered. Though these days, being overwrought seems the norm. You're one of the few, Albert, who seems able to maintain his balance in all circumstances."

"Lucy might tell you otherwise. I think you have a need, my friend, to see me as better than I am. And do you know what? I suddenly realize that I don't like it. You're denying me the right to become passionate and upset, just like everyone else." Parsons was startled by his own words, but Spies had hardly heard him. His mind had shifted back to the meeting planned that night in Haymarket Square.

"You *must* be one of the speakers," he said to Albert. It came out as a command, not a request. "You and only you can draw the needed distinctions, can rechannel all this turbulence into calmer waters."

"What distinctions?" Spies's renewed vehemence puzzled Albert.

"The ones I've just been drawing, for heaven's sake!" Spies sounded downright snappish. The Spies Albert knew had always been among the most judicious and well grounded of men.

"I'm sorry, my friend," Parsons said. "Now you're getting *me* rattled—though you think I never am. You've told me so much in the last few hours, I can't keep it all straight."

Spies slumped into a chair, shaking his head with remorse.

"No, my dear Parsons, I'm the one who is sorry. Desperately sorry. To have raised my voice at you, the most decent man I know, is unforgivable."

Albert sighed deeply. "Perhaps we should start all over."

Spies burst into laughter. "No—not *all* over! If we recapitulate the entire conversation, we'll both go mad!" The two men smiled; the tension was broken.

"Nobody else in Chicago is so entirely trusted by both the English- and German-speaking communities as you. So you must speak tonight at the protest meeting."

"If I possibly could, I would," Parsons said quietly, "but, alas, I'm already committed elsewhere."

"Where? What could possibly take precedence?" Spies sounded as if he was about to flare again.

"I've promised Lucy. The American Group is meeting tonight to discuss ways of encouraging the sewing girls to join the eight-hour struggle. Lucy and Lizzie have worked hard to organize them but the girls seem to be losing heart."

Spies tried to conceal his exasperation. "Surely Lucy would understand that the Haymarket meeting is more important."

"No, I doubt that she would. The plight of the sewing girls has become a passion for her. I've given her my solemn promise to attend the meeting.

It's set for seven o'clock, here in the *Alarm* office."

"Well then, you can attend both meetings!" Spies said, brightening. "Haymarket is scheduled to start at seven-thirty, but given how long it takes a crowd that size to settle down, I'm sure the proceedings won't begin till eight, or even eight-thirty. I could speak first, then you could come over straightaway at the close of your own meeting. Say, about nine o'clock."

"But I can't be sure when it will end. And I can't leave before it does. That would send the wrong message—as if I didn't think the gathering important enough to see it through to its conclusion."

"Nonsense! You could simply explain that you were urgently needed elsewhere."

Parsons smiled. "Spies, you're not a married man."

"Lucy shares your politics. She would completely understand."

"She might. She might not. I intend to hold to my commitment."

"You're in thrall to her, that's what," Spies said, sounding testy again.

"Indeed I am. And she to me. I hope that someday you'll be as lucky."

Neither man spoke for a moment. Spies knew he was behaving badly, but distemper, so unfamiliar to him, had him firmly in its grip. Albert broke the silence.

"Spies, let us stop this at once. We have done quite enough quarreling for one night."

Spies gratefully seized the olive branch. "You're right. I must accept your decision. I've been pressing you too hard. I don't recognize my own adamancy. But I do recognize how unattractive it is."

"I have an idea. If the tone of the meeting at Haymarket does go awry in some way and you feel that you need me, send a messenger and I will come at once. Yes," he said, smiling broadly, "even if our gathering is still in session."

Spies seized hold of Albert and gave him a fierce hug. "Thank you, my dear friend . . . that's a great relief, a great relief . . . I can't tell you . . ."

"Both our meetings will be boring and brief," Parsons said with a laugh, "and by nine o'clock we'll be sitting in a booth at Greif's downing beer."

Chicago

Sam Fielden had been so busy hauling a load of stone to Waldheim cemetery that he didn't get to read the newspaper until after he'd washed down his horses. It was then that he saw the announcement calling for a meeting of the American Group that evening.

Though bone tired, he felt duty-bound to attend; as treasurer, he had to be there in case an outlay of money was decided on. Hurrying home, he had a quick meal with his wife, pregnant again (for which she credited her spiritualist adviser) after the loss of their young son to dysentery. He gave her a huge hug, the only kind he knew, gently rocked the crib of his sleeping baby girl for a few moments, and then reluctantly headed out to catch the streetcar.

He arrived at the offices of the *Alarm* at eight o'clock to find that only fifteen members had gathered in the first-floor business office and that the meeting, awaiting the arrival of the Parsons, hadn't yet been convened. Milling around and greeting friends, Fielden learned of the simultaneous gathering taking place in Haymarket Square.

Albert, Lucy, and the two children, accompanied by Lizzie, decided to walk from their flat on Grand Street to the *Alarm* office. They were in high spirits, Albert regaling them with tales of his most recent trip. When he pushed out his stomach in imitation of a self-important trade union official he'd met, the children were so delighted that they strutted around in imitation of their father, bellies stuck out, noses high in the air.

In the midst of the hijinks, they ran smack into two reporters, one from the *Times* and one from the *Tribune*, at the corner of Halsted and Randolphs Streets. Since Albert knew the two men and considered them among the more honest press representatives, he paused to answer their questions. Mr. Owen of the *Times* asked for an update on the Haymarket gathering. He wasn't headed for Haymarket, Albert said, and knew nothing of what might be taking place there. He was on his way, he explained, to another meeting entirely, one that had been called to discuss the plight of the city's sewing girls.

"But we've heard you were scheduled to speak at Haymarket," Mr. Owen said.

"Well, you heard wrong," Parsons said jovially. "*I've* heard that you reporters have taken to carrying revolvers."

"We're not that frightened!" Owen said good-naturedly.

"You see—it shows how silly most rumors are," Parsons said.

"Does that include the rumor that you're in possession of dynamite?" the *Tribune* reporter asked, unsmilingly.

Parsons laughed and shook his head from side to side in disbelief.

"He's a very dangerous-looking fellow, isn't he?" Lucy chimed in merrily.

"Now we really must be off to our meeting," Parsons said. "It's on the South Side, and I'm afraid we're already late for it." Lizzie suggested they board a streetcar to make up for the lost time, and they bid the reporters a friendly good-bye.

It was nearly eight-thirty when they finally arrived at the meeting, and it was immediately called to order. The needed decisions were quickly taken. No one had to be persuaded that the sewing girls were desperate for help. It was agreed to print circulars, appoint organizers, and hire halls for meetings. Parsons made a motion, passed unanimously, that the American Group contribute five dollars—four dollars for handbills and one to pay carfare and incidental expenses. Fielden, in his official capacity as treasurer, handed Lizzie the money and she promptly handed him a receipt—along with a big kiss on the cheek, which made Fielden blush wildly.

"You must admit," Lizzie whispered to Lucy, "that a strong body and a sweet good-nature are a rare combination in a man."

"Personally, I like 'em frail," Lucy parried. "Easier to keep in line. I don't want nobody lookin' like Moses handin' me down his commandments!"

By now it was approaching nine o'clock, and there being no further business, the group was about to adjourn when Balthazar Rau, business manager of the *Arbeiter-Zeitung*, came hurriedly into the room. He'd been sent, he explained, by Spies. The Haymarket meeting, Rau reported, had turned out a tame affair, drawing only a few thousand people and no speakers other than Spies himself. He needed relief. Having promised he would go if summoned, Parsons felt he had to comply. The American Group voted to adjourn, and almost everyone headed over with Parsons and Fielden to Desplaines Street, half a block north of Haymarket, near the mouth of Crane's Alley.

In his four consecutive terms in office, Mayor Carter Harrison had won the good opinion of Chicago's working-class. Even before he mandated the eight-hour day for city employees, Harrison had shown his sympathy for labor in numerous ways. He'd supported ordinances calling for stricter factory and tenement inspection; had fended off the anti-saloon reformers, whose campaign threatened to destroy a beloved German American cultural institution; had resisted attempts to interfere with union organizing and the rights of free speech and assembly; and had publicly stated that he would never call in state or federal troops to put down a strike. Unlike so many officials of the day, moreover, Harrison had never had his hand in the till. If the city's business elite was bemused by such unorthodoxy, it was downright incensed when Harrison dared to appoint a few socialists to local office in the city's department of health.

Bombarded with predictions from the police hierarchy in general, and from Inspector Bonfield in particular, of impending "revolutionary violence" at the Haymarket Square meeting, Harrison had decided on the evening of May 4th to have a look for himself. He'd come deeply to regret appointing Bonfield as an inspector, now that his brutal ways had escalated—Bonfield had of late become fond of repeating to reporters his now favorite slogan: "The club today saves the bullet tomorrow." Harrison believed his presence might restrain Bonfield's eager pursuit of conflict. He'd been told that Bonfield had, with the approval of Chief Ebersold, already concentrated a disproportionately large police force of some two hundred men at the Desplaines Street station and that he'd put additional reserves on alert at other precincts around the city.

The outdoor meeting still had not started when Mayor Harrison arrived. A large, striking man of sixty-one, he was immediately noticed. But the mayor was leaving nothing to chance: he periodically placed himself under the one streetlight in the area to illuminate his presence, and when he moved genially through the crowd he occasionally paused and struck a match under his face, although somehow his cigar never materialized. A friend accompanying Harrison expressed fear that the mayor was making himself a target for potential trouble-makers, but Harrison insisted that he wanted "the people to know that their Mayor is here."

His presence had been well established by the time Spies, shortly before eight-thirty, mounted one of the two Crane Plumbing Company wagons abutting the alley and finally began his speech. He'd originally been scheduled to talk in German, but because of the absence of other speakers, had decided at the last minute to switch to English. With his very first sentence, he aimed to set a calm, deliberate tone. "There seems to prevail in certain quarters," he began, "the opinion that this meeting has been called for the purposes of inaugurating a riot, hence the war-like preparations on the part of so-called law and order. But let me tell you at once, that this meeting has *not* been called for any such purpose. Our object in gathering is to explain the eight-hour movement and to throw light on various incidents in connection with it, chief among them, yesterday's events at the McCormick plant."

Pleased at the tone and tenor of Spies's words, Mayor Harrison had just begun to let himself relax a bit when several angry voices called out from the crowd, "Hang McCormick!" "Let's get the bastard!" Could Bonfield have been right after all? The mayor pulled his black slouch hat down over his forehead in a reflexive gesture of self-protection.

"No!" Spies instantly shouted back. "Make no idle threats! There will be a time, and we're fast approaching it, when monsters who destroy the lives and happiness of the citizens will be dealt with like . . . like wild beasts"—Spies seemed stunned by his own words. Trying to soften their impact, he quickly added, "But that time has *not* come!" Then, as if again mysteriously overpowered (perhaps, he later thought, by a collective rage not exclusively his own) he burst out, "When the time has come, you will no longer make threats, but you will go and act." Spies silently cursed himself. He was defeating his own conciliatory purpose. Alarmed, he steeled himself to stay in control, and out poured a string of pacifying words. They came just in time; Mayor Harrison was nervously fingering his watch chain and scanning the crowd to catch sight of Bonfield should he, after all, be needed.

But for the next half hour Spies spoke in such soothing, even platitudinous, terms that Harrison felt confirmed in his original estimate that the rally was likely to be merely tedious, no threat to civic peace.

At nine o'clock Parsons and his party arrived at Desplaines, and Spies, with relief, immediately waved his friend over to the wagon. As Parsons jumped up, the crowd cheered. Spies briefly introduced him then went over to sit with Lizzie, Lucy, and the children on top of another wagon. Parsons spoke for nearly a full hour, and throughout sustained the temperate tone that had kept mysteriously giving way during Spies's talk. Parsons mostly revisited familiar ground: the just grievances of the workers, their right to control the fruits of their own labor, the greed and intransigence of the ruling class.

The name Jay Gould stirred a few people in the crowd to jeer and shout imprecations. But Parsons held firm. "This is not a conflict between individuals," he emphatically responded, "but the time for a change of system. Socialism aims to remove the causes that produce the pauper and the millionaire, but does not aim at the life of the individual. Kill Jay Gould, and like a jack-in-a-box another or a hundred others will, under the existing social conditions, spring up in his place."

With that, the crowd, or what was left of it, subsided. Popular though Parsons was, his speech had for the most part been shopworn, and people had steadily drifted away. The event in all respects was turning out to be a rather dispirited, even soporific affair. By ten o'clock, when Parsons yielded the platform to Fielden, the last speaker of the evening, no more than three hundred people were still milling indifferently about. Fielden whispered to Parsons that he intended to talk for only a few minutes.

Mayor Harrison felt he could safely leave for home. He decided that on the way he'd do well to stop off at the Desplaines police station, only a block from the Haymarket gathering, and give Bonfield the benefit of his first-hand impressions. He chuckled at the thought of informing the zealous inspector that not a single bloody pike had thus far been thrust into the air.

When Harrison entered the station, he was taken aback. Despite the lateness of the hour and the lack of incident at Haymarket, the large contingent of officers remained on full alert. Bonfield himself had on his blue overcoat and boxy official hat—as if prepared to dash out the door at a moment's notice. His thick black eyebrows and his roguish smile made him look more like a French legionnaire than a Chicago policeman. At the sight of the mayor, Bonfield's smile gave way to a frown.

Harrison strode directly up to him. "There's no need for this," he said sharply, looking around at the armed officers. "I've just come from the rally, and the tone throughout, with a few minor lapses, has been moderate and unthreatening. Nothing has occurred, or seems likely to occur, to require the intervention of the police."

"I entirely agree with you, Your Honor," Bonfield replied. His voice was smooth, his expression benign, but the hunched tension in his shoulders conveyed anything but compliance. "I've had plainclothes detectives at the meeting from its onset and they confirm your characterization of the proceedings."

That came as a relief to Harrison. "Very well, then. I suggest you give the order at once for your reserves at the other stations to go home."

"The order, sir, has already been issued." The surprise on the mayor's face pleased Bonfield. He despised the man for his womanish scruples— and for how easy it was to circumvent them.

"And what of the men assembled here?" Harrison asked.

"With all due respect, Your Honor, I think it's advisable to hold them on standby until the meeting has actually concluded. We've heard rumors of plans for a violent confrontation to coincide with adjournment."

"There have been rumors of every kind and description," the mayor responded tartly, "and not a single one has proven true."

"I'd take it as a personal kindness, sir," Bonfield said deferentially, "if you'd allow me the peace of mind of holding my men here for just a short while longer."

Bonfield sounded downright humble, and the mayor, in his decency, was moved by it. "Very well, Mr. Bonfield. But not a moment more than is needed."

"Exactly my intention, sir." Bonfield respectfully bowed his head, chuckling inwardly at the gullibility of the old fool. "I am the one," he thought contentedly, "who will decide what is needed, and when."

Convinced that all was well, Harrison bid Bonfield and his officers good evening, and left for home.

Back at Haymarket, Fielden had been speaking for only a few minutes when a sudden gust of cold wind swept in off the lake and the darkening sky threatened a downpour. Parsons yelled up to Fielden that they should adjourn to Zepf's Hall, a popular tavern nearby.

"There's a meeting of the furniture-workers union going on there," Fielden called back. "Don't worry, I'll wrap it up in two or three minutes, and we can all go home."

"The children are getting cold," Parsons said, "we'll go on ahead to Zepf's and meet you there."

Seeing the Parsons group leave, and with the weather growing more ominous, a number of others, including Adolph Fischer, decided to call it quits; no more than a few hundred people remained to hear Fielden's closing remarks.

Aiming to end on a forceful note that might reenergize the dispirited crowd before it scattered into the night, Fielden, eyes bloodshot and voice hoarse, told the crowd in his blunt way that there was "no security for the working class under a social system that had shot down the men at McCormick's in cold blood." He implored them to "have nothing more to do with the law, except to lay hands on it and throttle it until it makes its last kick."

The two plainclothes detectives hanging back in the crowd raced over to the Desplaines station. Fielden, they breathlessly reported to Bonfield, was inciting people to riot. Before they had even arrived, Bonfield had had an officer follow Harrison from the station with instructions to report back the moment he saw the mayor mount his horse and ride away. That report had arrived five minutes before the plainclothesmen and Bonfield had already ordered his men to shoulder their Winchester repeater rifles and fall in line outside the station house, which they were already doing.

For weeks Bonfield's men had been conspicuously practicing advanced techniques of crowd control, marching shoulder to shoulder up and down Chicago's streets, alarming the citizenry with their militaristic maneuvers. Lucy had written an article about it for the *Alarm*. "What foreign enemy," she wrote, "is about to invade America?" She answered her own question: "The only sovereignty at risk, the only lives, are those of American workers."

With his men now assembled in front of the station, Bonfield ordered them to march at once, and in strict formation, to Haymarket Square. "And *on the double!*" he called out, fearful the meeting would disperse before he got the opportunity to break it up. His throat was dry with excitement, his penis swelling uncomfortably in his tight-fitting pants.

The police, 180-strong, arrived at the square just as Fielden was finishing his remarks. "Any animal, however loathsome," he yelled, "will resist when stepped upon. Are men less than snails or worms?"

Bonfield and his second in command, Captain Ward, strode directly to the front of the wagon on which Fielden stood. "I command you in the name of the people of the state of Illinois," Ward called out loudly, "immediately and peaceably to disperse."

"But we *are* peaceable," Fielden said quickly.

Ward repeated his command, this time louder still.

"All right then, we will go," said Fielden, "We were about to anyway."

He stepped down from the wagon. At the precise second his foot touched the ground, a noisy device sputtered overhead, giving off a faint glow and landing directly in the front ranks of the police. It exploded with enormous force, killing one officer, Mathias Degan, outright, badly wounding half a dozen others, and shattering windows throughout the area.

After a moment of stunned silence, the police regrouped, firing round after round directly into the crowd. The noise was so loud that some mistook it for cannonry. As Spies dismounted from the speakers' wagon, an officer aimed his revolver directly at his back. Seeing the officer out of the corner of his eye, Spies's brother, Henry, grabbed the weapon just as it went off—and fell to the ground with a bullet in the groin. Unaware, Spies was pushed along by the fleeing, panicky crowd.

Amidst shrieks and groans, people fled in every direction to escape the onslaught of bullets and clubs, scattering down the side streets with the police in enraged pursuit, firing in every direction. Not satisfied with a single revolver, Bonfield grabbed the weapon of a fallen officer and started blazing away double-fisted. The Desplaines station sent out a riot alarm and patrol wagons from all over the city descended on the area. Within minutes some thousand officers had made a clean sweep of the three blocks surrounding Haymarket, ruthlessly clubbing anyone who dared to linger.

The wounded, their moans filling the air, lay strewn across the pavement; those able to crawl away pulled themselves into nearby stores; others, dragged by friends, disappeared down alleyways. One young boy bled to death in a drugstore at the corner of Halsted and Madison. In the weeks ahead roughly equal numbers of officers and civilians—seven in most estimates—would also die of their wounds, and the total number of seriously wounded would rise above a hundred. It had all happened in five minutes.

Mayor Harrison arrived home at 10:20, got undressed, and was about to get into bed when he heard what sounded like a cannon go off in the distance. Raising his bedroom window, he was bombarded with the noise of small arms and revolver shots coming from the direction of Haymarket Square. Dressing quickly, he rode on the gallop back to the Desplaines Station.

When Harrison pushed open the door to the station, a jolting scene of devastation met his eyes. Some two dozen wounded officers lay scattered on the floor and benches, their groans filling the air as a handful of doctors and nurses attempted to minister to them. Several of the injured, ashen and silent, blood oozing from multiple wounds, were clearly near death.

Harrison, stunned, went straight up to Bonfield. "What in God's name has happened?" he demanded, his eyes dancing with disbelief and anger.

"When we arrived at Haymarket, sir, my men—"

Harrison broke in. "What were you doing in Haymarket?! I had your distinct promise that—"

"The decision to hold my men on standby," Bonfield said calmly, "to which Your Honor graciously acceded, proved to be a wise one. The final speaker, Samuel Fielden, did indeed—just as predicted—attempt to incite the mob to violence. We had no choice, as defenders of law and order, but to hasten to Haymarket to prevent a bloodbath."

"But a bloodbath," Harrison said, glancing over at the wounded, "seems to be precisely what you precipitated."

"Not at all, sir. These noble men have prevented a far greater disaster."

There's no point arguing with this man, Harrison told himself in exasperated anger. In his arrogance, he'll lie through his teeth. I must attempt to get what facts I can, and deal with his insubordination later.

"And when you got to Haymarket," Harrison said evenly, "what happened?"

"I ordered the mob to disperse, sir," Bonfield said. "But instead, it opened fire on the police. In self-defense, my men were forced to fire back. Then some villain in the crowd threw a bomb directly into our ranks."

"A bomb?"

"Yes sir, a bomb." Maybe that'll open the old fool's eyes, Bonfield thought to himself. "Some of my men say it came from a window, others say from within the crowd itself. Several insist it was thrown from the wagon on which Fielden was giving his speech."

One of Bonfield's lieutenant's suddenly spoke up. "It's also been suggested, sir," he said to Harrison, "that the bomb may have been intended for the crowd, not the police. We'd been driving the people forward at such a rapid pace that had the bomb struck a mere two or three seconds earlier, it would have landed where the workers had just been standing . . ."

A fierce glance from Bonfield silenced the lieutenant. "That view, Your Honor, has already been discredited."

A reporter from the *Inter-Ocean* newspaper stepped forward and asked the mayor what he planned to do. "I can't tell yet . . ." Harrison replied. "This is the sort of thing where a man must be guided by the facts, and the facts alone, not theories. This disgusts and saddens me . . . But I will protect this city."

Albert was looking out of the window of Zepf's saloon, with Lizzie, Lucy and the children seated at a table not far off, when the sound of the explosion ripped through the air. It was so loud that Adolph Fischer, seated at another table, feared that the police had attacked the meeting with a Gatling gun. Immediately after, volley after volley could be heard and people started rushing into Zepf's to escape the hailstorm of bullets, some of which whistled into the saloon through the open doors before the owners were able to rush over and close them. Just before they did, Spies staggered in, panting from exhaustion.

Lizzie and Lucy dashed over to aid him, while Albert scooped up the children in his arms and tried to soothe them. "Don't be frightened, little ones, don't be frightened." Lulu's face lit up with excitement at all the unexpected liveliness, but Albert Jr. buried his head in his father's shoulder, shut his eyes tight and screamed.

Someone shouted that for better protection they should vacate to the saloon's back room, and nearly everyone quickly moved there, shutting the door behind them. There they sat in total darkness until, after some fifteen minutes, someone opened the door and told them the firing had ceased and all was quiet.

The street in front of Zepf's was deserted. At the moment, no police were in sight, and the people who'd been inside the hall quickly scattered in various directions. "We're all in danger of imminent arrest, you realize," Spies said. "Let's not make it easy for them by sticking together as a group." He embraced the others quickly, then swiftly left the building. The Parsons and Lizzie hurried down Desplaines Street toward home.

Lizzie was the first to speak. "If any of our people are in danger, Albert, it is you. You dare not stay in the city."

Albert looked startled and said nothing, but Lucy immediately seconded Lizzie's view. "Lizzie's right. You're the best-known labor leader in the city. The administration's going to have to blame this massacre on somebody, and you can be sure it won't be themselves. You've got to leave, at least for a few days, until the hysteria passes."

"I couldn't possibly," Albert said firmly. "It's not an option. I can't leave our friends behind."

"They'd all agree with me, I'm certain of it," Lizzie said with unexpected passion. "They love you. They want you safe."

"You don't want to be taken unawares," Lucy added, knowing that Albert wouldn't consent unless appealed to on grounds of what was right for the movement. "Once you're at a safe distance, you can see what's needed for the good of the whole and make your decision accordingly."

"I don't think I ought to go," Albert repeated, but this time with less vehemence.

"I insist." Lucy sounded implacable. "You must go for our sake."

Albert looked puzzled, allowing Lucy to press the advantage. "Think of the effect on the people's morale if you were locked away in Bridewell. And what of our own children? Do you want them to see you dragged in cuffs from our home? What would they do with their father locked away for months, or years? What would I do?" She threw her arms around him, and Albert buried his face in her neck.

"You really think I ought to go?" he said quietly.

"Yes—go!" She held him at arm's length, making a strenuous effort not to let the qualms she felt show in her face.

"Me, too! Me, too!" Albert Jr. clamored, folding himself under his father's arm.

"Next time, sweetheart," Albert said quietly, "I promise . . . next time . . ." He turned to Lucy. "Where will I go *to*?" he asked plaintively.

"You'll go straight to William and our house in Geneva," Lizzie said.

"Perfect!" Lucy exclaimed. "The police won't immediately make the connection, and by the time they do, William will have secured a more distant hideaway for you."

Reluctantly, Albert gave his consent. But he warned the two women that he wasn't convinced and might easily have a change of heart within a day or two.

"Well don't come knocking on *my* door," Lucy said, "Just take yourself straight to the Desplaines police station. Bonfield will give you a warm welcome, even if I won't." Lucy suddenly looked as if she might burst into tears.

Albert took her in his arms and kissed her. "Lucy . . ." he whispered.

They held on to each other tightly, until Lucy, who had started to cry, pushed Albert away. "Now hug the children, quickly," she said, between tears. "You mustn't tarry a minute longer." Albert gathered the children into his arms, squeezing them tightly.

"Ow!" Albert Jr. yelled. "That hurt!"

"Oh, my poor boy," Albert said, "I'm so sorry . . . it's just that papa loves you and Lulu so . . ." Lulu giggled and ran to her mother's arms, with Albert Jr. close behind. Lucy gave Albert one last, fierce embrace, then, without looking back, hurried off with the children.

Albert and Lizzie headed directly to the depot of the Chicago & Northwestern Railroad, where Lizzie purchased one ticket for Turner Junction, the nearest point to her home in Geneva. They waited nervously in a dark corner of the platform for the train to arrive. When it finally did, and Albert boarded, Lizzie, her face covered in tears, stood waving good-bye as the cars pulled slowly out of the station.

By the next morning, a tide of hysteria had spread across the country: Chicago's City Hall had been dynamited! Half the city was in flames! Anarchists were looting and pillaging at will! A plot had been revealed to seize control of the government in Washington! The Red Revolution was sweeping the country!

The panic was fanned by the press. Newspapers everywhere denounced Mayor Harrison for "misguided liberality" in allowing fanatics like Spies and Parsons to speak freely in public. Invective that poured from the editorial pages matched, in slightly more decorous form, that from the pulpits. Editors and preachers vied to outdo each other in vilifying the ill-defined horde of socialists and anarchists as "assassins," "fanatical brutes," "inhuman rubbish," "rag-tail cutthroats." Neither publishers nor preachers paused to mention possible police culpability for the Haymarket carnage, but instead filled their pages and podiums with praise for the officers' extraordinary valor. The fact that many ordinary citizens—not revolutionaries, not police officers—had also died in the skirmish was skimmed over.

The *Chicago Times* singled out Parsons for special vituperation, calling him a "fiend, who for months past has advocated the torch and dagger," mentioning as well that he "is the husband of a negress, and a most arrant coward withal." The only part of the attack that surprised Lucy was being described as a "negress"; she hadn't realized the matter had become grist for public discussion—and she didn't like it.

There were other shocks to come. Within twenty-four hours of the bloodshed, Grand Master Workman Terence Powderly issued a statement to the effect that no *honest* workingman could or should be found marching under the red flag, "the emblem of blood and destruction." When Lucy learned of Powderly's statement, she spat on the ground in indignation. "The Grand Master *Traitor!*" she hissed.

She next learned that Albert's own union, Typographical Number 16, had adopted a resolution denouncing "the heinous acts of the mob at the Haymarket," making no mention of the gratuitous provocation by the police. Lucy decided that if possible, she'd conceal the resolution from Albert. He would be gloomy enough about the misunderstandings and self-sabotage common among working people.

Bonfield was up early the following morning. Determined to use his new status to maximum advantage, he gathered his men together and sent them off across the city with explicit instructions to run as many labor activists to ground as possible and to ransack their meeting places. Bothering with neither warrants nor itemized charges, Bonfield soon had his jails bursting with hundreds of prisoners, cuffed and beaten at will.

Zepf's Hall was among the first places locked and bolted, followed by Greif's, where a raiding party, led by Bonfield himself, discovered a meeting of striking freight handlers in progress. He demanded that the presiding officer have everyone present raise his right hand and pledge that he had "no sympathy with the socialists who committed the dreadful crime of last night." Every hand went up. Grinning, Bonfield then closed the place down.

Sam Fielden took a bullet in the knee soon after the police opened fire in Haymarket. It passed through his leg, and he was in severe pain as he escaped from the square and hobbled home. The next morning the police roused him from bed, declared his wound superficial, and marched him to Central Station. As Fielden was being booked, the officers taunted him as "a murder-preaching devil" and made jokes about his "ratty eyes" and "moss-filled whiskers." Chief Ebersold decided that Fielden was faking his wound and ordered him to remove the bandage on his knee. When Ebersold saw the torn flesh, he quickly looked away; then, pointing to Fielden's forehead, he told him that the bullet should have gone in *there*. Fielden was removed to the basement lockup.

George Engel had been at home playing cards on the night of the Haymarket meeting. Certain that Spies, Fielden, and Parsons would make what Engel liked to call "their usual bland, cautionary remarks," he decided that he'd heard enough of their prudent clichés. He and Spies were in fact no longer even on speaking terms, having squabbled bitterly about the advisability of armed struggle. Yet when a friend burst into Engel's home that night with the news that a bomb had been thrown, Engels expressed disdain for the act. "Violence is admissible," he said, "only when it emanates from the masses, not from a maverick individual."

When the police arrived to search the Engels's apartment, an officer discovered a portable furnace made of galvanized iron. It resembled a plumber's furnace, yet was suspiciously odd in shape. Engel claimed he had no knowledge of where it had come from—"I currently work as a painter in a wagon factory"—or what it was used for. They decided to take the furnace along to the station. Chief Ebersold thought it might be a "blasting machine" used for the manufacture of dynamite. On inspection, though, the mysterious contraption turned out never to have been fired, and in any case was clearly not designed to produce explosives. Engel was arrested anyway.

At 8:30 A.M. on May 5, a contingent of seven plainclothesmen, led by Detective James Bonfield, Black Jack's younger brother, came bounding up the stairs at 107 Fifth Avenue, home to the *Alarm* and the *Arbeiter-Zeitung*. Lucy and Lizzie had gone there at dawn, after a few hours of restless sleep, determined to print a refutation of the official lies circulating in the city. Schwab, Fischer, and Spies had also arrived early at the *Arbeiter*, with the same goal in mind.

Recognizing Spies, Detective Bonfield turned directly on him: "Are you not the fiend named August Spies?"

"That is my name," Spies answered quietly, "but not my disposition."

"Look here, men!" Bonfield shouted to the other officers, while pointing at Spies's face. "Look at that grimace, that row of wolfish teeth! And he claims not to be one of Satan's fiends—ha!"

Trying to maintain his composure, Spies blandly asked what he could do for "our unexpected visitors."

"You can get yourself ready to accompany us," James Bonfield shouted. "We're officers of the law. You're under arrest." At this, according to the *Times* account the next day, "the faces of the cowering wretches, whose utterances and writings have caused so much misery and recent bloodshed, paled to the color of ashes . . . Fischer stood perfectly still, as if frozen in Hell. Michael Schwab trembled like an aspen and could hardly button his coat. This office was performed for him in no very gentle manner by the justly incensed officials."

Bonfield ostentatiously picked his nose, then walked up to Spies and rubbed his encrusted finger on the arm of Spies's jacket. The three men were then dragged to the street, thrown into the waiting police van, and taken to Central Station at City Hall for booking.

Neither Lucy nor Lizzie was arrested. After their friends had been taken away, and though fighting back tears, the two women immediately went back to getting out an emergency issue of the *Alarm*. They'd been at it for about an hour when Oscar Neebe suddenly appeared in the doorway. He'd been working on the outskirts of the city and had only just heard about the chaos of the night before. He rushed over to the *Alarm* immediately.

Lucy and Lizzie had barely begun to catch Neebe up on events when they were interrupted by the sound of a second contingent of officers bounding back up the stairs. This time they were accompanied by Julius Grinnell, State's Attorney for Cook County (who had earlier advised

Inspector Bonfield to "make the raids first and look up the law afterward") and Mayor Harrison, who, given the pressure of public opinion, had decided to modify his previous stance, or at the least to go on a raid. His face was ashen but determined.

Five of the officers raced up to the third floor, which hadn't been inspected during the prior raid, and finding several printers still at work there, immediately arrested them. Meanwhile Mayor Harrison was sternly demanding that Neebe give an account of himself and his connection to the *Alarm* and the *Arbeiter*.

"I am a friend of August Spies," Neebe said simply. "I do not work for either paper."

"How do you support yourself?"

"I was once a tinsmith, and a good one, but when I supported the railroad strike in 1877, I was fired."

"And now?" Harrison asked impatiently.

"My brother and I started a small yeast company. That is my current livelihood."

"Do you have employees?"

"No, sir. But if we did, they'd work an eight-hour day."

Harrison, a decent man under indecent pressure, felt Neebe was being pointlessly provocative.

"As you may be aware," he said, with some annoyance, "I am a supporter of the eight-hour day."

"Yes, sir, I am aware. You are known as a friend of working people."

Harrison's features relaxed slightly. "I've tried to be. But you people don't always make it easy." Lucy and Lizzie exchanged a furious glance.

The officers and State's Attorney Grinnell had by this time made their way down the narrow flight of stairs with their prisoners in tow. Harrison turned to follow them, then took a step back into the room.

"I want your word," he said, "that your press will not publish any more inflammatory articles."

"The truth is often inflammatory," Lucy shot back. "Are you asking us not to publish the truth?"

"Do not push me too far, Mrs. Parsons," Harrison answered evenly. "I stand between you and those howling for your immediate imprisonment."

Neebe quickly stepped forward. "I give you my word, sir, that I'll personally read this morning's edition, if we can manage to get one out, now that you've arrested our typesetters. You have my guarantee that nothing incendiary will appear."

"Well then," Lucy said, almost under her breath, "that means either a newspaper of blank pages, or ones filled with glowing tributes to the brave officers who filled Haymarket Square with blood. Perhaps we should invite Inspector Bonfield to write for us."

Neebe beseeched her with his eyes to hold her tongue, an appeal Lizzie reinforced by silently squeezing Lucy's arm.

Harrison, ignoring Lucy, spoke directly to Neebe. "I will hold you to your word," he said sternly. "Should you break it, the consequences, as you must realize, will be severe." With that, Harrison turned his back and departed.

"Let's get to work at once," Lucy said, preempting any discussion of her exchange with Harrison. "Given our constraints, we should focus on getting out the *Arbeiter* in circular form."

"Can we do even that?" Neebe asked. He was on the board of the Socialistic Publishing Society, which sponsored the *Arbeiter*, but had no hands-on experience with newspaper work. "I mean, the entire staff, even the printer's devil in the composing room, has been arrested. There are only the three of us left."

"We *must* do it," Lizzie said. "We must show that we can't be crushed."

"What about the *Alarm*?" Neebe asked.

Lucy laughed. "From worrying about being able to get out one paper, you now want to publish two?! No, Neebe, for the moment we must put the *Alarm* aside. I only hope," she added sadly, "that it *is* for the moment."

Just then, the racket on the stairs announced that the police had returned yet again. But this time, it was an entirely different group of officers who barged into the room seething with determination. The detective at their head immediately set his men to work breaking into files, drawers, and boxes, scattering their contents on the floor and rummaging through the piles to pick out "inflammatory" material that could be taken back to Central Station and used as "proof" of the "terroristic intentions of the conspirators."

While his men were at work, the detective abruptly wheeled on Lizzie and, without explanation, told her she was being placed under arrest. When she protested, he told her he'd knock her down if she didn't shut up. When Lucy tried to intervene, another officer pushed her into a chair, called her a "black bitch," and threatened to knock her to the floor too. The raiding party, with Lizzie in tow, then left.

Lucy was furious, Neebe stunned.

"I don't understand," he said hesitantly. "Why did they take Lizzie and not us?"

"It's simple," Lucy said, as she paced angrily among the heaps of manuscripts, letters, and galley proofs scattered over the office floor. "They'd have too much trouble concocting a case against you as an extremist. That simply isn't your reputation, or history."

Neebe felt slightly offended, as if Lucy had told him he wasn't a true activist, not important enough for the police to bother with. "I've been one of the leading organizers for the bakers and the brewery workers," Neebe said, feeling sheepish about his own defensiveness.

Lucy was barely listening. Her thoughts were with Lizzie. Who could help, who should she notify? Should she telegraph William in Geneva, or would that jeopardize Albert's hiding place?

"Besides," Neebe continued, "you *are* known as an extremist. Why didn't they arrest you?"

"For an obvious reason," Lucy said evenly. "They're hoping I'll lead them to Albert. The public is furious that the Chief Fiend has eluded arrest . . . I'll have to be very careful," she added quietly, as if to herself.

She started to gather up her things. "I must check on my children, Neebe. I wouldn't put anything past the police."

"What about the *Arbeiter*? Should we give up any hope of getting it out?"

"Certainly not! The working people of Chicago need to have something to read besides the filth and lies in the *Times* and *Tribune*. I'll be back as quickly as I can. Probably all we'll be able to manage is a one-page statement. If you could draw that up while I'm gone, we can then take it to Burgess, our printing contractor, and have several thousand copies run off. I shouldn't be gone more than two hours."

By the time Lucy reached home, the police were already there and, despite her arrival, continued, without a word, to ransack the premises. Five-year-old Lulu had apparently been taking it all in stride and was contentedly playing with a rag doll. But a terrified Albert Jr. was cowering in a corner, tears streaming down his face. When Lucy was finally able to dry his eyes and get him to speak, he told her the police had wrapped him in a rug and spun him around on the floor, all the while shouting at him: "Where's your father hiding? . . . You better tell us, kid . . . Your old man's a murderer . . . We're gonna string him up just like a nigger . . . You'll never see him alive again . . ." An outraged Lucy screamed so ferociously at the officers—"Gangsters! Bandits!"—that they physically restrained her. Yet they still chose, for the moment, not to arrest her, certain she knew Albert's hiding place and might lead them to it.

The rest of the day was consumed in a grim game of cat and mouse. Lucy, with both children in tow, dodged into untenanted houses and ran through buildings and backyards, trying to shake the police from her trail long enough to allow her to contact comrades. Yet the police never lost the scent. By late afternoon, exhausted, and thinking she'd shaken them off, she decided it was safe to duck into a friend's flat—only to have the police burst in right behind her and tear the place apart in a frenzy of frustration.

Their efforts at intimidation having failed, the police finally put Lucy under arrest—*four* separate times before the day was over, releasing and rearresting her in a bizarre pattern designed to undermine her caution, and perhaps her reason. During each incarceration, Lucy hurled invective at them, refusing to answer a single question. Yet they kept releasing her, convinced she'd eventually slip up and lead them to Albert.

She never made it back to the *Arbeiter* office, but Oscar Neebe resolutely carried on alone. When he finished writing up the one-page circular, he took it to the Burgess Printing Company, as Lucy had suggested. But they refused to print it. Burgess himself whispered to Neebe that the *Chicago Times* owned the building in which his firm was located and had threatened to cancel his lease if he dared ever again print the *Arbeiter*.

For hours Neebe ran from printing firm to printing firm, everywhere getting the same frightened refusal. Finally a small socialist outfit clandestinely got the circular out, and Neebe hand delivered it to a variety of workers' clubs and saloons. "We have taken the place," the circular read, "of our arrested comrades. Should further arrests occur, then will others step into our places . . . Forward and unceasingly forward will this movement continue, in spite of the chicanery of the ruling classes." A copy of the circular fell into the hands of the *Chicago Times*, which, in an editorial on May 8th, pronounced its language "amusing."

By May 10th, less than a week after the bomb had gone off in Haymarket, hundreds of people were in jail and most of the labor press closed down, much of it permanently. And the raids continued unabated. Captain Michael Schaack outdid even John Bonfield in sustaining the public's fear, periodically announcing the discovery of yet another cache of arms, the uncovering of yet another anarchist plot to paralyze the city. Schaack was greatly aided in his efforts by a secret fund of one hundred thousand dollars provided by the Chicago business community; immediately after the Haymarket incident, three hundred leading members of the Citizens Association, including Marshall Field, Philip Armour, and Cyrus McCormick, met and put together the purse. Buoyed by his newfound notoriety as Savior of the City, Schaack became obsessed with seeing bombs and daggers everywhere; to keep public anxiety at fever pitch, he even suggested that the police themselves organize new anarchist groups to replace the ones they'd broken up—and then raid them.

His men finally found the evidence of dynamite they'd sought so desperately, when, ten days after the explosion at Haymarket, they surprised the young carpenter Louis Lingg in his tiny hideaway on Ambrose Street, having been tipped off by his ex-landlord, coworker, and purportedly militant comrade, William Seliger (who was given a handsome reward and repatriation to Germany). Lingg had arrived in Chicago from Germany only ten months before, already, as he himself phrased it, a full-blown advocate of "rude force to combat the ruder force of the police." When the officers burst into his room, Lingg put up a fierce struggle. He very nearly choked one of them into unconsciousness before another managed to land a powerful blow on Lingg's head with his club, knocking him off his feet and allowing the police to overpower and handcuff him. Searching Lingg's trunk, the officers found two bombs, two pistols, and a large number of shells and cartridges. The *Chicago Daily News* announced the thrilling news of Lingg's capture the next day: "The police are confident that at last the man who threw the dynamite bomb into the ranks of the police on the night of May 4th is under arrest." The paper neglected to mention that Lingg had not attended the Haymarket rally.

Lizzie was held incommunicado for four days after her arrest, during which time no charges were specified and no visitors or legal counsel allowed. Then on May 9th she was abruptly released, again without explanation. She went straight to Lucy's flat, where she learned that the police had raided her Geneva home while she'd been imprisoned. Lucy hastily reassured her that William and Albert had earlier vacated the premises, having realized in time that a raid was imminent. Lizzie left for her home within the hour.

Albert had arrived in Geneva midday, the 5th of May. Holmes had greeted him warmly and caught him up on the various reports in the morning papers—that the anarchists had torched Chicago and that they and their allies were being lined up against the wall and shot. Albert's initial impulse was to return at once to the city. He told Holmes that whatever was going on, his place was in the thick of the action.

Holmes had a difficult time preventing him from rushing back that very night; after hours of pleading and argument, Albert would only agree to delay his departure until morning. If the next day's papers confirmed the earlier rumors, Holmes assured him, they would go to Chicago together.

The morning papers contravened reports of fire and massacre, but revealed alarming enough news: almost their entire circle, including Lizzie, had been arrested, a massive search for Parsons—who had been declared public enemy number one—was in progress and it was said he would be instantly detained, if not killed, the moment he set foot in Chicago. With Lizzie in custody, they realized it would only be a matter of hours—or minutes—before the police arrived to search the Holmes residence.

Decisions had to be made at once. Albert still tried to argue for a return to Chicago, but Holmes sternly told him that he owed it to his family and his comrades to stay alive, that it was romantic folly to throw his life away when, after the hysteria died down, he might yet play a constructive role. Albert chafed and stormed, but finally yielded. He agreed to go into hiding.

Holmes immediately sent word ahead to a political comrade, Daniel Hoan, in Waukesha, Wisconsin, warning him to expect the arrival of "a friend." Albert shaved off his mustache, changing his appearance to a remarkable degree: his pale, unlined face made him seem closer in age to eighteen than thirty-eight. He then removed his collar and neck scarf, tucked his pants in his boots, smudged some dirt on his clothing, and, with a few additional adjustments, managed to make himself over into the archetype of an unemployed young tramp.

Holmes advised him to head for Elgin, where he could catch a train for Waukesha. They warmly embraced, telling each other that they'd soon be reunited. Holmes watched from the doorway as Albert, affecting the hunched, meandering gait of an idler, wandered casually down the empty road. Early the next morning, the county sheriff, his deputy, and a Pinkerton detective arrived at the Holmes residence. They searched it over and over, with mounting fury at finding nothing and no one.

Daniel Hoan, a simple, earnest man in his mid-fifties, was reading when he heard the knock. He knew at once that it must be Parsons. "Come in and God bless you," he said as he opened the door, his eyes shining, his hands fidgety with excitement. "The Lord sent you here, and you've come to the right place. You're as safe here as if you were my own child."

Albert thanked him warmly, and gratefully ate the food Hoan soon put before him. Then the two men set about inventing a persona for him. They settled on "Mr. Jackson," an itinerant carpenter who—so the neighbors would be told—would be staying for some weeks to work at Hoan's small pump factory and to make repairs on his house. Hoan produced some old clothes, including a big gray coat and a wide-brimmed hat, to lend credence to his visitor's new identity.

Within a few weeks Parsons's gray-flecked hair and beard had grown long and he refrained from coloring them with the black dye he'd used for years. Between the baggy clothes and the scraggly steel-gray beard, he soon had the ladies of the village lamenting the strangely unkempt appearance of a man capable of such interesting, articulate conversation. Several of them talked of clubbing together and buying him a nice new jacket.

He mingled freely with the townspeople, on the premise that he'd be far more suspect if perceived as skulking in the shadows, as a man with something to hide. The villagers took an immediate liking to his modest manners and lilting voice, his keen intelligence, and the kind, gentle way he regaled the local children, as he worked to repair the eaves on Hoan's house, with tales of the hard lives of the slaves and of those who toiled these days in the great factories of the city. Hoan once overheard Parsons telling the children, "Men and women are always as good as their conditions allow them to be."

Waukesha was a snug, lovely village of green hills, winding paths, and clear springs. Before beginning work in the morning at the pump factory, Parsons would go out for an hour's ramble and soon found a favorite spot on Spence's Hill, overlooking the valley, to which he'd return every evening. The tranquility of the place had a double-edged effect on him; even as the quiet soothed his spirit, it allowed his raw emotions, blessedly numbed during the workday by a busy routine, to resurface—his aching longing for Lucy and the children, his anxiety over the unknown fate of his imprisoned friends.

After he'd been in Waukesha for two weeks, Parsons was able (thanks to a string of anonymous emissaries) to get a letter through to William Holmes, and through Holmes a few words of reassurance to Lucy. "I continue to think," he wrote in the letter, "that I should return to Chicago," and he asked Lucy to seek counsel among their friends about when his reappearance would most likely prove beneficial.

Word came back, again circuitously, that their friends were divided. Most of them felt that he ought to stay away for the foreseeable future, that his return would jeopardize his own life while doing nothing to alleviate the plight of his comrades. Even those who argued that his return might somehow prove useful, urged him not to be precipitous. A grand jury had been impaneled on May 17th but had not yet handed down indictments. A recently formed Defense Committee had been unable to find a single hall to rent and, on May 22nd, had been forced to hold its first meeting in one member's private office. The message from Chicago was, in sum: all is in flux; bide your time.

On May 27th, the Grand Jury announced its indictments. Engel, Fielden, Fischer, Lingg, Neebe, Parsons, Schwab, and Spies were named as "accessories before the fact" in the "murder" of Mathias Degan, the policeman who had died instantly when the bomb exploded in Haymarket Square, and in the deaths of the six other officers who had subsequently succumbed to their wounds.

The only name on the list that caused surprise was Neebe's. Though a tireless labor organizer, he wasn't affiliated with the IWPA and had never spoken in favor of armed self-defense. Only years later did it become known that the owners of one of the breweries whose workers Neebe had helped to organize had spent ninety thousand dollars in persuading members of the grand jury to include him in the indictments. As soon as they were handed down, Neebe was arrested, but as if in acknowledgment that the case against him was weak, he was allowed to post bail. The other defendants—except Parsons—were already in custody and were promptly transferred from Central Station to the Cook County jail to await trial on June 21st.

A few labor unions and the Defense Committee provided Neebe's bail and they also hired twenty-eight-year-old Moses Salomon, and his twenty-six-year-old associate, Sigmund Zeisler, who'd just been admitted to the bar, to represent the prisoners. Both were gifted men, but neither had an established reputation, nor the commanding presence in court that might have compensated for it. The Defense Committee was given the responsibility of finding a senior associate to head up the legal team.

William Perkins Black was among the most prominent corporate lawyers in Chicago. A dignified, handsome man of forty-four, Black, at age nineteen, had been awarded the Congressional Medal of Honor during the Civil War for heroism at the Battle of Pea Ridge. It was widely agreed that he had a brilliant future, even though he'd failed in his initial bid for Congress in 1882; running as a Democrat, he'd lost by a handful of votes after giving what his wealthy friends viewed as an inexplicable and ill-advised speech defending the "generous impulses" of the Russian populist movement. Despite that "misstep," many predicted that Captain Black (as he was known) would be Governor before his fiftieth birthday.

Black and his modest, attractive wife, Hortensia, had all the right credentials and connections. Though serious, civic-minded and unpretentious people, they adhered to the conventions of their class: carriage drives and calling cards, tailor-made clothes, dancing lessons with the Borniques (the esteemed husband-and-wife instructors of the moment), and periodic dinners at Rector's, Henrici's or Kinsley's—opulent and exclusive onyx palaces that boasted expensive French wines and specialized pastry chefs. For Captain Black there was a steady routine of lunches at the Chicago Club, where he discussed business and politics with the city's elite, and regular exercise at the Chicago Athletic Club, which, understanding the need of its select membership never to be seen sweating in public, contained carefully secluded handball, squash, and racquetball courts.

On the evening of June 1, a five-person delegation from the Defense Committee called on Captain Black at his home. The delegation was headed by Dr. Ernst Schmidt, a moderate socialist who'd run for several city offices, a man known for his cultivation and learning. Schmidt disliked "extremism" and hadn't joined the IWPA, but he was determined to see that the imprisoned men got proper representation and a fair trial.

Captain Black received the delegation in his study and told them, courteously but without preface, that he was aware of why they had come. He was also aware, he said, that they'd already approached several other attorneys to take on the case and had been turned down.

"That's true," Dr. Schmidt replied, "turned down out-of-hand. The gentlemen in question told us that regardless of what their personal feelings about the justice of the proceedings thus far might be, they were not prepared to risk the consequences of being associated with so unpopular, not to say disreputable, a cause."

"And why would you believe that my response would be any different?" Black asked.

"Because," another delegate said, "you were willing to risk—and lose—election to Congress in order to defend another unpopular cause, that of the Russian populists. And because you're known to be a man of the utmost integrity. In the face of injustice, you could not help but speak out."

Black smiled wryly. "I thank you, sir, for so generous an estimate of my character. But I must tell you that if I had known it would cost me the election, I might never have mentioned the Russians at all."

"Forgive my frankness," Dr. Schmidt said, "but I don't believe you."

"Ah!" Black said, chuckling. "I can see that in the hope of winning me over, you've decided on a strategy of outrageous flattery."

"Not at all," Dr. Schmidt replied. "We describe your character as we see it. And what we see is a love of truth."

Black rose from his chair and slowly began to pace the room. "Are you aware, gentlemen," he asked after a few moments, "that I have met both Mr. Spies and Mr. Parsons?"

There was a murmur of surprise among the delegation. "No, Captain, we were not aware of that," Dr. Schmidt said.

"Yes," Black continued, "I went to hear them speak several times. I was present at that famous gathering at the West Side Philosophical Society, when Parsons gave the derisive crowd a well-deserved tongue lashing, yet somehow did so with suffusing grace. It was quite remarkable to witness."

Emboldened, another delegate asked if Captain Black counted himself a socialist.

Black laughed. "Good heavens, no!" Then he added, quietly, "But I am informed about conditions, and aware that socialism is the product of despair."

Regretting that he'd said more than intended, Black quickly brought the conversation back to the business at hand. "Even if I was inclined to take on your assignment," he said, "I have no confidence that I could execute it competently. You must understand, gentlemen, that I'm a corporate lawyer and have negligible experience in criminal cases."

"We can offer you a retainer," another member of the delegation eagerly put in, misreading Black's moral hesitations for financial ones. "Contributions have begun to pour into the Defense Committee, mostly small sums from ordinary people, but the amount is adding up."

Black felt offended, and his voice stiffened slightly. "I can assure you, gentlemen, that the size of my fee, or even whether there is a fee, would play no role in my deliberations."

Dr. Schmidt hastened to agree. "Of course not," he said with some fervor. "We"—diplomatically, he gestured at the entire delegation—"simply wanted you to know that money for legal expenses does exist. We wouldn't want you to think you'd be without support staff or secretarial assistance."

"I'm glad to hear that so many people are sending in contributions," Black said. "And frankly, I'm a bit surprised, given the intensely hostile climate."

"We were as well, and deeply touched. People have sometimes sent in as little as ten cents, all they could afford, but from every state and territory of the Union and from as far away as Upsala and Bombay. The response is very gratifying."

"This case can be fought and won," one delegate added emphatically.

"And for that to happen, gentlemen, you need a properly qualified attorney," Black replied. "I'm flattered that you're willing to entrust me with this assignment, but I cannot allay my own doubts in regard to my suitability."

Seeing Schmidt's crestfallen look—he seemed on the verge of making some anguished plea—Black hastened on. "What I am prepared to do is find you a lawyer who does have the skill and experience to handle the case. But I'll need a few days. I must make inquiries. And I must hone my powers of persuasion." Black again expressed his gratitude to the delegation for coming to him, and then politely saw them to the front door. They, in turn, thanked him for his time and courtesy.

Over the next few days Captain Black, true to his word, tried his luck with a number of colleagues experienced in criminal law. Uniformly, their eyebrows lifted in astonishment at the proposal, then lowered in suspicion of Black. Why was he on such a mission? Was he a secret sympathizer? Had they misjudged him? Was this respected member of society in covert alliance with its enemies? Most of the men Black approached responded with outward civility, pleading disqualifying outrage at the bomb-throwers, or crowded dockets, or both. But one senior member of his own firm came straight at him, irately accusing him of helping to foment social disorder and predicting, if he persisted on so quixotic a path, social ostracism and professional ruin.

The reaction of the legal world deeply shook Black. Not with fear that he'd ruined his future prospects, but with anger at what he viewed as his colleagues' professional dereliction of duty. Someone had to provide these men with legal counsel. Since no one else would, he realized ruefully, he would, after all, have to take on the case himself.

But before telling Schmidt and the others of his decision, Black wanted his wife's blessing. The result of representing these despised renegades might make the Blacks outcasts, too, and the Captain didn't feel he could comfortably accept the assignment without Hortensia's consent.

Initially, she was shocked and upset. "How can you think of doing such a thing?" she said, nearly in a whisper. "It would threaten all our prospects, perhaps even our livelihood."

"I can't gainsay a word of that," Black said gravely. "But what alternative is there? To let these men go undefended? That would make a mockery of my duty—not only to my profession, but to myself."

"Yourself? What duty, what principle, obliges you to cast us into a pit?"

"My oath to uphold justice." Black said quietly. "I couldn't live with myself if I failed to see that these men get a fair trial."

Neither of them spoke for a few moments. Then Hortensia said, "If I asked you not to take the case, would you go ahead anyway?"

Black felt his throat seize up. He could hardly breathe. "My dearest wife . . ." he said softly, "I know your kind heart. You wouldn't ask that of me . . ."

Hortensia turned silently toward the window and stared out at the trimmed lawn, at the velvety greenness of late spring sparkling in the June sun. When she turned back into the room, her face was free of anger, though there was a hint of melancholy around her eyes.

"You're a noble man, my dearest William. I'm not worthy of you. But I will stand by your side. Firmly by your side."

✳

Thanks to Daniel Hoan, Parsons was able to get hold of the Chicago papers every day. It was there that he learned of his indictment for conspiracy, unlawful assembly, and murder, and where he read, too, the fierce editorials demanding summary justice. Even the labor press, it seemed, was divided, with the *Knights of Labor*, the working-class paper with the largest circulation in the city, declaring that the anarchists "were entitled to no more consideration than wild beasts." At the state convention of the Knights on June 2nd, a resolution passed that offered sympathy to the families of those policemen injured or killed during the Haymarket melee—but not to the families of the equal number of civilians maimed.

The rantings in the Chicago press made the danger of Albert's returning to the city obvious. Yet he persisted in arguing for its necessity. In a second letter smuggled to Lucy, he asked her to confer again with the defense attorneys about the issue of his return. "I promise to abide by their advice," he wrote, "but in my own view, a trial, if an impartial jury can be secured, could only result in my acquittal—since I had no knowledge of the bomb, nor any hand in planning the Haymarket meeting. Even if the attorneys are uncertain if a fair-minded jury can be secured, I'm ready to come to the bar," he wrote Lucy, "if it's judged that my presence during the trial could in any measure prove helpful to my codefendants."

On June 18th, three days before the trial was due to begin, Lucy met with the defense attorneys—who now included a fourth member, William A. Foster. Once Captain Black had made his decision to head the team, he knew that he'd have to persuade a criminal lawyer to join it. Foster, a recent arrival in Chicago from Iowa, proved willing to accept the assignment. Though neither learned nor urbane, Foster, at forty, had had considerable experience in criminal cases and was known as a tough-minded advocate who relished controversy and welcomed a contest of wits. With his wavy red hair, indifferent dress, and constant tobacco chewing, Foster contrasted sharply with the cultivated Captain Black. But Black understood the importance of being complemented rather than duplicated.

After Lucy summarized the contents of Albert's letter to his legal team, Foster was the first to respond. "I feel strongly," he said, "that your husband should not return. It would be suicidal, given the rancorous public senti- ment against him. He's now in a place of safety, surrounded by a cordon of friends, and every effort of the police to discover his whereabouts has failed. He should stay put."

Captain Black offered a rejoinder in the form of a question: "But do you not think, Foster, that if Parsons came into court of his own volition, that the heroism of his gesture could not but favorably impress the jury, and from that, spill over into a softened view of the character of all the defendants?"

"I do not," Foster bluntly replied. "I think, sir, if you will allow me to say so, that you have an overly idealized view of human nature. *You* might regard a voluntary surrender as heroic, but I suspect most will see it as an act of supreme stupidity."

Black was startled at Foster's gruffness. He sat back in his chair, let his chin rest on his hands, and lapsed into silence.

Salomon, one of the two younger members of the legal team, took on the job of responding to Foster. "I might agree with you," he said, "if I thought there was a significant chance of the jury voting for conviction. But there is absolutely no evidence that Parsons ever counseled, aided, abetted, or advised the throwing of a bomb at the Haymarket meeting. He's demonstrably innocent and any dispassionate mind must draw that conclusion."

"It seems to me," Foster said laconically, "that dispassionate minds are at the moment notable for their scarcity."

It was Zeisler's turn to comment. "There's also the matter of Parsons's history. What he did or didn't do at Haymarket will, it seems to me, not weigh as heavily on the scale as the fact that he's been widely known for years as an agitator. He's argued over and over—and this is a matter of public record—against the injustice of the present social system, and warned repeatedly that the fixed refusal of the moneyed classes to ameliorate conditions will plunge the country into revolution. True, he's personally deplored a resort to violence, but he's persisted in predicting that it will soon overwhelm us."

"And what does that lead you to conclude?" Captain Black asked, pensively.

"I can't draw any firm conclusion," Zeisler replied, shaking his head in frustration. "I merely mean to warn that what we see as Parsons's transparent innocence isn't a widely shared opinion. The prosecution will insist that Parsons's words over the years are ultimately responsible for inspiring the bomb-throwing at Haymarket."

Captain Black turned to Lucy. "I would very much value your own view of the matter," he said.

Lucy had sat silent and erect throughout the discussion. Even now, as she spoke, she barely moved. "I do not choose to give an opinion," she said firmly. "I believe that Albert will do what he believes is wise and right. In making that decision, he wishes to take into consideration the views of his attorneys." It was clear from Lucy's tone that she would not be drawn out further.

"Well then," Black said after a moment's pause. "I suggest a formal vote. There is obviously a range of opinion in the room and we need to attach our names to it. What say you? Should Parsons turn himself in?" Black and Salomon voted in the affirmative, Foster in the negative, and Zeisler abstained. Captain Black said that he would compose a letter to Parsons conveying the vote and the essence of the discussion. "I'll express my personal belief that we'll be able to establish his innocence and secure his acquittal, and my further belief that the effect of his participation in the trial cannot but be advantageous to his codefendants. But be assured, gentlemen, that I'll also convey the counterview expressed here today, preeminently by Mr. Foster, that his return is fraught with very real danger to his own safety and freedom."

All four men pushed back their chairs as if to rise in adjournment when, to their surprise, Lucy spoke again: "I believe, gentlemen, that my husband is more aware than even Mr. Foster of the degree of hazard involved in the step he is about to take. On his behalf, I thank you for the earnest consideration you've given his inquiry."

***

Parsons had felt from the start that he should stand trial with his comrades, but hadn't wanted to appear indifferent to the opinions of those closest to him. The letter from Captain Black, though conveying a divided vote, fell on the side of his return. From Lucy, he heard that Lizzie and William Holmes had expressed strong opposition to his "delivering himself to the Philistines." But Lucy, he knew, disagreed with them, though she'd steeled herself against openly expressing an opinion.

On June 19th Parsons sent word through Daniel Hoan that he'd be starting for Chicago the following evening. That afternoon he suggested to his friends in Waukesha that they accompany him to Spence's Hill, his favorite spot. For a time he sat quietly apart, letting the balmy spring air caress his spirit. Then he rejoined the group, his mood cheerful and affectionate. At one point, in a burst of boyish humor, he laid himself out full length on the ground and rolled down the long hill—jumping up at the bottom, flushed and laughing. He later told Hoan that he had no faith in the courts.

That night, one of Hoan's sons hitched a team to a light wagon and they, carrying Parsons's city clothes in a basket, set off on the twenty-mile ride to Milwaukee. From there he caught a 3:00 A.M. train to Chicago. As the train neared Kinzie Street, where it always slowed down, Parsons decided to jump off, thinking he'd be at greatest risk of being spotted if he went all the way in to the depot. But the train was moving faster than he thought, and he hit the ground with a thud, rolling over and over down the incline. He looked up to see a young Irish policeman staring down at him, asking if he was hurt.

"No, I thank you. A bit shaken up is all. I be fine." Parsons affected the slow, ungrammatical speech of a poor country farmer to match his ill-fitting clothes and scraggy beard.

"Why'd ya jump off, anyway?" the officer asked.

"'Cause the Kinzie stop is near to where I be headed," Parsons answered, keeping his composure but fearful of more questions.

"Then you know where you're goin', do ya?"

"Yes indeed, officer. Been there many a time. Thanks for your concern. Good day to you, sir." Parsons hurried off.

"Take better care now," the officer called after him, oblivious to the opportunity that could have catapulted his anonymous life into full-scale celebrityhood.

Parsons went straight to the home of a friend, who greeted him with hugs and tears. While Albert changed clothes, shaved off his beard, and blackened his moustache and hair, the friend sent off a note to inform Lucy that her husband had safely arrived. Her heart in her mouth, Lucy set out with the children. Over the past six weeks, she'd been kept under constant surveillance, never able to leave home without being followed. Assuming that detectives were dogging her steps on this morning, too, she acted as if she were out on a casual walk—pausing to tie Albert Jr.'s shoelace, encouraging Lulu to linger over an attractive bed of flowers—even as she felt near to bursting with wild impatience. Luck was with her: she and the children managed to slip into the friend's house without being seen. She and Albert fell into each other's arms and Lucy, who never cried, burst into racking sobs.

Word was at once conveyed to Captain Black that Parsons had arrived in the city and was prepared to turn himself in. Various comrades worked all morning to complete the necessary arrangements. At 2:00 P.M. Albert and Lucy embraced, assuring each other that all would be well. Albert fiercely hugged Lulu and Albert Jr., then stepped into a waiting hack and told the driver to go directly to the Criminal Courthouse.

Captain Black was pacing agitatedly in front of the building when the cab pulled up and Albert stepped out. Black silently gripped Albert's hand and offered him his arm, and the two men mounted the stairway leading into the building. As they entered the courtroom and headed toward Judge Joseph Gary's bench, several people instantly spotted Parsons and word of his presence spread like an electric current through the court. Then, just as Captain Black was about to address the bench and dramatically announce that Albert Parsons had come to surrender himself for trial, State's Attorney Grinnell, who'd been appointed chief prosecutor in the case, jumped to his feet and shouted, "Your Honor, I see Albert Parsons in the courtroom! I move that he be placed in the custody of the sheriff."

Infuriated at Grinnell's attempt to convert a surrender into an arrest, to deflate the magnanimity of Parsons's act, Black angrily addressed the bench: "Mr. Grinnell's motion, Your Honor, is as gratuitous as it is cruel. As should be apparent, Mr. Parsons has himself made the decision to appear in court." Parsons broke in to say, "I present myself for trial with my comrades, Your Honor."

Judge Gary told him to take his place among the defendants and ordered that another chair be brought. Walking over to the dock, Parsons was warmly greeted by the others and shook hands with each. Smiling, he sat down among them.

Part Seven

The Diary of
Albert R. Parsons

June 22, 1886

So it is done. I sit here in my cell, early morning, waiting to be taken to court for the second day of the trial. I hardly slept last night, thinking of Lucy and the children, of how frightened little Lulu became when the bailiff broke apart our embrace yesterday and gruffly told her: "Go home with your mother." But I mustn't linger over such scenes, of which, I fear, many more are to come, if I'm to sustain my spirits, to say nothing of my sanity.

Which is why I'm turning again to this journal after more than five—or is it six?—years. I must stay occupied, or as much as is possible in this chicken coop they've put us in on the upper tier of the Cook County jail. "Murderers Row" they call it—guilty before being tried—and it is accessible only by a flight of narrow iron stairs at one end of the corridor. Each of us lives in a stone cell that measures six feet by eight and has wire grating on the front just large enough to squeeze our fingers through (poor Neebe, with his huge hands, can barely manage it, and with some pain). My cell, number 29, is the first on the tier, then Fischer follows at 30, Fielden at 31, and so on down the line, with Spies, Engel, Schwab, and Lingg in the middle and Neebe in the last cell. The air barely circulates, but the thick stone walls make it less stiflingly hot here than in the courtroom.

We'll be in court every weekday from 9:30 to 5:00, which will leave many hours still to fill. For most of them, we'll be confined to our cages, with two armed guards constantly pacing back and forth in front of us. In the courtroom as well, we sit jammed together in a row to the left of our counsels' table, closely guarded—on the assumption, I presume, that we'd otherwise be lobbing bombs at the packed rows of spectators.

Twice a day we're allowed short visits, and are also permitted to exercise in the narrow corridor that runs in front of the cells. But we're never allowed out of doors. When locked in our cells, we can call to each other, most easily to our immediate neighbors. We can have brief private conversations only in passing. Under these conditions, time hangs heavily. At least the authorities allow us writing materials and books, and surely these will prove my salvation.

As Spies and I passed each other in court yesterday during an adjournment, he said to me, "You know you've run your neck right into the noose, don't you?" He said it with a sort of mocking admiration, his eyes twinkling with affection. I heard nearly the same words from one of our counselors, a Mr. Foster, as we were being escorted from court later in the day, but in his case they were said with considerable anger, which took me by surprise. He's a rough sort and told me straight out that if I'd been set on turning myself in, I should at least have waited until the jury had been impaneled. That way, he went on, I'd have had a separate trial, and at a time when the public's bloodlust was no longer at fever pitch. I'd also not be in jeopardy, as I now am, of having the "infamous" materials presented in court against "anarchist fanatics" like Lingg and Fischer (how did a man who employs such words get assigned to our case?) rub off on "a more moderate type" like me.

Affronted at Foster's bad temper, I replied curtly that I felt it my duty to stand by my friends in adversity. That seemed further to excite his ill will—I don't know what else to call it. "I suppose," he said with sarcasm, "that you think it was the *manly* thing to do. Well, I have news for you, Mr. Parsons: manliness doesn't demand that one play the fool and willfully subject oneself to the prejudices of an inflamed public opinion. I can assure you that in the city they're not calling you manly for having turned yourself in. They don't even credit you with sincerity—other than with a sincere eagerness to play the martyr. That, and a sincere contempt for the law, a function of your having foolishly decided—am I not right?—that you'll escape punishment because you're the only American-born prisoner among the eight."

Foster's wrath so baffled me that I held my peace. Telling Spies about the exchange later, I learned something of its cause. Yesterday morning, apparently, just before I turned myself in, Foster made a motion for separate trials for each of the defendants, and he and Judge Gary had a bizarre exchange over it. Foster proclaimed that although the court as a matter of justice ought to grant his motion, he didn't expect that it would. To which Gary gave an acid reply: "Well, Mr. Foster, I shall not disappoint you"—and promptly turned the motion down. In response, Foster aimed his tobacco wad at the cuspidor ten feet away and hit it dead center. This produced some tittering, and a few gasps, in the courtroom, but infuriated Spies. "How dare our own counsel," he said, "and on the very first day, further prejudice our case by going out of his way to insult the court? Surely Foster knows—everyone knows—that Gary is strongly biased against us as it is."

"*I* didn't know it," I said, "He's long been outspoken against unions, but I thought he had the reputation for presiding in a fair and impartial manner."

"That's his reputation," Spies replied, "but whether it's warranted you can soon enough decide for yourself. I think he's dead-set against us. And Foster's grandstanding will only make matters worse. Captain Black is as good a man as ever lived, but I find it inexplicable that he's added Foster to our legal team."

"Perhaps," I said, "Foster is the only criminal lawyer he could get. Didn't Foster volunteer his services after Black had been turned down everywhere?"

"Yes, shrewd lout that he is. He must have decided, as a new arrival in the city, that he could win attention—and clients—by participating in such a trial."

June 24

I'm beginning to see what Spies means about Judge Gary. The process of jury selection has begun, and hour after hour has passed without a single candidate being deemed acceptable. Nor has one industrial worker been called; it's as if a whole class of people has been disqualified before the process even began. Gary apparently disregarded the standard procedure for safeguarding a fair trial—drawing the names of prospective jurors out of a box containing many hundreds taken randomly from the rolls of the citizenry.

June 26

It seems—we're learning as we go along—that when choosing jurors in a murder case, the law allows for an unlimited number of challenges based on "cause," or demonstrable bias, but Judge Gary has been overruling every such challenge. This forces Captain Black to use a "peremptory" challenge when he wants to disqualify a prejudiced juror. The trouble is, the number of peremptory challenges allowed is limited (each defendant is allotted twenty). With Judge Gary overruling him on every motion to dismiss for cause, the Captain says he must begin accepting as jurors men who show *some* degree of fairness and candor. Otherwise, he warns, we'll run out of peremptory challenges and have to accept a far more viciously hostile set of jurors. He told us today, shifting his body uncomfortably, that we should prepare ourselves for the possibility that we'll end up with a jury convinced of our guilt before hearing a word of testimony.

June 27

Our wives have been present in court every day, though the strain on them is terrible. Our children are allowed only a brief moment on our knees before being yanked away by a guard. Judge Gary seems hugely pleased with himself for allowing us to glimpse our children each day. He's presented it as a magisterial act of generosity and mercy, oblivious to what a cruel mercy it is.

June 28

Two more days of jury examination. Still only three jurors impaneled. What with the oppressive heat and fitful sleep at night, I can hardly keep focused on the proceedings. The tedious questioning, the blurred procession of men, the repetition, have made me numb. My mind wanders back to Waukesha, to Spence's Hill overlooking the valley, the budding spring foliage, the clean air . . . Schwab, on the other hand, who sits next to me, seems utterly absorbed. He leans forward intently lest he miss a single word. A scholar in all things . . .

June 29

Lucy has visited faithfully every day. The only absent wife is Meta Neebe, a fragile soul who's taken her husband's imprisonment hard and has fallen ill. We're rarely allowed to be alone with our wives in our cells, and must mostly talk through the grate or sit, in full view of the guards, in the small alcove at the end of the corridor. Still, it's a great comfort just to hold Lucy's hand and feel her warmth. Ever a believer in action, she's been doing battle, working closely with the Defense Committee to organize picnics and raffles to raise money, writing articles for the labor press—or what's left of it, the police having shuttered the *Alarm* as well as the *Arbeiter*. When I ask her about the children, I can tell by the way she avoids my eyes that she's trying to spare me.

"Oh, they've long since gotten used to your being away," she said today, "since you're always off giving speeches or the like . . ."

"Do they understand what a prison is?" I asked, knowing full well that seven-year-old Albert Jr. surely does.

"I tell them the truth," Lucy said, "that the bad people have put you here because of your struggle to help the poor."

"And what does Albert say to that?"

"He asked if they are poorer than us." Lucy made an effort to laugh, but it came out constricted, almost like a gargle. She did tell me that she's been losing customers at the dress shop at a rapid clip and that we might have to consider moving to a cheaper flat. That she would mention the possibility means it's a foreordained conclusion.

June 30

More stuporous monotony; still only four jurors have been chosen. Two days ago Judge Gary announced the appointment of one Henry Ryce as a special bailiff to seek out and summon men who might qualify as jurors. "A necessary expedient for speeding up the selection process." But Captain Black tells us that Ryce has privately boasted that he intends to summon only such men as will force Black to use up all of his peremptory challenges, and that this is the real reason Judge Gary has appointed him.

July 1

Bailiff Ryce has been doing his masters' work well. He had the gall today to summon a man who's kin to M. D. Flavin, one of the policemen killed at Haymarket, and then called a close friend of another dead officer's family! In both cases Gary overruled Captain Black's challenge for cause—as he did with a man who said flat out, "I hardly think you could bring proof enough to change my negative opinion of these anarchists." But the most outlandish moment came when one potential juror admitted that he believed we were guilty and felt his belief would prove a "handicap" in hearing evidence impartially; to which Judge Gary replied, "Nonsense! The more a man is aware of his handicap, the more he will be on guard against it." Such blatant bias on the part of a presiding judge is nearly beyond belief, were I not already familiar with the lengths to which the propertied class and its minions will go in defending their privilege.

Foster told me that before I turned myself in, he had already tried arguing before the bench that the trial was taking place far too soon after the deaths in Haymarket and entirely too near the home of the families of the policemen who were killed. But Judge Gary turned a deaf ear to him.

July 2

Louis Lingg deeply intrigues me. Before the trial, we'd never met. Since he speaks little English, and I no German, we can't talk together. Yet from simply watching him, I've gotten a strong sense of his admirably fierce, independent character. He sits in court hour after hour reading a book or staring idly ahead, not deigning to acknowledge the activity around him, making the clear point that he doesn't accept the court's legitimacy. His defiance is made more impressive still by his remarkable physical presence. He has a powerful build (Spies says he's a dedicated gymnast) and exudes a kind of smoldering, volcanic energy. He has as handsome a head as I've ever seen: curly chestnut hair, pale white skin and piercing blue eyes. A veritable Greek god—a contemptuous, wrathful one.

July 3

I was allowed a visit today with Lizzie and William, a short one because both are "notorious radicals." During the whole of it, a guard stood directly outside my cell. Lizzie, dear soul, was fighting back tears the entire time. I tried to convince her that I remain cheerful and that despite the prejudicial way jury selection is proceeding, I remain confident that I'll be able to establish my innocence. Lizzie smiled wanly and started to say something, but I saw her catch herself mid-sentence, fearful of dampening my spirits.

William told me that in the wake of Haymarket, eight-hour strikes have been failing almost everywhere; workers are more fearful and the police quicker to use their muscle. These cycles are inevitable, I said, and a temporary downturn mustn't be viewed as a permanent defeat. We're on the right side even if, at a given moment, it's the losing one. I must believe that nothing in "human nature"—that grab-bag phrase for whatever can't otherwise be explained—prevents like-minded people from discovering their common interests and acting together to secure them.

I asked Lizzie for her frank assessment of how Lucy and the children are faring, and she assured me that I need never worry about Lucy: she's steadfast in her optimism and formidable in her energetic pursuit of my vindication. As for the children, Lizzie thinks they're basically doing well, though Albert Jr. is of an age where he has some understanding of what's at stake, and concomitant fears for his father's safety. Lizzie thinks it would be advisable to send both the children to Waukesha until the trial is over. "But wouldn't they then be bereft of both father and mother?" I replied. Lizzie says they'd be in good and loving hands and that the distance is not so far that Lucy couldn't visit often. In Waukesha the children would be given little or no news of the trial, and therefore not be subject to constant frights. Besides, their absence would free up Lucy's time for advocacy. I can see some merit to the plan, but I'm not convinced. A loving mother close at hand seems to me the best stay against dread.

July 4

Independence Day. We had a shortened court session so that Judge Gary, chief prosecutor Grinnell and other Defenders of the Republic could go off and perform their various patriotic duties—from saluting the state militia as it parades by to responding to toasts of congratulation at the Union League Club for having corralled the wild-eyed terrorists bent on destroying Our Sacred Liberties (like the liberty to pay starvation wages so they can erect their second marble palace). How they'd laugh at the suggestion that true patriots concern themselves with the welfare of the whole people . . .

July 7

The tedious process of jury selection grinds on, in stifling heat and in still more stifling monotony. Hundreds upon hundreds of men have been summoned over the past few weeks and yet only seven have been seated. Not that those seven could be called impartial; each has admitted to varying degrees of distaste for socialists and anarchists, and shown considerable gullibility about what they've read in the mainstream press about us.

Counselor Zeisler explained to me why we persist in challenging for cause when it's obvious Judge Gary will continue to overrule: "To make a strong case, should the jury convict, for an appeal to the Supreme Court to set aside the verdict because of Gary's erroneous rulings." That word "convict" made me swallow hard. Knowing our innocence—though it's true I can't vouch for Lingg—and the enormous weight of evidence that supports it, I've been pretty steadily optimistic up to now. I've always known that conviction was a possibility, since the "weight of evidence" has no influence with tyrants. Zeisler isn't one to overdramatize.

July 10

Today a juror was accepted who admitted that he thought the *accusation* of guilt is presumptive evidence of its truth! Captain Black withheld a peremptory challenge, deciding that an uninformed mind was preferable to one filled with fixed convictions. Alanson Reed, a merchant of considerable standing in the city, has also been seated, even though, under questioning, he declared a strong aversion to socialism. Black has some slight acquaintance with Reed and has from time to time heard rumors that he's something of a free-thinker—at least as defined within entrepreneurial circles! Thus has Bailiff Ryce cleverly shrunk our range of choice. It was either Reed or the candidate who proudly declared earlier today, "If I am seated on this jury, I will hang all the damned buggers."

July 12

I had a strange dream last night. I was a young boy back in the Brazos River Valley on my brother's ranch, riding bareback on a wild Mexican mustang. I was all alone and full of joy. I suddenly caught sight of a woman lying by the side of a hill. Kneeling down beside her, I discovered it was my beloved Aunt Ester, the slave and house servant in my brother's family who mostly raised me. She woke up, took me in her arms, and gently rocked me back and forth. A huge crow suddenly landed on her face and began clawing at it. When I tried to fight the crow off, it turned into a rattler and bit me on the neck. Screaming out in pain, I woke up. The guard was banging his stick against the mesh of my cell. I couldn't understand where I was. "Parsons!" the guard kept calling out, not unkindly. "Parsons—wake up, wake up! You've roused the whole cellblock with your yelling." By then I'd come to my senses, but as I lay awake in the dark I felt profoundly shaken. Aunt Ester's face has remained before me all day.

The dream follows on a letter I had yesterday from my brother, announcing his intention of coming to Chicago to attend the trial once it begins. The news came as a great surprise and stirred up conflicting emotions. William and I haven't seen each other in some fifteen years, and during the Reconstruction period we sharply differed in our politics. He once announced his intention of writing a book warning against the dangers of the superior white race submitting to "mongrelization." My marriage to Lucy put an end to all contact between us.

Yet now he writes that he's had a change of heart politically. In Virginia, where he currently lives, he's joined the Knights and has written a pamphlet denouncing Northern monopolists who manipulate the economy for their own advantage, determined to prevent the South from rebuilding (so he hasn't changed beyond recognition!). He tells me straight out that he doesn't share my "extreme" views, yet he's apparently gone out of his way to contradict reports in the press that he's repudiated me.

"I've issued a statement," William writes, "declaring my belief that you are fighting for principle and applauding you for having the courage of your convictions. I have also expressed my anger and amazement that your voluntary surrender has not won you more credit. Speaking as a general in the Confederacy, I've declared that among belligerents in actual war, such an act of intrepidity as yours would have insured your honorable discharge; and that among savage tribes such a surrender would have insured your elevation to the chieftainship."

He even sends regards to Lucy, and expresses his anticipated pleasure in making her acquaintance and getting to know our children. When I told all this to Lucy today, I thought she might be dismissive and say something along the lines of "too little, too late." But instead she seemed merely indifferent, brushing off the news of my alienated brother's reappearance as being about as significant as the addition of sugar water to the prison diet.

July 15

This morning Captain Black used up his last peremptory challenge. The seating of the very next, and twelfth, juror was therefore a foregone conclusion. The gentleman turned out to be one H. T. Sanford, who said he had no reason to believe that newspaper accounts of our guilt were false, and gratuitously added, "I have an opinion in my own mind that the defendants encouraged the throwing of that bomb."

It has taken twenty-one days and the processing of 931 candidates to produce this jury of "twelve good men and true"—which is to say, a jury with only one man born on foreign soil, and with no industrial workers. Mr. F. S. Osborne, a head salesman for the Marshall Field department store, has been chosen as foreman. At the announcement that the jury process had been completed, cheers filled the courtroom. With so partisan a jury, there's understandable cause for gloom, and some of our comrades have given way to it (especially poor Schwab, who is as tender as a dove). Yet I go with Captain Black in his conviction that if the verdict goes against us, it'll never stand up in a higher court. Besides, he doesn't believe the verdict will go against us.

Immediately after the jury was seated, State's Attorney Grinnell leapt to his feet—as if a jack-in-the-box had been sprung—and launched full steam into his opening remarks. That he aims for melodrama above truth was instantly apparent. "For the first time in the history of our country, people are on trial for their lives for endeavoring to make anarchy the rule, and ruthlessly and awfully destroying life."

As if he begins to understand what Anarchism means! He equates it, or wants the jury to, with nihilism and violence, which in fact are the polar opposites of what we actually stand for. We believe that human beings are innately social and that once freed from the tyranny of traditional pieties and institutionalized authority would form communities based on mutual affinity and assistance. Anarchy is a belief in human possibilities. The Grinnells of the world want us to believe that slavish obedience to authority is all that protects us from our own bestial nature. Dutiful sons of Calvin, they see life as the war of each against all. We stress the responsibility of each for all and insist that human nature, inherently compassionate and companionable, makes such a social goal feasible. I suppose that does make us "traitors" of a sort—traitors to the ingrained American view that success in life is best measured by the accumulation of status and goods, and that an individual's "failure" is caused solely by his own moral deficiencies.

Grinnell's ignorance and distortions set my blood a-boil. The man has no commitment to truth. He sees this case as the opportunity of a lifetime, and would happily sacrifice our lives to advance his career. He describes our characters and motives in the vilest of terms. I myself came in for an extra share of abuse today: "Parsons is a coward who never did a manly thing in his life—all the more shameful for someone born on our soil."

But it was Spies who got the worst of it. Grinnell portrayed him as some sort of moral monster, intent on destruction for its own sake, a man who relentlessly preaches the doctrine of bloodshed and riot. He insists that Spies is at the center of a secret, diabolical conspiracy to bomb the city to ruins; accuses him of personally instigating the violence at the McCormick plant—and then running away from the scene to save himself; of planting secret words in the *Arbeiter* to signal the other plotters that the moment for a general uprising had arrived; of then attempting to use the Haymarket meeting to inaugurate a citywide orgy of bomb-throwing, an attempt foiled only by the "timely and wise" intervention of police inspector Bonfield; and so on, and so on. Throughout, Grinnell's voice throbbed with such histrionic zeal that if ever the term *extremist* applied to any man it surely belongs to him. To top it off, he had the gall to tell the jury, his eyes droopy with fake sincerity, "I hope I shall not at any time during this trial say anything to you which will in any way or manner excite your passions." How does the man live with himself?

The jury seemed mesmerized throughout, but that doesn't mean, I like to believe, that they're foolish enough to swallow Grinnell's wild fabrications whole. Captain Black tells us that much will hinge on the plausibility of the link Grinnell will try to establish between the bomb-thrower's act and the words we've spoken and written over the years that purportedly encourage such acts. The key to Grinnell's strategy was revealed, the Captain said, when he told the jury that "perhaps none of these men personally threw that bomb, but each and all abetted, encouraged, and advised the throwing of it, and therefore are as guilty as the individual who in fact did throw it. They are accessories." In case Grinnell can't produce the actual bomb-thrower—though Captain Black says he'll try to pin the deed on Rudolph Schnaubelt, Schwab's brother-in-law and a member of the IWPA—he's cleverly laid the groundwork for arguing that the actual murderer need not be named, nor even indicted, in order for the jury to find *us* guilty.

July 16

Grinnell today called as the first witness "for the people," Inspector John
Bonfield. As he moved to take the stand, applause broke out in the packed
courtroom. Judge Gary lightly pounded his gavel for order, but his avun-
cular smile contradicted any suggestion of a reprimand. Bonfield spoke
with the snappy assurance of a man confident of his audience, even as he
boldly lied to it. He claimed some thousand people were in Haymarket
when the police arrived—in fact there were maybe two hundred—and
then described how, immediately after the bomb exploded, "firing poured
in on us" from all sides, "from seventy-five to a hundred pistol shots before
a shot was fired by any officer." Yet even the mainstream press reported
that the police opened fire with such reckless speed that they managed to
kill several of their own officers. Mayor Harrison himself has described
the crowd as peaceable and unarmed.

Following Bonfield's brief appearance, Gottfried Waller took the stand.
We knew in advance that he'd be testifying for the prosecution, indeed,
that he'd be the centerpiece in building its case for a "widespread conspiracy." Still, seeing one of our own IWPA stalwarts, a dedicated social
revolutionary, in the embrace of our enemies, was painful to behold.
His drooping shoulders and downcast look gave the appearance of a man
unhappy with his assignment. But I may well be imagining or embellish-
ing what I would like to believe is true.

As the man who chaired the notorious meeting of May 3rd at Greif's
Hall, Waller's testimony carried special authority. Yet the story he told
was full of distortions and outright lies, as Fisher and Engel, the only
defendants present at that May 3rd meeting, later assured us. According
to Waller, Engel presented a plan at Grief's, which the group adopted,
that called for an armed response to revenge the recent massacre at the
McCormick plant. The signal for the uprising would, according to Waller,
be the appearance of the word *Ruhe* (quiet, rest) in prominent letters in the
Arbeiter. In the paper's edition of May 4th, *Ruhe* did appear, in the "Letterbox"
column of announcements, which meant (so the prosecution would have
the jury believe) that in Haymarket Square that evening, the Revolution
would begin. Yet Waller himself admitted that at the May 3rd gathering
at Greif's, the pending Haymarket meeting was scarcely discussed and
the possibility that the police would attempt an intervention there was
never once mentioned. If a "conspiracy" *had* been decided upon at Greif's,

no one seems to have dreamt that it should or would commence the very next night at Haymarket. Indeed it was specifically suggested that men carrying arms should stay away from that meeting altogether!

Tonight in the cellblock, Engel told us that the "plan" he's accused of having presented at Grief's on May 3rd was nothing more than a vague suggestion that workers stop turning the other cheek and start responding to force with force. Those at the meeting, he said, had been equally vague when expressing agreement with him. Nobody had spoken of particular timetables or detailed strategies. Most of those present, Engel says, simply shared his view that one day, a proletarian uprising would take place, and when it did, they would be ready to lend their support. What the so-called conspiracy amounted to was a group of men expressing their conviction, widespread in the working-class, that the shape of the future has been unavoidably set.

I'm sure Engel is telling the truth, though I suspect he's downplaying the rage he expressed that night at Greif's. It had been but a few hours, after all, since the slaughter at the McCormick plant. Spies had poured his outrage into his overwrought editorial. And had I been in town, I might well have given way to some sort of ill-considered passion. So might any one. Only those indifferent to suffering—the Cyrus McCormicks of the world—can maintain composure in the face of human misery.

In any case, by the time our counsel was done with Waller, his credibility had been shredded. Captain Black got him to admit that he had no idea why the word *Ruhe* appeared in the *Arbeiter* on the fourth—that no "gong" had in fact been sounded—and to admit, further, that Spies, the paper's editor, was ignorant of the significance of *Ruhe* as any sort of "signal"; he had simply inserted it in the "Letterbox" in the same automatic way he did other announcements that came in to the paper.

Waller even admitted on the stand that it was after the police had threatened him with indictment for conspiracy that he'd agreed to cooperate. He further acknowledged that he's been at Central Station every day for the past two weeks discussing the shape his testimony should take, and matter-of-factly added that the police had written out portions of it for him to memorize. He even revealed that he's been financially compensated for his time and that Captain Schaack has helped him find a job. Perhaps Waller's had a change of heart. Why else would he have played so directly into Black's hands?

I would have assumed that the revelation of perjured testimony and police complicity in it would immediately result in the declaration of a mistrial, if not the dismissal of the indictments themselves. But apparently my naiveté is bottomless. When Waller stepped down from the stand, the trial proceeded with a recess so short, we barely had time to stretch our legs.

July 20

Having failed thus far to prove the existence of a "conspiracy," let alone any persuasive connection between the meeting at Greif's on May 3rd and the events that took place at Haymarket on the fourth, the prosecution has shifted its focus on to Rudolph Schnaubelt, who was indicted with the rest of us but has disappeared. To make his case against Schnaubelt, Grinnell's been calling a ragtag string of witnesses to the stand. His two "stars" have been a Mr. M. M. Thompson, who works in dry goods at the Marshall Field Company, and a Mr. Harry L. Gilmer, whose employment history seems as clouded as his sense of truth.

Thompson testified that during the Haymarket rally, he followed Spies and Schwab into Crane's Alley and overheard the words *pistol* and *police* exchanged. Moving closer, Thompson claims to have heard Spies say, "Do you think one is enough, or hadn't we better go and get more?" A few minutes later, Thompson insists, he heard Schwab say, "Now, if they come, we will give it to them." At that point, according to Thompson, the two were joined by a third man. Spies handed the man a large object, which he put in his right-hand pocket. That was Grinnell's cue to whip out a photograph of Schnaubelt, whom Thompson dutifully identified as the third man in question.

On cross-examination, it emerged that Thompson had never previously seen either Spies or Schwab, that between the word *pistol* and the word *police* he had heard nothing at all, and, most damning, that he himself doesn't speak German! Thompson tried to claim that Spies and Schwab conversed in English that night, but Captain Black called up witnesses who established beyond question that the two men, when together, *always* spoke German. "It hardly seems likely," Foster acidly told the court, "that two men plotting a murderous crime would revert to using a language more readily understood by bystanders—and would speak up loudly enough to be overheard by a man standing some six feet away."

Other witnesses conclusively demonstrated that Schwab went to Haymarket from the *Arbeiter* office that night solely to give Spies a message imploring him to come at once to address a meeting in progress at the Deering plant. Unable to find Spies after searching for him in the crowd for fifteen minutes, Schwab went off to Deering to fill the speaking engagement himself. In short, Spies and Schwab never even crossed paths that night in Haymarket!

Unfazed at having had one star witness demolished, Grinnell promptly called a second. Gilmer proved, if anything, a still greater disaster for the prosecution. He claimed that after the police had entered Haymarket, Spies climbed down off the wagon and joined several men in Crane's Alley. "One of them was him," Gilmer said, pointing to Fischer, seated in the dock. Spies had then, according to Gilmer, lit a match to some object another man was holding. "A fuse then commenced to fizzle," Gilmer testified, "and the second man then tossed it into the column of police." Once again the photograph of Schnaubelt was produced, and once again the witness identified him, without hesitation, as the man who threw the bomb. A pat enough narrative—but alas for the prosecution, markedly different from the version Gilmer had earlier given to a reporter from the *Chicago Times*. In the *Times* interview, Gilmer had never mentioned Spies at all and had insisted that one and the same man lit and threw the bomb, and the man he described bore not the slightest resemblance to Schnaubelt.

The prosecution offered no corroborating evidence for Gilmer's testimony—in either of its versions. Captain Black, on the other hand, produced *thirteen* witnesses to the effect that Spies had not left the wagon after the police arrived until Captain Ward gave the order to disperse. When Spies did then step down, someone tried to shoot him and he was saved by his brother lunging between him and the would-be assassin. As for Fischer's purported role in the bomb-throwing, Captain Black proved that at that fateful moment, Fischer was not even in Haymarket Square, but rather at Zepf's Hall. That Gilmer was a venal and inveterate liar was testified to over and over again by the nine neighbors and acquaintances Captain Black produced. Two of them went so far as to insist that Gilmer was "not to be believed even under oath!"

What a wondrous debacle! Our spirits soared. After the hearings ended for the day, Lucy came by with some roast chicken and we feasted on the imminence of our vindication and release. Captain Black and his wife, Hortensia—she's attended every session—stopped by, and they seemed as pleased as we with how things are going. Captain Black did feel compelled to remind us that the prosecution is far from finished. He predicted that they'd next shift their focus on to Lingg; having failed to establish him as the bomb-*thrower*, they'd now try to target him as the bomb-*maker*. "No, I fear we're not yet done," the Captain said, though his face shone with satisfaction. "We can raise a toast soon enough, I hope," he said, "but perhaps not just yet."

July 24

Captain Black's predictions have proven accurate. The prosecution spent the last four days proving that Lingg manufactured bombs. Not a difficult feat, given the contrivances and tools found in his flat, in combination with the "eyewitness" testimony of his landlord and onetime comrade, William Seliger, now turned state's evidence, who claims to have assisted in the bomb-making. What did prove difficult to establish was any link between Lingg's bombs and the one thrown in Haymarket, or between Lingg and ourselves—since most of the defendants had never met Lingg prior to the indictments and the few of us who had, knew of him in a distant way only.

Several professors of chemistry and the like were called upon to examine the few fragments of the Haymarket bomb that have been recovered. They testified that they'd found comparable percentages of various metals—though in different proportions, they acknowledged—in that bomb and in the ones Lingg had manufactured at home. This was still a long way from proving that it was one of Lingg's bombs that had been thrown in Haymarket, and even further away from proving that Lingg himself had thrown it—since it's been clearly established that the closest he ever got to Haymarket that evening was some two miles distant.

When Captain Schaack testified, he managed to drag Johann Most into the picture, knowing that the mere mention of the leading advocate of terror would frighten the jurors. Schaack claimed on the stand that Lingg told him, when incarcerated at Central Station, that he'd learned to make bombs from Most's pamphlet, *The Science of Revolutionary Warfare.* Which may or may not be true, but the whole point of saying so was to allow Mr. Grinnell to read the *entire* pamphlet aloud to the jury—without bothering to establish whether the rest of the defendants had ever seen it (I, for one, have not).

July 25

The trial's become the leading attraction in the social calendar. Even during jury selection, the courtroom was packed, but now fashionable young ladies are attending in droves, delighted to put aside their needlecraft and dancing lessons in favor of this modern-day Coliseum, where dangerous heretics and foreigners are forced to fight for their lives to amuse a dulled aristocracy. And there they sit in the front rows, dressed in their finery, munching candy, giggling among themselves as they inspect the defendants and call each other's attention to this one's depraved lower jaw or that one's shifty eyes. If they catch one of their number staring overlong at the handsome Spies or Lingg, the giggling redoubles as they mock her.

Judge Gary often invites several of the more socially prominent, or attractive, young matrons to sit with him on the bench, and he chats away with them even while testimony is in progress. Today he outdid himself. A particularly comely woman sat beside him and he entertained her as if the two were fellow guests at a seaside resort, drawing pictures for her amusement and then helping her complete a puzzle that had been vexing her!

On Sundays, special guests of the court are allowed to wander among the jail cells, to inspect the beasts at close range. Lingg has found the perfect strategy for dealing with the parade of visitors: when they approach his cage, he uses his gymnastic skills to swing from the cell bars, grunting and scratching himself like an orangutan.

Meanwhile the jury members, in contrast to the prisoners, are being treated with the utmost deference and courtesy. They're living in an expensive hotel directly across from the courthouse and on Sundays are given carriage rides along the promenades of the rich. If they want to visit home, all they need say is that a family member is feeling indisposed.

July 26

I know perfectly well from my own experience that even among the rich there are a few of exceptional sensitivity. After all, we've had two prominent men of property willing to testify to the utter unreliability of Gilmer as a witness, despite likely retribution from members of their class. And our own Captain Black, who long traveled in the highest social circles, has jeopardized his standing and income in defending us. Mrs. Black, who rumor has it was initially against her husband accepting the assignment, has shown profound concern for our plight and, at the cost of increasing social isolation, openly expresses her sympathy for us to her privileged circle. Good and compassionate people are to be found everywhere, yes, even among the upper crust. Most of the young women who appear in court do so infrequently, and sometimes but once. But a few attend the sessions regularly, and follow the proceedings with the utmost attention and seriousness. One such is Miss Nina Van Zandt, who's been here nearly every day, often accompanied by her elegant mother, Mrs. James K. Van Zandt.

On one of the first days of the trial, I scanned the room, as I always do, for Lucy. And there she was seated between two of the more fashionably gowned female spectators, who looked to be mother and daughter. I noticed that the seats directly next to the three were unoccupied, though such is the size of the crowd that there aren't ever enough seats to go round. Then it suddenly dawned on me that this must be Lucy's client Nina Van Zandt and her mother, about whom she's told me so much.

I'm amazed at the audacity of the Van Zandt women, seating themselves so visibly at Lucy's side. During an adjournment, moreover, they came up to the docket with Lucy to be introduced to me. Mrs. Van Zandt did seem somewhat ill at ease, but Nina chatted away as breezily as if we'd all just met at a fancy dress ball.

Then this evening, still accompanied by her mother, Nina (as she insists we call her) visited the prison for the first time. Since they're not relatives of the defendants, they were allotted only a few minutes. But the daughter managed to exchange pleasantries with several of us, and she sat alone for a brief spell with Spies, who later told us how sincere she seemed in her determination to help.

July 27

Since six of us were not even present at Haymarket at the time the bomb was thrown, the prosecution has been leaning hard on Spies and Fielden. Having failed in his earlier effort to identify Spies as the man who tossed or at least lit the bomb, Grinnell is now trying to portray Fielden, the gentlest of men, as determinedly bent on violence that night. One witness has claimed that Fielden called outright in his speech for the killing of policemen, and Lieutenant Quinn has sworn on the stand that as the police approached, Fielden cried out, "Here they come now, the bloodhounds! Do your duty men, and I'll do mine!"—a claim that three eyewitnesses, and Fielden himself, emphatically deny. Several other officers have insisted that Fielden fired directly at the police, but State's Attorney Grinnell has been notably sloppy in getting them to coordinate their stories: One officer has Fielden firing *before* the bomb exploded, another immediately afterwards; one has him firing while still on top of the wagon, another after having taken cover behind it. As if all this wasn't muddle enough, two police lieutenants have categorically stated that "*no* shot was fired before the explosion of the bomb."

In any reasonable mind such vagaries and contradictions would be regarded as a mockery of jurisprudence, an indelible stain on the veracity of Grinnell and his motley array of witnesses. The case would by this time have been thrown—or laughed—out of court. But instead Judge Gary has occupied himself with the strenuous demands of playing host to fashionable Chicago, and to mechanically overruling all of Captain Black's objections on points of law. The prosecution, knowing it has in Judge Gary an automatic ally, has marched blithely on, treating an unmasked bit of perjury here, an exposed set of contradictions there, as mere peccadilloes, acting much as a chipper schoolboy might when reprimanded for poor penmanship.

As each of the prosecution's tactics has backfired—"exploded" would be the more apt description—it's simply proceeded on to the next, like a patent medicine salesman quick to suggest calomel when the patient throws up the previously touted Castoria. Having to date failed to prove that any of us threw the bomb, or fired at the police, or suggested in speeches from the wagon that anyone else do so (in this regard, Mayor Harrison himself took the stand to reaffirm what he's now said many times over: that the speeches given at Haymarket that night were "tame"), Grinnell has perforce fallen back on his last hope for making a case against us: that through our earlier speeches and writings we urged and abetted violence. Captain Black tells us that over the next few days, before the prosecution begins its summation, it will try to convince the jury that our persistent advocacy of force in the years prior to the throwing of the bomb in Haymarket makes us as guilty of murder as the person who actually threw it. He warns us that this latest shift in tactics could prove more formidable than anything preceding. "I have been reading consecutive runs of the *Alarm* and the *Arbeiter*," he told us gravely, "and I must say to you in all frankness, gentlemen, that they contain numerous sentiments that I do not personally share and which, more importantly, can be used to prejudicial effect against you."

Spies, in his sardonic way, asked Captain Black if the First Amendment, guaranteeing freedom of speech, had recently been abolished without his having noticed.

"No, Mr. Spies," Black gently answered, "but nor has it ever been consistently applied."

July 28

After a dozen years apart, William and I saw each other this morning. The change in him is marked. He's grown bald and portly, and more than a little blustery. But I'm deeply grateful to him for standing by me. He's already paying the price, he tells me: shunned by neighbors, hints passed that his post as inspector of customs at Newport News may be in jeopardy. But he feels it's his duty to defend me—not my views, most of which he finds "grievously wrongheaded," but my right to express them. An old states-rights man, he's grown concerned in recent years over the proliferating power of the corporations. "Nobody else is standing up to Jay Gould," is how he puts it. We talked about all sorts of matters, and at some length; the guards tend to be permissive when the visitor is a bona fide relative. Having practiced law for a time, William is keenly interested in the judicial procedures of the trial. He's been astounded, he says, at the flagrant bias of the proceedings, and is utterly confident of an outright acquittal. Seeing William again has moved me deeply, flooding me with memories.

July 30

For three full days, the prosecution has been relentlessly reading aloud excerpts from the *Alarm* and the *Arbeiter* into the official record, along with portions of our other writings and speeches. They've done their homework. They seem to have found every reference any of us ever made to violence in any form, and they heighten the negative effect by taking words out of context. They even read Lucy's "To Tramps," and Lizzie's article, "Dynamite!" into the record, despite the fact that neither has been indicted or is on trial. The prosecution drags them and others in because it's trying to establish the existence of a widespread and vicious conspiracy of which the eight of us who are actual defendants constitute but a small part.

Both Lucy and Lizzie, at the time they wrote those pieces, were mesmerized by Johann Most, and I remember trying to get them to tone down certain sections. But they would have none of it, and the articles appeared in the *Alarm*, to my discomfort, as originally written. I'd pretty much forgotten the contents and was startled at some of it, especially Lucy's assertion that tramps who couldn't find work and were in danger of perishing from exposure and hunger should remember that "the voice of force is the only voice which tyranny has ever been able to understand." But this heated rhetoric came at times of great public excitement, when hyperbole was the national style. Lucy's article had been in direct response to the 1885 events at Lemont—which went unmentioned in the courtroom—when the militia had bayoneted and shot quarry workers who'd gone out on strike for a living wage.

Just as we hear nothing in the courtroom of the murderous action of the soldiery against the people, so we've heard nothing of the violent rhetoric—more than a match for anything Lucy or Lizzie ever said or wrote—with which the propertied classes and the press have egged the troops on. None of us can forget, even if the court has managed to, the *Chicago Tribune*'s suggestion that when a tramp asks for bread, "put strychnine or arsenic on it and he will trouble you no more." Or the blunt prescription offered by Tom Scott, president of the Pennsylvania Railroad, during the 1877 strike: "Give them the rifle diet."

Why aren't these people being tried for murder, or its incitement? They advocated and *initiated* violence, yet remain at liberty. The prosecution wants to convict us of murder on the basis of our opposition to the current social order—for our political views—yet hails the Captain Bonfields, who have committed actual deeds of murder, as "saviors of law and order."

Yesterday, the prosecution inflamed the jury, without interruption or caution from Judge Gary, with a display of the dead Officer Mathias Degan's torn and bloodied vestments. Grinnell was allowed to play the role of Marc Anthony pointing to the rent in Caesar's garment where Brutus "plucked his cursed steel away." But there's no dispute whatever about the cause and place of Degan's death, only as to who committed the deed, and the vengeful, prejudicial display of his sadly stained raiments did nothing to solve that mystery, nor was it intended to.

Why not exhibit the tattered garments I saw young girls wearing in Canton when I spoke in the Ohio coal region last February?—show the jury pictures of those tiny, emaciated little children scraping snow from the railroad tracks, hunting for a few nuggets of coal that a passing train might have dropped?

Why not display the bodies of the strikers barbarously killed at Martinsburg by militia bullets during the Great Railroad Strike? Or the body of the teenage boy, his brains oozing out of his head, shot dead by the Chicago police on the Halsted Street viaduct for the crime of happening to be on the street during a police rampage?

Why not hear the testimony of the mill workers I talked to in Allegheny, hear how they're kept running twelve hours a day firing six boilers at a time while regulating the steam in them, knowing that the least oversight could cause a boiler explosion that would kill forty or fifty mill workers—which has happened more than once. Why haven't they put on the stand the widows of the brakemen whose heads have been lopped off by bridges because the railroad barons refuse to install proper safety equipment?

July 31

For the fourth day, the prosecution drones on, reading a mountain of words from the *Alarm* and the *Arbeiter* into the record in an effort to prove that we inspired the bomb-throwing through our writings, befuddling the minds of honest workingmen with our crafty prose and arguments. In short, we're "accessories" to murder and, by Illinois law, thereby subject to the same punishment as the murderer himself. But the reasoning is utterly circular: without knowing who the man is, how can one claim what did or did not influence him?

The prosecution's also trying to persuade the jury that we, the eight defendants, are the leaders of a well-organized conspiracy that settled on the specific date of May 1, 1886, for the commencement of a reign of terror (and here *we* thought we were inaugurating a drive for the eight-hour day!). But as Lucy eloquently argued in the *Labor Enquirer*, the fact that only one bomb was thrown itself disproves the notion of any sort of widespread conspiracy or coordinated uprising—the bombing of police stations and the like—that the prosecution insists was part of the "plot." The singularity of the Haymarket bomb argues instead for a maverick act, perhaps of a man demented, or of one beaten by the police and determined on revenge—or, for that matter, of an *agent provocateur*. With the identity of the man unknown, how can the prosecution persist in arguing that he was part of a conspiracy, or that he knew any of us or that we were together involved in such a plot? Yet persist it does, and with every sign of confidence that its garbled logic will be believed.

Captain Black continues to remind the court that we are on trial for the specific crime of murder and that all the material being read into the record is therefore irrelevant and inadmissible. It establishes no connection at all between our opposition to the current social order—openly stated by us, never concealed—and the bomb-throwing in Haymarket, let alone with the organizing of a "general conspiracy" or a plot to inaugurate a reign of terror on May 1st. Yet Judge Gary continues to accept the material from our writings as "germane and admissible evidence." And Captain Black protests into the wind.

August 1

Mayor Carter Harrison has taken the stand. "I was present at the Haymarket meeting," he said today, "from its start until near the close of Mr. Parsons's speech, when not one-fourth of the crowd of some eight hundred people remained. I wish to state plainly before the court that at no point during that time did I have the sense that I was witnessing an 'organized conspiracy,' let alone the inauguration of a so-called Reign of Terror."

Coming from the leading official in the city, that unadorned statement produced a considerable murmur in the audience. Grinnell shook his head from side to side in scandalized disbelief, a smirk of disapproval distorting his features. But it could not neutralize the impact of the mayor's words, nor stop him from proceeding. "It is true," he went on, "that the speakers made several evidently bitter remarks, but they were not sustained. I feel certain, in any case, that the majority of the crowd were idle spectators, mostly laborers or mechanics, not English-speaking people, mostly Germans. I am also certain that no speaker called that night for the immediate use of force or violence. If anyone had, I should have dispersed them at once. I saw no weapons at all upon any person."

I believe Mayor Harrison has today destroyed his political career. Would that I could believe that he has convinced a single soul.

August 2

Restricted to my cell for so many hours, and with the trial dragging interminably on, I have to struggle to maintain my spirits. As do all the others, though Lingg, Fischer, and Engel seem, as viewed from the outside anyway, the steadiest and most stoic (though who can say, finally, what awful sorrows they bear within).

The intense heat is, on most days, nearly intolerable. I try to keep my mind off it by writing in this journal, but I stain nearly every page with drops of sweat; substitute tears is how I think of them, tears that I force back whenever I think about my little ones. How I miss them, Lulu's sweet squeal as she jumps up and down on my lap, Albert Jr. insisting I read him *Ben Hur* "just one more time." It may be many a week before I set eyes on them again: with closing arguments about to begin, we've decided, after all, to send them off to our friends in Waukesha, sparing them the worst of the emotional strain.

August 4

The children left today. I managed to keep a cheerful face when they came to say their good-byes and assured them we'd be together again very soon. Ah, if only I believed that . . . I feel as if my heart has been ripped out . . .

August 6

I've begun to take up whittling, having watched Lingg occupy himself with his jackknife for hours on end. I'm currently working on a steamboat; if it turns out well, perhaps I could raffle it off to bring in some money for Lucy—you know, "Carved by the hands of the anarchist beast." She may soon have to close the shop. Yet she never misses a visiting hour, bringing me little treats and the immense comfort of her touch. We speak openly of all contingencies, concealing nothing from each other of our fluctuating hopes and fears.

Today she was annoyed with William, who's staying in a nearby hotel and calls on her regularly. "He treats me more like your housekeeper than your wife," Lucy told me. "You know, he's quite fond of the sound of his own voice. Yesterday he went on and on about the 'misguided' notion that workers might eventually, out of desperation, take up arms, insisting that free democratic elections were sufficient to solve all grievances." 'Why,' I asked William, 'had *he* taken up arms after Mr. Lincoln won fair and square in a *free, democratic election?*' That seemed to startle him," Lucy giggled, "but he soon regained composure and shifted to lecturing me about the dangers of excessive reading. He says it will jeopardize my health. Reading, it seems, *overstrains the female's weaker brain.*"

"William's the one who reads too much—too much purported Science."

"Then your dear brother added, fatefully, 'The particular talents of *your* people, after all, lie in other directions.'"

"Uh-oh . . ."

"I swear I kept my temper, though I could hardly let that pass without comment. 'My people,' I told William, 'are the American people. And my talents are 'particular' only in the sense of being unusually broad and deep." Lucy laughed. "William looked utterly confounded. Which I took to be a decided advance."

Nina Van Zandt visited the jail today. She's been seeing Spies with increasing frequency, and the two have begun to work together on his autobiography. Because she's not related to him, she has to surmount the various obstacles that the prison authorities put in the way of her visits. But the prominence of her family, and her own tenacity, have consistently won out. She's as ardent and strong-willed as Lucy. Instead of ending up as friends, as they have, they could easily have become antagonists. And might yet, I suppose. Forceful people aren't fond of sharing space.

After Nina left, Lucy startled me by saying, "Nina's in love with Spies."

"Did she tell you that?"

"She didn't have to. It's written all over her."

"Oh, I think you're mistaken."

"All the telltale signs are there: the hushed, adoring tone when she mentions his name, the way she blushes at the sight of him, her insistence, even when no one's challenging him, that he's the most misunderstood of men. How can you *not* see it?"

"I suppose," I finally said, "because I don't want to. What possible future can they have together?"

Lucy gasped. "Albert, do you realize what you just said? They'll have the same future that you and I will. A good future. A long future. You've heard Captain Black say that the odds are in favor of acquittal. Why do you doubt him?"

"Foster is more pessimistic," I said, hoping the conversation would end there.

"Only in regard to *this* jury," Lucy countered. "Even Foster believes that if the jury convicts, you'll all be set free on appeal."

Her tone was so assured that I hesitated. "Foster used those words?"

"Words to that effect."

"I see," I said quietly. And we dropped the matter there. We grasped each other's fingers through the grating, and held on tightly.

August 7

Some newspaper reporters have been digging into my life as a young man in Waco. One, from the *Chicago Herald*, has turned up considerable detail, much of which I'd forgotten, about my early reputation as a "wild young'un." He's even discovered the names of several women I squired, and one I lived with briefly before I met Lucy. None of this made me turn a hair—I never claimed to have been a straight-backed Yankee, and in those years, "wild" was what was expected of a young male in Waco.

But now matters have taken a serious turn. The reporter's latest piece is about Lucy's early life, and she's in a towering rage over it. The article insists she's a negro and claims that before she met me she'd been married to a man named Oliver Gathings, an ex-slave! That's certainly news to me, yet I realize it could be true. I've long since learned that Lucy will never reveal her past in full, not even to me. She may not know it completely herself, may never have disentangled all the conflicting bits of stories handed down to her. Or chosen not to, since gaps and fragments can be useful . . .

When visiting hours came around today, I could hardly believe my eyes: there was Lucy standing outside the cell grating, her eyes breathing fire, with the *Herald reporter in tow*! She didn't even bother to greet me. "Tell him!" she said angrily. "Tell this fool reporter everything you know about my past—and I mean *everything*."

Since both of us are well aware I don't know much, I realized that she wanted me to take my cues from her. "Tell the fool!" she repeated, as if I were deliberately hesitating or withholding information.

Not knowing what she wanted me to say, I began with a digression about our political struggles while living in Texas.

"No, no!" Lucy said impatiently, cutting me off in the middle of a sentence. "Not all that tired old Reconstruction stuff. This here reporter"— she gave his shoulder a poke—"wants to hear about *important* matters, like who was sleepin' with who. Affairs of the bed, not affairs of state. Here in Chicago, reporters leave that boring stuff to the *North American Review*."

At which point the reporter sheepishly introduced himself to me as a Mr. F. W. Peters and assured me he was not interested in gossip at all, but rather in sketching the "human" side of our story, implying that his aim was to make us more sympathetic to the reading public. Between his misrepresentations and Lucy's, I looked for the safest way out: "I can tell you this," I said to Peters, "I've never heard a word about this man Oliver Gathings, whether from Lucy or from anyone else. Are you sure he exists?"

"Oh yes, sir, he still lives in Waco."

"Sounds to me like he's trying to get a bit of publicity for himself," I offered blandly. "Some people will say anything to get their names in the paper. Take me, for example, why I've gone so far as to denounce wage slavery just to get my picture plastered on the front of the *Herald*." My effort at humor went unappreciated. Lucy shot me a furious look, and Mr. Peters stared in embarrassment at the floor.

"Well, I'll tell you two things here and now, Mr. Peters," Lucy said, glaring at him, "and after I say them I'll have nothing more to say. One is that my heritage is Mexican and Creek Indian. And the other is that I have no idea who this man Oliver Gathings is. Now you can either accept that and print an apology in your paper, or you can bring me up on charges of bigamy. You practically have, anyway. You might better spend your time 'investigating in depth' the recent lynchings in Carrollton, Mississippi. Apply some of your research skill to probing why vigilantes lynched a black man simply because he tried to defend a black woman from being gang-raped; and why then, for added sport, they shot up a courthouse and killed thirteen more black people. I'd be willing to bet that the private lives of those Carrollton men would make for some mighty spicy—excuse me, 'human interest'—reading."

With that mouthful, Lucy turned her back and strode off down the corridor. Mr. Peters tipped his hat to me and without another word, was gone.

August 13

The closing arguments are in their third day. Messrs. Walker and Ingham for the State have done little more than repeat, at excruciating length, points already made many times over during the course of the trial. Walker even dared to characterize the Haymarket protest meeting as "an unlawful assembly." Why? Because it was held, he declared, for the deliberate purpose "of committing riot." This, after mountains of testimony, including that of Mayor Harrison, that the meeting was very nearly impromptu and was throughout utterly peaceful—that is, until the arrival of Bonfield and his men, who *were* determined on violence; therein lies the true conspiracy.

Walker said of the defense witnesses that "not a one of them is an American citizen or a naturalized citizen"—inaccurate, and a brazen attempt to arouse nativist sentiment among the jurors. In the same spirit, Ingham advised all men who do not believe in private property to take themselves off to live among the Hottentots of Africa or the Fiji Islanders. He chose those places, I suspect, because of the color of their inhabitants' skin.

Ingham *twice* reminded the jury that they must not entertain a verdict of acquittal simply out of "fear of the consequences"—meaning, out of any humane reluctance to see us hanged.

August 14

Today it was our turn. Mr. Foster opened for the defense, and for once his caustic temperament served us well. I'll never like the man, but I have newfound respect for his abilities. He went straight to the heart of the case—and for the jugular. "There is one question and only one question," Foster said, his voice rancorous, and glaring directly at Judge Gary. "Are these defendants responsible for murder? The elaborate—and refuted—charge of conspiracy has been designed to divert attention to immaterial issues. The defendants should never have been called upon to resist the conspiracy charge, since holding opinions about the desirability or likelihood of social revolution, and announcing those opinions publicly, are the right of every citizen as guaranteed in our Constitution."

Judge Gary chose precisely that moment in the argument to whisper into the ear of a fashionably gowned lady sitting close to him on the bench; she covered her mouth with suppressed mirth. Dumbstruck at Gary's provocation, Foster stopped in the middle of a sentence. The silence managed to restore Gary's attention.

"If we are to start hanging men for their political views," Foster continued, his voice edgy, "what then should be the fate of those newspaper editors and public figures who have so frequently called, as the defendants have not, for initiatory violence? The editorials of *Tribune* owner Joseph Medill have happily envisioned, and I quote him directly, 'communistic carcasses decorating the lamp-posts of Chicago.' Should not such a call to murder be strenuously punished? And what penalty should be meted out to the proprietors of the *New York Tribune* who have stated in print that 'these brutal creatures'—meaning men who go out on strike—'can understand no other reasoning than that of force and enough of it to be remembered among them for many generations.'

"Surely such vicious sentiments deserve stern rebuke. Or would you prefer to say that every newspaper shall be protected in the expression of opinion except for the *Alarm* and the *Arbeiter-Zeitung*?—though neither has ever urged, as the *Tribune* has, throwing hand grenades at our fellow citizens?"

I wanted to stand and cheer, though fully aware that the pugnacity of Foster's summation will lose us more sympathizers than his irrefutable arguments will gain us friends. In one sense, the most important sense, I suppose, it hardly matters. By this late date, surely most if not all of the jurors have long since made up their minds.

August 15

Yesterday, Foster took me aback with his brash showmanship. Today, Captain Black surprised me in quite an opposite way. The dear man's appearance alone alarmed me. Though I've seen him every day for months, when he stood before the bar this morning I was suddenly aware how much whiter his hair is since first we met and how much more lined his face. Not six months ago, he seemed to personify the handsome, dignified military hero. Now, his figure is slightly stooped and his eyes dart back and forth with uneasy anxiety. An old man stood before us.

And his performance today seemed far off his usual mark. My heart sank. Has Captain Black lost confidence, grown fearful that we're likely to be convicted? If so, why? He's been buoyant throughout, sometimes to the point where he's had to make a patently obvious effort to modulate his optimism rather than raise our hopes unduly.

Lucy's been worried for some time that Captain Black's effectiveness has become compromised by his steadily deepening, and evident, admiration for us.

"He's lost objectivity," she said just a few days ago.

"He's become a friend," I replied, "and to some extent a political sympathizer, even. Friendship, perhaps, will make him a stronger advocate, will make him more determined to represent us in the most effective way possible."

"That, surely, would be his wish," Lucy said. "But admiration can be hazardous. When you think well of a person, you're mystified at attacks on their character and tend to dismiss them out-of-hand, rather than take pains to *prove* them mistaken"—which is a lawyer's responsibility.

It was only today that I fully grasped what Lucy meant. At one point Black referred to government, to "*all* government," as "resulting ultimately in despotism," thus making himself sound for all the world like the dedicated anarchist he is not. He then went on to describe us to the court as men of "the broadest feelings of humanity, men who have consecrated their lives to the betterment of their fellows. Is it such a horrible thing," he asked, "that a man should sympathize with the sufferings of common people, that he should feel his heart respond to the desires of oppressed workingmen? We would, I might suggest, profit from having more such men in our midst."

That was enough to produce a broad smirk on Grinnell's face and several titters in the audience. Then came a string of compliments so exorbitant that I felt embarrassed. And concerned. Captain Black's hyperbole could have serious consequences.

What he did was to compare our "self-sacrificing idealism" with that of John Brown and —Jesus Christ! Black described Jesus as "the great Socialist of Judea," the man who "first preached the socialism taught by Spies and his other modern apostles." As for John Brown, Black told the court that Brown's attack on Harper's Ferry "might be compared to the Socialists' attack on modern evils."

The analogy to John Brown was dangerous enough, since most white people strongly disapprove of his having taken up arms to free black slaves.

But likening us to Jesus Christ was assuredly a blunder; in my view, a serious one, though I don't doubt for a moment that the good Captain spoke from his heart.

When Grinnell stepped up to deliver his summation, immediately after Black had concluded his, he took shrewd advantage of the Captain's miscalculations.

"Government is despotism? Does not our splendid nation put the lie to so misguided a statement?" The courtroom resounded with patriotic applause. Smiling, Judge Gary gently tapped his gavel for silence. "Fortunately for the defendants," Grinnell went on, "one of their counsel, Mr. Foster, is untainted with the perfidious anarchism of his clients."

Grinnell paused for more applause, but none was forthcoming; the crowd didn't want Foster praised, not even backhandedly; he had shown far too much biting contempt for the court and its spectators.

Grinnell hurried on. "Mr. Black describes the defendants as humanitarians. Surely the court, unlike Mr. Black, has not forgotten that these men have been openly preaching treason and murder in this city for years. Is the advocacy of murder his definition of *humanitarianism*? Yet Captain Black goes further: he claims for the defendants the similitude and mantle of Christ, of the Savior of mankind! Is the case for the defense descended so low, is it so mean, that he who was for peace should be compared to these wretches here?" Boos and shouts filled the courtroom.

Judge Gary took his time in restoring order. Grinnell then proceeded to repeat all the accusations made against us over the past weeks about conspiracies and terrorist plots. He then sunk to new depths. Standing directly in front of the jury box for maximum effect, he warned the jurors, his voice heavy with foreboding, that should they vote to acquit, "all the slimy vermin who have taken cover in the holes and byways of the city during this trial, will flock out again like a lot of rats."

Applause once more filled the courtroom, and the jury members, their bodies tensed with excitement, their eyes glistening with pride, looked for all the world like dedicated troops about to set forth into climactic battle. Grinnell, seasoned veteran that he is, sent them off with a firm set of instructions and a fulsome expression of confidence that they would do their duty.

Where Foster and Black had settled for rather perfunctory thanks to the jurors, Grinnell heaped praise on them for what he called "their selfless, noble service" and "the kind attention" that they had given him through-out the arduous trial. Then, in a masterstroke, he asserted his certainty that the jurors, as men of the tenderest conscience, would do their duty courageously, "even if that duty is an unpleasant and a severe one."

Lest the jury, despite its "fine-tuned sensitivity," somehow be in doubt as to precisely where their duty lay, Grinnell proceeded actually to list us in terms of comparative iniquity, the ranking carrying an automatic implication of what the appropriate amount of punishment should be: Spies, Fischer, Lingg, Engel, Fielden, Parsons, Schwab, and Neebe. Grinnell explicitly severed Neebe from the rest of us. He was declared less than a full partner in the murderous conspiracy that the police had "so timely aborted," deserving of punishment, to be sure, but of a decidedly lesser magnitude than the rest of us.

Tonight, back in the cellblock, we had some nervous sport speculating on the standards of iniquity Grinnell might have used in ranking us. I took a good deal of kidding for having come off so badly in the competition. Spies made sad-eyed banter with me: "Do visit us from time to time," he sighed, "if you can tear yourself away, that is, from the beer gardens!" It was not a good joke, but it came from a brave heart . . .

August 17

Time is hanging much heavier than usual, as we await Judge Gary's instructions to the jury, due the day after tomorrow. Only Lingg, Fischer, and Engel methodically pursue their usual routines, speaking in firm good spirits about the rightness of our cause. But the rest of us are showing signs of the accumulated strain, from sleeplessness to an inability to concentrate on reading or writing.

I've resorted to whittling a second steamboat, this one more elaborate and carved from a single piece of wood. My skills have grown. I've even been able to carve a rudder, and two human figures to place in the forecastle. Passing my cell today and seeing my handiwork, Lingg broke into a rare smile and nodded his head approvingly.

I find that the whittling not only diverts my mind from brooding about what lies ahead, but induces a kind of reverie. I move back in time and become a boy again, daydreaming about Aunt Ester cradling me and telling me never to forget the value of every single life, about galloping exuberantly along the banks of the Brazos, my hair flying wildly in the wind, the sweet smell of jasmine filling my nostrils. How strange life is . . . who could have guessed that the heedless, happy boy hunting antelope near the riverbank would some day be sitting in a stone-cold Northern jail, denied the right to breathe fresh air or glimpse the sky, awaiting other men's verdict on the degree of his criminality. How little we can guess, when young, of what lies ahead, how little we bother our heads with so meaningless a topic as "the future." Yet sitting here now in this cheerless cell, I recognize full well how easily my life could have taken a radically different turn—and how ultimately mysterious is the fact that it did not. This isn't a matter of regret, but of curiosity. Why was it that I didn't follow a path similar to William's, didn't become a rancher, say, or a cotton factor in Galveston—certainly far more logical and common choices for a lad of my background than defending negroes (let alone marrying one) and joining hands with immigrant workers . . .

August 18

Nina Van Zandt has become a near-daily visitor—it would be daily, if she could get permission. She came by my cell today to see how I was, and we chatted briefly through the grating. She seemed rather more distracted and her face more strained than usual, the lines around her eyes crinkled with anxiety. When I asked about it, she told me in an agitated voice that a rumor was gaining currency about a new sheriff soon to be appointed, a man named Matson, who had the reputation of being a stickler for discipline. She's fearful that Matson might curtail her visits to Spies or indeed ban them altogether. I tried to reassure her, but since I had no real grounds for optimism, my words rang hollow.

"If Matson is appointed," Nina said, her eyes clouding over, "Mr. Spies and I are discussing some alternative plans . . ." Her voice trailed off ambiguously. Clearly she regretted having said that much, for when I asked what kind of "alternatives" they had in mind, she evaded my question and soon after bid me a hasty good-bye. How curious . . . Surely they can't be planning a jailbreak! That would be suicidal.

August 19

Judge Gary gave his instructions today to the jury and it has now retired to begin deliberations. In essence, he told the jurors, without being able to cite a single legal precedent, that we could be found accessories to murder even though the identity of the bomb-thrower and the specifics of our relationship to him could not be established, and especially if the jury feels that in print or speech we ever encouraged the commission of murder. Captain Black is furious at the prejudicial nature of Gary's instructions, yet sees a bright side: should we need to take the case to an appeals court, he feels confident Gary will be reversed and reprimanded for his blatant bias.

The general prediction is that the jury will be out several weeks at least, given the complexity of the issues and the fact that Grinnell, by "ranking" the defendants during his closing remarks has all but mandated gradations of punishments to correspond to the implied gradations in guilt.

We'd been back in our cells but a few hours and were celebrating the joyful news just arrived that Sam Fielden's wife has given birth to a son, Sam Jr., when Captain Black suddenly reappeared, looking more distraught than I've ever seen him. He struggled to regain his composure, but it was only moments before he blurted out the shocking news: the jury has already reached a verdict—after deliberating for a grand total of three hours!

"Can you imagine it?" Black stormed. "Three hours! With two months of complex testimony to sift through, convoluted evidence to evaluate, scores of intricate definitions and rulings to appraise . . . Why, in three hours they could hardly have *read* the sixty-nine counts of the indictment, let alone considered the surrounding material. Oh gentlemen"—here the good Captain looked as if he might break down—"I must tell you in all frankness that . . . that this unseemly haste greatly . . . greatly concerns me. A speedy verdict very likely means that the jury, ignoring Grinnell's proposal of rankings, has taken the easy way out and opted for a . . . a uniform verdict. What that verdict is, we will know soon enough . . . Court has been reconvened for 10:00 A.M. tomorrow."

Captain Black begged leave of us almost immediately after delivering the stunning news, saying he had to consult at once with the rest of the legal team. I don't doubt they'll be up the entire night. As will we.

August 20

Shortly before ten, they led us into the courtroom. To my amazement, it was nearly empty, the public having been excluded—though judging from the noise coming up from the street below, a large crowd had gathered to await the verdict. The courtroom itself was heavily guarded, and only immediate family members were present. Lucy was sitting with Spies's mother and sister; she blew me a kiss and never took her eyes off me thereafter.

The jury entered promptly and took their places. Judge Gary asked if they had reached a verdict. They said yes and handed a piece of paper to the clerk, who read it aloud. The jury has found all but Neebe guilty of murder and has fixed the penalty at death. Neebe is sentenced to fifteen years at hard labor. Schwab's wife became hysterical and her shrill screams rent the air.

I looked around at my comrades. All appeared calm, though Spies and Schwab had gone notably pale and Neebe appeared dazed—he had felt certain of acquittal. I, too, felt shaken, having foolishly thought that my voluntary surrender would have ruled out the death penalty. But I was determined not to show that I'd been taken by surprise. I put on a smiling face, took my red handkerchief from my pocket and, being near a window, waved it to the crowd below. A guard instantly stopped me, but as soon as he released my arm, I grabbed the curtain cord, rapidly formed it into a noose and dangled it out the window. The crowd below went wild—the verdict pleased them.

Captain Black made a motion for a new trial, but Judge Gary postponed any hearing on it until next month. The guards then immediately led us from the courtroom. Fielden lost his footing and I had to hold him up for support.

6:00 P.M.: There have been comings and goings all day. Lucy's anger is holding her together. Captain Black told us he'd heard from a colleague that Grinnell has expressed regret at having "forgotten" to mention in his summation, as he'd intended, that "Parsons was entitled to some consideration for having voluntarily surrendered himself."

On hearing that, Lucy became so irate that I feared for a few moments she might lose control. "'Forgotten'?!" she hollered. "The bastard wants you dead *and* wants credit for having tried to save your life! He's slime, he's hypocritical slime! . . ."

Later in the evening, Captain Black saw to it that he and I were alone together in my cell.

"I . . . I wanted to tell you . . ." he stumbled, "that . . . that the verdict has profoundly shocked me . . ." I put my hand on his shoulder to calm him.

"Oh my dear Parsons," he said, barely managing to suppress a sob, "I . . . I should be the one comforting *you*."

"The verdict didn't surprise me much," I said quietly. "The court reflects the country. And the country is overwhelmingly against us."

"But the widespread feeling in legal circles—including the prosecution itself, I'm told—was that at most only four of you could get the death penalty, Spies, Lingg, Fischer, and Engel. The consensus was that you, Fielden, and Schwab, if found guilty at all, would receive a limited term of imprisonment. As for Neebe, it was universally believed that he'd be acquitted outright."

"You did your best, Captain," I said. "You must remember that. You have no cause to blame yourself for this outcome, none at all. All of us, I assure you, feel the same."

Black seemed deeply grateful for my words, and became a bit more cheerful. Just before leaving the cell, he turned back and begged me not to lose courage. "Even aside from the pending motion for a new trial," he said, "we have any number of avenues of appeal left open to us—the state and federal Supreme Courts, and also a direct petition for pardon to Governor Oglesby. Be of good heart," he said, even as his melancholic eyes conveyed a different message, "the fight for your freedom is but begun."

The evening edition of the *Tribune* bears this banner headline: "THE SCAF-FOLD WAITS. SEVEN DANGLING NOOSES FOR THE DYNAMITE FIENDS." The paper also carries a fund-raising appeal for a purse of $100,000, to be presented to the jury "with the thanks of a grateful people for their noble work." According to the *Tribune*, "There is every reason to believe that the fund will be rapidly oversubscribed."

Part Eight

My dearest husband,

I rush to get this note off to you. In two hours the first talk of the tour begins. My body aches with exhaustion, I have no tears left to cry. I long to be with you but know I must push on. I still can't believe that Judge Gary denied a new trial. The sentence will not come to pass, my dearest, it will not . . . I'm confident of that . . . Many besides myself are spanning the country to raise funds and support. And now that Leonard Swett—*Lincoln*'s friend!—has replaced Foster, a man never in sympathy with our ideals, Captain Black is of the opinion that the State Supreme Court will overturn the verdict. You must believe that, you must stay strong.

That seems almost foolish to say, having heard your speech to the court this morning. William and Lizzie whisked me to the train so quickly, I couldn't share my reactions with you—to your speech and to the others. For all these months you've had to sit there while perjurers and rogues poured venom on your head, spat out like adders the vile poison of their tongues, with you not permitted to say a word in rebuttal. Surely Gary got far more than he bargained for when he finally allowed you the floor—a mere ten weeks after passing sentence! What dignity and defiance you showed, my darling, what passion! You must have felt the shiver that ran through the courtroom when you asked, "Can it be that men are to suffer death for their opinions?" And I hope you saw Judge Gary shift uncomfortably in his chair when you warned the prosecution that it was deceiving itself if it thinks that the strangulation of seven men, or the carrying of their bones to potter's field, will settle anything or will prevent the American people from rising up and insisting that the Constitution of our country not be trampled underfoot at the dictation of merchant princes and their hired tools. Albert, your inspired words will ring through the ages.

What touched me the deepest was what you said at the very end about regretting nothing, not even now. And then, the way you went over to Captain Black's chair and gently put your hand on his shoulder, as if speaking the words directly to him, knowing that, justifiably or not, he carries a terrible burden for the part he played in advising you to leave Waukesha and turn yourself in. I saw his eyes cloud over with relief and regret, and with the tenderest gratitude that in the hour of your direst need it was *his* feelings that concerned you. I'm not a sentimental woman, but I need to say, dearest, that the generosity of your soul deeply humbles me—me, the least humble person you know!

Yet I'm not so partial that I couldn't recognize the splendid way every one of the men acquitted himself. There wasn't a weak speech, though of course each spoke in a manner reflecting his own temperament, of which several, as I believe I have often enough made clear, don't particularly appeal to me. I've always thought Schwab a dull man, ponderous as a professor. And while Fischer and Engel's militant views are close to my own, their flat, stodgy personalities are decidedly not.

But the other four—oh, how each tore at my heart, even as my whole being flushed with pride at their exalted words and bearing! When Spies, his eyes ablaze with bitterness, said, "Let the world know that in A.D. 1886, in the state of Illinois, men were sentenced to death because they believed in a better future," Nina grabbed my hand tightly and burst into tears, matching my own. And we cried again when Neebe, that simple, unassuming soul, told the judge that he was sorry he was not to be hung with the rest of the defendants and asked the court to let him share their fate. Fielden was equally moving when, in his straightforward way, he recounted the hardships of his youth as a child laborer in the mills of Lancashire and told how his suffering had made him hate injustice and devote himself to trying to make life easier for future generations of children. A woman sitting near to us, a stranger to me, let out a stricken cry, as if pierced to the heart.

And then there was Lingg. He embodied defiance, evoking in me not tears, but a fierce anger equal to his own. The fact that he spoke in

German, with every sentence needing translation, added to the power-ful impression he made. It was as if a creature from another world had come to pass irrevocable judgment on us. It sent shivers through me. Imagine!—only twenty-two years old, under sentence of death, and yet composed enough to hurl his scornful thunderbolts at his tormentors! I'll never forget his closing words. I've committed them to memory and will live by them forever: "I die happy on the gallows, so confident am I that the hundreds and thousands to whom I have spoken will remember my words. When you shall have hanged us, then *they* will do the bomb-throwing! In this hope do I say to you: I despise you. I despise your order, your laws, your force-propped authority. Hang me for it!"

How artificial it feels to share these thoughts with you in a letter, but such is now our lot. With William and Lizzie rushing me off right after the sentencing, I barely got to throw my arms around you and say more than a word to the others. And now it's to be six long weeks before I lay eyes on you again! It's hard to bear, but nothing like what the rest of you are living through. Embrace everyone, and try to write often. It is for now our only lifeline . . .

I've arranged the tour in a way that will allow me to spend a few days in Waukesha with Lulu and Albert Jr., which will be a blessed inter-lude. By all reports they're well looked after and happy—or as happy as possible separated from the two people who love them most in the world . . .

I send you a thousand kisses . . . Be of good courage!
              Ever your devoted Lucy

✳

Cook County Jail, Chicago
October 16, 1886

Dearest Wife,

I felt our parting deeply and—now I can confess it—came very close to begging you not to go. "It won't matter," I wanted to say, "our enemies are too powerful, the chances of a reversal too slim to spend our pre-cious remaining time apart." But I felt you needed to go, needed to feel through intense activity, on which you always thrive, that cheering audiences would somehow translate into sympathetic judges. Not wanting to dampen your optimism, I held my peace. In confessing this now, do not think I've given up all hope; I speak of odds and priorities, not certainties.

And you are getting the cheering crowds! We follow your progress in the papers closely. I've noticed how much space they give to describing your appearance, which obviously fascinates them: your "copper-colored skin," your "piercing black eyes," your "deep, mellow voice." How transparent it all is. They're dying to simply call you "a negress," and I note one or two of the New York papers have. It must irk you. But at least they're reporting what you say as well as how you look, and your words are full of power and truth. I particularly like what you told the crowd at Cooper Union about Philip Armour being "a slaughterer of children as well as of hogs" and the contrast you drew between Armour employing ten-year-olds and our anarchist dream of taking the little ones out of the factories and putting them at play, where they belong.

To be frank, I liked certain of your remarks in New Haven somewhat less—the part where you talked about how "every great reform needs its martyrs" and how if your husband did end up on the scaffold, "his death will only help the cause." Lucy! What you say may be true, but keep in mind that it is *your husband* who you seem to be offering up so gladly for sacrifice! It gave the husband himself, I can tell you, a bit of a chill—and I'm not sure it endeared you to your audience, either. We of course agree, dear, that none of us individually are of any importance when compared to the success of the cause, but State Supreme Court justices might understandably feel disinterest in saving the lives of people seemingly so eager to sacrifice themselves! The fact is, I've never had what people call "a martyr's complex." I do not court death, nor have I ever seen myself as a singular creature marked for some special destiny. I love life too much to seek for a way of voluntarily quitting it. Yes, I'll bow to necessity, should it come, but I'll not welcome it. Don't be cross with me for refusing to censor my thoughts. We've always prided ourselves on speaking our minds to each other and must go on doing so.

Everyone here is deeply grateful for your energetic work. Captain Black tells us that you collected $750 last week alone! At such a rate we'll have no trouble raising the $12,500 needed for the appeal to the Illinois Supreme Court. You see—you are our agent and banker rolled in one, and we're well aware how much strain this puts you under. None of us is feeling exactly serene these days, though we do our best to present an unflappable public face. I was glad to hear you say how well we succeeded during our final statements to the court. But it's a terrible thing to realize that as "symbols," we dare not openly express the terror that sometimes sweeps over us.

Oh what I would give to see you and the children . . .

Your devoted husband,
Albert

＊

Philadelphia, Pennsylvania
October 20, 1886

Oh my dearest Albert,

I've hurt you deeply and without dreaming for a minute that my words would cause such pain! When I got your letter, dearest, my impulse was to rush back to Chicago and hold you in my arms. Lizzie (she's joined me here for a week) had to keep repeating over and over that I must meet my lecture obligations, that I can help you best by pleading your cause to the people. But I'll have no peace of mind until you tell me that you'll never again doubt my love, or think for a second that I could ever "gladly" sacrifice my dear husband's life. Albert, Albert, you are the dearest person in the world to me, you've given meaning to my life from the first moment I laid eyes on you at my uncle's ranch. You must promise that you'll keep the certainty of my love close to your heart every second! You speak in your letter of the strain of maintaining a cheerful public face. Do you not see that the same is true for me? I'm probably better at it than you, my nerves are less delicate, but when I thunder from the platform about "the crimes of the capitalists," do not doubt that inside my heart is weeping. I know how to give the crowd hell, but I am also living in one.

And remember, too, that not everything you read in the newspapers— no, not even in the labor press—is true. Surely you, if anyone, knows that! How many times have you seen yourself misquoted, a particular sentence highlighted in a way that distorts your meaning? Sometimes when I read an account of a speech I gave the night before, I can barely recognize the sentiments as my own, to say nothing of the complete absence of feeling and gesture that accompanied and gave sense to the words.

Let me caution you in one other regard. As you and I agreed before I left, the country's enormous interest in the trial and verdict presents an opportunity that must be seized. Whenever a speech of mine is announced, whether to an IWPA local or to the privileged young men at Yale, the turnout is almost always tremendous. Some of my audiences are ignorant about labor conditions, and even at trade union meetings I find astounding misconceptions about the meaning of anarchism—they think we're nihilists and dynamiters, and they know nothing of our vision for a more humane society. *They desperately need education*, and I'm giving it to them. I continue to be told that I'm a striking presence on the platform and a forceful orator, and that I've begun the job of leading the *masses* toward anarchism.

And do you know what, Albert? I enjoy hearing the compliments. I admit it. I enjoy the attention and admiration. I try not to blame myself for the personal gratification the tour is bringing me, though I hear whisperings that I "love notoriety" and have become "bombastic with self-importance." Well, let them whisper! I have nothing to apologize for, certainly not for being forceful and effective, however widely those qualities are disapproved of in a woman. You always said I was ambitious and—thank you!—did not think it a fault. None of us is free of ego, though many pretend to be. The egoism, however, must be kept subservient to the cause.

I want to confess something else to you: I'm relishing the opportunity to speak my own mind. I say "confess" because I realize that some of what I say won't meet with your approval, especially when I insist that any and all means are justified in destroying a social system that is itself based on the constant employment of violence. I know you have far graver doubts on this point than I, and I know, too, that emphasizing such a point at this critical moment runs the risk of heightening public sentiment against you. I'm trying my best to strike a proper balance between the need truthfully to proclaim what I stand for, and the need to declare your innocence of advocating force for any purpose other than self-defense. I wrestle with this dilemma constantly, and believe that I'm successfully fulfilling both missions.

Please tell me that you believe in me and what I am doing on your behalf . . . I could not go on if I thought otherwise . . .

Ever your devoted Lucy

*

Cook County Jail, Chicago
October 25, 1886

My Dearest Lucy,

You and I are no strangers to misunderstandings and disagreements. That we've not had many more in our married life puts us apart from most couples. Given the nervous strain under which we live, it's remarkable that we don't strike out at each other more often. Your letter said all that need be said. I do not doubt your love. We know our hearts beat in unison.

I have considerable news for you, much of it, alas, unsettling. Sam Fielden has had word of his beloved father's death in Lancashire; he is low in spirit. Neebe, too, is under great strain. His wife, Meta, has fallen seriously ill and her recovery is in doubt. You remember what a timid soul she is, how reliant on Neebe for all practical decisions. Indeed, she's so afraid of getting on a streetcar by herself that her visits to the jail have been infrequent. As the weeks have led into months, Neebe's absence from home has driven her into a kind of emotional paralysis. The doctors talk vaguely of a "nervous collapse," since they've been unable to pinpoint any physical disorder. She seems to weaken by the day; let's hope her decline can yet be arrested.

Also, Hortensia Black has come under attack. It seems Judge Gary's verdict stunned and infuriated her—I suppose the good Captain, in his optimistic way, had been leading her to expect a quite different outcome. In her anger, Hortensia sent off a letter to the *Chicago Daily News* defending us in the most outspoken way. In case you've not seen it, I'll quote part of what she wrote: "I have never known an anarchist, did not know what the term meant, until my husband became counsel for the defense. When I learned the facts, I became assured in my own mind that the wrong men had been arrested . . . During all of that long trial a kind of soul crucifixion was imposed upon me. Often I would recall reverently those words of my Divine Master: 'For which of my good works do you stone me?' . . . Anarchy is simply a human effort to bring about the millennium. Why do we want to hang men for that, when every pulpit has thundered that the time is near at hand?"

The press is heaping scorn and outrage on her. As you can imagine, the reference to Jesus, which parallels Captain Black's during his summation in court, has generated the most indignation. She's been called everything from a blasphemer to a "moral degenerate." It's been very hard on her, but I've selfishly taken comfort in learning that so noble-hearted a woman believes in our goodness and innocence.

When is your next visit to the children? Much too much time has passed since they've seen either of us.

All my love,
Albert

*

Bridgeport, Connecticut
November 5, 1886

Dearest Husband,

I had intended to write before this, but I've been utterly consumed with a nonstop series of speeches, dinners, rallies, and the like. Even now, I must be brief, since a committee is due any minute to cart me off to address the local IWPA.

In terms of political importance, the biggest event has been the Knights of Labor convention. I'll save all details for when I see you—only three more weeks!—but (this much you may already know) the sympathetic resolution that passed did so over Powderly's furious opposition. He said the defendants are owed not sympathy but "a debt of hatred" for managing to turn the public mind against "decent, law-abiding workers and their legitimate demands." He's not alone among trade-unionists in endorsing the court verdict. They're terrified of being identified with "extremists." Yet more and more people are realizing how biased and unfair the trial was, and the tide of opinion among the working class is turning in our favor. Powderly's threat to expel any affiliate of the Knights that expresses support for us is being increasingly defied by the local assemblies.

Powderly told the editor of the *Labor Enquirer*, Burnette Haskell, who told me, that he's long had proof—some of it, he claims, provided by your brother!—that all eight of you *are* assassins. "If you have proof, sir, than why have you withheld it?" Haskell asked. "Because I'm not a detective and it's none of my business," Powderly dared to reply—he who has made it his business to defame us over and over again. His latest sally is to insist that I'm not your proper wife, that we live together but are not married. He also asserts that I am a woman of "bad reputation" and adds, in his sly way, that no woman, "white or negro, who tramps around the country," can be thought of as respectable.

Can you believe it?! I suppose if *he* were under sentence of death he'd counsel his wife to spend her time in church, or maybe in sewing samplers of the Virgin Mary to hang in their living room! The contemptible man is doing everything he can to undermine my credibility, but Haskell has taken up the challenge for me. He angrily informed Powderly that you and I are "regularly married," and that as for the attribution to William, your brother has publicly defended you throughout, and is currently hard at work on a book about the corruption and bias of the trial. None of which, Haskell told me, seemed to make a dent on Powderly. So be it. The leader of the labor movement in America is now our declared enemy. But the average worker is not. Johann Most has written a reply to Powderly in *Die Freiheit*, referring to him as "the Grand Master Rat"! Most may not be your favorite person, but he does get some things right.

Please try not to concern yourself overly about the children. I got to see them briefly last week—and will again by midmonth. They're being cared for devotedly by the Hoan family and other friends. Albert Jr. is reading well enough to follow some of the newspaper stories (though the more hostile sections are concealed from him) and he's constantly plying everyone with questions about when you will be released, when he will see you again, etc. "Soon," everyone reassures him, "very soon." He seems to understand that you're being held unjustly, and is very angry at the bad men who are hurting his father. Lulu was briefly ill; there was some fear of a glandular disorder, but though there's still no diagnosis, the fever and sore throat have abated and she seems very nearly her old self.

I know how eager you are to hold the children in your arms, but we must put their welfare first. When I return at the end of the month, I'll have to permanently close down the dress shop. Even if I had enough customers left, I wouldn't have the time to fill their orders. That means we'll no longer be able to afford the apartment. I'll have to find a third-floor walkup somewhere, doubtless with minimal amenities; that, in my opinion, would be too difficult an adjustment for the children after the open spaces and beauty of Waukesha. They are better left where they are. Possibly I could ask the Defense Committee to supplement our rent and we could stay put. But I think we agree that the receipts from my lecturing should be spent entirely on legal costs. We can talk more about all this once I'm back in Chicago . . .

As you know, I'll only be able to stay for a few short days because once the stay is issued, as I'm certain it will be, the Defense Committee wants me to undertake a western tour. The more I lecture, the more militant I become, though I try hard not to go too far, lest it jeopardize our appeal. Did I tell you that in Orange, New Jersey, when an armed guard tried to prevent me from entering the hall, I kicked in the door? No one laid a hand on me after that, and I did get to deliver my speech.

I forget, have we shared our reactions to the unveiling of the Statue of Liberty in New York Harbor? Mine was simple: why did no one think to plant a bomb?

They've come for me . . . I must close—we are late.

> Ever,
> Your Lucy

✳

> Cook County Jail, Chicago
> November 12, 1886

Dearest Wife (despite what Powderly says!),

Your exuberance comes bounding through your letters. How I envy you, out among people, *breathing the air*! Sitting here in this stone cell, forced day after day to perform the same mechanical routines, I remember well the thrill of standing up before a crowd, their appreciative cheers filling me with a sense of purpose. I say this not to elicit pity, but to encourage you to enjoy the acclaim and the sense of purpose it gives. Don't enjoy it so much, of course, that you decide not to come back. Just think, dearest, in less than two weeks we'll again be together, or as together as we can be with iron mesh separating us and armed guards breathing on us.

And don't become *so* militant that you arrive with a posse and try to shoot our way out of here—which in Waco, I don't doubt you would have done! Lizzie reports from the week she spent with you, that "militant" is putting it mildly. Even she, who is practically your political twin, confesses to having been startled now and then at your vehemence. Breaking down the door in Orange, New Jersey, was apparently less dramatic than some of your rhetoric, at least as Lizzie reports it. I chuckled over substituting "Hangman Gary" for "Judge Gary," and I've never entirely discounted the possibility that you're apparently averring as absolute truth, that an *agent provocateur* threw the bomb in Haymarket as part of a Wall Street conspiracy to destroy the eight-hour movement.

But unless your audience is entirely composed of committed revolutionaries (and that can't be true, given the large size of your crowds), I have to say that you sound in danger of provoking your audience rather than persuading it. You're your own person, and I have no right to advise restraint. But I do agree with Lizzie, who says she several times felt the need to chide you when you repeatedly called the police "vermin" or said that had you been in Haymarket and heard "that insolent command to disperse," you would have flung the bomb yourself. Such rhetoric does nothing to soften the hearts of the people, to say nothing of the authorities, towards us.

But let me turn to another subject. I cannot say this strongly enough: I need to see my children, I need to hold them to my breast, hear their sweet, silly squeals, nuzzle their necks. So strong—selfish, if you like—is the need that I'm willing to risk having them feel dislocated. They're young and resilient; they'll soon bounce back from being moved from Waukesha to Chicago. I don't mean that Albert Jr. and Lulu should stay in Chicago indefinitely, but I *must* have them with me for a while. As my own spirits sink—I've tried not to write you about this—my soul needs to feed off the joy and hopefulness in their innocent eyes.

Don't be alarmed; I haven't fallen into any viselike depression, but my fluctuations of mood are more pronounced now than earlier (though I continue to show, being a good platform performer, a cheerful face). Captain Black feels certain that the appeal he filed with the State Supreme Court ten days ago, asking for a stay of execution, will be granted. And that will give us the needed time to argue for a retrial. Should he be right, I have no doubt my spirits will come surging back.

Call me a sentimentalist if you like, but the newspaper photos of the Statue of Liberty now standing proud and tall in New York Harbor, sent a thrill through me. Think of it this way, dear: the statue represents what our country will one day become. I know you believe this, too, though you enjoy playing the chortling cynic far too much to admit it. People who lack optimism never become social reformers—they're convinced that nothing can ever be changed for the better. Which is not true of either of us.

I am ever your faithful and loving,
Albert

*

TELEGRAM
MILWAUKEE, WISCONSIN
NOVEMBER 25, 1886

ALBERT: THRILLING NEWS JUST ARRIVED. JUSTICE SCOTT GRANTING STAY OF EXECUTION. THE WAY NOW OPEN FOR MARCH APPEAL TO STATE SUPREME COURT. GLORIOUS. HOME IN FEW DAYS. TWO THOUSAND AT RALLY LAST NIGHT. WE WILL WIN. LUCY.

*

Cook County Jail, Chicago
January 29, 1887

My Dearest Wife,

The pen feels like lead in my hand. It actively rebels against having to resort yet again to letters after having had you in Chicago these past two months. Even though you were on the road many of those days, it was a great comfort to know you were never too far away and would soon be returning. And oh, the joy of seeing my little ones again, however briefly; I could hardly bear letting them go back to Waukesha. Yet what choice do we have, now that you're again too far away for visits and can't return here till April. My heart sinks at the thought. But I'll stop. We must try and remain strong.

I'm writing immediately following the wedding to give you all the particulars, as promised. As you know, many of our friends thought the whole idea ill-advised. Hortensia and Captain Black were especially upset, feeling the marriage would infuriate Nina's social set and make it more difficult to plead Spies's case. I'd never seen Hortensia more vehement; she confided to me her conviction that Nina was impetuous and shallow, a mere publicity seeker, unworthy of Spies and unable to transcend the values of her class. I wanted to say that if she, Hortensia, has, then why is it so unthinkable that Nina could do the same? Certainly she and her parents have shown every sign of understanding our plight, and Nina has defended us most passionately to the outside world. The Van Zandts have risked much, including their personal safety. The family's house has several times been assaulted—rocks and mud thrown, windows smashed—with Nina and her parents forced to huddle, terrified, in the basement.

In any case, after Matson took over as sheriff and barred Nina from visiting, what options did she and Spies have? Only if Nina officially became *Mrs.* Spies could she demand visitation privileges (though Matson is still doing his best to hold her to a minimum). Besides, Spies was determined to go through with the marriage. The press, of course, insists that it's all calculation on his part, that he wants to use her fortune for his legal defense and her class influence to win him a reprieve. But that "fortune" is rapidly disappearing. Nina's aunt, the wealthiest member of her family, has completely disinherited her, and as for her "class influence," not a single neighbor on East Huron will so much as acknowledge the Van Zandts on the street.

No, I believe the bond between Nina and Spies is real, their affection deep. Who is to decide whether it's deep enough to be called love—surely not those wealthy families who these days connive to sell their daughters to the highest bidder among the European aristocracy.

In anticipation of the nuptials, Nina had filled Spies's cell with flowers and put down a lovely small carpet to cover the harsh stones. But Sheriff Matson at the eleventh hour refused permission for the ceremony to be performed in the prison and the couple had to be married by proxy, with Spies's brother standing in for the groom and taking the vows in their family's home. Under the circumstances, what can we dare wish the couple? "Happiness" would be fatuous. Courage, maybe? . . .

Did you see that Henry George has come out in support of our appeal? He's written in the *Standard* that we have been "convicted by a jury chosen in a manner so shamelessly illegal that it would be charity to suspect the judge of incompetence." We already have the country's leading journalist, Henry Demarest Lloyd, and its leading man of letters, William Dean Howells, on our side, and both continue to champion our cause. In Howell's most recent statement, he declares that we "are condemned to death on a principle that would have sent every ardent antislavery man to the gallows."

But we need many more such "notables" to declare themselves if our pending appeal before the State Supreme Court is to carry the needed weight. When the famous speak up, the nabobs take some heed, whereas the opinions of common folk, the "riffraff," count for little—except of course at election time . . . Thus far, though, George, Lloyd and Howells stand nearly alone. We hear that in Europe some well-known figures are rallying to our side, including William Morris, Annie Besant, and George Bernard Shaw. But our patriotic judges will doubtless take umbrage at "foreign interference" in our domestic affairs.

I must stop. Having just seen you, the shadow-exercise of a letter is too painful.

> Kisses to you, my dearest wife,
> Albert

P.S. Here's a bit of pathos for you: I've had to apply to the Defense Committee for money to buy undergarments and socks! If that doesn't move your hard heart, try this: I've been told that in all likelihood I'll be turned down! Have they decided my chances of surviving are too poor to justify the outlay? Perhaps you could put in a good word—insist that $3.00 from your fund-raising be set aside to keep your husband looking (if not sounding) respectable.

✳

> Omaha, Nebraska
> February 15, 1887

Dearest Husband,

Your letter of January 29 has just caught up with me, and I hasten to send you a few lines lest you think I've disappeared into the bowels of some midwestern prison. The fact is, I *was* jailed in Columbus, but not for long. After I was refused a hall in which to speak, I confronted the mayor. He told me, "Shut your anarchist mouth," and when I tried to reply, barked at the guards, "Take her down!" I was thrown into a large, filthy cell, where I found four other women, locked up on charges of "disorderly conduct." Which I suspect means they're down on their luck and friendless. They were living on bread, water, and salt doled out twice a day. When my supporters came to visit me, I sent them out to get some proper food for the women. They all but wept with gratitude. I was let out the next day.

Nebraska is the seventeenth state I've been in during the past four months. I've lost count of how many speeches I've given, how many pamphlets I've sold, how many tens of thousands of people have heard my message. And yet I remain full of energy, and yes, hope.

I don't understand the reaction of Hortensia and Captain Black to the marriage. Could it be that their class bias is surfacing? Like you, I think the world of them; without their advocacy we would have been thrown to the wolves long ago. But something tells me their disapproval of Nina hasn't much to do with concern about generating hostility to Spies. After all, having already been labeled the most dangerous fanatic of the lot, he could hardly fall lower in the public's estimate. I believe it has more to do with the Blacks' discomfort with "mixed" class marriages. Being good people, I doubt they're in touch with their own prejudice. You may think me batty, but I'm not.

I don't share your pleasure at Henry George enlisting in our cause. At bottom, I think the man's an ambitious opportunist. As you know, he'll be running as an independent candidate for Mayor of New York in the upcoming election, and he wants to win. Which means, I suspect, that the next bulletin from Mr. George about the Haymarket defendants will be much less favorable towards us. I hope I'm wrong. Alas, I rarely am: it's my cross! (Yes I know—and yours).

I've met up several times with Lizzie and William, who are maintaining a fund-raising schedule nearly as hectic as my own. Lizzie said to me point-blank one day that she'd gladly trade her life for yours, if she could. And she means it. William told me a touching tale about Fischer. It seems that back in November, before the stay of execution had been granted, William went to say good-bye to all of you in prison before leaving on the first leg of his tour. He said Fischer took him aside and asked him to tell his old comrades in St. Louis that they must not mourn him, that he was glad to die for his principles and "would not change places with the richest man in America." The story brought tears to my eyes. I've never felt personally close to Fischer, as you know, but the words he spoke represent my own attitude exactly, and I believe yours. We're privileged to serve . . . Hold steady, my dearest love,

Lucy

P.S. Does Captain Black have any prediction as to how much longer the State Supreme Court will take before delivering its opinion?

*

Cook County Jail, Chicago
March 10, 1887

Dear Jailbird,

Well, congratulations on your first night in jail. I know you did it solely to compete with me, but I need to point out that one night is hardly in a league with those of us entering our tenth month of confinement. I know: you're only a woman, doing the best you can with your limited resources!

If your prison record doesn't put me in awe, your prescience in regard to Henry George most assuredly does. No sooner do you predict his defection, than it comes to pass. He's now saying in his newspaper that on "rereading the trial transcript" he's forced to conclude, contrary to his earlier view, that the anarchists *were* condemned on sufficient evidence. With his talent for backtracking, my guess is that he'll make an excellent run for Mayor.

As for Hortensia and Captain Black, I think your intuition has failed you. None of us can entirely scour from our souls the vile class and race prejudices bred into us as children, but surely the Blacks have gone as far as anyone. It's typical of you, dear, to hold out for 100 percent, but by that standard the entire world would be held "unsuitable" as comrades . . . No, the Captain hasn't offered a prediction as to the length of the Supreme Court's deliberations. The tedium and tension of this endless waiting is taking its toll—with the usual exception of Fischer, Engel, and

Lingg, who are superhuman in their ability to remain at least outwardly calm, even indifferent. The story William told you about Fischer is integral to his character. In the corridor the other day he told me how much he resents the criticism he's read against your "inflammatory" speeches. He defended you passionately and expressed utter contempt for those who would modify their words and principles simply because the capitalists have managed to get a few of us behind bars. "The true battle," he says, "is for the future, not for a piddling seven lives!" Your exact sentiments. Mine, too, except as one of the piddling seven, my conviction comes wrapped in the deepest melancholy. I'm only human. I want to see my children grow up and watch my Lucy continue to storm across the landscape. My mood is best when I keep busy. I've begun to write both a reminiscence and a history of Anarchism.

Some of our other comrades are not bearing up well. When Fielden and Schwab say good-bye to their wives and children after a visit, they often burst into tears. (By the way, you should see the way Lingg happily romps with the children; his essential sweetness emerges and he plays like an innocent child himself—hardly the ogre created by the press.) Spies keeps himself busy working with Nina on his autobiography, but his pale complexion and sad eyes give away the truth of his condition. The worst news of all I save for last: Meta Neebe has just this week succumbed to her illness, leaving poor Neebe a wreck of a man.

All of us get at least a brief lift in spirits from the mounting volume of mail that pours in, and also from the variety of visitors who come from all over, including a few from Europe. You'll be amazed to hear that none other than Wilhelm Liebknecht, the great German socialist, visited us, accompanied by Karl Marx's youngest daughter, Eleanor, and her husband, Edward Aveling! We had to talk through the iron grating, of course, but Mrs. Aveling could not have been more staunch in her support. She and her husband have been addressing mass meetings in New York and elsewhere ardently insisting that we're being condemned not for what we've done, but for what we've believed. In New York, she told me, she quoted her father's words during the massacre of the Paris Communards: the executioners "are already nailed to that eternal pillory from which all the prayers of their priests will not avail to redeem them."

As thrilling as her visit was, I've had one visitor who moved me even more: my old friend Ollie Canby from Texas! Can you believe it?! I haven't laid eyes on him, nor exchanged a word of correspondence since we left Waco nearly fifteen years ago. As far as I can remember, he was away on cattle drives for such long stretches that you never met him, but I've spoken of him often. A more decent man, and a more profane one, never lived. He now has a belly as large as his heart, and a wife and three children. He never got the ranch he dreamed of owning one day—he mostly does menial labor—but he has no bitterness about it, and dreams on. I don't know how he managed to afford the trip, but he came all the way from Waco just to see me. We talked about the old days through the grating. Even as teenagers during the War, he was always protective of me, always afraid I'd get myself killed.

"And now," he told me, his eyes clouding over, "you've gone and done it . . . Never shoulda let you outta my sight . . . It's the damn Feds! We shoulda won that war!"

After Ollie left, I sat down and had myself a good cry.

This will probably be my last letter before you return. I count the days . . .

Your loving husband,
Albert

Chicago

1887

The attorneys on both sides presented their arguments before the Illinois Supreme Court for three days. The defense detailed the legal errors and personal biases that in its view had disfigured the trial from start to finish. The prosecution insisted on the validity of its previously detailed definitions of *conspiracy, incitement,* and *accessory.* On March 16th, the six elderly judges of the court, sitting in Ottawa, a town due west of Chicago, retired to conduct their deliberations.

Days passed into weeks. Weeks into months. Yet the justices failed to reappear. A quick decision had been expected, and as spring gave way to summer, concern and puzzlement over the protracted delay grew throughout the land. As autumn approached, the country was still standing on one foot, and the prisoners, stifling in the heat and monotony of their daily routines, came fully to agree with the declaration Neebe had made during the trial that he preferred to die at once rather than by inches. Captain Black became so incensed at the delay that he again invoked to a reporter the imagery of Jesus suffering on the cross—which created such an outcry that he (at Hortensia's urging) issued a statement claiming that he'd been misquoted. "Given the stockpile of perjury already accumulated on the other side," he bitterly confided to Hortensia, "the Lord will forgive a thimbleful from us."

Then suddenly, on September 13th, Justice Schofield sent word from the chambers that at ten o'clock the following morning, the Supreme Court would announce its decision. The cramped, packed courtroom filled to overflowing hours before the justices filed in on the morning of the 14th. Speaking for the full court, Justice Magruder, looking notably frail but firm of voice, slowly read the opinion, page after page of it, aloud. In nearly every particular, the opinion sustained the rulings and verdict of the lower court. Only Justice Mulkey suggested even the slightest degree of dissent, writing that he did "not wish to be understood as holding that the record is free from error, for I do not think it is," but without specifying what errors he had in mind and while emphasizing that he was "fully satisfied with the conclusion reached. " The court refused to order a new trial and fixed the date of execution for November 11th. The State had won.

The mainstream press hailed the decision, and the country's "respectable elements" drew a collective sigh of relief. The defendants themselves tried to appear stoic. "I never expected anything else," Fischer told one reporter, and Spies sarcastically told another that "if the people of this great country are satisfied that free speech should be strangled, then what use for me to complain?" Albert had earlier predicted the result, telling a labor reporter that the propertied classes would "bulldoze" the supreme court into ratifying Judge Gary's verdict: "What a spectacle for 'free America'" he told the journalist, "Men put to death only because they made speeches that were offensive to the ruling class." Now that his prediction had been confirmed, Albert tried, in his public statements, to take the high ground: "I have done my duty to myself and the people, and I shall fearlessly stand the consequences. How can I do otherwise when I know that I have not committed a single crime against my fellow men or violated one clause of the Constitution?"

Captain Black had been shocked at the decision, but he was far from alone in believing that despite the setback, the sentence of execution would never be carried out. There were, Black insisted, still real grounds for hope. Two options remained: taking the case to the United States Supreme Court and, should it fail there, making a direct appeal to Governor Richard Oglesby for a commutation or pardon.

Backed by a strong team of prominent attorneys—ex-Confederate general Roger A. Pryor, ex-Union General Benjamin Butler, and the widely respected John Randolph Tucker of Virginia—Captain Black appeared before the United States Supreme Court on October 27th and for two days argued for a writ of error. On November 2nd, the Court gave its unanimous answer. Chief Justice Waite announced that the Supreme Court lacked jurisdiction, since "no federal issues" were involved in the case. The Court's critics were quick to point out that among the federal issues in question are the rights of free speech and assembly, and due process of law. The legal battle, in any case, had reached a dead end; no avenue of appeal remained open through the courts.

That same night, Oscar Neebe, the only one of the eight defendants who had not been condemned to death, was removed from the Cook County jail and taken to the state prison at Joliet to begin his fifteen years of hard labor.

Nine days remained before the scheduled executions. All eyes and efforts turned toward Governor Richard Oglesby.

The Defense Committee had already launched a petition drive for commutation of the sentences. Hundreds of people now stepped forward in a burst of sympathy to help distribute the petitions. Nina Van Zandt and her mother were frequently recognized by their disapproving peers as they stood on street corners soliciting signatures, and garnering curses. Lucy had to contend with the police. It was a rare day when a patrolman didn't poke his club in her ribs and order her to move on. Finally, one afternoon, she was arrested. The judge who heard the case—having expected, from all the negative publicity, an unmanageable tigress—was unpredictably moved at Lucy's wan, exhausted appearance, gave her a minimal five-dollar fine, and ordered her released at once.

Petitions, telegrams, letters and resolutions poured into Oglesby's office. They came from around the world, from the eminent and the unknown, from George Bernard Shaw and mill workers in Rhode Island. "In the name of humanity . . ." many of them began, and often closed with variants of "return them to their families, leave them, we implore you, to the judgment of history." There was reason to believe that Oglesby might prove responsive. In the prewar period he'd been an active abolitionist, deeply sympathetic to the sufferings of the slave. "I'm told by many," Captain Black reported to Lucy, "that the governor has a good heart." Lucy said she was delighted to hear it, "but hearts are notoriously fickle." She was putting her hopes, she said, in the recent unmistakable shift in public opinion. "To that, the governor might respond."

Though Oglesby thought of himself as "a decent sort," he was decidedly a politician, and one particularly reliant on the good opinion of the business and professional communities. Ideally he would have liked for the heart lobe that pumped sympathy for the oppressed to be consonant with the lobe that pumped hands for votes, lest an electrical cross-current create a dangerous arrhythmia. And he was glad that some of the voices being raised in behalf of clemency came from prominent citizens. Among the forty thousand signatures on the petitions were those of William Goudy, head of the city's bar association, and Marvin Hughitt, president of the Chicago & Northwestern Railroad. No less a figure than Potter Palmer was known to have spoken up in favor of commutation at a secret meeting of some fifty members of the city's elite, though the strong opposition of Marshall Field had prevented any additional support from materializing. Other powerful business leaders, including George Pullman, Cyrus McCormick, Jr., and Philip Armour, let it be known that they considered the carrying out of the death penalty essential to the future preservation of law and order.

The signals were mixed, public opinion passionate and divided. Governor Oglesby hunkered down in his office, pondering the tangle of charges and disclaimers, hoping for a thunderstruck inspiration worthy of Solomon.

✳

The children clamored noisily up the iron flight of stairs, shouting "Papa! Papa!" at the top of their lungs before they'd even reached the entry to the cellblock. Hearing their cries, Albert jumped to his feet with such exuberance that he nearly overturned the small table at which he'd been writing, deeply engrossed, just a moment before.

Rushing to the front of his cell to glimpse the children at the earliest possible moment, he caught the eye of the guard standing nearby. "Don't worry, Mr. Parsons," the guard said, smiling, "I'll let them in the cell, your wife, too. Just don't snitch on me to the sheriff, or you'll soon enough be gettin' a less kindly type watchin' over you!" Albert thanked him fervently and turned back to find Lulu and Albert Jr. racing down the corridor toward him, Lucy following behind.

It had been many, many months. Once inside his cell, the children scampered all over him, Lulu climbing up to his shoulders, Albert Jr. hugging him around the waist, then smothering his face with kisses. With Lulu perched on his neck, Parsons pretended to gallop around the tiny cell as she squealed with delight and as Albert Jr. brought up the rear whooping at the top of his lungs.

Shouts and greetings filled the cellblock as the other prisoners became aware of the children's arrival. Fischer, in the cell next to Albert's, called over in a ponderously cheery voice, "Don't hurt your papa now, we must save him for the State!" He'd meant to make a joke, but jokes were not Fischer's forte and the children, as if understanding the literal import of his words, did quickly quiet down. Lucy had brought some toys with her and scattered them over the cell floor for them to play with so she could talk to Albert.

"Remember what Aunt Lizzie said, Lulu," she called over. "If you run around too much, you'll shake out the medicine."

"What's wrong?" Albert asked in alarm.

Lucy tried to make light of it, though she was deeply worried at the frequency of Lulu's fevers. "Oh, she's had a little bout of sickness again, that's all."

"What does the doctor say?"

"You know doctors are useless for this sort of thing," she said vaguely. Then, seeing Albert's stricken look, she hastily added, "She's been to half a dozen doctors. They all say the same thing: it's nothing serious, just a bit of catarrh that she'll soon outgrow. Lizzie's been dosing her with Drake's Plantation Bitters, which seem to help."

Lucy abruptly took a small newspaper from her purse and handed it to Albert. "Now feast your eyes on *this*!" she said triumphantly. When he unfolded the paper and grasped what it was, his face lit up. The heading read: "*THE ALARM.* NOVEMBER 5, 1887." "You've done it!" Albert cried. "You've brought it back to life! But how—how did you ever manage it?!"

"*I* didn't do anything," Lucy said. "All the credit goes to Dyer Lum. Remember him? We all met at the Greenback-Labor convention in 1880, and we occasionally published an article by him in the *Alarm*. He's now a staunch IWPA man."

"Remember him? Why, Dyer Lum visits the jail constantly, mostly to see Lingg. Haven't the two of you ever run into each other here?"

"No, I had no idea . . ." Lucy was surprised. "All I knew was that he'd sold his bookbindery in New York and moved to Chicago after he heard about the Haymarket bombing."

"How did Lum ever manage it? I didn't think anyone could resurrect the *Alarm*."

"He's been at it for a year, trying to raise the money. He put in all his own savings, $1,500."

"And none of you told me what he was up to?"

"We were so afraid he wouldn't be able to carry it off . . . Oh, and by the way, can you guess who Lum has chosen as his assistant editor?"

"You."

"Almost as good—Lizzie!"

"Oh Lucy," Albert said softly, his voice breaking, "maybe it hasn't all been in vain . . ."

"In *vain*?!" Lucy's exhaustion dropped from her like a veil. "Don't ever think that, not ever. Albert, Albert, it's been far, far from in vain!"

The children, startled at their mother's vehemence, dropped their toys and climbed back into Albert's lap.

"All right, all right," he said to Lucy, smiling gently, "I'll believe you . . . or try to . . ."

✳

With only days left before the scheduled executions, rallies and marches proliferated across the country and around the world. The protest meetings drew huge crowds; resolutions were passed ranging from fierce denunciations of "judicial bloodletting" to prayerful calls for impartial justice. And from London came a telegram to Oglesby petitioning for commutation that was signed by, among others, Oscar Wilde, Edward Carpenter, William Rossetti, George Bernard Shaw, Friedrich Engels, Olive Schreiner, and William Morris.

Terence Powderly continued to insist that the Knights avoid all taint of association with those who "abetted violence," and the local assemblies of the Order remained bitterly divided over the question of clemency. Yet the more conservative Samuel Gompers joined hands with a number of other prominent labor leaders in calling the pending executions "a disgrace to the honor of our nation," and in begging the governor to commute the sentences to life imprisonment. Gompers wrote Oglesby that his own organization, the American Federation of Labor, and the anarchists "were fighting for labor upon different sides of the house," that he believed the Chicago police were themselves accountable "in some measure" for the violence at Haymarket, and that in any case the execution of the anarchists

would make them martyrs and give impetus to "this so-called revolutionary movement." If this country could grant amnesty to Jefferson Davis,
Gompers wrote, "it ought to be great and magnanimous enough to grant
clemency to these men."

Everyone was aware that even if the public outcry should succeed in
personally moving the governor in the direction of clemency, state law
would prevent him from acting unless the prisoners submitted a formal
appeal requesting mercy and making some acknowledgment of regret,
however hedged, for past "mistakes."

The problem came in trying to persuade the condemned men to send
such letters of appeal to the governor. Lingg, Engels, Fischer, and Parsons
refused outright. Insisting that they were innocent of all charges, they
held out for unconditional release. "If I cannot obtain justice from the
authorities," Fischer wrote Oglesby, "and be restored to my family, then I
prefer that the verdict be carried out as it stands." Fischer and Engel's wives
begged them to reconsider, but everyone knew it was futile: they'd never
agree that staying alive was more important than adhering to principle.

As for Albert, many, including Captain Black, believed that he would
ultimately yield to entreaty and bring himself to cooperate with those
attempting to save his life.

Schwab and Fielden, from the beginning, were amenable to submitting a formal appeal to Oglesby, though they insisted that the wording
be carefully crafted; they had no intention of admitting to thoughts they
had never entertained or acts they had never committed. Spies, to the
surprise of many, finally gave way to Nina's pleas, and to his own intense
desire to stay alive, and said that he would be willing to at least discuss
signing a joint letter with Schwab and Fielden.

Speed was of the essence. Working around the clock and adjusting
every word for maximum nuance, a letter was finally constructed that
won the approval of Fielden, Schwab and, more reluctantly, Spies. The
brief, two paragraph letter began with a firm declaration by the three:
"We never advocated the use of force, excepting in the case of self-defense,"
and moved on to assert, "We have never supported, or plotted to commit,
an unlawful act." That said, the required obeisance followed: "If, in the
excitement of propagating our views, we were led into expressions which
caused workingmen to think that aggressive force was a proper instrument of reform, we regret it. We deplore the loss of life at the Haymarket

and"—this was added at the insistence of Spies—"at McCormick's factory as well." "I think I am making a mistake," Spies said, as he took up his pen to sign the letter.

Over the next two days, Fielden and Schwab sent second, supplementary letters to the governor, in which they ate just a bit more crow than Spies had proven willing to. Fielden admitted to having now and then been so "intoxicated with the applause of my hearers" that he had sometimes given speeches that were "irresponsible," that could have been taken as recommending a resort to violence. "But," he added—for Fielden was far from craven—"it is not true that I ever consciously attempted to incite any man to the commission of crime . . . I was not engaged in any conspiracy to manufacture or throw bombs and I had not the slightest idea that the meeting at the Haymarket would be other than a peaceable and orderly one."

Schwab's second letter, a mere three sentences long, made essentially the same points: "Many utterances of mine were expressions made under intense excitement, often without any deliberation, and were injudicious. These I regret, believing that they must have had a tendency to incite to unnecessary violence oftentimes. I protest again that I had no thought or purpose of violence in connection with the Haymarket meeting, which I did not even attend."

Captain Black could hear Lucy's hissing voice from the end of the corridor, and as he got closer to Albert's cell a few of her words became distinct: ". . . a coward, he's a coward! . . . Radicals in Germany are denouncing him as a traitor . . ."

As Black approached, he could pick up Albert's hushed protest: "Be quiet, for heaven's sake—Spies will hear you!"

"I don't care if he does," Lucy said, lowering her voice nonetheless.

"You're being much too harsh . . . Spies was under intense pressure . . . you cannot judge another man's—"

By this point Captain Black was standing directly opposite the cell, and Albert abruptly left off. All three made vague efforts at apology, though no one was sure for what. To end the general embarrassment, Black quickly asked if he might have a few words alone with Albert. He knew Lucy would be offended—which the suspicious look in her eye confirmed—but he'd heard just enough in coming down the corridor to realize that he stood his best chance with Albert if they conferred alone. Lucy covered over for all concerned by claiming that in any case she'd been on her way out.

When the two men were alone, Black began by telling Albert that his refusal to sign any petition for executive clemency was being widely construed as obstinacy, folly, or some combination thereof, bespeaking a character so self-righteously intransigent that he had only himself to blame if he ended on the scaffold.

"And exactly who is saying these horrid things?" Albert asked, still buoyant from Lucy's visit.

"Among others, several of your codefendants."

"Meaning, I presume, Schwab and Fielden. Though not, I'm fairly certain, Spies. Mind you, Schwab and Fielden are speaking out of their love for me, their wish to 'save me from myself,' as they might put it, not out of a need to defend their own willingness to petition the governor. I know these men well. They have bowed to the entreaties of their families and appealed for clemency, but have done so, I can assure you, with a heavy heart."

"Why do you exempt Spies?"

"Because Spies is about to rescind his appeal to Oglesby, and himself become one of the 'obstinate intransigents,' making it unlikely he'd simultaneously deplore their 'folly.'" From the moment Spies signed the appeal, he's been in anguish about it. He's talked to me at length and has concluded that he made the wrong decision."

"I have a copy of Spies's latest letter to the governor. Have you seen it?"

"I know the gist of what he's been planning to say; we've gone over several drafts together, but no, I haven't seen the final version."

They spoke in a whisper, to avoid being overheard. Captain Black handed Albert his copy of Spies's letter and sat back. It was only two pages long, and Albert, thinking he was already familiar with its sentiments, started to skim the letter when an unfamiliar paragraph brought him up short. He looked up at Black in astonishment. "*This* section I haven't seen!" He held up the letter and read softly from it: "'If a sacrifice of life must be, will not my life suffice? I offer it to you that you may satisfy the fury of a semi-barbaric mob and save that of my comrades. If legal murder there must be, let one, let mine, suffice.'"

Albert let the letter fall into his lap. "There's the measure of the man," he said quietly. "Who will dare call Spies a coward now?"

"There's no chance, of course," Captain Black said gravely, "that Oglesby will accept the offer. Which does raise some question as to why he made it. To repair his reputation among his comrades, of course, and to remove all doubt of his devotion to principle. But I suspect there may be another reason, one of which Spies himself may not be fully aware."

Albert looked puzzled, and Captain Black quickly went on, "In my opinion, Spies doesn't believe that any of you, ultimately, will go to the scaffold. He's an idealist at heart. How does he put it at the end of his letter to Oglesby?—something about 'men whose only crime is that they long for a better future for all.' It surely follows, in Spies's logic, that the State would never be callous enough to put such men to death. Spies is convinced there will be a last-minute reprieve. He doesn't understand that the State isn't fond of idealists."

The Captain deliberately paused for effect. Then he solemnly turned his gaze on Albert. "But Spies is wrong. And that is what I've come to tell you tonight: he, Engel, Fischer, and Lingg will hang, they will most assuredly hang. There is no chance whatsoever at this late date of saving them."

Albert showed no sign of surprise or alarm. "I believe you're right," he said quietly. "But why do you omit my name from that list?"

"For a very good reason. Because I believe strongly that *you* can be saved."

Albert shifted uncomfortably in his chair. "If, you mean, I agree to meet certain requirements."

"Yes. Even State's Attorney Grinnell and Judge Gary have hinted they could accept commutation in your case, so long as *you* request it. After all, you're American-born, you surrendered yourself voluntarily, and your speech in court, the depth of your sincerity, made a strong impression. The governor has let it be known to me—the hint was unmistakable—that he believes you are entitled to some special consideration."

"If I agree to sign an appeal to him."

"I urge you to do so. I beg of you to do so. If for nothing else, than for the sake of your wife and children."

"Lucy is not urging me to sign."

"Is she urging you not to?"

"She's refused to offer an opinion, to say a single word on the subject."

"But she's denounced Fielden, Schwab, and Spies for signing. I heard her as I was coming down the corridor."

"Yes, but I'm her husband!" Albert's laughter eased the tension. "She's rather fond of me, you know, much as she enjoys trying to out-radicalize me. She doesn't want me to die. And you know something, Captain? I don't want to die, either. I'm a young man still. I'm only thirty-eight. I'm not at all tired of life."

"Then *live*, Parsons!" Captain Black burst out. "It is within your power."

"William and Lizzie Holmes don't agree with you. They believe Oglesby and his masters are playing a clever game, holding out the possibility of amnesty in order to make me crawl. They're not satisfied with murdering me; they also want to disgrace me. And once they've done that, they'll murder me anyway."

"William and Lizzie are wrong! They could not be more wrong! Do you think I would for a moment suggest that you sign an appeal if I didn't believe Oglesby was sincere in his offer?"

"Of course not, Captain," Albert said gently. "I've always known you to be a man of absolute integrity. I feel certain that William and Lizzie are mistaken and that you are right: that if I sign an application for pardon, my sentence will be commuted."

Captain Black sighed deeply. "I'm at a loss, Parsons. I cannot understand your reluctance. I'm at a loss what to say further that might bring you round." Black's face was full of pain. There was a brief silence between the two men, then Albert spoke, his voice eerily calm.

"I'll tell you what the real secret of my position is. But I do so in utmost confidence. Can I have your word that you'll say nothing of it until after November 11th?"

"Yes, of course," Black answered, leaning forward intently. His stomach turned over at the casual way Parsons referred to the date.

"It's like this, Captain. I have the faint hope—the odds are a thousand to one—that in refusing to apply for executive clemency I may yet save the lives of the four comrades who also reject it. If I were to separate myself from Lingg, Fischer, Engel, and Spies and petition the governor, I'm certain that would spell their doom. If there's any chance of saving them it's by my standing firmly at their side, making their cause my own. That way Oglesby cannot pardon me without pardoning them as well."

"But he'll never do that!" Captain Black cried out. "In refusing to sign, you're not cornering the State into pardoning the others, but rather giving it a legal reason for putting you to death. After all, they're not that eager to keep you alive!"

"Yes, you're almost certainly right. I expect my strategy will fail to free them, and instead I'll end up sharing their fate on the gallows. But I'm at peace about that. I'm ready."

There was nothing more Captain Black felt he could say. He knew that Parsons's refusal to apply for clemency was in fact the only chance the other four men had to escape the gallows. And he realized that Parsons was immovable in his determination to give them that chance, even as he fully recognized it would almost certainly cost him his life. Captain Black took Parsons by the hand and, with tears in his eyes, simply said, "Your action is worthy of you."

On the morning of November 6th, the prisoners were suddenly told that they must vacate their cells at once. They were swiftly moved into the small area at the end of the corridor. The guards then began a methodical search of the cells. Within a short time, a shout went up from the two guards rummaging through Lingg's bedding. In a wooden box under his bed they'd found four narrow pipe bombs hidden beneath layers of newspaper.

The discovery, immediately released to the press, caused a sensation. The mainstream papers highlighted the most melodramatic interpretation: that the bombs had been intended to destroy the prison, perhaps to facilitate an escape, perhaps to allow the prisoners to take down as many of the "enemy" as possible with them. Rumors were already flying in the city that the anarchists were conducting secret drills and planned to free the prisoners by force on the eve of their execution.

The Citizens Association at once donated supplementary arms to the police: four hundred Springfield rifles and bayonets, twelve thousand rounds of cartridges, and a Gatling gun. The state militia was put on alert and two companies of the United States Sixth Infantry Regiment in Salt

Lake City were ordered aboard trains headed directly for Chicago. In the next few days, Captain Schaack and Superintendent Ebersold fanned the flames with fabricated announcements of the discovery of a cache of dynamite here, a hidden store of Remingtons there. Only Bonfield found amusement in the feverish alarm: "There is no reason to fear a disturbance," he told a *Tribune* reporter, "anarchists are natural cowards. After all, when the police opened fire at Haymarket, they ran away instead of standing their ground like men."

Captain Black and the Defense Committee were deeply upset at the discovery of the bombs, fearful it would reverse the mounting sympathetic trend in public opinion and cripple the effort to win commutation. They moved quickly to counteract the negative publicity. The four bombs, Captain Black pointed out to reporters, were far too small to cause serious damage, and yet too large to be passed through the narrow wire meshing of the cells; in other words, Lingg could only have meant to employ them for self-destruction—a theory Lingg refused to corroborate. He denied any knowledge of the bombs.

That, in turn, fed speculation that the police had themselves planted the bombs in Lingg's cell in a deliberate effort to discredit the growing movement for clemency. That was the view taken by Albert and Lucy, among others, and Lucy publicly mocked the police for their ineptness. "More intelligent men," she told a reporter, "would have placed a bomb in one cell, a fuse in another, dynamite in a third and percussion caps in a fourth—thereby plausibly making the case that some sort of genuine conspiracy existed."

Unlike Lucy and Albert, Spies was convinced that Lingg was aware of the bombs, having persuaded some friend to smuggle them in. Spies had never much liked Lingg, and the two men had barely spoken in the preceding nine months. Spies now lashed out publicly at Lingg, writing a letter to the Chicago press (which Fielden and Schwab also signed) that characterized Lingg as a "monomaniac," a man willing to sacrifice the lives of his fellow prisoners for a cause he did not even understand and—reversing the theory that Lucy and Albert had put forth—accusing him of putting the bombs in his cell in a deliberate attempt to thwart the growing momentum for clemency. A furious Lucy refused ever to speak to Spies again. Which prompted an equally furious Nina to cut off all communication with Lucy.

The big question now was what effect the discovery of the bombs would have on Governor Oglesby. On the very next morning, November 7th, Oglesby announced that he was setting aside November 9th to receive at the Statehouse all those who desired to present appeals for clemency.

On that same morning of November 7th, John Brown, Jr., the eldest child of the Hero of Harper's Ferry, sent a box of Catawba grapes to each of the condemned prisoners, along with a note that asked them to accept the grapes "as a slight token of my sympathy for you, and for the cause which you represent. Four days before his execution, my father wrote to a friend the following: 'It is a great comfort to feel assured that I am permitted to die for a cause, not merely to pay the debt of nature, as all must.'"

On November 8th, when Lucy appeared at the jail for her daily visit, she was for the first time subjected to a thorough body search, as were all the other wives, and although nothing suspicious was found, they were told there would be no visits that day. Lucy wheeled angrily on the guards and accused them of deliberate humiliation. "Someday," she spat out, "the men you keep in dungeons will turn the key on *you*—and leave you there!" She swept out.

That evening chartered railroad cars left from Chicago for the State Capitol at Springfield. They carried the attorneys, many of the family members, and the leading supporters of the prisoners. But not Lucy, nor Lizzie and William, who announced that they would refuse to "demean" themselves. Some three hundred other sympathizers, many from outside the state, arrived at Springfield throughout the evening and into the early morning hours.

At nine-thirty the next morning, Governor Oglesby seated himself at a table in the back of the gilded "audience room" in the Capitol and announced to the hundreds of people assembled before him that he was prepared to hear appeals in the Haymarket case. Captain Black, with his wife, Hortensia, seated at his side, opened the proceedings with a lengthy and eloquent plea for clemency. The governor periodically interrupted to ask that a point be clarified or an argument repeated. Throughout the day Oglesby listened to every presentation with an unwandering eye and the keenest attention.

And for more than eight hours, with only a short recess in the early afternoon, the parade of petitioners wound on. Notables such as Henry Demarest Lloyd and Samuel Gompers joined their voices to those of spiritualists, housewives, relatives, farmers, and labor organizers to urge the governor, in the name of humanity and common justice, to be merciful.

Though many spoke with passionate fluency or, more effective still, with hesitant, touching grace, little was said, after so many months of public debate, that could be considered new or surprising. That is, until the very end of the day, when Captain Black announced that he had in his possession letters from August Spies and Albert Parsons to the governor, and requested a private audience confined to a small number of people, at which he could read them aloud. The governor immediately granted the request, and some dozen people retired to his private chambers.

The Spies letter was the one—only now actually delivered to the governor—in which he requested that he alone be executed and his comrades spared. Hearing it, the literal-minded Oglesby seemed visibly moved, perhaps far more so than Spies had been when writing it, since everyone recognized the suggestion couldn't possibly be implemented.

Albert's letter, on the other hand, had been earlier seen by no one but Lucy, Captain Black having pledged not to open it until he was facing the governor. The letter's contents, brief and shocking, shattered the Captain's hope that it contained a plea for clemency. Parsons requested—with a harrowing irony apparent to everyone but the governor himself—that since he was to be hanged for being at Haymarket the night the bomb was thrown, he felt the governor ought to know that his wife, two children, and Lizzie Holmes had also been present. Accordingly, Parsons requested a reprieve long enough to enable the other four to be indicted, tried, convicted, and sentenced to death, so that they might all go hand in hand into the Great Beyond. "My God!" the governor burst out, his face suffused with agony, "this is terrible!"

After a resonant pause, Oglesby recovered his wits long enough to announce that he would render his decision on clemency the following day. Less than forty-eight hours remained before the executions were scheduled to take place.

That night in his prison cell, Parsons took out his pen to compose another letter, this one to his two children. "As I write these words," it began, "I blot your names with a tear. We will never meet again. Oh my children, how deeply, dearly your Papa loves you. Of my life and the cause of my unnatural and cruel death, you will learn from others. To you I leave the legacy of an honest name and duty done. Preserve it, emulate it. My children, my precious ones, I request you to read this parting message on each recurring anniversary of my death in remembrance of him who dies not alone for you, but for the children yet unborn. Bless you, my darlings. Farewell."

✳

At 8:55 on the morning of November 10, the sound of an explosion resounded through the corridor of the jail. A guard standing in front of Lingg's cell saw a puff of blue smoke roll out from it and immediately yelled, "It's Lingg!" The other guards raced toward the area. They found Lingg lying on his bed, with his head over the edge of it, and everything in the cell—bed, pillow, walls and floor—splattered with blood, flesh, teeth, and bits of bone. Turning his body over, the guards discovered that Lingg was still breathing: a sound like a clogged gurgle was coming from his mouth. How he could still be breathing astonished them. The entire lower part of his face, including the larger part of his lips and most of his tongue, had been torn away, leaving a hideous, gaping wound that extended nearly to the angles of the jaw. His nose had collapsed into itself, a mass of sunken, flabby flesh. A bit of chin remained and the trace of an upper lip. His eyes were closed.

Yet he was fully conscious. The jailers carried him from his cell to an office across the way and medical help was immediately summoned. The doctors decided to attempt surgery, without anesthesia, to save him, perhaps because someone with a taste for grim humor had asked how healthy a man had to be before he could be hanged, perhaps out of determination to thwart Lingg's last wish—to die by his own hand.

Three doctors took turns working on him, inserting their probes, twisting their blunt instruments into his bleeding flesh in a tableau of excruciating Inquisitorial horror. Throughout the ordeal Lingg never once groaned, though his body now and then involuntarily twitched with agony. He desperately wanted to escape his tormentors and die, but for six hours his powerful body refused to cooperate. Then suddenly, around 3:00 P.M., he lapsed into a coma and expired. The guards threw the corpse into a bathtub, to await its expected companions.

Nina Van Zandt was convinced that the police had murdered Lingg, but few others who knew him accepted that theory. As Engel said, "Why kill a man the day before he's due to be hanged?" No, it was generally accepted that Lingg, who had personified defiance throughout his trial and imprisonment, was determined to rob the State of jurisdiction over his mind or his body.

The only real puzzle was how he'd managed to get the explosives to kill himself. Many assumed that his girlfriend, Ida, had somehow smuggled in the dynamite cartridge. But it turned out to have been Dyer Lum, the new proprietor of the *Alarm* and a far more militant revolutionary than anyone had suspected. It was he who had passed Lingg the cartridge, concealed within a cigar casing. Since the prisoners were allowed to smoke, the cigar had gone unexamined when the police had searched Lingg's cell three days earlier. When he was ready, Lingg had calmly placed the cigar in his mouth and lit it.

In its front-page article on Lingg's suicide, the *Chicago Tribune* devoted the last paragraph to triumphantly reminding its readers that at least his death "closes the mouths of those anarchistic sympathizers" who had been claiming that the police planted the bombs found in Lingg's cell on November 6th in order to discredit the movement for clemency.

When William Dean Howells heard the news of Lingg's death, he told the press, "All over the world people must be asking themselves, 'What cause is this really, for which men die so gladly, so inexorably?'"

The news that Lingg had killed himself was immediately telegraphed to the State Capitol at Springfield. An hour and a half later, at four-thirty, reporters crowding the rotunda were told that Governor Oglesby would shortly issue his decision on the clemency appeal.

He appeared in person soon after, looking somber and uncomfortable. Reading directly from a prepared text, he began ominously: "My careful consideration of the evidence has failed to produce upon my mind any impression tending to impeach the verdict of the jury or the judgment of the trial court or of the Supreme Court affirming the guilt of all these parties."

Michael Schwab's wife, Maria, standing in the rotunda, turned pale and looked as if she might faint; just the day before, the governor had revealed that State's Attorney Grinnell had joined with Judge Gary in recommending commutation for Schwab and Fielden, because of their "respectful and decorous" conduct throughout the trial and their appropriately remorseful petition. Everyone had been confident that their joint recommendation would be followed, which the governor's gloomy introduction now seemed to contradict.

But in truth, Oglesby had simply decided, in keeping with his self-protective nature, on a cautious, long-winded prelude. His primary concern was setting himself to rights with the business community; it had been deluging him with petitions demanding that he stand firm. To secure his standing with the propertied classes, Oglesby declared at the top of his statement that he entirely agreed with the court's conclusion that all seven men were indeed, through their "violent" speech, guilty of being accessories to murder. The governor then went on to announce that Parsons, Fischer, Engel, and Lingg, later implicitly joined by Spies, had, by demanding "unconditional release," precluded him from even considering the question of clemency in their cases; they had doomed themselves.

All prudential bases covered, Oglesby finally felt able to declare that in the cases of Schwab and Fielden he was—"in the interest of humanity, and without doing violence to public justice"—commuting their sentences to life imprisonment.

When word of Oglesby's decision reached Lucy that evening, she rushed to the Cook County jail, accompanied by Lizzie and William. They found the entrance to the prison blocked by a solid phalanx of police. Lucy tried to push her way through, but was brusquely thrown back. Stunned, she looked as if she might pass out. An anxious Lizzie hurried to her side, and the touch of her hand seemed to bring Lucy back.

Within a few seconds, she was again pressing toward the line of guards, her eyes now clouded with anger. She yelled up into the face of the nearest officer, "What time are you going to murder my husband?!" The guards stood like statues, eyes averted, silent. Spotting the sergeant in charge, Lucy went straight over to him.

"I know for a fact," she shouted, "that some of the other wives and family have been allowed inside the jail earlier this evening to say a final good-bye. Why am I being denied the same privilege?"

"I have no idea, madam," he said gently, "but I feel sure that if you return in the morning, entrance can be gained."

Believing him, and in any case having no other option, the three left.

When the prisoners were told of Oglesby's decision, they expressed no surprise and limited distress. Spies chatted amiably with the guards, then sat down and wrote Nina to "be strong; show no weakness." When a prison chaplain dropped by Engel's cell to offer consolation, Engel told him that he needed none. "I feel content," he told the chaplain, "that I've been true to the only religion I recognize—'to wrong no man and to do good to everybody.'" Fischer asked for a bottle of champagne and wrote his typographical union requesting that he be buried with "our beloved red emblem," and without "religious humbug" or "sentimental songs."

As for Parsons, he kept up a steady stream of cheerful conversation with the deputy sheriff assigned to him, turning melancholy only when expressing concern for Lucy and his children. At one point late in the evening, a telegram arrived from his brother, William, and Parsons read its last line to the deputy.

"Listen to this, will you?" he said, his voice full of affectionate mirth. "These are my beloved brother's final words to me: 'I am proud of your sublimity, fortitude, and hereditary heroism.' Can you believe it? Here I am about to march to the scaffold for my principles and William wants to give credit not to me, but to the family blood!" The deputy tried his best to chortle, but felt at a loss for words; it wasn't William's sentiments, but Albert's smile, that unsettled him.

It was only when the lights were turned off in the cellblock shortly after the death watch changed at 1:30 A.M., and each man sat alone in his cage, that the silence grew heavy and the mood darkened. Before long, loud noises ascended from the courtyard below, the cacophonous sound of dozens of saws and hammers working feverishly away. The scaffold was being erected.

Since no one could sleep, Albert decided he'd try and distract his friends from the noise with an impromptu recitation of poetry and song. He recited stanza after stanza of John Greenleaf Whittier's "The Reformer":

> The noblest place for men to die
> Is where he dies for man—

oblivious to the irony that just weeks before, Whittier had refused to sign William Dean Howells's petition for mercy.

Albert then sang his favorite of all the songs that he'd performed over the years at parades and rallies—his beloved "Annie Laurie." His sweet lyrical tenor soared at the refrain:

> And for bonnie Annie Laurie
> I'd lay me doon and die.

It carried hauntingly along the row of cells, reverberating over the stone walls.

✳

At that very moment, Captain Black was sitting on a train headed back to Springfield. He'd no sooner returned to Chicago that morning than a telegram had arrived from New York City, which had kindled a spark of hope. The telegram read:

I HAVE PROOF SHOWING ANARCHISTS TO BE INNOCENT. GUILTY MAN IN NEW YORK—LOCATED. HAVE TELEGRAPHED TO GOV. OGLESBY. PROOF IS UNDER OATH. HOW SHALL I COMMUNICATE IT?
  (SIGNED) AUGUST P. WAGENER
  COUNSELOR-AT-LAW

Captain Black quickly established that Wagener was a real person, and a reputable one, and chose to interpret the telegram as meaning that the actual bomb-thrower had made himself available to testify.

Black arrived at Springfield at 8:30 A.M.—three hours before the scheduled executions—and was immediately ushered into the library of Oglesby's private residence. The governor had also received the telegram from New York and, discarding all preliminaries, asked Captain Black what meaning he assigned to it.

"From all I can discover," Black said, "the contents and the signer are authentic."

"If so," the somber-faced governor asked, "what are you proposing?"

"A sixty- to ninety-day reprieve, Your Honor, to allow time to return the bomb-thrower to Illinois and to take his testimony, which will surely throw critical light on the events at Haymarket and the responsibility for what took place there. Having admired the fair-minded way you've conducted this inquiry, I feel sure you'll want to give the condemned men every legitimate chance to save their lives."

Saying he needed to be alone to consider the matter, the governor retired to an inner room. Twenty minutes later, he reappeared and rejected the request for postponement. Months later, when Lucy tried to locate Wagener and get to the bottom of his story, he was no longer to be found at his given address and had left no forwarding one.

*

November 11 dawned bleak and cold on a city gripped by fear. Rumors abounded that anarchists had planted bombs in the basement of the jail-house and intended either to blow it up or to storm it, in a last-minute effort to free their comrades. Many in the city thought a catastrophic outbreak of some sort inevitable, even though it was known that Parsons had several days earlier put out a plea to the workmen of Chicago not to resort to any form of violent protest.

"A diversion, a ruse," Superintendent Ebersold had said when told of Parsons's statement. "He's trying to throw us off guard." Proud of his superior insight, Ebersold ordered police units, supplemented by militia troops armed with Gatling guns and cannon, stationed throughout the city, with the larger portion concentrated on the blocks and rooftops sur- rounding the Cook County jail. Factories closed and stores boarded up their windows. Most of the well-to-do stayed indoors; the few men who ventured out armed themselves with revolvers. Those thought in the most danger of reprisals from the "mob"—among them, Judge Gary, Grinnell, Ebersold, and Bonfield—were given special police protection.

The day before, as an additional precaution, a secret court session had convened and issued the necessary legal papers for allowing the police to "arrest at will and put down summarily" any anarchist found loitering suspiciously in the vicinity, broadly defined, of the Cook County jail. The blocks immediately adjacent to the prison were sealed off with ropes and all traffic in the area suspended. Three hundred policemen armed with Winchester rifles surrounded the immediate perimeter of the jailhouse.

In New York City, seven thousand workers marched through the streets to protest the pending executions.

✳

Having dozed fitfully for an hour or two, the prisoners were awakened early for breakfast. Albert washed his face, drank some coffee, and ate fried oysters, pronouncing them "tasty." He felt anxious about how Spies, the most high-strung among them, was faring and felt relieved, when the four men greeted each other across the line of cells, to find that his friend seemed composed.

Albert wondered why Lucy and the children had not yet appeared. To chase their image from his mind, he sat down to scan the morning papers. But suddenly his cell door was thrown open and the turnkey admitted a man announced as "the Reverend Doctor Bolton." Albert listened patiently to the reverend's assorted admonitions to repentance and assurances of grace, but when he finished, politely told him that he thought religion was superstition and preachers were Pharisees. Reverend Bolton, plainly shocked, retained his poise. "So great is the Maker's magnanimity," Bolton said, "that He is able to disregard even the crudest forms of blasphemy." He then bid Parsons, or rather his Soul, a hasty farewell. "Remember," Albert called out to the reverend's back, "I didn't send for you."

✳

Early that morning Nina and her mother drove in their carriage to the jail and asked permission to say good-bye to Spies. A deputy sheriff told them that they had already had their final visit and turned them brusquely away. Returning to their home, the Van Zandts closed the curtains on every window and locked every door. A neighbor who snuck up close to the house reported with satisfaction that he'd heard sounds of moaning and intense crying coming from within.

✳

The deputy sheriff had told Lucy, when turning her away the previous night, that she and her two children would be admitted for a final farewell at eight-thirty the following morning. Lucy slept a fitful few hours, then at dawn aroused and dressed Lulu and Albert Jr. The morning was cold and Lulu had again been running a fever, so Lucy bundled her up in three layers of sweaters. Lizzie and William arrived promptly at seven-thirty to escort them downtown. Once there, William went off to the offices of the Defense Committee and the others proceeded to within a block of the jail, where they ran directly into the cordon of police guarding the approach.

Lucy identified herself to the police officer standing on the corner and told him that she'd been promised admission.

"Not at this entry point," he blandly said, "but I think it likely that if you pass on to the next corner, the officer there will let you through."

But at the next corner, the lieutenant in charge, refusing eye contact, stared above Lucy's head and said, "You must first obtain an order from the sheriff."

"And where is the sheriff to be found?" Lucy asked, her panic rising.

"If you proceed to the west corner of the next block, straight ahead, you'll find facilities for sending a message to him." But when Lucy arrived at the third corner, no one seemed to know anything about where the sheriff was or how to reach him.

And so it went for some two hours, as the dispirited band of four were shuttled, under this excuse or that promise, from pillar to post of the prison. Never once did an officer say outright, "You positively cannot see your husband; you are forbidden to enter the prison." Instead, there was always the suggestion that if she passed quietly along, at some unspecified place a path would open and she and her children could make their farewells.

Precious little time now remained before the scheduled executions at 11:30. Lucy's nerves had become unstrung, unwonted tears streamed down her face; and the children were shivering in the cold, little Lulu's eyes glassy with fever.

Desperate, Lucy humbly begged the officer in command at the prison corner where they now stood to at least allow the children in for one last blessing from their father, one final image that might linger in their hearts. The officer told her to go away. Her agony suddenly spilling over, Lucy started screaming at the policeman, "Kill me in the same way you're murdering my husband!" Lizzie took Lucy in her arms and tried to soothe her, but to no avail. Her shrieks pierced the air and three police officers, desperate to shut her up and promising to "see what we can do about getting you inside," dragged her around the corner, where she, Lizzie and the two children were thrown into a paddy wagon.

Thus were they finally taken "inside," Lizzie locked in one dank basement cell, Lucy and the children in another. All four were stripped to the skin and searched, even the children, who screeched in terror. The search completed, the heavy doors of the cells clanged shut and they were left, without light, water, or food, to sit and wait.

✳

Promptly at eleven-thirty Sheriff Matson, the county physician, and several deputies appeared at the entrance to Spies's cell. With reporters crowding around, Matson, his voice tremulous, read the death warrant aloud as Spies stood with his arms folded across his chest, his face impassive. Spies was then ordered to step out from his cell into the corridor, where a leather belt about an inch and a half wide was bound around his chest to pinion his arms just above the elbows, and his wrists were handcuffed behind his back. The sheriff's party then proceeded to the other three cells and repeated the same procedure. As Albert's arms were being restrained, he looked up and saw Sam Fielden, tears pouring down his face, standing at the grating of his cell. "Good-bye, dear Sam," Albert called out, giving him a wan smile.

The solemn march to the scaffold began, with the sheriff in the lead and reporters crowding in on all sides. Albert turned to one of them and asked sardonically, "Would you care to follow?"

The scaffold had been erected in the north corridor, with benches below it that seated two hundred people. They'd been gathering since six o'clock that morning. Every seat was taken and the room buzzed with agitated talk. But the moment the sound of the approaching procession was heard on the iron stairway, an instant and absolute silence descended.

In a few seconds the prisoners appeared, each with a deputy by his side. When they reached their respective places on the trap, they were turned to face the spectators. Each man remained composed, but each in his own fashion. Spies gave the audience a slightly contemptuous look, then fixed his eyes on some invisible object above their heads. Fischer, erect and confident, glanced boldly around, as if immensely curious about who these people might be. Engel radiated happiness, the guest of honor at some noteworthy event. Albert looked merely reconciled and stared straight into the faces below him. His own face was ashen.

The impression had prevailed that the condemned would be allowed to say a few final words, but as the deputies stooped down and buckled leather straps on the feet of each prisoner, it was apparent that a swift conclusion had been determined.

As the nooses dangling overhead were lifted from their hooks, there were several audible gasps from the spectators. Spies was the first to have the rope placed around his neck. It was drawn a bit too tight and a deputy loosened it to ease Spies's discomfort; he gave a faint smile in acknowledgment of the kindness. Next it was Fischer's turn. Entirely self-possessed, he bent his head forward slightly to facilitate the adjustment of the noose under his left ear. When Engel received his, he turned his head several times to say a word or two to his deputy; judging from the smile on Engel's face, he could have been thanking him for placing the nation's highest decoration around his neck. When Albert's turn came, he stood unmoving, seemingly resigned, but with a faraway look in his eye. For an instant, Aunt Ester's face appeared to him, suffused with loving grace.

Shrouds were thrown over each man's shoulders, fastened at the neck and waist. Then came the white caps, tied loosely under each man's chin, completely blocking out the light of day streaming in from the windows. The caps were known to mark the last of the preparations. The moment had arrived.

Suddenly, from under his hood, Spies's voice rang out like a thunder-clap: "There will come a time when our silence will be more powerful than the voices you are strangling today!"

"Hurray for anarchy!" Fischer immediately shouted.

"Hurray for anarchy!" Engel echoed more loudly still.

A deputy was tying the last fastening in Albert's shroud when Fischer yelled out again—"This is the happiest moment of my life!"

Then Albert, his voice firm and strong, was heard to say, "Let me speak, Sheriff Matson! Let the voice of the people be—"

The trap door dropped, cutting Albert off mid-sentence. The four bodies plunged downward, then swung in the air. For a moment they seemed lifeless, then one by one they began to contort violently, the limbs contracting, the chests swelling with spasms, the arms convulsing. It was nearly eight minutes before the last of the four went entirely limp.

The bodies were left hanging for another ten minutes, then cut down and placed in plain coffins to be turned over to the relatives.

The doctors, during their final examination of the bodies, discovered that none of the necks of the men had been broken. All had died from slow strangulation.

At twelve-fifteen, the prison matron pushed open Lucy's cell door and barked, "It's over." She slammed the door shut again, leaving Lucy and her children alone in the darkness. From the adjoining cell, Lizzie could hear their moans and sobs and, in a frantic effort at comfort, repeatedly called out their names. But there was no response, and the terrible moaning continued.

Three hours later, Captain Schaack abruptly appeared and told them they could go home. Though weak with exhaustion, Lucy planted herself firmly in front of Schaack and angrily protested the way they'd been treated. Schaack shrugged his shoulders, said he knew nothing of the matter, and told them they must leave at once.

Coda

The funeral cortege was the largest ever seen in Chicago. Two hundred thousand people lined the streets. Lucy wore heavy black crepe and rode in the first carriage with Lizzie and other friends. The five black hearses, Lingg having been reunited with his comrades, were entirely covered with flowers and wreaths. The cortege moved slowly down Milwaukee Avenue to the accompaniment of muffled drums. Onlookers threw red flowers from the streets, windows, and bridges. The faces of many in the crowd were streaked with tears, including several policemen guarding the line of march.

The city had prohibited the display of banners or flags, but an aging Civil War veteran stepped suddenly to the front of the hearses, unfurled a small American flag, and carried it, unchallenged, to the end of the march.

Thirty special trains carried some ten thousand people to the burial grounds at Waldheim Cemetery, ten miles west of the city. Many in the crowd wore red ribbons, the women on their bonnets, the men on their coats.

The sun was setting as Captain Black stepped forward at the cemetery to speak his brief eulogy. "We are not here," he said softly, "beside the caskets of felons consigned to an inglorious tomb. We are here by the bodies of men who were sublime in their self-sacrifice."

Other, angrier speakers, followed. "You, the workers of Chicago," one of them shouted, "have permitted five of your best to be murdered in your midst . . . You've shown that you know how to bury your dead . . . You've loved faithfully and well. Now let us *hate*! . . . Vow it in the sight of these coffins . . . Shake off the yoke . . . Be free!"

What Became of Them . . .

CAPTAIN WILLIAM BLACK lost most of his legal practice and income in the years immediately following the Haymarket trial. But with the passage of time he gradually regained a clientele. For the rest of his life, Black remained an outspoken admirer of the Haymarket defendants, and became politically active as a Populist Democrat. He died in 1916 at age seventy-four.

INSPECTOR JOHN BONFIELD AND CAPTAIN MICHAEL SCHAACK were charged in 1889 with serving as fences for stolen goods and were suspended from the police force. Bonfield formed his own private detective agency, but it soon went bankrupt. Schaack retired to a farm in Wisconsin.

SAMUEL FIELDEN, along with NEEBE and SCHWAB, was pardoned by Governor John Peter Altgeld in 1893—an act that cost Altgeld his political career. Fielden went back to the stone-cutting business for a time. Then, on receiving a small inheritance from a relative in England, he bought a ranch in Colorado, where he and his family raised cattle and chickens. He sporadically engaged in labor politics. He died in 1922 at age seventy-four.

JUDGE JOSEPH GARY served on the bench, an honored member of the legal profession, for forty-three years, until the day before his death in 1906 at age eighty-five.

LIZZIE AND WILLIAM HOLMES continued to write for anarchist and labor publications. In 1893, after the Altgeld pardons, they moved out west, settling in New Mexico. Their home became a gathering place and refuge for political radicals. Lizzie died in 1926, William two years later.

OSCAR NEEBE remarried shortly after his pardon, and he and wife ran a tavern together near the Chicago stockyards until his death at age sixty-five in 1916.

MICHAEL SCHWAB never recovered from his years in prison. After being released in 1893, he barely scraped together a living running a small shoe store, out of which he also sold books. He died in 1898, age forty-five, from the tuberculosis he'd contracted in prison, leaving his wife and four children.

NINA VAN ZANDT, after a prolonged period of mourning and isolation, twice remarried and divorced. Her parents lost most of their money and Nina was eventually reduced to poverty. She eked out a living running a boardinghouse on Halsted Street, where she provided cheap lodging for workers and free lodging for the homeless. She remained politically active for the rest of her life. She died in 1936 at age seventy-five.

The Parsons Family

LULU EDA PARSONS died from a disease of the lymph glands at age eight, two years after her father's execution.

ALBERT PARSONS, JR. became a churchgoer, and also dabbled in Spiritualism. At age eighteen, over his mother's strong objection, he enlisted in the Spanish-American War. In 1899 he was committed to the Illinois Northern Hospital for the Insane, where he spent the rest of his life, dying of tuberculosis in 1919 at age thirty-nine—the same age as his father when executed.

LUCY PARSONS remained ardently political for the remainder of her long life. Bereft of husband and children, for years under constant surveillance and threat of arrest, she devoted herself to editing Albert's unpublished work, writing for a variety of radical periodicals, and lecturing widely on public issues. In 1894 she addressed Coxey's Army, the march of the unemployed on Washington. In 1905 she took part in the founding convention of the Industrial Workers of the World (the Wobblies). In the 1930s she spoke out in defense of Sacco and Vanzetti and the Scottsboro Boys. And for decades, she continued her efforts to organize the workers at the McCormick reaper plant. After the Russian Revolution, she became increasingly interested in Communism, but never joined the Party. Blind in her later years, Lucy continued her activities on all fronts, and on November 11, 1937, she addressed the fiftieth anniversary commemorating the execution of the Haymarket defendants. For the last thirty years of her life, she lived with George Markstall, and they died together in a fire that consumed their small wooden house in March 1942. She is buried next to the Haymarket monument.

A Note to the Reader

This novelized account of Haymarket and its participants adheres closely to the known historical record. That record, however, is skimpy. There is abundant public material—recorded speeches, newspaper articles, trial transcripts, and the like. But very little has survived that documents the private lives of those involved, and almost nothing in the way of diaries or intimate letters—those subjective road maps that reveal the most about personal experience, temperament, inner states of being, and relationships. Most of this I've had to invent, including Albert Parsons's journal, the exchange of letters between him and Lucy, and nearly all of the novel's dialogue, ruminations, and interactions. In doing so, I've tried to stay true to the outlines of character hinted at in the surviving shards of documentary evidence. Ollie Canby is the only fictitious person in the book. The real names of everyone else have been used throughout.

Acknowledgments

I owe an enormous debt to two people. My partner, Eli Zal, not only read every version of this novel over a four-year period, but did so with immense patience and insight. Jill Schoolman at Seven Stories Press gave me—several times over—brilliant notes on what still needed doing; and when I balked and moaned, gently waited me out. I also want to offer special thanks to Tom McCarthy who, during the book's production phase, benevolently solved a multitude of problems.

*

A number of primary sources have been of great help to me. I especially wish to cite and credit the following:

Foner, Philip S., ed. *The Autobiographies of the Haymarket Martyrs*. New York: published for A.I.M.S. by Humanities Press, 1969.

Keil, Hartmut, and John B. Jentz, eds. *German Workers in Chicago: A Documentary History of Working-Class Culture from 1850 to World War I*. Urbana: University of Illinois Press, 1988.

Lawson, John Davison, ed. *American State Trials*. St. Louis: F. H. Thomas Law Book Company, 1919.

Lum, Dyer. *A Concise History of the Great Trial of the Chicago Anarchists in 1886*. Chicago: Socialistic Publishing Company, 1887.

Parsons, Albert Richard. *Anarchism: Its Philosophy and Scientific Basis as Definied by Some of Its Apostles*. Chicago: Mrs. A. R. Parsons, 1887.

Parsons, Lucy E. *The Life of Albert Parsons, with a Brief History of the Labor Movement in America*. 2d ed. Chicago: L. E. Parsons, 1903.

Roediger, Dave, and Franklin Rosemont, eds. *Haymarket Scrapbook*. Chicago: Charles H. Kerr Pub. Co., 1986.

Among the dozens of secondary works consulted, the following have been indispensable:

Ashbaugh, Carolyn. *Lucy Parsons, American Revolutionary*. Chicago: Charles H. Kerr Pub. Co. for the Illinois Labor History Society, 1976.

Avrich, Paul. *The Haymarket Tragedy*. Princeton, NJ: Princeton University Press, 1984.

Bruce, Robert V. *1877, Year of Violence*. 2d ed. Chicago: Ivan R. Dee, 1989.

Calmer, Alan. *Labor Agitator: The Story of Albert R. Parsons*. New York: International Publishers, 1937.

Crouch, Barry A. *The Freedmen's Bureau and Black Texans*. Austin: University of Texas Press, 1992.

David, Henry. *The History of the Haymarket Affair: A Study in the American Social-Revolutionary Labor Movements*. 2d ed. New York: Russell and Russell, 1958.

Duis, Perry R. *Challenging Chicago: Coping with Everyday Life, 1837–1920*. Urbana: University of Illinois Press, 1998

Foner, Eric. *Reconstruction: America's Unfinished Revolution, 1863–1877*. New York: Harper and Row, 1988.

Lindberg, Richard C. *To Serve and Collect: Chicago Politics and Police Corruption from the Lager Beer Riot to the Summerdale Scandal : 1855–1960*. Carbondale: Southern Illinois University Press, 1998.

Nunn, William Curtis. *Texas under the Carpetbaggers*. Austin: University of Texas Press, 1962.

Phelan, Craig. *Grand Master Workman: Terence Powderly and the Knights of Labor*. Westport, CT: Greenwood Press, 2000.

Schlereth, Thomas J. *Victorian America: Transformations in Everyday Life, 1876–1915*. New York: HarperCollins Publishers, 1991.

Voss, Kim. *The Making of American Exceptionalism: The Knights of Labor and Class Formation in the Nineteenth Century*. Ithaca: Cornell University Press, 1993.

Weir, Robert E. *Beyond Labor's Veil: The Culture of the Knights of Labor*. University Park, PA: Pennsylvania State University Press, 1996.